P9-BYS-397

She's determined
to be naughty…
He's daring to be nice…

"I could stay here all night,"
Jack murmured against Rebecca's mouth.

She sighed, her lips barely moving beneath his. She clutched his arms; her fingers locked around his biceps.

"What is it?" He brushed his lips against hers in a sensuous glide. "What do you want?"

She stilled. It seemed she had stopped breathing. "I want you," she said simply.

He sat frozen. Stunned.

He'd sensed that she wanted him, of course. He hadn't expected her to say it, though—at least not this early. He'd planned to take all night to coax her free from her innate shyness, calming her, softening her, making her comfortable, willing. Making her not only want him, but *need* him.

Her voice fired his blood in a thousand different ways, but he couldn't submit to either her wishes or his body's demands. Not yet.

"Becky…" His hand slid down her neck, between her shoulder blades and lower, until it rested on the small of her back.

He did kiss her then. The tug of her hands on his arms was irresistible.

PRAISE FOR
JENNIFER HAYMORE'S
NOVELS

A Touch of Scandal

"4½ Stars! TOP PICK! Haymore delivers a second fascinating, powerful, and sensual novel that places her high on must-read lists. She perfectly blends a strong plot that twists like a serpent and has unforgettable characters to create a book readers will remember and reread."
—*RT Book Reviews*

"Jennifer Haymore's books are sophisticated, deeply sensual, and emotionally complex. With a dead-sexy hero, a sweetly practical heroine, and a love story that draws together two people from vastly different backgrounds, *A Touch of Scandal* is positively captivating!"
—ELIZABETH HOYT,
New York Times bestselling author

"An author to watch . . . *A Touch of Scandal* is a wonderfully written historical romance. Ms. Haymore brings intrigue and romance together with strong, complex characters to make this a keeper for any romance reader . . . The characters come to life with the turn of each page."
—TheRomanceReadersConnection.com

"A classic tale . . . Reading this story, I completely fell in love with the honorable servant girl and her esteemed duke. This is definitely a tale of excitement, hot sizzling sex, and loads of mystery."
—**FreshFiction.com**

"4 Stars! Kate and Garrett were wonderful characters who constantly tugged at my heartstrings. I found myself rooting for them the whole way through . . . If you like historical romances that engage your emotions and contain characters you cheer for, this is the book for you."
—**TheRomanceDish.com**

"These characters are just fantastic and endearing. I just couldn't wait to find out what happened on the next page."
—**SingleTitles.com**

A Hint of Wicked

"Full of suspense, mystery, romance, and erotica . . . I am looking forward to more from this author."
—*Las Vegas Review-Journal*

"A clever, provoking, and steamy story from an upcoming author to keep your eye out for!"
—**BookPleasures.com**

"Haymore is a shining star, and if *A Hint of Wicked* is any indication of what's to come, bring me more."
—FallenAngelReviews.com

"Debut author Haymore crafts a unique plot filled with powerful emotions and complex issues."
—*RT Book Reviews*

"A unique, heart-tugging story with sympathetic, larger-than-life characters, intriguing plot twists, and sensual love scenes."
—NICOLE JORDAN,
***New York Times* bestselling author**

"Complex, stirring, and written with a skillful hand, *A Hint of Wicked* is an evocative love story that will make a special place for itself in your heart."
—RomRevToday.com

"Jennifer Haymore is an up-and-coming new writer who displays a skillful touch in her erotic tale of a woman torn between two lovers."
—SHIRLEE BUSBEE,
***New York Times* bestselling author
of *Seduction Becomes Her***

"Recommended for readers who enjoy steamy Regency-era romance . . . there's a surprising lightness and tenderness to the love story."
—*Historical Novels Review*

"A story of life and death, revenge and true love . . . filled with passion, intrigue, and suspense . . . I look forward to reading much more historical romance from Jennifer Haymore."
—ArmchairInterviews.com

"Sweet and satisfying . . . refreshingly honest . . . a gripping read."
—LikesBooks.com

"A new take on a historical romance . . . complicated and original . . . the characters are well crafted . . . surprisingly satisfying."
—TheRomanceReadersConnection.com

"The characters in this book are easy to love . . . I can't wait to read the next book!"
—TheBookGirl.net

"What an extraordinary book this is! . . . What a future this author has!"
—RomanceReviewsMag.com

ALSO BY JENNIFER HAYMORE

A Hint of Wicked
A Touch of Scandal

A Season
of Seduction

JENNIFER HAYMORE

FOREVER

NEW YORK   BOSTON

This book is a work of fiction. Names, characters, places, and incidents are the product of the author's imagination or are used fictitiously. Any resemblance to actual events, locales, or persons, living or dead, is coincidental.

Copyright © 2010 by Jennifer Haymore
Excerpt from *Confessions of an Improper Wife*
Copyright © 2010 by Jennifer Haymore
All rights reserved. Except as permitted under the U.S. Copyright Act of 1976, no part of this publication may be reproduced, distributed, or transmitted in any form or by any means, or stored in a database or retrieval system, without the prior written permission of the publisher.

Cover design by Claire Brown
Cover illustration by Alan Ayers
Book design by Giorgetta Bell McRee

Forever
Hachette Book Group
237 Park Avenue
New York, NY 10017
Visit our website at www.HachetteBookGroup.com.

Forever is an imprint of Grand Central Publishing. The Forever name and logo is a trademark of Hachette Book Group, Inc.

Printed in the United States of America

First Printing: October 2010

10 9 8 7 6 5 4 3 2

ATTENTION CORPORATIONS AND ORGANIZATIONS:
Most HACHETTE BOOK GROUP books are available at quantity discounts with bulk purchase for educational, business, or sales promotional use. For information, please call or write:

Special Markets Department, Hachette Book Group
237 Park Avenue, New York, NY 10017
Telephone: 1-800-222-6747 Fax: 1-800-477-5925

For Lawrence.

Acknowledgments

With deepest gratitude to my agent, Barbara Poelle, and my editor, Selina McLemore. Thanks so much for your belief in me.

A Season
of Seduction

Chapter One

London
November 3, 1827

Tonight I will be his.

Becky closed her eyes as her maid, Josie, sprinkled rosewater on her hair, and a shudder spiraled up her spine. *Jack Fulton.* The dashing sailor who'd recently returned to London after many years at sea. Tonight would be the first time she'd touched a man intimately in four years. Tonight, she would give herself to him, wholly and completely.

She'd been acquainted with Jack for a month now, but she knew little of his true nature, and he knew little of hers. When they were together, they conversed easily about the past and the present, but they lived in the moment and never dug beyond the surface.

She preferred it that way. Nevertheless, there was something about him that made her yearn to burrow beyond his hardened shell and discover what lay beneath that rugged, handsome surface.

She shook herself a little to toss away the thought. Josie's round face scrunched in disapproval as a tendril of hair dislodged from Becky's coiffure, and the maid gave a long-suffering sigh before she went back to smoothing her mistress's hair.

Becky opened her eyes and stared into her friend Cecelia's dressing room mirror. It was hypocritical of her to want to learn more about Jack Fulton. She certainly didn't want him delving into *her* soul. She'd locked herself up tight long ago and never intended to reveal herself again. Not even to a lover. As long as she kept her heart safely guarded, tonight would set her free. Jack couldn't hurt her—she wouldn't allow that to happen. He *could*, however, release her from the lonely prison that had held her captive for years. He could make her feel alive again.

"You're thinking about something, Becky. I see it in your face."

Becky met her friend's gaze in the mirror. Cecelia, Lady Devore, clasped her hands behind her back. She stood in the center of the room, one of her guest bedchambers. Her white satin dress with its high collar and broad belt of embroidered crimson emphasized the slightness of her build, and the sweep of her chocolate-colored hair accentuated her elegant swan's neck and pointed chin.

Earlier this evening, Cecelia had fetched Becky from her brother's house on the pretense of taking her to the opera. But there would be no opera for Becky tonight. Instead, Cecelia would deposit Becky at a respectable hotel where she intended to have a not-so-respectable tryst with a seafaring rogue who possessed a hint of the gentleman. Or was it that he was a gentleman with a hint of the rogue?

There was no denying that Jack Fulton came from respectable stock—his father was one of the king's privy councilors, his eldest brother possessed parliamentary ambitions, and his middle brother was a captain in His Majesty's Navy. Jack wasn't at the pinnacle of the aristocracy, like Becky's family or even Cecelia's, but his bloodlines were quite dignified, indeed.

One look at him, though, and anyone could detect that there was something enticingly disreputable about him. An air of danger—of roguishness—that made Becky's pulse flutter and her limbs turn to mush. His looks appealed to her in a startling way. She was more familiar with the sleek, pale, soft bucks of the London *ton*, but Jack was suntanned, with a permanent crease between his eyebrows and lines fanning from the edges of his eyes that deepened when he smiled. His hair and sideburns were trimmed short and were a color of brown just a shade lighter than his eyes. His lips were light pink, and they had a wicked curve to them that matched the glint in his eyes. Together, those eyes and lips had featured in her erotic dreams for the past month.

Cecelia cleared her throat softly, jerking Becky from those scandalous thoughts.

"Yes..." Becky admitted slowly. "I *am* thinking about something."

Cecelia's dark eyes gleamed with understanding. Still, she wanted Becky to voice it. "Tell."

Becky glanced at her maid and dismissed her with a small movement of her hand. In complete silence but with a mulish pucker to her mouth, Josie corked the bottle of rosewater, set it on the table, curtsied, and went away.

When the door clicked shut, Becky said, "I think tonight is the night."

"Do you?" Cecelia's voice was soft. Satin rustled as she glided over the carpet, closer to the dressing table. "You've grown fond of our Mr. Fulton, haven't you?"

Resting her crooked arm on the shining oak surface of the dressing table, Becky wiggled her fingers. The last two fingers on her left hand tingled often, but she'd learned to take comfort from the sensation. The tingling was a part of her, like her bent, badly healed arm. It reminded her of a time in her life she'd do well not to forget.

"It's not that I've grown fond of him, per se. I've grown fond of...parts of him."

"Ah." Cecelia's lips tilted with mischief. "Parts you wish to become more intimately acquainted with."

Becky's cheeks heated, and she shifted uncomfortably in the chair. "Well, yes, I suppose you could put it that way."

Cecelia's renowned bluntness extended to matters most people kept to themselves. This was one attribute of her friend that had originally drawn Becky when they'd met during the Season earlier this year. She found Cecelia's matter-of-fact approach to mankind's baser nature both refreshing and shocking.

When London society had left en masse after the Season ended, Becky's family had remained. Cecelia had stayed in London, too, citing an utter loathing of country life. With most of society gone, Cecelia and Becky had turned to each other for company almost daily. Even now, however, despite their months of friendship, Becky still blushed often in the other woman's presence.

Cecelia's brow smoothed, and her lips softened into an expression of compassion. She laid an elegant, long-fingered hand on Becky's shoulder. "I am pleased for you. It has been so long."

Four years had passed since Becky had last lain with a man. She'd been so eager with her husband—eager to learn and eager to please. She had reveled in every touch they'd shared. Until things had turned sour.

"Too long," Cecelia added.

Becky blew out a breath and gave her friend an exasperated look. "Indeed, you are quite spoiled, Cecelia. Most widows never touch another man after their husbands die."

Cecelia, whose natural demeanor was one of haughty aristocracy, managed to appear even haughtier. Her thin, dark eyebrows arched into peaks. "Well, that is their loss. I lost my husband the same year you lost yours, and as you know, many men have warmed my bed since." She shrugged. "I shall offer no apologies for it. I love men."

Becky twisted her lips. "Really? I wouldn't say so. As a whole, I'd say you take a rather cynical approach to the male sex."

Cecelia laughed lightly and patted Becky's shoulder. "Of course you are right. I daresay men are most appealing when they're in my bed naked and occupying their mouths with pursuits other than talking."

Tiny hairs danced on end at the back of Becky's neck, and she wrenched her gaze away from her friend. When they'd last met, Jack had kissed her. The erotic touch of his lips had sent electric bolts shooting through her body, reminding her that no matter how long she kept it confined, her innate passion would never disappear.

"You're ready, Becky." Cecelia gave her shoulder an encouraging squeeze.

"I'm not certain."

"I know it is what you want. And I know that whatever should happen between you and Mr. Fulton tonight, you're well equipped for it."

In the past few months, Cecelia had drawn Becky outside the tight confines of her loving but protective family. Late one night after a few glasses of claret, Becky confessed her secret desires to her friend, and Cecelia had taken it upon herself to candidly teach her all about how a widow should properly manage an affair—from the seduction to the culmination to what must take place afterward.

She was as ready as she'd ever be.

"I feel so heartless." Staring into the mirror at Cecelia, she ran a fingertip along the smooth neckline of her white muslin overdress. She'd worn a heavy silk opera dress to Cecelia's house, but that dress now hung in the oak-paneled wardrobe across from the dressing table. She intended to remove the overdress before she went to him tonight. The translucent gown underneath would make her intentions clear. "Somehow it feels wrong—immoral—to approach such intimate topics so carelessly."

Cecelia shook her head firmly and clasped her hands behind her back. "You mustn't feel that way. I believe this is one of the weaknesses of our sex—we become so overwrought in matters of carnal love that we are unable to see them for what they are."

Becky frowned up at her friend in the mirror. "And what are they?"

"Simple fleshly pursuits. Completely separate from matters of the heart."

"Surely there must be an overlap between matters of the flesh and matters of the heart."

"Sometimes there is," Cecelia admitted. "But that is generally not the case. It is a rare specimen of a man who allows his carnal desires to trickle under his skin in such a manner." Smiling, she waved her hand. "Yes, yes, I know your brother is one of them. But one need only survey the men of our class to prove my hypothesis."

Becky returned her friend's smile, then rose from the dressing table. She was ready. Trustworthy Josie, despite her impertinence, remained ever tight-lipped about her mistress's affairs and would remain here until Becky returned in the morning. Cecelia would accompany her to the hotel, leave her to her privacy with Jack, and return for her at two o'clock.

"No doubt you are right." Becky straightened her spine. "Never fear, Cecelia, I will remember everything you have taught me. My heart will remain uninvolved. Whatever becomes of the time I spend with Mr. Fulton, I shall possess fond memories of all that we will share."

Cecelia took her hand and squeezed it, smiling at her.

Becky hoped she was telling the truth. She *wanted* to be telling the truth. Yet she was terrified, for though she would try with all her might to heed her friend's warnings, she feared Jack Fulton had already melted away a piece of her armor and had begun to burrow beneath it.

Drawing on the gloves the butler had just handed him, Jack glanced at the Earl of Stratford. "Everything in place?"

Stratford nodded, then cocked a blond brow. "I feel it imperative to ask you one final time: Are you certain about this course? I am not personally acquainted with the woman, but her family is formidable. If they were to discover that you planned it—"

Jack raised his hand. "Easy, man. No one else knows. No one will ever know."

Stratford was the only man in London he trusted with his plan. Jack had returned three months ago after a twelve-year absence from England to discover most of his childhood acquaintances had matured into weak, foppish creatures. He'd met the earl one night at a tavern on the Strand and discovered he was neither.

In the past weeks, Jack had learned a little of the man's past. Like Jack, the earl had suffered a great loss. That experience had done much to form the man he was today. He was well known as a profligate rake, immoral and debauched. He was the kind of man the mamas of the *ton* cautioned their innocent daughters against.

Despite the abundant warnings against him, however, with his devil-may-care indifference, his stylish good looks, his sandy blond hair several shades lighter than Jack's, and his pugilist's build, Stratford managed to lure every female that came within his proximity. The earl managed his reputation with a devilish glint in his blue eyes and a carefree smile. If Jack hadn't been accustomed to such feelings himself, he never would have recognized the bone-deep misery and weariness within his friend.

The two men walked through the front door of the earl's townhouse and into St. James's Square. The sun streamed through a thick haze, and leaves and rubbish tumbled down the street, propelled by a stiff breeze. The wind had whipped away the sooty smells of the city, leaving the crisp scent of the late autumn air in its wake.

Staring over the windswept square, Jack tugged at the black woolen lapels of his coat, pulling it more tightly about him. Two carriages rattled past, followed by several men on horseback and a milk cart. He glanced at his friend, who had paused at the top of the stairs to button his stylish dark gray topcoat.

"I need this," he said, just loudly enough for the earl to hear over the sounds of the street.

Stratford paused, his hand on the stair rail. An amethyst ring winked at Jack from the earl's fourth finger. "I know."

Jack spoke flatly. "It is the only way. I haven't much time. I'll not run from England with my tail between my legs."

"Of course." Stratford's tone was mild, but he gazed at him from beneath the brim of his hat, his blue eyes probing. "I'd choose a different course. But I am not you."

"No," Jack agreed, his voice tight. "You are not."

The earl shuddered, the stiffness in his shoulders evaporated, and he descended the remaining two steps with easy grace. "I possess no desire to be shackled to anyone. Ever."

Neither had Jack. Not until he'd seen Lady Rebecca— *Becky.* He'd first glimpsed her six weeks ago at the British Museum. He'd followed her at a distance, observed how she'd clutched her arm to her chest as she studied the artifacts in studious silence while her companions gossiped and chatted amongst themselves. A part of him had softened. Standing apart from the others, she looked fragile and distant. She was beautiful, delicate, seraphic. But something about her, some dark edge he couldn't quite place his finger on, reminded him of himself.

In the ensuing days, he'd learned she was the widowed sister of the eccentric Duke of Calton. At the tender age of eighteen, she'd lost her husband and then she'd injured her arm badly in a carriage accident, which explained the way she'd guarded it so carefully at the museum. Though four years had passed since the accident and the death of her husband, her family reputedly hovered over her and protected her virtue as though she were a virgin debutante.

As Jack learned more about her, understanding dawned. She was the answer to his dilemma.

He'd discovered that Cecelia, Lady Devore, was a bosom friend of his target. Fortunately for him, the lady had been one of Stratford's conquests, and they remained on civil terms. Stratford had arranged an introduction, and upon meeting Jack and hearing of his interest in Lady Rebecca firsthand, Lady Devore's cool, cunning gaze had swept over him, and she'd agreed to discuss the prospect of presenting him to Lady Rebecca.

The next day Lady Devore sent a note naming a date, time, and place—a room in a small, elegant, but unassuming hotel near the Strand.

He'd seen Lady Rebecca five times. Lady Devore had chaperoned the first meeting, but they'd met alone since. They'd dined, they'd played chess, they'd talked late into the night. She had played the pianoforte for him while he'd watched raptly, his body hardening at the way her teeth grazed over her lower lip as she focused on the notes.

He was tired of being teased. He was tired of shaving through her layers of shyness. He knew she wanted him—he witnessed it when her eyes followed him across a room, when her breath caught as his fingertips grazed her cheek. He'd kissed her two nights ago, and she'd responded with breathless passion.

She was ready.

More important, he was running out of time. He would be married—or dead—before Christmas.

Tonight would seal their future.

Tonight would be the first night of the rest of his life with Lady Rebecca Fisk.

Becky took the coachman's hand and stepped out of the carriage, drawing her hooded, fur-trimmed cape close against the chill. She stared at the edifice of the hotel as Cecelia slid out and came to stand beside her.

The unremarkable façade of Sheffield's Hotel was painted a somber gray to complement the slate of the sky it stood beneath on this chilly November afternoon. Behind the façade, however, stood a stately place, with common rooms on the ground floor and twenty well-appointed and expansive guest chambers on the floors above. Cecelia had advised Becky to take a suite of two rooms on the top floor at the end of the corridor. The door to the suite opened to a sitting room containing a pianoforte, a marble hearth, and elegant French furniture. Double doors in the back of the room led into a bedchamber Becky had never entered. She'd have the opportunity tonight—although she knew it was more likely she'd have eyes only for Jack Fulton rather than the bedroom décor.

Cecelia squeezed her hand. "Are you ready?"

"Yes." Deliberately, she added a steel edge to the timbre of her voice. "Yes, I am."

She wanted this to happen tonight. More than she

could adequately convey to Cecelia. Even though she knew Cecelia would understand.

"Let's go, then."

Cecelia pulled her bonnet low on her brow, and Becky drew the hood of her cape over her head. They walked in side by side. The hotelier, Mr. Sheffield, stood at the door as if he'd spent all day waiting for them to appear. He bestowed a friendly, guileless smile on them both.

"Ah, Mrs. Fletcher and Mrs. James. How lovely to see you again."

They'd given him false names. Cecelia had explained she always used her maiden name when she engaged in trysts outside her own home. Her maiden name was a common one, and though she was a member of the aristocracy and hardly invisible, it did offer some measure of anonymity. Becky's maiden name was James, an even more common name, so she had followed Cecelia's lead.

Both ladies offered their greetings to Mr. Sheffield, Becky without meeting the man's eyes. This was very awkward for her, because she was certain Mr. Sheffield knew that she'd reserved his finest suite to meet in secret with a man. Yet, whenever she did chance to glance at him, she saw only graciousness. There was no judgment in his expression.

She didn't understand his reaction—it was not one she'd have expected from anyone, even someone she was paying.

Mr. Sheffield led them into his tiny but tasteful and well-appointed office. The whole downstairs level of the hotel smelled of coffee, tobacco, and nutmeg, but most of the other rooms were larger, and space diffused the scents. Still, it wasn't an unpleasant combination, though it was one that struck Becky as entirely masculine. It didn't come as a surprise, either, since the hotel appeared to cater mostly to wealthy merchants in London for business.

Mr. Sheffield turned to a strip of wood lined with keys hanging on pegs. "I've had the rooms cleaned especially for you tonight, Mrs. James. There is a buffet of selected cheeses, breads, and fruits, and the bottles of spirits you requested await you." He paused. "And, of course, your guest has already arrived."

In an instant, burning heat suffused her face. "Thank you, Mr. Sheffield."

He pressed the key into her hand, and she closed her fingers around it and turned away to his hopes that she had a very nice evening.

Cecelia chuckled as they turned down the passage. "You're adorable."

Becky's blush deepened, and she choked out, "Adorable?"

"How flushed and flustered you become every time we come here. As if Mr. Sheffield doesn't deal with this kind of thing every single day."

"Is that why he doesn't judge?" Becky murmured, wondering whether all those men she saw in the corridors and common rooms weren't here on business at all, but to engage in torrid affairs with their mistresses.

"Of course it is. You pay him well, you don't destroy his property, and you're respectful. What right has he to judge?"

"He knows what I am doing? Why I am here?"

"Of course he does."

Becky sighed as they mounted the stairs. Truly, the world was much different from how it had been presented to her when she was younger. She had always been taught that there were certain moral laws everyone abided by and everyone upheld. There was right and wrong, good and bad. In her marriage, she'd seen true evil, and in her family she'd seen true good. But so many other actions and thoughts blurred in the center of the spectrum.

"People are so complicated," she murmured as they stepped onto the landing of the first floor and turned the corner to mount the second set of stairs.

"That they are," Cecelia agreed.

"Deeds are complicated, too."

Cecelia was quiet for a moment. "Yes," she finally said. "That's also true."

The strong, cloying scent of ambergris and carnations heralded the approach of another lady. The swish of skirts preceded the large woman as she bustled toward them. Startled, Becky looked up and met a set of heavy, dark-ringed hazel eyes. The woman stared at her for a long moment, and a flash of recognition jolted through Becky.

The woman turned to Cecelia. "Excuse me," she said in a haughty voice. She twisted her skirts out of their way and continued her progression down the stairs.

By the time she disappeared, Becky and Cecelia were at the landing. Becky paused, gripping the top of the stair rail. "I know her," she whispered.

Cecelia frowned. "Really?"

"That was Lady Borrill. Her husband sits in Parliament with my cousin Tristan. They're friends. I knew they'd been staying at a hotel while their townhouse was being refurbished, but I didn't know it was this one."

Cecelia glanced back down the stairs. "Well, she didn't seem to know you."

How could she not? Becky had met Lady Borrill several times. It was certainly true that she had never struck Becky as the most intelligent woman of her acquaintance, but Lady and Lord Borrill had even come to visit Calton House for a month the winter before Becky had come to Town for her Season.

"She just gave me the cut direct," Becky whispered.

Cecelia gave her a dark look. "You cannot know that. More likely she simply didn't remember you."

"I...don't think so. Oh, Cecelia, she must know what I'm doing here."

"Of course she doesn't."

"How can you be so sure?" Even though Becky kept her voice quiet, her words emerged in a low wail. "I'm at a hotel in town, when she knows full well I live at my brother's house. Why else could I possibly be here?"

"You are with me," Cecelia explained patiently. "She doesn't know anything about me. The first assumption, of course, would be that you are here to visit me."

Becky closed her eyes. She clenched and unclenched her fists, deliberately releasing her tension. Lady Borrill truly had no reason to cut her. Surely she hadn't known her, in her dark cloak with her covered hair. If she had recognized Becky, of course she would have stopped to inquire after her family's health.

She was being ridiculous. "You're right. I suppose I'm just on edge."

"Perfectly natural." Cecelia's mouth relaxed into a smile. "Come." She held out her hand. Becky took it, and Cecelia's tight squeeze reassured her even more as they walked down the corridor.

"I envy you," Cecelia said in a near whisper.

Becky raised her eyebrows. "Why?"

Cecelia sighed. "There's nothing quite like the first time..."

"But...it won't be my first time."

A real grin split Cecelia's face. "Oh, but you don't understand, my dear. There is a physical first time, which you've already experienced, and a visceral first time, which I think is what you have in store tonight."

Becky shook her head and released a nervous chuckle. "I don't think so." She'd enjoyed making love with William. As fleeting as those moments were, and as abruptly as they'd ended, she'd taken true pleasure from the experience. Despite the horror of what had happened afterward, there was no sense denying it.

Cecelia just smiled knowingly. They'd reached the end of the corridor and stopped before the tall, white-painted door that led to the suite.

With a final squeeze of her hand, Cecelia dropped it. "I'll leave you here, Becky. My coachman will come round for you at two o'clock."

Becky leaned forward and kissed her friend's cheek. "Thank you."

Cecelia's laugh tinkled pleasantly, reminding Becky of a tiny waterfall. "It is my pleasure. I know you will have a perfectly lovely time."

She glided down the hall, her heels clicking over the wooden floor. Becky stood staring at the door until she couldn't hear the sound of Cecelia's footsteps anymore. Then she took a deep breath, thrust the key into the lock, and turned it.

Chapter Two

At the sound of the door handle, Jack turned from the crystal decanters at the sidebar, a tumbler of brandy in his hand.

Lady Rebecca closed the door and glided in, her steps whispering over the dark gray and blue swirls of the carpet. She reminded him of the Queen of Winter, icy perfection, petite, sleek, and flawless. Her behavior was aristocratic, reserved, her demeanor stiff and chilly, at times downright cold.

A smile twitched at the edges of his lips. He'd watched her melt, turn warm and soft, and bloom like the spring. His goal was to see that happen again tonight, and Providence willing, many more times in the days to come.

After acknowledging him with a nod, she stripped off her cloak, turned, and hung it on the gilded coat rack that stood beside the door.

His pulse had leapt to his neck when she'd entered,

and now it sped. He clutched the glass of spirits and froze as every nerve in his body spun in somersaults.

She wore a diaphanous gown of gauze, reminiscent of the turn-of-century styles of France rather than the stiff, thick fabrics of today's fashions. It clung to her feminine shape and molded her into an Aphrodite. The neckline swooped low, revealing the plump top curves of her breasts, and a fine braided gold rope was belted just below, gathering the fabric to draw attention to her décolletage and hint at the dark shadows of her nipples. The skirts hugged the subtle flare of her hips and revealed an outline of the willowy legs beneath. She stood there, breathless, like a beautiful offering.

She trusted him, he realized with a jolt. She trusted him not to hurt her.

A dagger point of guilt sliced through all the masculine cravings roaring through him and pricked at his soul.

Damn it. There was no other way. He took a steadying breath.

"Do you like it?" The melody of her voice chased away his guilt, and his gaze snapped to her face.

"I do," he murmured. "Very much."

Some of her stiffness receded. "I'm glad."

He turned back to the sidebar and retrieved the glass he'd poured for her. "Sherry?"

She took it with a grateful smile, wrapping her pale, delicate fingers around the glass. "Thank you."

He followed her to the silver sofa at the center of the room and waited until she settled on the sleek cushions and took a sip of her drink before lowering himself beside her.

This was where he'd kissed her the night before last. He could see the memory of it in the depths of her gaze. She possessed the most fascinating pair of eyes he had ever seen. Sometimes a dark, midnight blue, other times—like now—the deepest indigo.

The need to take her mouth again burned through him, and his body hardened in anticipation. He schooled himself to temperance, however. Tonight was special. He couldn't botch this.

For a long moment he stared at her. Then he tossed back his brandy and set the tumbler on the side table.

Reaching out, he clasped the back of her pale neck and drew her to him. She came without resistance, with a sigh—a near desperate sound—escaping her lips.

He pulled her close, closer, until their lips met in a touch that lit the fuse running through his veins.

Her lips were like rose petals. So soft, so enticing. Delicate and sweet.

He held her there. Closing his eyes, he breathed in flowers and spring. Proof that she had already begun to thaw. Their noses bumped as he brushed his lips over hers. She held still, waiting, her skin warming, anticipation humming over her flesh.

"I could stay here all night," he murmured against her mouth. "Right here."

Again, he bussed her lips, a light graze. He firmed his grasp on her neck, keeping her steady, and touched his tongue to her upper lip, rewarding himself with the tiniest taste of her.

"Jack," she sighed, her lips barely moving beneath his. She clutched his arms; her fingers locked around his biceps.

"What is it?" He brushed his lips against hers in a sensuous glide with every word. "What do you want?"

She stilled. It seemed she had stopped breathing. He opened his eyes to discover that she'd closed hers. She held herself immobile, a flawless porcelain statue.

He drew back just enough to study her face. Its oval shape, smooth skin, red lips. The dark sweep of thick eyelashes and the midnight arcs of her brows. The silky black hair he suspected was naturally straight, curled to frame her face.

Her lips parted, and he resisted the urge to touch them again, either with his own lips or by tracing them with his fingertip.

"I want you," she said simply.

He sat frozen. Stunned.

He'd sensed that she wanted him, of course. In all their previous assignations, she'd been receptive to his every advance. She'd confirmed it by wearing that sheer gown tonight.

He hadn't expected her to say it, though—at least not this early. He'd planned to take all night to coax her free from her innate shyness, calming her, softening her, making her comfortable, willing. Making her not only want him, but *need* him.

He'd met her five times before, each time honing his strategy for tonight so that he could execute it without a hitch. The seduction had been timed perfectly. It was flawlessly planned.

Hearing her voice her desire fired his blood in a thousand different ways, but he couldn't submit to either her wishes or his body's demands. Not yet. Not for—he slid his gaze to the clock on the mantel—another hour.

He gritted his teeth. *Damn*.

"Becky…" His hand slid down her neck, between her shoulder blades and lower, until it rested on the small of her back.

He did kiss her then. The tug of her hands on his arms was irresistible. Their lips met in a fierce clash, and he groaned inwardly. She was an intoxicating mix of fiery hot aggression and sweet question, tentative yet brave. Fierce yet submissive. Darkness and lightness.

His breath caught, and Becky stilled, leaving the kiss suspended as if in midair.

"What is it?" she whispered, her words a soft puff of breath over his cheek. "Why do you hesitate?"

Drawing her closer within the confines of his arms, he tugged her onto his lap. Tilting her head, she gazed up at him, still trusting.

He traced his fingertip along her hairline then across the smooth skin of her cheek. She was so young and looked even younger, but an air of experience radiated from her, giving the impression of someone much older.

She reached back for her sherry and took a healthy swallow of the liquid, grimacing a little as she lowered the glass.

Sliding off his lap, she moved away from him and set her glass on the table. He watched as she erected those barriers again, turned chilly and distant. Spring retreated as quickly as it had come.

She stared straight ahead. "I don't understand."

He frowned. "What do you mean?"

"I truly don't understand why you're here with me." Sighing, she pressed her fingertips over her injured arm. "I am a novice at this, Jack. Surely that truth must be unappealing, when you can have your pick of any widow in London with a much broader arsenal of sensual skills than I have. So why—"

The sick feeling in his gut tightened until it felt as if a cannonball had lodged there, and he covered the hand that was restlessly kneading her arm. "If I wanted anyone else, I wouldn't be here. You must know that."

"But why?" Her dark blue gaze searched him, trying to seek out the truth, and he knew he must lie to her once again.

"You've intrigued me from the beginning."

That was no lie. Perhaps this would be more a matter of omission of facts than lying.

"Why?"

"Because you remind me of myself," he said before he could think about the wisdom of that response.

"What do you mean?"

He slid his fingers up her crooked arm. "You have suffered. You have experienced pain."

She shuddered.

"You're a beautiful woman, Becky. A perfect lady. But ever since I first saw you, I've wanted to know you better."

"Where did you first see me?"

"At the British Museum."

"I remember that day. It was the first time I saw you, too."

"Was it?" He thought she hadn't seen him at all.

"Yes. You leaned against the wall, your stance so casual, yet you watched everyone with sharp eyes. You seemed so interested in the people surrounding you."

He gave a low chuckle. He'd only been in London for a short time, and he'd been studying the people of England, of his homeland, comparing and contrasting them with the people he'd encountered on his travels.

"I found you...intriguing, too," she said. "Appealing. I wanted to know who you were, but none of the ladies I was with was acquainted with you."

"I asked Stratford about you that afternoon," Jack said, "and in turn he questioned Lady Devore. And here we are."

Her brow furrowed. "But what could you have seen in me that day? I was doing nothing but studying the artifacts with my companions."

He shook his head. "*You* studied the artifacts. They chattered. You set yourself apart from them."

Her frown deepened. "Unknowingly."

"Nevertheless, you did. I watched you. I couldn't place it, but there was something very different about you."

"And now you have learned more about me, and you understand it is because of the loss of my husband that I appear distant at times. And because of the carriage accident that left my arm crippled and deformed."

His fingers, which had been trailing up and down her injured arm, stopped, tightening over her elbow, and she flinched.

His grip loosened instantly. "Am I hurting you?"

"No," she murmured. Yet her eyes glistened.

"Your arm speaks of a tragedy, but please don't call yourself crippled and deformed. I'll never think of you as either."

She took a steadying breath. "But what of you?"

"What of me?"

"You said I reminded you of yourself because of my suffering. You seem to know all about my suffering. Now you must tell me of your own."

A wry chuckle escaped him. "I shouldn't have hoped you'd forgotten about that, should I?"

She shook her head, her expression somber.

He knew he must reveal the truth to her, but how much of it? There must be more omissions, and now, most certainly, there would be lies. But these were lies he was accustomed to telling. She'd hear some of the story in the next few days, of that he had no doubt.

How much easier it would be to take her straight to bed. To possess her sweet, delicate, willing flesh. To seduce her, to bring her to rapture, to dive deep within her, and experience the fulfillment he'd been anticipating for what felt like forever. His body commanded him to act.

But he'd taken it this far. Surely he could control his base desires for a while longer.

"Twelve years ago, I was a youth of eighteen." At her nod, he continued. "I was...well, I was involved in a scandal."

Twelve years ago, Lady Rebecca had been a child of ten sheltered in the Yorkshire dales. She'd have heard nothing of the events that had defined him for the past twelve years.

She cocked her head. "What kind of scandal?"

"It concerned a lady I had known since childhood and her husband, a marquis. Society assumed I was involved only because of my previous connection to the lady..."

"Involved in what?" she asked.

He faced straight ahead, staring at the small but

elaborately carved marble fireplace. Someone had built the fire earlier, and it crackled cheerfully behind an Oriental screen. Flexing his fingers, he laid his hands on his knees, giving the appearance of relaxation. He hated talking about this. Hated it. But it had to be done—she would probably hear the story in a way that would transform Anne into a whore and him into a depraved seducer of married women.

Unexpectedly, nerves flickered in his gut. He'd planned this, but he never spoke of his past, of his exile, of Anne and the events surrounding her death. Yet Becky was important. She must know the story—at least the parts of it that would ultimately be revealed to her by parties who would depict his role in a less favorable light. She'd need ammunition with which to respond to the cruelty of the gossipmongers, of those who would try to destroy his association with her just for the sheer joy they would glean from doing so.

"The marriage was tumultuous. It was well known that the marquis had taken a mistress, and his wife—her name was Anne…" There, he'd said it. Her name. He hadn't spoken her name aloud in years. It emerged more smoothly than he ever would have imagined.

Becky frowned at him. "Yes?"

"She was very unhappy."

Becky gave a compassionate murmur.

"Late one night, the marquis was murdered between the door of his club and the mews."

"Just a moment." Becky raised her hand to prevent him from continuing. "I believe I've read about this. The Marquis of Haredowne was murdered in…1815, wasn't it?"

"Yes," Jack said, his voice as taut as a mooring line

under the strain of a gale. One strong gust, and it would break.

Her brow furrowed in thought. "I recall he was shot by footpads intending to rob him, but the sound of the gunshot attracted the attention of passers-by, and they ran away before they could steal anything."

"That is the general understanding of what happened."

"His wife died the very same day, didn't she?"

He nodded, his throat dry.

"But she died of natural causes while he was murdered. It was a terrible tragedy."

"Yes. It was. A tragedy of the very worst kind."

"Oh, God." Straightening, she stared at him with widened eyes. "Before the authorities could make sense of what had occurred, a young gentleman was implicated in the crime."

"Yes."

"That was you," she whispered.

He nodded.

"You were accused of murdering the Marquis of Haredowne." She blinked at him owlishly, as if the truth of it did not register. No doubt it did not. No doubt she was as innocent as a young widow could be.

How she took this would determine their fate. Jack was not oblivious to the fact that such information would frighten the wits out of most London society misses. This news might very well send her bolting out of his life forever. He could only pray that she was as unique as her actions had hinted.

"I was cleared of all suspicion," he said.

"I remember that, too. A witness came forward with an alibi, and a judge decided it was impossible for the young gentleman—you—to have committed the crime."

"That's right." Jack caught himself fidgeting and forcibly stilled his body and lightened his voice. "How can you know so much of this? You were just a child at the time."

"Haredowne was a peer, so it was a well-publicized case. I read about it years later."

And it seemed she had remembered every detail. Jack gazed at her with newfound respect.

"But you—" She broke off, still staring at him in shock. "That was you." Taking a great, gulping breath, she shook her shoulders as if flinging away some burden. "What happened?"

"Afterward, you mean?"

"No—I mean, were you there when he was killed? Why is it that you were accused?"

He noted that she had put as much distance between them as the sofa would allow. He must tread carefully here.

He remained very still. "I was accused because of my prior relationship with the marquis's wife. It was rumored that we were lovers."

Becky was silent. He glanced at her to see her studying him with a frown, and he turned away, closing his eyes so he wouldn't detect any hint of horror in her eyes.

He and Anne had been lovers when they were younger, but not then. They hadn't touched each other since the day she had come to him weeping that she was to marry the Marquis of Haredowne.

"Was the rumor true?" Becky asked.

Jack spoke through a tight jaw. "No. It wasn't." His voice shook with the power of his conviction. "I have done many unprincipled and dishonorable things in my life, but I draw the line at touching married women. I wouldn't cuckold any man." Not even as despicable a man as the Marquis of Haredowne.

Becky's luxurious, black velvet eyebrows swept downward as she blinked, and then those indigo eyes fixed on him. Her voice was little more than a whisper. "I believe you."

Jack pushed his hand through his hair. "In any case, because of that rumor, suspicion immediately turned to me."

She nodded, but she still pressed her body against the arm of the opposite end of the sofa. God, he wanted to snag her waist and haul her back onto his lap. His fingers itched to stroke that porcelain skin again. He couldn't touch her, though—not until he soothed her fears.

"The witness came forward explaining that I was elsewhere at the time of the murder, and the charge was dismissed two days after the marquis's death."

She nodded.

"Nevertheless, there was an enormous scandal. I'm sure you can imagine."

An expression of complete understanding crossed her face. "Oh, yes. I can imagine."

Jack had learned some about her family. They were no strangers to scandal. Nor were they as snobbish as Anne's family had been. While Anne's father would accept nothing less than a peer for his daughter, Becky's own brother had married a woman from the lower orders—the current Duchess of Calton had once been a maid.

From the start, everything he'd learned about Lady Rebecca Fisk, her past, and her family had convinced him that this was the right course for him to take. Every moment he spent with her strengthened that conviction. He liked her. He wanted her. More important, he *needed* her.

"My father sent me away," he continued. "He ordered me to vanish until the gossip abated. I didn't officially return to England until August of this year. Before then, the last time I'd set foot on English soil was in the spring of 1815."

A long, painful silence ensued.

Revealing it all had been more difficult than he'd expected. But it was over now. All he could do was wait. And hope.

"You were gone for so long," she murmured.

"Twelve years."

"But you explored the whole world in that time."

"Well, not the *whole* world."

She sighed. "I have always dreamed of exploring the world. Africa, Asia, Polynesia. I am fascinated by indigenous cultures. But I'd especially love to visit America."

"America? Why?"

"I imagine the Americans to possess many of the qualities I admire: curiosity, adventurousness, bravery, practicality. I've always envisioned them to be enterprising and imaginative." She gave him a wistful smile. "Though I'm sure my girlish conceptions have little to do with their real character."

"No, I think there is much truth in them. As with any place, however, America is filled with all kinds of people."

"I wish I could travel—go wherever I wanted and do whatever I wished to do. I wish I could be a sailor . . . but alas, I am a woman, and a duke's sister. It is not meant to be."

"Yet you have traveled within the United Kingdom?"

She hesitated. "A little. I have been between London and Yorkshire, where Garrett's seat is, several times." She stared at the fire. "I have been to southern Scotland for a few days, and I lived for a time with my husband in Warwickshire. But really, I haven't seen much of the country. I have a house in Cornwall from my mother, but I've never been there."

Cautiously, he took her hand in his own, turning it over in his palm. It was so soft, so fragile. "If you could pursue a profession, what would it be?"

She took a long moment to consider, and finally she smiled. "I'd be a surgeon."

"Really?" She'd surprised him yet again. He could hardly see this delicate, elegant creature sawing bones, sewing up wounds, and issuing draughts to the dying.

"Yes, I believe I would," she said, her voice grave. "I think it must be a most gratifying profession. A heart-breaking one, but ever so worthy."

"Very true," he said, remembering Smith, the surgeon on the *Gloriana*. He'd drowned last autumn in a gale off the coast of Jamaica, along with three other sailors. Smith was his friend, and a good man. It took a special kind of man to be a surgeon.

Becky brought her knees close and wrapped her arms around them, gazing at him. "Why didn't you return to England sooner?" she asked finally. "Twelve years is such a long time."

"I wasn't welcome. My father, as you know, is a member of Parliament, and my brothers have their own

ambitions. They didn't want their scapegrace of a youngest
brother ruining their chances for success."

"That's so cruel."

"I understand their hesitation in allowing my return,
and I cannot blame them."

That wasn't a lie, not really. After twelve years, he was
as distant from his closest family members as anyone
could be. He'd seen his father and eldest brother once
since his return, and the meeting had been stiff and
formal, and eminently uncomfortable. He had no wish to
repeat the experience. "My father was sworn to the Privy
Council last year, so my absence was certainly not detri-
mental to his career." He took a breath. "England is my
home, though, and I intend to make a life here now that I
have returned."

She nodded. "Yes. Of course."

He fetched his glass from the side table. Rising, he
went to the sidebar to refill it with brandy as she sipped
at her sherry.

As the amber liquid streamed into his tumbler, he
said, "Tell me about your husband."

She recoiled, and he instantly regretted the command.
He couldn't fathom why he had brought up her husband—
except, he thought ruefully, for the fact that he had
revealed a part of himself, and now he wanted her to
reveal something about herself in return. It was childish
of him, really.

Jack returned to the sofa, set the glass aside, and took
her hand again, pressing his palm against its silky
warmth. "Forgive me for that. You needn't answer."

"My husband." She swallowed hard and stared at him,
as if she were determined to answer no matter the cost.

"He...it was an elopement. I hardly knew him. At first, I was madly in love with him." She took a deep swallow from her glass, finishing the last drops of the sherry, and then she lowered the empty glass to her lap.

He frowned at her. "But not later?"

"No. Not later. William wasn't..." She looked away, and tendrils of deep pink crawled across her cheeks. "He wasn't a good man."

The effect of her words was instant. Red tinged his vision. His skin prickled hot as memories rushed through him like a flash flood, too quick for him to control. His fist clamped over her hand. "Did he hurt you?"

"Yes." His hand tightened over hers, and her brows drew together in a frown. "What's wrong, Jack?"

He loosened his fist and brushed the fingertips of his other hand over her twisted elbow. "He wasn't responsible for this?"

"No. Not directly. The accident occurred a few days after he died." She shook her head, confused. "Are you angry with me, Jack?"

He tried to smile at her, but he feared it emerged as more of a grimace. His reaction had nothing to do with her, really. Just with his memories. Why had his mind made that connection the instant she'd said William Fisk hadn't been a good man? She was a different woman with a different husband in a different time.

"No, I'm not angry with you."

"Why...?" Understanding dawned in her expression. "You're angry with him."

He knew nothing of what had happened between her and her husband. Becky was different from Anne. Becky was safe. Whatever William Fisk had done to her, the man was dead. Trying to calm his racing blood, Jack spoke through his teeth. "I cannot abide a man who abuses innocents."

She gave a small, bitter laugh. "I'm no innocent."

"Perhaps you're more innocent than you think you are."

"No. I am a widow. I have seen…" She paused, and her gaze grew distant. "Too much," she finished quietly.

He rubbed tender circles in the fleshy part of her palm. God, he was being an ass. None of this was her fault. Whatever had happened to her, it was over. It was over for him, too. By now, he should be better able to control his memories.

"I'm sorry," he said.

"About what?"

"Whatever it was that hurt you. And I'm sorry for reminding you of it."

She gave him a faltering smile. "I am sorry you were hurt as well."

They sat in companionable silence for several long moments. With every minute that passed, his body grew in awareness of hers. In the past twelve years, he'd felt lust once in a while—especially when the *Gloriana* sailed into port after long months at sea. Yet the feeling Becky evoked in him was different. Lust was there, and it was more consuming than ever, but there was more to it than that. A tenderness. A longing to tuck her against his body, hold her close, and simply breathe her in, as if her sweetness and essence would filter through him and bring him peace.

Those thoughts were nonsensical, he knew that. The fact that he actually liked her was certainly a bonus, but

there was no sense in fooling himself into believing anything but his desperate need for money had instigated
their association.

He pressed gently on the soft pad of flesh below her
thumb. "When I touch you..." He paused to search for
the right word to describe the heady feeling touching her
gave him. "It's potent."

"Potent," she whispered. She released his hand and then
took it again, lacing her fingers with his. "Yes. It is."

She raised his hand, still tangled with hers, and
pressed slow kisses to each of his fingers. "I love your
hands. They're so large, and your fingers are so long."
She stroked along the calluses on his fingers. "Hardened
by work, yet graceful. So masculine."

He closed his eyes, thoroughly seduced by her simple
touch.

This was business, nothing more. A seduction, nothing
more. He required something she possessed, and he knew
how to go about obtaining it. Certainly there would be
some side benefits to the arrangement, he thought,
breathing in her blossoming essence. He liked Lady
Rebecca Fisk, and he respected her. He'd take good care
of her, and he'd never deliberately cause her pain.

But if he hadn't needed her fortune, he never would
have made the effort to meet her.

Chapter Three

Cecelia had counseled her to be practical, so Becky would grit her teeth and be practical. She had not come to Sheffield's Hotel tonight to hear proclamations of love—in fact, such a proclamation from this man would scare her to death and would likely have her fleeing to Yorkshire before dawn.

The fact of the matter was, she wanted him. Desperately. She'd never have him, though, if they continued to discuss such dour, depressing topics. Since he seemed so hesitant to seduce her, it fell to her to do the seducing.

Staring at his rugged face, she lowered his hand and brought it to her lap. "I like your taste."

He raised a brow. "My...taste."

"Yes."

"What do I taste like?"

She sat back, considering. "You taste clean, like soap."

He grimaced.

"Not like lye," she reassured him, then took a moment to consider. "Like velvet."

"Does velvet have a taste?"

"I think it must. Soft and smooth."

"I see. I think." He frowned.

"There's a bit of male in there, too. Brandy. And something salty, that reminds me of the sea."

"Not such pleasant things?"

"Things that remind me I'm kissing a man," she corrected. "Which I'd much prefer to kissing a woman, after all."

She smiled a little, and so did he. Their gazes met, and they both sobered. The smile slipped from his face. "Becky, I..."

She pressed a finger to his lips. "I am glad you told me about your past. It means very much to me to know that you have been forthcoming and honest with me."

He didn't meet her eyes. Instead, he raised his hand to trace the plunging neckline of her dress. She sucked in her breath as his skin rasped over the curve of her breast, the sensation rough, his touch gentle. She stared at his face, but he stared at the place where his finger dragged over her flesh, his eyes dark with intent.

He paused at the bottom of the vee where the fabric gathered between her breasts. His lips curved, and he took on the sinful expression of a pirate about to plunder a treasure-filled ship.

She'd kept herself locked up so tightly for so long. Now she was releasing one of the locks—just the one that had to do with her carnal longings. Several locks still remained, however, and she checked over them systematically. There was the one that kept the glass case enclosed around her heart—that one was shut tight. There was the one that protected her trust—her guard—and that, too, was safe. And there were the ones standing sentinel over her soul, her mind, and her brain. Those wobbled a little, and she took a moment to reinforce them.

What happened between her and Jack would only be skin deep. What she wanted tonight was simple. She wanted him to touch her. All over. She wanted those rough fingers to rove over her body, to graze every square inch of her.

Currently those fingertips traced the exposed skin of her upper breast. She closed her eyes, focusing on the heated trail of his touch. His hand rounded over her breast, his fingers pressing against the delicate flesh, his palm over the thin layer of muslin that separated her skin from his.

Her nipple responded in an instant rush of sensation, tautening, seeking more. Becky grasped her sleeve and pulled the gown off her shoulder, sliding the fabric from between them.

His palm was burning hot. He shifted his hand, his skin gently abrading the sensitive puckered tip of her breast, and she gasped.

"You like being touched here," he murmured.

She couldn't lie to him. She couldn't pretend to be some demure maiden. She couldn't pretend to be anything but what she was.

"Yes."

He lowered his dark head, tugged her closer, cupped her breast in his hand, and closed his mouth over the tip.

She grabbed his shoulder, pressing him more tightly

against her. The movement of his lips on her was exhilarating. She was so sensitive here, and the strong movement of his lips bordered on painful, but, oh, it was such an exquisite pain. A pain that made gooseflesh break out on her forearms, sent tingles to her toes, and made her whole body shudder with delight.

He pulled down her other sleeve, revealing her other breast. Closing a hand over the one he'd just taken into his mouth, he moved to the opposite side, suckling, licking, moving his mouth over her flesh in ways she hadn't known were possible. Sliding up his shoulders, her hands wove into the softly curling hair at his nape. His thumb brushed over the nipple still damp from his kisses, sending bolts of light through her to coalesce at her center.

A certain feeling welled deep within her—it was an elusive feeling, a sensation of rising toward some pinnacle, some height she couldn't describe and had experienced only a handful of times.

Jack closed his teeth over her flesh and tugged. The feeling within her tightened, burned hotter, a ball of light condensing, contracting, preparing to explode and flood her veins.

He soothed with his lips, feathering kisses over the place he'd just nipped, and Becky sighed. The light simmered, its flame low and pleasurable deep within her.

As if he knew she could not bear to be abandoned there, his lips left her breasts but his hands didn't. He cupped them both, his fingertips plucking, stroking, as his mouth traveled upward, over her chest and collarbones, and finally her neck.

Becky threw her head back to offer her flesh to him,

and he took it, all of it, just as she'd wanted. Alternating between gentle brushes, licks, and sharp sucks and tiny bites that left her gasping, he left no inch of her neck unexplored by his lips.

He traveled upward, explored her jawline, and finally returned to her lips, pressing a tender kiss at the corner of her mouth.

"Becky. I do want you. Never forget it."

"Why—?"

But the assault of his mouth cut off her words. No longer gentle, his lips took her on a careening journey of sensation. Hard, commanding, and thorough, he took her mouth under his control.

In response, she squirmed, she pushed, she pulled. She kissed him back, then retreated as his touch overwhelmed her senses. His body covered hers, heavy and hard, so manly, so large, so dominant. The fabric of his shirt, his trousers, and her dress tangled between them, but the hard ridges of his body touched her everywhere. A firm thigh, a strong arm maneuvered her down onto the sofa. The solid bulge of his erection pressed against her leg.

All of a sudden, Jack's body heaved up, and Becky realized she lay on her back, her skirts twisted around her thighs, her hair sagging from the coiffure Josie had spent so long arranging.

He gazed down at her, his dark eyes narrow with desire. Cool air whispered over her bare breasts, tightening her nipples even more.

Becky felt no impulse to cover herself. She stared up at him through half-lidded eyes, heated arousal swirling within her. She wanted him to look at her like that. She wanted him to stare at her bare breasts with lust in his eyes. Lust he felt for her.

His chest rose and fell. "God. What you do to me."

"What's that?" She meant the question to emerge like silk, as if she were an experienced seductress, but instead it rasped out, sounded raw and full of longing.

"You make me forget…" His words faded. Becky watched in fascination as his fingers worked to untie his cravat.

"Forget?"

The linen slid over his neck as he drew it away and tossed it over the back of the sofa. "You make me forget myself. Forget who I am, where I am, what I'm doing…"

"Isn't that how it should be?"

"Is it?"

"I…" Her chest went tight as his lips twisted into a wicked curve. That crooked smile would be her undoing. "I think it is."

She gazed at his fingers, rapt, as he slid free the buttons at his stiff, high collar. All at once, he pulled the shirt over his head, and all the air left Becky's body in a whoosh.

His torso was a thing of beauty. She'd never seen anything like it. Rippling with muscle, the skin deeply tanned, every inch taut and lean. The muscles in his abdomen expanded as he inhaled, and she dragged her gaze to his face.

He watched her with a bemused expression, and realizing she was gaping, she snapped her lips shut.

"You *were* married?" His voice was soft.

"I was." He raised a brow in question, but she didn't want to talk about William, about how different a specimen of man he was. She wanted to consider nothing but the man before her. "But I never saw *you* before."

"Do you like what you see?" His voice slid around her senses like a strip of satin.

"I do." She rose onto her elbows and tucked her legs beneath her. Rising onto her knees beside him, she slipped her arms around his waist.

His skin was smooth but taut, hairless but for the dark trail leading from his navel to the waistband of his black trousers.

Her breasts pressed against his side as she leaned into him, and the tight ball of heat within her flared at the contact. His arm snaked around her back, pressing her closer as she bent forward to explore him with her lips.

"There it is." She pressed her lips to the side of his chest. "That taste. Mm."

"Velvet?"

"Mmm."

His chest resonated as he chuckled. His hand slid up her back and into her hair, fumbling as he plucked away her pins.

She stroked his side, soaking up the warmth of his skin beneath her fingertips. She traced his navel and tickled the hairs trailing to his waistband, then traveled back up to the hard planes of his chest, circling the flat, small nipples.

She moved higher, completely focused on her exploration. He had a small scar at his waistline, a freckle on his left pectoral and one on his shoulder above it, and his nipples were small and round and a dusky pink, not as dark as her own.

He leaned against the back of the sofa, his hands

combing through her hair as she explored him, his breaths deep and even. When he released the last pin, her hair tumbled to her waist.

"You have beautiful hair."

"You have a beautiful abdomen," she returned, bent over the narrow strip of hair trailing from his navel. She touched the scar. "What happened?"

"Ah, that." He sighed. "Accident with a fishhook. The wound itself was less serious than the infection that resulted from it."

She shuddered. "Thank God you recovered."

She traced his waistband, then brazenly moved her hand lower, over the bulge delineated by the snug woolen fabric.

He seemed to hold still, suspended, as she explored the ridge of his erection, fascinated by its size, length, and girth. A glimmer of fear prickled along nerves that had been quiescent since she'd decided to pursue this course.

How was it possible for such a massive organ to fit inside a woman? How was it possible to feel pleasure at such a thing?

It had been a long time, indeed. She could hardly remember how William had done it. At first, he'd been very passionate with her, but whenever he'd joined with her the room had been dark. Furthermore, this particular part of his anatomy had come in contact with hers in only one specific location.

Despite Becky's bemusement, her body experienced no such hesitation. It heated, ached, craved, silently begged him to connect with her in this most intimate way.

A part of her, the ever-analytical part, told her that these feelings were natural, the instinctual human response to physical attraction. This instinct worked in a reciprocal fashion—by his evident state of arousal, she knew he wanted her, which in turn, made her own desire soar.

He'd moved her hair aside and was unbuttoning her dress, spreading the seams apart as he worked, his finger-tips moving down her spine. Cool air washed over her newly bared flesh, and she sighed.

"I want this off you," he said, tugging on the fabric covering her back. "I want to see you. All of you."

She cupped his solid length in her hand and looked at him from beneath her lashes. "In that case, it would only be fair for me to see you as well. *All* of you."

"You will, sweetheart." Again, that wicked smile. "I promise."

Becky swiped her hand up over him. Her fingers skimmed over the ridged muscles of his stomach, then higher to his chest. She traced his collarbones, then moved down his arm, fascinated by the bulges and cords of muscles that flexed underneath her hand.

She wished she were an artist. She would draw him. No—better to sculpt him, for it was his shape that took her breath away. His chiseled, sculpted body brought to mind a statue created by an Italian master and brought to life by the gods. Like Michelangelo's *David*. She'd never been to Florence, but she'd seen the likenesses in books.

Compared to Jack, though, David was a slender boy. Jack was taller, thicker, sturdier, stronger, and bigger from top to bottom, especially...

Heat crept across her cheeks as she returned her

fascinated gaze to that part of him that so intrigued her.

"Stand," he commanded in a low voice.

Her gaze shot to him. If she stood, her dress would fall down, and she would be naked.

He never took his eyes from her face. Gently, he took a stray wisp of hair that had fallen over her eyes and tucked it behind her ear. "You do want this, don't you?"

"I..." Her voice dwindled, and she lapsed into honesty. "It has been a very long time. And...I was married. What if...?"

What if she'd been right about matters of the flesh overlapping with matters of the heart? What if once she gave her body to him, she lost her heart as well?

Her shields would shatter. She would no longer be safe. She'd be as vulnerable as she'd been with William.

With a low noise that sounded like a cross between a growl and a moan of dismay, he yanked her tightly against him. Her breasts crushed against the smooth heat of his chest, and she sighed in bliss. The warmth and comfort of his bare skin pressed against hers was inexplicably pleasurable.

"I'd never willfully cause you harm, Becky. Never." His voice shook as he said it. The rawness of his tone bespoke his honesty. His body resonated with it, and she knew he told the truth.

She did trust him, as much as she could trust any soul. She truly hadn't allowed him to crawl under her skin— well, not *too* much. She'd already promised herself she wouldn't allow him—or anyone—to hurt her. If she kept up her guard, she could protect herself from pain.

"What if...?" Her voice trailed off again. There were so many "what ifs." What if he didn't find her up to his standards for a bedmate? What if it hurt? What if he were to get her with child?

She simply could not take this as lightly as Cecelia would. Such a joining held great significance. When she stripped off her clothes, she stripped away her only tangible shields. How could anyone take such a thing lightly?

She'd only known Jack for a few weeks. They weren't married. If Jack possessed any desire to wed her, he'd have gone to her brother rather than to surreptitious private late-night meetings at a hotel.

"No," he said quietly. "I won't hurt you. I will give you pleasure. No regrets."

"No regrets," she repeated softly. She slipped her arms around his waist until her right arm would straighten no further and laid her head on his shoulder. "I am not innocent, Jack, but then again, I suppose I am in some matters. Such encounters are very new to me. Before this night, the only man who had seen my bare chest was my husband. In the dark. I didn't quite understand it until now, but by removing my clothes, you render me vulnerable. I dislike being vulnerable...but..." She struggled for the right words. "In a primal, most frightening way, I wish to be vulnerable to you."

"It's all right." His fingers trailed down her back, to the place where her dress had fallen to her hips. She sank into his embrace, soothed by his touch. "I am not the kind of man who would take advantage of a lady and then spurn her. Whatever might happen between us, know that I will take every precaution to protect you, both in body and in spirit."

It was a pretty speech. Outwardly, she knew that, and she also knew that a man would say almost anything to entice a woman into bed. But the quiet vehemence in his voice did much to allay her fears.

"I want you, Becky. From the moment I saw you, I wanted to bed you."

She almost laughed. She had thought herself utterly debauched for thinking the exact same thing about him.

"But those feelings do not scratch the surface of all there is to this night. There is so much more."

It was true that she felt that way, but he was a man. What more could there be to him? She tilted her head to look at him quizzically. "Really?"

He smoothed a thumb over her lower lip, pressing gently. "You're beautiful, you must know that. You stand apart from the other ladies of the *ton*."

Her shoulders tightened. Talk of her looks always made her uncomfortable. She'd never truly felt a resident in her own skin. She often stared at herself in the looking glass and all she could see was a frightened, lonely woman, old beyond her years. A woman who'd made tragic, terrible mistakes, and nearly destroyed every person she'd ever loved in doing so.

"You don't like to be told of your beauty." It wasn't a question. He laughed softly, but there was bitterness in the sound. "Neither do I."

She remained silent.

"That's what it is, don't you see? I feel a connection to you that I never have with another person. I feel innately that there is something that binds us, something beyond carnal attraction."

His words placated her even as alarm bells screeched in her head. He was too serious. He was speaking of a more intimate connection than lust.

"Neither of us can know what the future will hold, but I have no intention of leaving you defenseless, no matter the circumstance."

She pressed a hand to his chest. "Noble Jack."

After a tense pause, he said in a low voice, "Never make the mistake of thinking me noble."

He made no sense. He went on about his honorable intentions—well, as honorable as intentions could be in such circumstances—and then said he wasn't noble. She narrowed her eyes. "Then you've been lying to me."

"No."

"You tell me how noble you are, in so many words, and then say to me that you don't possess the trait. How can that be?"

"Some things are simple. My desire to have you, and to please you while I have you. My desire to keep you safe from harm. Other aspects of me are more complicated and certainly less noble."

She nodded, and again awareness of her body pressed against his warm skin flooded through her. She sighed in contentment.

"You have taken me too far," he said quietly. "Every second I am not inside you my suffering increases."

"You don't look like you're suffering."

Reaching behind him, he grasped her hand and pressed it between them, pushing it down over the hard ridge of his erection. "You've teased me, ever since that first night we were alone. Now, it happens when I am with you, and when we are separated I can't stop thinking about you." He gave her a disgruntled look. "This tends to become highly uncomfortable for a man after a while."

Becky fought a grin. "I'd apologize if the wicked part of me weren't so wildly gratified to hear it."

His groan as she squeezed him was truly wretched, and Becky almost felt sorry for him.

"Come to bed with me," he said, his voice an arousing combination of entreaty and command.

She pressed her palm flat against the slight curve of his pectoral muscle and closed her eyes. "Yes. Take me to bed."

Jack rose, lifting her as if she were light as a feather. Her dress, still draped around her waist, bunched at her hips as he walked into the adjoining bedchamber, kicking the doors shut behind them as they entered the room.

The room was elegantly decorated. Art depicting landscapes of the Continent draped the walls. The carpet was lilac shot through with gold to match the similarly colored wallpaper. Candles burned from a pair of brass wall sconces, casting golden sparks of color through the room. The bed was the centerpiece. Tasseled golden ropes drew back velvet curtains of such a dark blue they appeared black, revealing an elegantly carved oak frame. A multitude of pillows in light purples, blacks, and golds covered the embroidered blue-black counterpane.

It was a room designed for illicit trysts. Becky tried not to think of Mr. Sheffield planning it thus, but she couldn't help it. A flush burned across her chest.

Jack pulled the counterpane and blanket down and laid her on the soft sheet, propping her head on one of the pillows. She gazed up at him as he hooked his fingers under the fabric of her dress, and she promptly forgot all about Mr. Sheffield.

"I don't want to tear it," he said when the material snagged over her bottom.

She lifted her hips, and the soft muslin slid over her pelvis, down her legs, and off her body, leaving her completely bare.

She focused on keeping her breaths even as his hands went to the falls of his trousers. She pressed her lips together and clutched the sheet beneath her in her fists as he kicked off his shoes and the wool slid down his narrow hips. Once he removed his trousers and stockings, he crawled onto the bed beside her.

He gathered her against him until they were pressed together from head to foot, face to face, his heavy erection nudging her thigh. "I'm going to take my time," he murmured, as if to himself. "It might kill me, but I will take my time." He cupped her cheeks in his palms. "Remember what I told you earlier."

"Remember...?" she asked faintly.

"I wouldn't hurt you for anything. Remember that."

"I...yes," she breathed. "I'll remember."

He kissed her tenderly, sipping at her lips as if she were ambrosia. She gripped his hard shoulders, her mind whirring, the aching need spreading through her body like a sweet poison.

Grazing over her skin, his hand left her cheek and traveled down her neck and chest to her breast, plumping and kneading, his fingertips scraping over her nipple, making her squirm and gasp into his mouth.

Moving his hand to the curve of her hip, he pulled her more firmly to him. Unable to help herself, she ground her body against him, needing him closer, wanting more.

"That's right," he murmured. His hand slipped lower,

right to the center between her legs, and she nearly lurched off the bed.

"Too fast?"

"No," she whispered. "No."

His hand tightened over her mound, and she gasped. Lightning blazed through her, hot sparks of pleasure.

His fingers pressed deeper. Becky held on to Jack for dear life as he began a slow glide over her sensitive, slick skin. "Oh," she gasped, her body arcing toward him.

She kept her eyes open, fixed on his face, despite the urge to slam them shut. His gaze remained on her, steady and determined. "I want you to come for me."

She made an incoherent noise. She'd been close earlier when he'd lavished attention on her breasts. Now, she didn't know if she could. The sensations were too powerful. Almost overwhelming.

His gaze, so focused on her, so steady. His sex, growing ever harder against her thigh. She squirmed against it, seeking it as she sought his touch. Light from the candles danced across his broad shoulders, making them shine bronze.

He was so beautiful. And his eyes were dark with want, brimming with lust. His lips were parted with need, his breath releasing in harsh rasps that drowned out the sound of her own exhalations and filled the room with his desire.

Yet he didn't push her down and make her his. He worked her slowly, patiently, until she whimpered. Her fingernails scored his shoulders. Her body shuddered from head to toe. The feeling—oh, it was beautiful and wicked and so heady she thought she might burst. It was a glowing sun of pleasure expanding within her, sending exquisite flames licking through her veins.

"Oh," she whispered on a moan. "Oh."

His fingers tightened over her, the pressure increasing. He pressed on that sensitive area, and she squirmed away, gasping, "Too much."

She would crawl out of her skin if he continued. He didn't. He gentled his fingers, tracing circles around that too-sensitive spot. Still, he studied her, watched her closely.

He was learning her body, she realized. Learning what made her groan, what made her squirm. What made her come.

He slipped a finger inside her, and she sucked in her breath and pushed her forehead onto his shoulder. She trembled as he moved inside her, learned about her most secret places, her unspoken desires, the places that made her sob with a need for release.

"Come for me, sweetheart. Come when you're ready."

His fingers pumped deep within her. She thought she might be torn apart, or that she might scream, or yell at him to stop or go harder, faster, do something to free her, to release the tension that had built so tautly inside her that her skin prickled with the need for relief.

She heard the roar of blood through her veins, her own harsh breaths, and his rasping exhalations overlapping both.

With a gut-wrenching sob, she came. The hot, tight ball condensing within her suddenly burst, exploded into a million sparks of agonized pleasure that shot through every nerve in her body. She froze, unable to move, to speak, to breathe, as it rushed through her, more powerful than any physical sensation she'd ever experienced.

He didn't stop. He stroked her through the powerful orgasm as her body clutched his fingers like a vise. She began to shake, her hands grasping at his back, trying to find purchase, and finally gripping his shoulders again. He was her lifeline. He kept her grounded, whole, kept her from falling completely apart.

"My God," she heard him say, as if from a distance. "My God, Becky..."

The contractions in her body slowly began to recede, and his expert fingers continued to keep her from falling, bringing her down gently back onto the soft sheet.

She was gasping, she realized. Loudly. Sweat—or was it tears?—caked a strand of hair to her cheek. Fresh tears leaked from her lids, and he kissed them away. "Don't cry. Please, sweetheart, don't cry."

A loud creak sounded from just outside the doors that led to the sitting room, and Becky froze. Jack jerked into action. He pulled away from her, tearing himself out of her grip and throwing the covers over her, hiding her body.

The doors banged against the inside walls as they opened. Assorted gasps reached Becky's ears. Panic surged, a cacophony in her head. Still in bed beside her, his torso bare but the sheet pulled up over his waist, Jack turned to the doorway.

She clutched the bedcovers to her neck.

"Rebecca!"

Oh, God. It was her brother's voice.

Chapter Four

Four years ago, Garrett might have yanked out a gun and shot Jack on the spot. But Becky's brother was a changed man, a calmer, happier one, less likely to jump into action without thought. His wife had come far in taming him.

Nevertheless, a powerful undercurrent of violence resonated in his voice.

Becky turned to the door and gasped at what—or rather *who*—she discovered standing there. Not only her brother. As if that wouldn't have been horrible enough. No, it seemed half the population of London crowded the door.

Becky's cousin Tristan stood behind Garrett, fury darkening his features. His wife, Sophie, was at his side. A large group of people Becky didn't recognize stood behind them.

"What is it? Let me see!" Lady Borrill thrust aside a

slender young man and burst into the room. Others closed
in behind her.

Becky had been in a life-or-death situation before.
She'd combated overwhelming panic and remained
strong. But at this moment, she wanted nothing more than
to shrink until she was pea-sized and disappear beneath
the covers, or better, vanish entirely and never show her
face to any of these people again. She stared dumbly at
them, unable to move, to speak. Her hands clutched the
bedclothes so tightly, her nails dug into her palms and
broke the skin.

For a long, charged moment, silence ruled. Then, all
at once, noise erupted. Some murmured, others shouted,
their words tumbling together. Garrett strode toward
Becky and Jack, his face white, his lips tight, his fists
bunched, looking for all the world as if he meant to
murder Jack Fulton with his bare hands.

Sophie lunged forward and grabbed his arm, trying to
hold him back. She spoke, but Becky could not discern
her words in the din.

She could discern Garrett's words, however, as he
shook Sophie off as easily as a horse might flick its ear to
rid itself of a fly.

"You bastard," he snarled, raising his fists. "That's my
sister you're defiling."

"What the devil are you doing?" Jack demanded.
"Leave this room. Now!"

Garrett surged toward the bed. "I'll kill you."

Sophie had turned to see the crowd gathered behind
them, and Becky heard her groan of dismay. "Oh, dear."

Garrett froze, his features a tight mask. Then he
sucked in a breath and whirled around. When he spoke,

his voice was a low, menacing command. "Get the hell out of here."

Nobody moved.

"Now!" he bellowed.

People leapt into action, and within seconds, the crowd cleared and the door closed, leaving only Sophie, Tristan, and Garrett in the room with Becky and Jack.

Again, Garrett advanced on Jack.

Jack surged up, raising his hands. "I'm happy to fight you, duke, but is this the time and place?"

"Yes."

Tension radiated from Jack. "Let's do this in a civilized fashion. Will this constitute a formal challenge? Pistols at dawn?"

"Fists," Garrett snapped. "Now."

Perhaps Kate hadn't tamed her brother as much as Becky had thought. Fear for Jack finally gave her back her voice. "No, Garrett," she breathed. "Leave him be."

Garrett's light blue eyes flicked to her and then away. His stance didn't change, nor did his demeanor. As usual, she hadn't affected him at all. Kate was the one person who could cool him, who could defuse his fury, but she wasn't present.

Tristan moved to stand beside her brother. He grasped Garrett's shoulder, keeping him—only temporarily, Becky knew—a safe distance from Jack.

Garrett's icy blue eyes flicked again to Becky, and a muscle jerked in his jaw. He looked at Jack. "Get off the damn bed."

Jack obligingly slid off, holding one of the pillows to his groin. The sides of his buttocks hollowed and flexed as he stepped away from the bed. Becky was helpless against the tiny flash of arousal at the sight.

Garrett pointed imperiously through the doorway leading to the sitting room. "Go in there and get dressed," he said to Jack.

Jack retrieved his trousers and glanced at Becky, who offered a quick nod. "As you wish." He strode out of the room.

Garrett bent and picked something up off the floor. It was the nearly transparent gown that Becky had worn. "Get some clothes on her."

Tossing the dress to Sophie, he marched into the sitting room. Tristan followed, shutting the doors behind them. Becky shuddered. At least she could be moderately hopeful that Tristan would prevent her brother from eviscerating Jack.

Lady Borrill had told them. She must have recognized Becky and then gone to Tristan and Sophie, who had been at a dinner with Garrett. Heavily pregnant, Kate hadn't been feeling up to going out tonight and had decided not to attend. But Garrett, Sophie, and Tristan had all gone to dinner in the same carriage. Somehow, Lady Borrill had communicated that Becky was here, involved in something not quite respectable, and of course Garrett had rushed to the scene, dragging along everyone else, without thought of the consequences.

Becky's brother was heartily indifferent to propriety. If he believed his sister was in danger, he'd charge into the fray without considering the consequences.

Becky swallowed down a choking sob.

Pressing her hand against the stylishly loose blonde knot of hair at her nape, Sophie hurried to the edge of the bed, the coffee-colored skirts of her evening gown swishing and her brow lined with concern. "Oh, Becky."

Becky knew she didn't mean to have that tone of censure in her voice. Still, Sophie never failed to make her feel like a naughty child. "Just give me my dress, if you please, Sophie."

Silently, Sophie handed it over, her lips pursing when she saw the sheer quality of the fabric as it fell over Becky's breasts. She looked around the room, evidently on the hunt for something for Becky to wear that would more adequately cover her.

Finally, she sighed. "Well, we'll have to drape the blanket over you before we take you in to see the gentlemen."

Becky wrapped her arms over her chest, trying to contain her shudders. "No. I've no intention of seeing the gentlemen. I've had enough of *gentlemen* tonight." Across from the bed stood a paneled door, presumably leading to the outside corridor, and she intended to use it. She had no desire to face Tristan or Garrett, and when it came to Jack, her mind was a confused jumble of emotion.

The most pressing thing to do now was prevent Garrett from killing Jack, and while Tristan could be counted on as a temporary measure, the only person in the world who could talk sense into Garrett was his wife. Becky would speak to Kate, and Kate would find a way to prevent a duel.

"What do you mean? Of course you must go—"

"No," she said. "Please, Sophie, just take me home. I want to see Kate."

Jack pulled his shirt over his head, and he rubbed the back of his neck as the other two men came into view. Hostile energy buzzed through the elegant sitting room.

The duke stared at him, eyes narrowed, jaw set. A blond behemoth of a man, he had a deep red scar the size of a shilling above his left eyebrow. If Jack hadn't faced men like this before, he might have been intimidated. But he'd been a sailor for too long. Men like this, while not a common sight in an opulent London hotel, were ordinary enough at sea.

The duke's cousin, Tristan, Viscount Westcliff stared at him from behind the duke's shoulder. This man looked far more at home in these surroundings than his counterpart did. He was taller but slighter than the duke. While the duke's shirt and cravat were rumpled beneath his dinner coat, Westcliff was impeccably dressed in a black satin-lined tailcoat with an immaculate white cravat held at his neck by a gold pin. His hair was dark brown, and his face was long and aristocratic. Just now, that face was expressionless, but there was a telling set to his jaw. Every movement the man made appeared to be calculated for precision, and his intelligent dark eyes seemed to miss nothing.

The Duke of Calton was far more expressive than his cousin. The man wanted to kill him, but something was preventing him. Dispassionately, Jack wondered what held him back.

After a long moment of silence, Jack released a sigh. He was ready for this, and he'd expected it. Ultimately, he loathed that he must manipulate these people—people who, despite their eccentricity, by all accounts and observations seemed of a very good sort.

"What the *hell* do you think you were doing with my sister? Do you know who she is?" Calton fumed.

"I know who she is." *How well I know*, he thought bitterly.

The duke stepped forward, Lord Westcliff at his heels. "If so, then you know I'd kill anyone who touched her, much less debauched and ruined her."

Inwardly, Jack cringed. He'd made himself look like a scoundrel of the first order this night.

He was a scoundrel, after all. If he wasn't, he wouldn't have lived the life he had. He wouldn't be doing what he was doing to these people right now. His gut curdled in self-loathing. Such a slick villain he was.

And for what? For his own skin. For goddamned Tom Wortingham—curse the bastard.

Jack held up his hand to stop Lord Westcliff from adding to what the duke had said. His voice was mild. "I'd hardly say she's been ruined. She is a widow."

The two men stared at him in a silence charged with animosity.

Jack took a moment to assess his main adversary. The key to men prone to fits of righteous violence involved a combination of appeasement and logic. Certainly not provocation, something which Jack by nature was far more inclined to.

Jack sighed. No more beating about the bush. Might as well get to the point. He dropped his hands at his sides and faced the two men head-on.

"I understand your anger." He made an effort to speak in a humble tone—and succeeded somewhat, a true testament to how important this moment was. "I have no wish to see this ordeal cause Lady Rebecca any pain."

It was God's honest truth. He'd have been disconcerted by that if he wasn't so determined to achieve his goal.

"Did you see who witnessed this spectacle tonight?" Lord Westcliff asked. "Do you understand what this will do to her reputation?"

"I don't want Lady Rebecca embarrassed," Jack continued. "To see her as the subject of ridicule or to have her honor besmirched in any way would grieve me." He straightened, firming his stance and his voice. "I'm willing to go to whatever lengths necessary to prevent it."

"You should have thought about all of that before you brought her here," the duke growled.

"Sometimes in such matters the heart speaks louder than good judgment."

"The heart?" Calton sneered. "Do you take me for an idiot? What I saw here was the speaking of flesh. Hearts had nothing to do with it."

"You're wrong about that," Jack said softly.

Westcliff leveled a hard gaze at him, as if trying to dive beneath the surface of his words. But long ago, Jack had encased himself within a steel barrier no one could cross. Nobody could dig into him. No one could see his true motivation. He wouldn't allow it.

He met Westcliff's dark gaze evenly. "I intend to make this right."

"Oh, Kate," Becky cried, falling into her best friend's arms.

Her sister-in-law's protruding belly prevented Becky from sinking too deeply into her embrace. The duchess was eight months pregnant with her second child. The first, two-year-old Jessica, was asleep in the nursery along with Kate and Garrett's adopted children. Jessica had been born in London and Garrett trusted the doctor who had delivered her, so he intended to keep the family here until this child was born. Sophie and Tristan had remained as well to lend their support—though if truth be told, they preferred London over the country.

Kate's dark braid hung down to her waist and she wore a soft flannel robe over her shoulders, but she'd been wide awake awaiting Garrett's return home when Becky had arrived.

"Shh." Kate's arms tightened around Becky's shoulder blades.

"I wish you'd been there. You could have talked some sense into him—"

"Shh. Everything will be all right."

"How can you know that?"

The child leveled a firm kick against its mother's stomach, and Becky loosened her hold. Kate smiled. "You see? He agrees. He's trying to make you see sense. Whatever it is, it cannot be that bad."

Becky plunked her body onto one of the palm-print sofas, gripped her knees, and tried to calm her panic.

"What happened?"

Becky closed her eyes. "I was in bed. In a state of undress. With a gentleman. Engaging in…in…"

Kate raised her hand to stop Becky from stuttering. "I see." She sounded mildly surprised but not disappointed.

"I…Lady Borrill saw me at the hotel, and I'm certain she went straight to Sophie and Tristan. And Garrett was with them tonight, and they all rushed in and saw…"

"Oh, dear Becky." Kate settled onto the sofa beside her and slipped an arm over her shoulders. "Garrett and Tristan will be angry at the gentleman, but that is to be expected. It is undoubtedly a wretchedly embarrassing thing to have your brother and cousin witness such a personal, private moment. But once their anger diminishes, all will return to normalcy. Never fear, when Garrett returns home, I will calm him down, and I am certain Sophie will do the same with Tristan."

"No doubt you will, if it isn't too late. Jack—the gentleman I was with—suggested a duel."

Kate stiffened. "Well. If they do plan to duel, it won't happen until tomorrow, at the very earliest. I shall remind Garrett that his child would like to know his father."

Tears pricked at Becky's eyes, and Kate's hand tightened on her shoulder. Kate would understand. Kate always understood her.

"Who is this gentleman, Becky?" Kate's voice was soothing, low.

"His name is Jack Fulton. He is the son of a privy councilor and has just returned to England after an absence of many years. Cecelia introduced us, and I was…attracted to him instantly." Heat crept over her cheeks. "The feeling was mutual. We've…met several times. Tonight was the first we were…intimate."

Kate sighed. "And Lady Borrill saw?"

"Yes," Becky whispered. "And there were others I didn't recognize—guests at the hotel…" She'd never fainted before in her life, but the palms printed on the chaise across from her began to drift back and forth across the upholstery. She gripped the arm of the sofa and squeezed her eyes shut.

Kate ground her teeth. "Lady Borrill is a notorious gossip."

"I know."

"The witnesses will make it known what happened tonight. There's no way around it."

"What am I going to do? Oh, Lord, but this family doesn't need another scandal. I'm sorry, Kate. I'm so, so sorry."

She leaned forward and pushed her face into her hands. After all she'd done to her brother, Tristan, Sophie, and Kate. Four years of demure living had done little to soften her guilt over the debacle of her elopement with William.

She'd finally decided to assert herself, to move beyond William's betrayal and prove to herself that she was a strong woman worthy of affection. She'd failed. Spectacularly.

Kate stroked her hair. "You once said that scandal could never touch you."

"No," she said bleakly. "Perhaps it cannot touch me, but it touches the rest of you."

From the folds of her gown, Kate procured a linen handkerchief. "I've told you time and again through the years that guilt is a pointless emotion. It accomplishes nothing at all. It is useless and unproductive, except to cause tremendous damage to those who feel it."

"It is not only guilt, Kate, but regret. I wish…" Lord, what did she wish? Not that she'd never met Jack, that he hadn't touched her. Selfishly, she coveted every kiss, every touch, and every word that they had shared, and she couldn't wish them away, no matter how much guilt and regret sliced through her.

"Do you care for this man? This Mr. Fulton?"

"I do." Cecelia would frown at her, or maybe she would laugh. But Becky wasn't admitting to love—that would be as impetuous and silly as falling in love at first sight with William Fisk four years ago. But she did care for him.

"Do you admire him?" Kate asked.

"Yes."

"He must be intelligent, then. Well-read."

Kate knew well the kind of man who would capture Becky's interest.

"And well-traveled," she said.

"Is he an honorable man, Becky?"

Becky considered this. He'd warned her that he possessed a dishonorable nature. And yet his actions proved otherwise. He was gentle, conscientious, caring. Even now, the memory of the look in his eyes when he touched her made her shudder. When the door had opened and all those people had poured in, his first thought had been to protect her from their curious stares.

"Yes, Kate. I believe he is honorable."

"There is only one clear answer, then," Kate said in a low voice. Sighing, she dabbed her handkerchief to Becky's damp cheek. "You must marry him."

Chapter Five

Early the following afternoon, Becky hurried to the nursery to see Kate. After Becky greeted the children, Kate instructed the governess to look after them, and then she drew Becky into the corridor and closed the door behind them.

"I received a letter from Sophie this morning." Kate looked exhausted—the babe was keeping her awake at night again. Kicking off her slipper, she leaned against the smooth plastered wall and awkwardly reached down to rub the arch of one slightly swollen foot. "It's still unclear who wrote the note informing Garrett of your whereabouts."

Becky crossed her arms. "I'm certain it was that awful Lady Borrill. She gave me the cut direct on the stairs and then took her scandalous news straight to Tristan and Sophie."

"Garrett isn't certain it was Lady Borrill. He told me

they'd left dinner and were on their way to drop Sophie and Tristan off when the carriage was stopped by a man on horseback. He gave the note to the coachman and then rode off before Garrett could get a good look at him."

"What, exactly, did the note say?"

"It said you were in trouble, and it gave the name of the hotel. Garrett ordered Pip to drive there straightaway, and when they arrived, Garrett flew out of the carriage, heedless of Sophie and Tristan on his heels. He stomped into the hotel, wrestled the room's location and a key from the proprietor, and then ran upstairs. All the shouting attracted some attention, but you know Garrett. He didn't pay it any heed." Kate lowered her foot back to the floor and looked at Becky, her dark eyes full of compassion.

"Garrett has summoned me to his study." Becky hesitated. "I came to ask if you would come with me."

Kate straightened, then took Becky's hand and pressed it to her heart. "You're my dearest friend, Becky, but he didn't ask me to come—he asked you. I think you must go to your brother alone."

For a flash of a moment, Becky considered pleading with her friend. She knew she tended to lean too heavily on Kate at times, and she knew she needed to start fending more for herself. It was part of the reason she'd taken such pains to befriend Cecelia.

Kate understood Becky. They'd experienced much tragedy, sadness, and love together. In the past four years, they'd grown as close as any two women could without the bond of blood.

"I know I should go alone," Becky finally said. "But I dislike confronting him without you there."

Kate smiled. "Why do you have such faltering confidence in your own ability to be brave? I have seen such bravery from you, Becky. It's just Garrett. You can face him, I know you can."

Garrett had seen her just a few hours ago in a very, very compromising position with a man he didn't know. Was he still intent upon killing Jack? She'd heard no further word of a duel, so perhaps Kate had nipped that ludicrous idea in the bud when he'd returned last night. He'd come home surprisingly early. Not long after she and Kate had settled into their conversation in the drawing room, they'd heard hoofbeats and run to the window to see the carriage drawing up to the house. Moments later, he'd stepped out, apparently unharmed. Becky had spent the remainder of the evening praying that Jack was similarly healthy.

Leaving Kate, she went downstairs. At the door to Garrett's study, she pressed her hands nervously over her cherry-striped taffeta skirts and fidgeted with the blond frill at her neckline. Then, taking a great gulping breath, she knocked.

"Come in," Garrett called, his voice gruff.

She pushed open the door, took a step forward, and then froze as her brother—and Jack—rose from their chairs.

"Rebecca," her brother said from across his gleaming mahogany desk.

Jack, who had risen from the mint-green velvet armchair opposite Garrett, gave a silent bow. He was dressed more finely than she'd ever seen him, in an embroidered dark wine waistcoat, a crisply tied cravat, dark gray trousers, and a black cutaway tailcoat that emphasized his broad shoulders and narrow waist.

"Good afternoon, Garrett." Her voice was shaky, breathless. "Mr. Fulton. I—I didn't expect to see you here."

Jack glanced at Garrett and then gave her an easy smile. "His Grace and I agreed to meet to discuss the...unfortunate event that occurred last night."

"I see." With precise movements, she turned to close the door. The finality of the click resonated through her skull.

She turned back to the gentlemen, who still stood facing her. Unclenching her fingers, she forced her shoulders to settle and inclined her head at Jack. "I'm relieved to see you in one piece."

"If I had known you feared for me," he said in a quiet voice, "I would have reassured you that I am very difficult to break, my lady."

"I'm glad to hear it." Keeping her back perfectly straight and her chin high, she crossed the carpeted floor and sat in the floral-print armchair beside Jack's. On that signal, the men returned to their chairs.

She tried to muster a smile at him as she ran her fingers over the roses embroidered on the arms of the chair. Awareness of his proximity, even after all that had happened, rang through her veins.

His smile carved grooves, too deep to be called dimples, in his cheeks. His eyes sparkled when he smiled, and his lips...oh, his wickedly erotic lips...

Garrett cleared his throat, and she tore her gaze from Jack to look at her brother. He sat as stiffly as his high, heavily starched collar, his narrow gaze focused on both of them.

He slid a pamphlet across the sleek surface of his desk. "It has already been printed."

Becky's heart surged to her throat. Jack took the paper and lowered it before him, his lips tightening.

"What?" she whispered. "What is it?"

Without a word, he handed it to her.

The open page showed a caricature of her and Jack. They were in bed in an indecent position. The artist had drawn enormous beads of sweat dripping from them both, and they both stared wide-eyed and gaping at the door, which overflowed with people holding lanterns. Becky's oval face was long and exaggerated, and her straight, dark hair flowed over the blankets. The artist had grossly misjudged the size of her breasts and had drawn them as enormous white globes of flesh as big as her head and spilling over the edge of the blanket, everything but her nipples showing.

At the forefront of the crowd stood Garrett pointing a pistol at them both, his face twisted in rage and the scar over his eyebrow flaming like a sun.

The caption read: "Society's hypocrisy—England's pious widows frigid by day but eager by night."

She gazed down at it. She would stay calm. She would be strong. Scandal would not touch her.

Becky lowered the paper to her lap and looked up at her brother and Jack, who studied her with guarded expressions.

"Well," she said. "This is unfortunate. But expected."

"I am disappointed in you, Rebecca," Garrett said.

"Because I said this was expected? Well, it was."

"No, it's not that. I'm disappointed that you . . . that you met with a man in this manner." He flung a hand toward the paper in her lap.

She took a deep breath. "Garrett, I understand that

what you saw was a very difficult thing for a brother to see—"

Garrett made a harsh, indecipherable noise.

"—but you must understand that I am an adult. Mr. Fulton is an adult as well. Whatever occurred between us was private, and it was very wrong of you—and of everyone else—to interrupt in such a manner."

"I had heard there was trouble stirring and that it involved you," Garrett said gruffly. "What would you have suggested?"

"Perhaps you might have tried knocking first? Perhaps you might have taken pains to ensure all of London didn't witness the event?"

She welcomed the anger that heated her cheeks. It was much better than the despair, embarrassment, and guilt that had run rampant since last night.

Garrett's narrow eyes grew narrower. "I did neither, and it is a good thing, too. Fulton has informed me that nothing was consummated between the two of you. If I had waited, if I had used manners and knocked on the door, no telling what might have ensued."

"What might have ensued is none of your business!"

She glanced at Jack, her cheeks growing even hotter. He watched her with a bemused expression, almost as if he couldn't believe she'd dare chastise her brother.

Garrett had the grace to look mildly contrite. "What's done is done, Rebecca. What we must face now is the fact that all of society will soon know of your affair with Mr. Fulton."

"That's true." She bowed her head. The anger seeped out of her as quickly as it had come. "I'm very sorry for that."

"Fulton and I have spent some time conversing on the matter..." He paused.

"Yes?"

"About how it can be resolved in the most expedient way possible."

"And?" She gripped the arms of her chair. Gooseflesh broke out over her skin. She knew what was coming.

"He has offered for your hand in marriage."

Wide-eyed, she turned to Jack. "You offered? *You?*"

She hadn't expected him to offer anything. She was far more inclined to believe Garrett had held a pistol to his head and demanded a proposal.

"Yes," Jack said. "Remember what I told you? I said I'd never leave you in the lurch, no matter the circumstance. I stand by my word."

"I promise you, you must not feel compelled to do any such thing. If my brother has forced you to—"

Jack raised his hand to stop her. "No. His Grace didn't force me to do anything. It was entirely my idea."

"But—"

"It is the most obvious solution," Garrett said. "Given what happened. It is the most expedient way to salvage your reputation and put the rumors to rest."

She swallowed hard. "Of course I do understand that is what will be expected after we have caused such a scandal. However, I care nothing for my reputation. You know that, Garrett."

"In principle, it is the right thing to do," Garrett said, and she detected a familiar edge of stubbornness in his voice. "And I know how you feel about scandal and reputation, Rebecca, but what about other members of your family who aren't as invulnerable to such things?"

Becky flinched.

Leaning forward, Jack reached out for her hand. "I should like nothing more in the world than to make you my wife."

Becky stared at him. This was a proposal. Jack Fulton was asking for her hand in marriage. He was asking her to spend the rest of her life at his side as his wife. He was asking for her trust and for her love. *Forever*.

"I've let a house for us near Richmond. It's not much, but you'll be close to your family, and I promise I will do my best to provide you with every comfort you require."

This was very different from the midnight proposal she'd received from William four years ago. There were no protestations of love today. Jack wasn't clutching her knees, desperately begging her to run away with him. Nor was he saying he couldn't survive another moment without her at his side.

There was no romance in this. Jack Fulton was proposing to her in her brother's study with her brother sitting across from them. His reasoning behind offering for her didn't go any deeper than the hope of softening the effect of a scandal and salvaging her reputation. This had nothing to do with her feelings for him, or his for her.

Heat tightened her chest. She shifted uncomfortably in her seat. She glanced between her brother and Jack. Tentatively, she reached out to take Jack's proffered hand, her arm heavy as steel.

"You don't know me," she whispered as he gathered her hand in his own.

"I do, Becky. I know enough to know that I will be happy with you. I think you will be happy with me, too."

She cast a desperate glance at Garrett. Surely he must understand how she was feeling! But her brother's face was hard and unreadable.

"But I don't know you, either," she said. "We've been acquainted for less than a month."

"I'm a simple man. There isn't much more to me than what you have already seen."

"His family and his origins are well known. Unlike..." Garrett's voice trailed off, and Becky knew he was going to say, "Unlike Fisk."

None of them had known the first thing about William when they'd taken him into their home. She'd known nothing of his past or his motivation when she'd tripped off to Gretna to marry him.

On the other hand, the whole of England was familiar with the Fulton family. Jack's father was a privy councilor, and they had all been the subject of public scrutiny. This was a very different matter than with William.

Garrett cleared his throat and addressed Jack. "I spent this morning looking into your personal affairs." In response to Jack's raised brows, her brother gave an unapologetic shrug. "People have attempted to infiltrate our family. Besmirch our name, steal our fortunes. It has happened more than once. Therefore you must see why it is important for me to ensure the moral quality of any man my sister associates with."

Assuming that she would agree to marry him, Garrett had already investigated Jack. Becky let out a nearly silent hiss of annoyance.

Keeping his hand in a solid clasp over hers, Jack gave an easy shrug, but his smile did not reach his eyes. "You are more than welcome to look into my private affairs as thoroughly as you wish. I will cooperate with all your requests."

Garrett returned his gaze to Becky. "There was a scandal that forced Fulton to leave England for several years."

"I am aware of that. He told me all about it."

"Did he?"

She glanced at Jack, grateful they'd talked about this last night. "Mr. Fulton was falsely accused of a crime but the charges were dismissed, and in their embarrassment and ambition, his family sent him away in the hope that society would forget the scandal."

"Did he tell you *why* he was implicated in the murder of the Marquis of Haredowne?"

"Yes, he told me that as well."

"Did he tell you he was in love with the marquis's wife?"

"Well..." She slid her gaze toward Jack. "No."

"That isn't exactly accurate," Jack said, his tone flat. He released her hand.

Garrett's icy blue gaze settled on Jack. "The lady's name was Anne Turling. She'd married the Marquis of Haredowne less than a year earlier, and you made it known that you objected to the marriage and wanted the lady for yourself."

Becky licked her lips and breathed steadily, in and out. Jack hadn't exactly told her *that*.

Jack's mouth tightened. He didn't answer.

"So when the marquis was shot, all eyes turned to you."

"But he didn't do it." Becky clenched her hands over the pamphlet in her lap. The page was still open to the caricature, and she tried not to look at it.

"No, he didn't," Garrett said, still staring Jack down. "The marquis was murdered outside his club in Chesterfield Street, and Fulton was at a bawdy house in Drury Lane at the time."

Becky sat very still. He hadn't told her he'd been visiting a whorehouse, either. But then again, why should he? It was none of her business that he was at a whorehouse, only that he hadn't been present at the murder. He was a young rake. That was what all young rakes did, though they attempted to hide such things from the innocent ladies of society. She shouldn't be shocked at all, for she was no innocent. She was a woman with experience far beyond her years, and she was aware of the profligacy that abounded in men of their class.

Garrett turned his gaze to Becky. "He was arrested, but there wasn't a trial. The charge against him was dismissed on the grounds that a man cannot be in two places at once."

Becky brushed her palms over her skirts as if to wash her hands of the matter. "I've no idea why we're discussing this. He wasn't guilty, and that's what is most important. In any case, it's irrelevant to the topic at hand."

None of it should concern her. Not the fact that Jack had visited whorehouses, not the idea that Jack had been besotted with Anne Turling, *especially* not the revelation that Jack had wished to marry the woman. It was twelve years ago, for heaven's sake.

"Lady Rebecca is right," Jack said. "It is irrelevant. Those events occurred many years ago, and I've spent many years trying to forget them."

Garrett leaned back in his chair. "The time after that unpleasant affair is somewhat of a blank, since you were at sea and no one could know anything of what transpired there besides the other sailors. However, when Tristan and I visited the docks this morning, we were able to locate a retired seaman from your ship, the *Gloriana*."

"Were you?" Jack said without intonation.

"He described you as knowledgeable but quiet. Seems that while you were well liked, you kept to yourself, for the most part. He did mention a few episodes of onshore debauchery, but that signifies nothing." Garrett shrugged. "I'd have been more concerned if there were none."

"Are you finished?" Jack said tightly. Becky glanced at him. A dark bronze had suffused his tanned cheeks. She couldn't blame him. No one liked having his privacy invaded, and Garrett was neither delicate nor subtle.

"These are things I already knew." She waved her hand in dismissal. "Well, for the most part, in any case. They don't affect my opinion of Mr. Fulton in the least."

"I want you to know about the man's past before we go forward, Rebecca." Garrett clasped his hands atop his desk. "Despite the scandals and the debauchery, I don't believe his intentions are malicious."

Well, if that wasn't a glowing recommendation from Garrett, Becky didn't know what was. She didn't believe Jack's intentions were malicious either. Yet...

Jack locked his gaze to hers. "The past is over. I'm only looking toward the future."

"How do you see your future, Jack?" she asked quietly.

"I see it here, in England. I want to make a home here, in the land where I was born." He paused. "And I want to do it with you."

"Why?"

"It's not only because of the scandal. That was just the catalyst. I would have offered for you eventually, but it took what happened last night for me to open my eyes to the truth."

Garrett shifted uncomfortably, but Jack ignored him. He slid off his chair and knelt before Becky, gathering both her hands in his own and squeezing them tight.

"I want to make things right. I want this. Please marry me. Please be my wife."

He looked so adamant, so honest. His words were a silvery lure, a promise of something bright and shining, something she hadn't thought herself worthy of since William's death. Hope. Happiness. Love. All of it real, and even safe. For a glimmer of a moment, she believed she could open her heart, reveal her soul, lower her hard-won shields, and be safe with this man.

The temptation was nearly overwhelming. She sat silent for long moments, locked in a battle between heart, conscience, and common sense.

Yes was on the tip of her tongue. It hovered there precariously, three little letters on the verge of tumbling out and sealing her fate forever.

She could stop the scandal. Salvage her reputation, and, more important, save her family from society's retribution. She could do the right thing, what everyone expected, what her lessons from childhood taught her was the only acceptable resolution.

She gazed at Jack. His dark eyes and sun-kissed brown hair that grew to a subtle peak at the middle of his forehead. The structure of his bones—strong chin, straight nose, eyes slightly turned up at the edges. The shallow lines that feathered from their corners. The rounded curve of his bottom lip. Last night, she'd touched her tongue to that lip, tasted it. She'd taken it between her teeth and nipped it. Lord, how she'd wanted him. Still wanted him.

Yet his face—it was the face of a stranger.

She stared down at their entwined fingers. His hand was so much larger than hers, so much darker. So masculine, so different.

So foreign.

Common sense was a trait she hadn't possessed four years ago. Without it she'd been lured into a miserable match with an evil man. Perhaps Jack wasn't evil or even deceitful, but could she throw herself into another marriage so recklessly? Would she end in the same endless mire of loneliness and misery she'd felt after she'd married William and realized he'd never love her?

Jack squeezed her hand, hard, and her gaze snapped up. His lips—lord, those beautiful lips—thinned. "Becky?"

"I . . ." She shook her head.

He hissed out a breath.

Oh, Lord. Perhaps it made her selfish beyond endurance, but she couldn't. She wouldn't ruin her life yet again. Not even to show the world that she could hold her head high and take responsibility for her sins. Not even to end a scandal. Not even because this man could give her a life-altering orgasm with just a few strokes of his fingers.

For years, she'd believed herself incapable of loving again. And the truth was, she didn't love Jack Fulton. How could she? She didn't know him.

He didn't love her, either. She saw the gentleness in his eyes. The admiration he felt for her. Certainly he possessed the desire to protect and care for her, even to make her happy. For some reason he truly believed he wanted to marry her. But he didn't love her.

Maybe it was true that society viewed marriage as a transaction rather than a means of joining two compatible people who loved each other. But that didn't make it right, or acceptable—not to Becky. Another woman of her class might go forward with this without a qualm, but long ago, Becky had realized she was different from most women.

As handsome and desirable as Jack Fulton was, no matter how he made her feel, she couldn't marry him. She couldn't ruin her life again. She couldn't traipse into a marriage knowing she had no in-depth understanding of the man she shackled herself to.

"I...don't know." She sucked in a breath. "I need...I need time."

Time was something Jack didn't have.

"How much time?" he demanded.

She shook her head. "I couldn't say."

Panic welled in his gut. He couldn't speak for a long moment.

Finally, he raised his head and stared at her. His voice was very quiet. "Why?"

"I told you before," she said. "I don't know you. Not well enough for—" She tore her hands from his and they flailed in a wild, all-encompassing gesture. "This."

Jack ground his teeth from the effort not to shout that they'd gone over this already, that he'd already told her she knew as much about him as was important to know.

God, he wanted this woman. He lusted after her. He wanted her in his bed like no one he'd ever seen. Those mad primal urges to make her his, to protect and care for her, to *love* her, merged with his pressing need for her money. Together, they were more than enough to make him go to any lengths to win her.

"There is a deeper explanation," Calton said. Jack looked over his shoulder at the duke as he continued, "Rebecca's first husband was a blackguard, and not only that, he was insane. He was out to ruin me and steal her money. And those were the least of his sins. My sister's hesitancy is completely understandable."

Like a punch in the gut, it struck Jack how similar he was to Becky's first husband, and he rocked back on his heels. He wasn't out to ruin the Duke of Calton, but God knew he wanted—no, *needed*—Lady Rebecca's money.

Yet he was different. He'd be damned if he would hurt her like the first bastard she'd married. She'd never need to know about the blackmail. He would make sure she didn't, because if she found out, she'd see the similarity to her first husband. She'd see it as a betrayal. It would hurt her, and Jack didn't want to see her hurt.

"I'm not that man."

"No, you're not him," she agreed. "We didn't know William at all and we gave him our trust, much to our detriment." Becky offered him a faltering smile. "I have since learned that most people are good. It is a rare man indeed who can live up to the standard of treachery set by my first husband."

"If you believe I'm not like him, then why do you hesitate?"

"I—" She bowed her head. "I just don't know you well enough. As much as I believe in you—feel in my heart that you cannot be anything like him—I cannot take the risk."

She sat more stiffly now, her hands clasped tightly in her lap, resting on that goddamned paper that made him want to go out and wring the smug little artist's neck. The caricature infuriated him even while it played perfectly into his plan. Yet apparently, it hadn't been enough.

He addressed the duke. "We agreed that marriage was the best course of action."

"Yes," Calton agreed. "But the choice is ultimately my sister's."

She exhaled a breath of relief, and for an instant, the devil in Jack regretted the fact that Calton gave her free choice in the matter.

"I told His Grace last night that I've no wish to see you suffer because of this, Becky," Jack said, looking meaningfully at the pamphlet. "I don't want anyone else to suffer, either." He rested his hands on his knees as if he had nothing to hide. "And I want you. God... You must know how much I want you."

He infused meaning into the word "want," because, damn it, he did want her. A *hell* of a lot more than he wanted the hangman's noose.

Her cheeks grew pink, and she slid a glance at her brother. "I feel wretched for having caused my family pain... again. There is nothing I desire less in this world, Garrett. But please understand my reasoning. My first marriage was so... difficult..." Gazing down at Jack, she swallowed hard. "I'm sorry, Jack, but I cannot marry you."

Chapter Six

A week after the world discovered her in bed with Jack Fulton, Becky pushed open the door to the drawing room and reeled to a halt.

Kate and Garrett stood in the center of the room locked in an embrace only slightly more decent than the one in which Jack and Becky had been discovered. They jerked apart, but Garrett's hand remained cupped protectively over Kate's belly as her skirt fluttered to the floor. One side of Kate's hair had been pulled free from its pins, and color flared high in her cheeks.

Becky froze in the doorway. "Oh...dear."

Garrett smiled. His smile could light up a room, and after his years of living in poverty and isolation, every one of his smiles was a gift. Though she often saw him grinning like a besotted fool at his wife, he rarely bestowed that gift on anyone else.

And he could smile, couldn't he? The object of his

affections was his wife, after all. Whatever they did together was perfectly acceptable.

Kate pressed the back of her palm to her flushed cheek.

"I'm so sorry...I was looking for my book." Becky gestured at the volume of *Antigone* lying on the palm-print sofa.

Garrett pulled farther away from Kate, but he clasped her hand, and a spasm of envy shot through Becky. Garrett and Kate were good people, and they deserved all the happiness and all the blessings they were given. Those had been many in the past four years, and Becky was thankful for it. Still, she couldn't help envying what they had.

"We were just sitting down for some tea." Kate made a vain attempt to correct her hair. "Please join us."

"All right." Becky seated herself on the sofa beside her book while Kate poured them some tea from the silver service set on the table.

"Perhaps you should tell her now," Garrett said as Kate handed her a cup of steaming liquid and sat beside her. Garrett took the matching chaise across from them, his back to the hearth.

"Tell me what?"

Kate hesitated. Then she lowered her cup to the saucer and placed it on the small marble table beside the sofa. "Please don't be angry with me, but I've invited Jack Fulton and his family to dinner day after tomorrow."

Becky gaped at her. "Why on earth would you...?"

"Fulton visited when you were with Lady Devore yesterday," Garrett said. "And Kate took it upon herself to ask him to return. When she learned his father and brother were in Town for a few days, she took pains to invite them, too."

Becky stared at Kate with wide eyes. Her sister-in-law raised her hand in a placating gesture. "I know it was rash of me, and I probably should have asked you first, but I do like him. He seems...well—" she cast Becky an apologetic smile, "—he seems quite besotted with you."

"I turned down his proposal," Becky reminded her.

"Not exactly," Garrett said. "If I recall correctly, at first you said you required time to think on it. You needed time to know him better. Kate is right—what better way to do that than invite him to dinner?"

"And his family," Kate added, tucking a stray strand of dark brown hair behind her ear. Kate always thought of family. To her, there was nothing in the world more important.

"I haven't heard a word from him," Becky said. "I thought he was finished with me. I assumed he'd decided to move on."

Those thoughts had plagued her for the past few days, filled her with doubt and even a glimmer of regret. A part of her wondered if, in her fear and distrust, she'd given away her final hope for happiness.

"He has no intention of moving on. He still hopes to convince you," Garrett said.

"Really? But why?" He'd been furious when she'd said no. He hadn't said a word, but he'd clenched his fists, and his lips had gone white. She'd believed she'd damaged his male pride beyond repair. "I'm surprised he'd even want to set eyes on my face again, much less dine here with his family."

"Sometimes love isn't so easy to relinquish," Kate said quietly.

Becky plucked her book up from the sofa cushion and clasped it to her chest. "Oh, for heaven's sake, Kate. He doesn't love me."

"Are you certain of that?"

"He hasn't known me long enough to love me. He hardly knows anything about me."

Kate's fingers slid up and down the curve of her belly. "Really, how can you know? Love is as variable as people are. How can you be so insistent that love cannot evolve after a month's acquaintance? Honestly, I fell in love with your brother even before we formally met." Kate and Garrett shared a secret smile before Kate turned back to Becky. "He seems so determined to have you. Why else would he persist? Why else would he agree to come to dinner? Why else does he seem so interested in ingratiating himself to our family?"

Becky closed her eyes. God, but she'd missed him these past few days. Her body yearned for him. She couldn't stop thinking about him, remembering the simple contentment of just sitting and talking with him, reliving the erotic pleasures he'd wrought on her body. She'd longed to see him again, even while she knew it was best if she didn't.

Kate's brow furrowed in distress. "I don't want you to feel compelled to join us for dinner. I understand if you prefer to stay in your room."

"It would be cowardly of me not to come." Rubbing her forehead with her fingertips, she looked through her fingers at her sister-in-law. "Tell me the truth, Kate. Do you think I should marry him?"

"What I feel has no bearing on what you should do. You must do what is right for you. Garrett and I only want you to be happy."

The scandal had escalated in the past few days. Now, when Becky walked on the street, ladies tittered behind their fans. Becky could hold her head high for now, but she was already tiring of it all.

A shudder of mixed anticipation and trepidation wound down her spine. "Dinner. Very well."

Kate smiled wistfully. "I must say I like Jack Fulton. I hope that someday things will work out between the two of you. I agree that it would put the scandal to rest if you marry him now, but it's certainly not worth risking your happiness to do that. Take your time to determine if it is the right course. But I truly hope you will give the gentleman a chance."

The day of the dinner engagement with Jack and his family arrived, and that afternoon, Becky sat in her favorite chair in the salon warming her toes by the fire, an unopened book on her lap. Tonight was the first time Becky would see Jack since the morning of his proposal over a week ago. But tonight, her entire family would be in attendance, including her sharp-tongued Aunt Bertrice, who'd arrived from Yorkshire for the holidays just this morning.

A knock sounded on the door and she looked up to see a footman peek into the salon. "You've a visitor, my lady. Mr. Fulton is here to see you."

Jack! She hadn't expected him to arrive before dinner. She jumped out of her chair, set the book aside, and shook out the flounces in her slate-colored skirts. "He's early."

"Yes, my lady."

"Please show him up."

A few moments later, Jack entered, bringing with him that masculine virility that shone about him like an aura. He was tall and broad and everything she ever imagined when she'd lain alone at night and envisioned perfection in a man.

Just inside the room, he stopped, a smile curving his wicked lips. The footman left, closing the door behind him.

"Thank God," Jack said, his voice an arousing amalgam of roughness and quiet. "I thought I'd never see you alone."

Her fingertips fidgeted in her skirts.

In two long, silent strides over the carpet, he stood before her. He hooked one broad arm around her waist and tugged her against him.

Every muscle in her body stiffened, but then his mouth descended over hers, and she melted.

His lips were the richest dessert, soft and creamy, passionate, as hungry for her as she was for him. She dropped her skirts, twined her arms about his neck, and kissed him back with the force of all the twisted emotions that had confounded her in the last several days.

If only it could always be like this. Her guilt and fear melted away, slid down her spine and pooled at her feet, leaving her fresh and pure and clean. Open to whatever he offered her.

He could make her lower all her shields. All he needed to do was keep kissing her, keep his lips pressed against her cheek, her eyelids, her jaw. Keep his hands firmly gripping her about the waist, holding her steady.

This was togetherness. If only they could stay like this, joined, inseparable...

But it ended all too quickly. He pulled away gently, then bent his forehead to hers. "I've missed you," he murmured, his breath a whisper over her lips.

"I've missed you, too."

"I'm going crazy for wanting you."

Should she tell him the truth? Admit that she wanted him, too? Had desperately craved his touch every day since she'd last seen him?

Once, she'd felt this way with William, but that had faded sooner than she ever could have predicted. It was all a figment of her wishful imaginings, this security she felt in Jack's arms. Even that had already proved false—for she'd been in his arms when all those people had stormed into the bedchamber last week.

He stroked the back of his finger down the side of her cheek. "You want me, too. I feel it." His lips moved to her ear, his breath dancing over her lobe. "Let's finish this nonsense. Marry me."

She sighed. As much as she wanted him, she couldn't suggest another evening with him in Sheffield's Hotel. He didn't want that anymore. He wanted more. He wanted too much.

Pulling back, he scraped a thumb over her brow, smoothing it. "I've made up my mind—I made it up a week ago. I want you. I'm ready to commit to marrying you."

She stared up at him, her forehead furrowed in consternation. "How can you say that so easily? How can you commit your life to someone you hardly know?"

He shrugged. "I've chosen my path. I will not be

dissuaded from it. Not now, not ten years from now. This is what I what. *You* are what I want." He gazed down at her face, his dark eyes intent. "Do you understand that?"

"I...think so." She turned away. "But it's not so simple for me."

"Why?" he demanded.

She crossed her arms tight across her shimmery gray bodice, closing herself off to him. "I never thought I'd marry again. I thought I'd live out the remainder of my days as a widow bluestocking."

He chuckled. "You? A bluestocking?"

Once again it struck her how very little they knew of each other. Scandal aside, he intended to spend a lifetime with her based on nothing but their immediate carnal attraction. They possessed only a sliver of knowledge of each other beyond it.

She remembered those long days at Kenilworth after she and William had married. William had grown distant, and she'd begun to realize they weren't as well matched as he'd led her to believe. She'd never felt lonelier.

Since William died, she'd surrounded herself with her family, and more recently, Cecelia, and though she was physically lonely, that feeling was nothing compared to the soul-deep aloneness she'd felt at Kenilworth.

It wasn't a difficult stretch of the imagination to think the same thing might happen with Jack. He was a bachelor rogue. Thirty years old, accustomed to gallivanting about the globe and taking lovers when the mood struck him. Accustomed to his freedom. Perhaps he'd loved a girl once, but that was long ago. Did he have the first idea how to know—to really *know*—a woman? Did he have the first idea how to be a husband? For that matter, did she have any idea how to be a proper wife?

"Becky?" He touched her hair, lightly stroking his fingers over the braided strands twisted at her nape. "I would make you happy," he said, his voice quiet but emphatic. "I swear it."

"Would you?" Turning back to him, she searched his eyes and found nothing but promise in them.

"I swear it," he repeated. His lips descended on hers again, sweet and warm. His gentle touch swept through her, softening her muscles and her resistance.

"Marry me," he whispered against her lips.

"No," she whispered back. Then she winced as he stiffened. "Jack...I..."

His hands curled around her shoulders, but he didn't pull away.

"I don't mean it to sound so final." *Give him a chance*, Kate had said, and she was right. It would be ridiculous, not to mention foolish, to dismiss Jack out of fear that he might be another William. "You must give me time."

The tightening of his fingers on her shoulders was subtle, but she felt it. "I want you, Becky. Now."

"I'm not ready."

With a harsh, frustrated breath, he drew back, thrusting his hand through his blond-streaked hair. "I'm going to convince you otherwise. You're afraid because of what happened to you last time. But you keep forgetting: *I'm not him*."

"I know. Just...please. Be patient with me."

"I'm not a patient man."

"It will take time for me to learn how to trust again."

"And once I win your trust?"

A small thrill wound through her at his insistence, at the steely determination in his eyes. "Then...if it can be done...yes. I will consider marrying you."

He squared his shoulders. His brown eyes bore into hers in direct challenge. "I will win your trust, then. It won't take long."

He seemed very convinced of that, but she knew herself better than Jack did. "I hope you're right," she said with a small smile.

"I am right. By month's end, we'll be at the altar."

He seemed to relish this challenge, and his cocky confidence melted her further. Her smile widening, she pressed her body against him, looking up at him from beneath her eyelashes. "Do you think so?"

"I know it." He lowered his lips to her brow. "I cannot wait to make you mine."

Jack sat stiffly, his fingers clamped around his wineglass, his neck prickling. He resisted the urge to yank off his cravat. He hadn't desired his father and brother's presence tonight, but the duchess had invited them, and he was in no position to naysay the woman.

To his annoyance, he'd not been seated near Becky. Instead, her aunt, Lady Bertrice, who incessantly peered at him through a monocle, sat on his right. Her magnified rheumy blue eye was so suspicious it made his skin crawl, though if he were being reasonable he'd remember there wasn't any way she could know anything. If the Duke of Calton could discover nothing of interest in his exploration into Jack's private affairs, surely an old woman couldn't either.

Still, he didn't like the way that blue eye pried under his skin.

Lady Westcliff sat on Jack's left, separating Jack from his father. Bertrand, Jack's eldest brother, sat across from them, flanked by Becky in a glorious cream-colored silk gown and Lady Devore. Jack's father and Bertrand behaved with an obsequiousness toward the duke and his family that made Jack's gut churn.

Viscount Westcliff, sitting at the duke's right, was the most affable presence at the table, deftly balancing the surliness of the duke with the fawning of Jack's family, and it was he and his wife who kept the conversation from sinking to banality—or ceasing altogether.

After the second course was served, Jack's father sighed and leaned back in his chair, resting one hand on his protuberant belly while the other lifted his wineglass, his little finger raised in an effeminate gesture. He spoke loudly, so his voice could reach the other end of the table. "I should like to thank you again, Your Grace, for convincing my son to take the proper course and do right by your lovely sister. I only regret that the lady has declined."

Everyone fell silent, and Jack glanced across to Becky. The edges of her lips thinned, and she stared at the table linen beyond her plate of oyster-stuffed venison.

The duke leveled a cold stare at Jack's father. "I convinced your son of nothing. He was the one who decided that marriage would be the best course of action."

Jack didn't look at his father. Not for the first time, he wondered how it was possible that anyone, much less a king of England, could have enough faith in the man to make him a privy councilor. Then again, the Right

Honorable Edmund Fulton had always sunk far more effort into his political career than he would with anything related to Jack. And considering King George IV—well, perhaps not so surprising, after all. Jack had never met the current king, but from all he'd heard, the man shared many traits and habits with Jack's father.

Jack had always been his mother's child, his mother's favorite. His father had showered his attention and his love on his two eldest sons, and Jack had never earned much notice from him, except on occasion as someone to vent his frustrations upon when life was not going his way.

When he was six years old, Jack had been blamed for the crops at Hambly rotting due to too much rain. When he was eight, he'd been accused of swaying a particularly important decision in Parliament. When he was twelve, he was solely responsible for the failure of an investment his father had made in a canal.

Between the ages of twelve and eighteen, Jack had gone away to school and had managed to avoid his father for the most part. But when he was eighteen, the murder of the Marquis of Haredowne had coincided with the failure of Jack's middle brother, Edward, to win a promotion to the rank of post captain in His Majesty's Navy. Of course, that was Jack's fault, too.

After the charges against him were dismissed, Jack was sent away forthwith, and weeks after he'd left England, his mother had died suddenly. Jack hadn't heard of her passing until months later. They'd been anchored in Sydney, and in the midst of his anguish and grief over his mother's death, Jack had received a letter from his father.

She'd died because of him, his father said. Because she was brokenhearted about the embarrassment Jack had caused to their family.

Jack knew it was nonsense. His mother had remained his most steadfast, staunchest supporter through every second of the ordeal. Yet a part of him had shriveled and died at those words, and he'd crumpled that letter, held a candle to it, and watched it burn, promising himself that he'd never again listen to a word his father said.

Becky's lips thinned further as Jack's father chuckled. "To be sure, sir, I never imagined my son settling down and marrying, especially into a family as fine as yours. He's a scoundrel of the first order, does naught but toss away his allowance on hells and women."

Jack ground his teeth. Not only were those words inaccurate—the man had interacted very little with Jack for the past twelve years—but they would do nothing to ingratiate Jack to the duke.

Jack had never understood his father. He never would. He could only count the hours until this night was over. He'd have to interact with his father and his brother—fortunately his middle brother had finally been promoted to the rank of post captain and was currently at sea—only at his forthcoming nuptials, and then he'd be free of them until the next family obligation arose, which Jack prayed wouldn't be anytime soon.

The duke shrugged. "You may trust I have looked into his affairs. I found nothing out of the ordinary."

Jack's father continued blithely. "Indeed, I never thought he'd be tamed. Fidelity is not a strong suit in our family, is that not so, Bert?"

Bertrand, who often left his wife in the country only to

be seen at various events in London with his mistress on his arm, choked down the wine he'd been holding to his mouth and swallowed, patting his napkin on his lips. Jack felt little fraternal affection for his oldest brother, who'd spent the better part of their childhoods reminding Jack and Edward of his superiority as the eldest son and heir.

The Duke of Calton's blue eyes narrowed into slits, and Lord Westcliff cut in, bringing his champagne glass to his lips. "We are certainly ahead of ourselves, aren't we? They are yet to agree on forging a permanent connection."

"Surely marriage is the best solution. Indeed, the *only* solution," Jack's father said.

Bertrand chose this moment to open his fool mouth. "What my father says is absolutely true. Ever since their— ah—*discovery*, my brother and the lady have been made fools of up and down the streets of London. I have heard that a playwright is fashioning the story of their discovery into a farce about the morality of the upper orders."

Jack thought that playwright would do better to base his work on his brother's life rather than his own, but he felt no impulse to respond. He couldn't open his mouth without showing his disgust for his father and brother's behavior, and he wouldn't show his loathing here. No matter how compelling the temptation to put them in their place, the truth was that he was of their blood, and he would not further the damage either was doing to his estimation in Becky's family's eyes.

Beside him, Lady Bertrice muttered something unintelligible and poked a fricasseed pea into her mouth.

Jack's father leaned forward and spoke past Jack and Lady Westcliff. "What was that you said, ma'am?"

Lady Bertrice swallowed her pea and raised her fork meaningfully. "Said it was a fine thing for my niece to suffer, when she is among the most principled of her class."

Jack's father and brother raised matching disbelieving brows. "Is that so?" asked his father.

"Mm." Lady Bertrice raised her monocle again and peered through it, her gaze sweeping from the duke at one end—still looking mightily annoyed—to the duchess at the other.

"I'd wager any one of you seated at this table tonight could easily surpass Rebecca in debauchery—both in thought and in deed."

Westcliff gave an easy chuckle. "No doubt you're right on that score, Aunt."

Lady Bertrice's enlarged eye focused on her niece, who sat at the other end of the table, across from her. Becky stared back at her aunt, her shoulders tight beneath the luxuriant silk.

"Of course, she could make it easier on all of us if she weren't so deuced stubborn." Lady Bertrice's eye slid toward the duke. "That comes from our side of the family, no doubt, because you're the same way, boy."

"It's not stubbornness." Becky spoke stiffly, still gazing at her aunt.

Becky had thrust away the openness she'd shown him before dinner; she'd stiffened and grown cold. With an aura of regal aloofness and a crown of ebony hair, she'd transformed into the Queen of Winter in ivory silk. She was beautiful.

"Pray tell me what it is, then, if it not be stubbornness," Lady Bertrice demanded.

"It's common sense."

Jack's father choked out a short laugh. "Common sense? Really? How can it be common sense to encourage a scandal?"

"Indeed," Bertrand added, "I should think that sense requires—no, it demands—marriage."

Becky shook her head as she carefully placed her fork on her plate and then looked up at Jack's brother, who sat beside her to her left. "It doesn't, in fact. Common sense demands caution. Marriage is a permanent state and hence it requires a thoughtful, careful approach. Jumping into it in a reckless fashion could wreak far more damage than playwrights, artists, and gossips could ever hope to."

She spoke from personal experience, Jack knew.

"I agree, Becky," Lady Westcliff said. "And you point out a common shortcoming of our class—the tendency to leap into such matters without forethought."

The duchess sat at the end of the table opposite the duke. She had spent most of the evening in contemplative silence, but now she spoke. "Indeed," she agreed. "I always am saddened to see the unhappy marriages prevalent in our class. So many wives voluntarily spend months separated from their husbands, and when I search for the root cause, it is invariably because their marriages were founded on financial considerations rather than a mutual regard."

Lady Westcliff and the duchess were attempting to steer the conversation to more general topics and away from Becky and him marrying. Jack was grateful for it. They'd been sitting here for over an hour, and during that time, he had observed the weight of the pressure building on Becky's shoulders and felt powerless to stop it.

This wasn't the way to go about winning her. This dinner was a mistake. They could prattle on about propriety, expectations, and scandal for the rest of her life, but that wasn't what she wanted. It wasn't what she needed.

She wanted peace. She needed to be freed from her fear. The way to do that was to be with her alone. To talk to her, to touch her. To prove that he was different from William Fisk; that he was the man who could bring her the happiness she believed was impossible to attain.

Jack's father slapped his hands on the table. "I see!" he exclaimed. He flashed a jovial smile across the table at Becky. "I finally comprehend your hesitation, my lady. You know as well as I do that my son is a wastrel—of course he is! He's got nothing, whereas you are rich as Croesus, and he could very well be after you for your money." His grin widened. "I do not envy you, child. Still, there is the matter of propriety and duty, is there not? And the matter of this wretched scandal. If you don't do whatever you can to stop the talk, it will only worsen. There are children in your family who could be affected by this years from now."

Becky's lips curved stiffly. "Thank you, sir."

Jack's father's eyes widened. "Why...you're welcome!"

"The solution is now clear," she said, her voice quiet but with a steely edge.

"Well, that's excellent!" Jack's father blustered.

She was impressive, so cool, so elegant, her back straight, her violet eyes cold and clear. She possessed far more strength than Jack had originally given her credit for. First she'd eschewed propriety and risked permanent exile from society with her refusal to marry him, and now Jack sensed that she was on the verge of giving his father the set-down of his life. Despite knowing that her solution wouldn't be compatible with his bid to become her husband, Jack's admiration for her soared.

"You're correct about the scandal escalating and you're correct about its effect on my family," she said with chilly politeness.

Bertrand muttered his assent. Her family stared at her, forks poised—some in midair—and Jack's gut tightened at their expressions. They knew what was coming, just as he did.

Becky stood. Instantly, Jack thrust his napkin aside and rose. All the other men followed suit. Snagging his chair leg on the expensive Persian carpet, his father was the last to rise.

She addressed the entire table. "By continuing with our association, Mr. Fulton and I are only adding fuel to this fire. I shall retire from London until the scandal has been put to rest. I intend to remove myself from this situation entirely." Her dark blue gaze traveled to Jack. "Forgive me, Mr. Fulton, but I believe this is the best course of action."

So many feelings crashed through him—respect, excitement, affection, dread, alarm—he could hardly push a word out. "Becky—"

She dipped her head in a semblance of a curtsy, swiveled, and left the room.

Chapter Seven

Jack caught Becky as she placed her hand on the banister and planted her foot on the first step. He grabbed her wrist, stopping her, and she turned to face him.

"Don't go."

She shook her head helplessly. "There is no other solution."

His grip on her wrist tightened, his skin warm against her chilled flesh. "Yes, there is. Marry me. We'll work everything else out later."

Her lips twisted. She leaned toward him, lowering her voice. "What if we cannot 'work everything else out'? What if we find ourselves locked in a miserable match for the rest of our lives?"

"That won't happen." His voice was firm, the look in his eyes hard and determined. She didn't understand how he could be so assured, but then she remembered. Of course. He'd never been married before. He didn't know how awful it could be to be married to a person who despised you.

"Let go of me, Jack." Her voice was quiet but strong.

He loosened his grip but didn't release her.

She glanced in the direction of the dining room, and seeing no movement, she turned back to him. "What if your father is right? What if you *are* a wastrel and a scoundrel? What if all you want from me is my fortune? What if you prove to be as inconstant as they are?"

She'd heard rumors about his father's and brother's infidelities. She wasn't blind or deaf, and these were the things the married and widowed ladies of London society gossiped about.

Jack's eyes locked onto hers. "I am not like them. You know in your heart I am not like them."

She gazed at him for a long moment, tempted to agree, to say she knew she was being hopelessly stubborn and that she believed him.

Instead, she shook her head. "No. I don't."

Anger flashed, sharp and hard, in his dark eyes, and his jaw muscle flexed as he ground his teeth.

"How can I?" she asked. "We've spent only a few hours together." Even less time than she'd spent with William before throwing her life at him. "It's not enough."

"Don't go, Becky. Don't leave London."

Across the hall, the door opened, and Kate bustled up to them, her skirts rustling. She paused when she reached the bottom of the stairs, inclining her head at Jack. His fingers slid from Becky's wrist.

"Good night, then, Mr. Fulton." Without another word, Kate grasped Becky's hand and marched her up the stairs. Jack didn't say anything, but Becky felt the heat of his stare as they disappeared from his sight.

She didn't realize she'd been holding her breath until they entered her bedchamber. She exhaled, then inhaled deeply as Kate closed the door firmly behind them.

"Sorry I took so long." Kate plunked her encumbered body onto Becky's bed. Her cheeks were pink with the exertion of their flight up the stairs. "There were certain feathers to unruffle at the dinner table."

Becky sank into her soft peach armchair. "It's quite all right. I managed." She tried to smile at Kate. "And thank you for unruffling those feathers."

"It's my fault for inviting the lot of them. I truly had no idea that Mr. Fulton's father and brother would be so..." Sighing, Kate changed the subject. "Are you really going to leave us?"

"I think so."

"But where will you go?"

Becky shrugged. "I don't know. Calton House, or..." She paused, thinking of the one other place she might go. Seawood—her house in Cornwall. It was the one thing in the world that belonged to her and her alone. But she'd never been there before, never seen it, had no idea what to do with it...

"Calton House," she repeated, her voice firm. It was the house she'd grown up in. Familiar and safe.

All spark drained from Kate's vivacious brown eyes. "Oh, Becky."

A knock sounded on Becky's closed door, and Becky's chest tightened. She swung her gaze to the door, and when she said nothing, Kate asked, "Yes?"

"It's Cecelia."

Becky's shoulders sagged with relief. "Come in."

Cecelia blew in, a compact, elegant ball of energy. She took the time to close the door with a firm *snick*. Turning to Becky, she shuddered. "What an abominable man that elder Mr. Fulton is, and that awful Bertrand takes after his father. Indeed, they are nothing like the youngest Mr. Fulton at all. Are you quite all right, Becky? And do you truly intend to leave London, or was that just a threat?"

"I feel it is best that I leave."

"Where will you go?"

"To Calton House in Yorkshire."

"Please don't," Kate begged, her voice a near whisper. She pressed her hand to her belly. "You were there for Jessica's birth, and I so want you to be there for this babe as well. I...I need you."

"Oh, Kate." Helplessness surged through Becky. Kate was right. She couldn't leave London, because she must be there for the delivery of her sister-in-law's child. Yet she *must* leave London, to escape the scandal and Jack Fulton. "Truly, I don't want to go, and I don't want to leave you, but..."

"When is the babe expected?" Cecelia asked.

"Not for a few weeks yet," Kate said. "But there is always the possibility that the child might come early."

Cecelia gave a brisk nod. "I've the perfect solution, then. You shall come to my house. Jack Fulton needn't know you're there at all. It is quiet at Devore House, I rarely see visitors, and you can have the time and space to be alone and think without the pressures of your family." She cast an apologetic glance at Kate. "No offense, Your Grace."

Kate didn't seem angry at all; instead she appeared relieved. "None taken, my lady." She turned to Becky. "I understand that you need some time to be alone, and I heartily approve. Lady Devore is right—it is the perfect solution. We will not make it known that you've remained in Town, and you'll have some time to yourself to mull things over. And I'll have the assurance that you'll be close and can attend to me the moment I need you."

Becky rose from her armchair and went to sit beside Kate on the bed. "Forgive me, Kate. You're all so torn between wanting me to be happy and wanting this scandal to go away, I can feel it, like a black cloud hanging over us all. You don't want to exert pressure on me, and yet it's difficult for me to hold on to my resolve under the force of it."

Kate squeezed her hand. "I'm so sorry that you feel coerced. I promise you, it's not intentional."

"I know," Becky said. "Truly, I do. But I still feel it."

Kate nodded gravely, and tears shone in her eyes. "Then it's for the best that you go. For a little while. I do hope you'll return to us soon."

"I will. I promise."

The three ladies spoke for a few minutes longer, arranging for Becky to stay a few weeks at Cecelia's house and for Kate to send a message if she went into labor so Becky could be present at the delivery.

After they fetched Josie and helped the disgruntled maid to pack, Becky's luggage was loaded onto one of Garrett's carriages, and at midnight, the carriage drew into the drive at Devore House. Cecelia led Becky to the guest bedchamber she'd used to prepare for her assignations with Jack, and Josie helped Becky undress. She fell into the bed and, after an hour of staring at the dark ceiling, sank into a fretful sleep.

When she awoke late the next morning, bright shafts of sunlight streamed through the crack in the rose-embroidered damask curtains.

Josie helped her to dress in a pale pink muslin morning gown, and by the time she descended to breakfast, the midday hour was fast approaching. Cecelia's breakfast room boasted tall, narrow windows looking over a small garden. The curtains were open this morning, and sunlight streamed into the room in bright golden shafts. Gleaming white wainscoting offset the yellow silk damask that covered the walls. An oak sideboard stood along the far wall, and a complementing round table dominated the center of the room.

Cecelia rose to greet her, saying she'd only just come downstairs as well, and offered her a light breakfast of warm chocolate and a poached egg, some bacon, and toast.

Becky seated herself at the table opposite Cecelia, and as a servant set her meal in front of her, Cecelia reported that in the last few days, rumors had run rampant through Town. Not only had Becky's true wicked nature been revealed, the gossips said, but after the world had caught her red-handed in debauchery, she'd spat in Jack Fulton's face and turned him down. Jack was portrayed as the hero of this most unfortunate event—he had proven his true gentlemanly nature by attempting to salvage her reputation by offering for her.

After Cecelia gave her the news, Becky sighed. "It seems to me that ladies always bear the brunt of such scandals while men are easily forgiven. Yet I am no guiltier than he is."

Cecelia's lip curled. "Absolutely true. It's just another

example of the unfair burdens society places on woman."

Becky leaned back in her chair and took a sip of her thick, sweet chocolate. "Well, I am happy the brunt of the blame has gone to me rather than anyone in my family."

Cecelia raised a sleek black brow in question, and Becky lowered her cup. "I like to consider myself immune to scandal. If they disparaged Garrett and Kate, Tristan and Sophie, or any of the children, they would truly harm me. But they can call me selfish and wicked till the world comes to an end, and I will bear it."

It was true—at least part of it. She *was* wicked—her dreams last night proved it. She'd dreamed of Jack Fulton's lips caressing her body. Dreamed of his hands, how they'd touched her, stroked her to the heights of passion. She'd awakened more than once to find her own fingers moving over the places his fingers had gone, as if to replicate his touch, but it seemed impossible to evoke the sensations in her body that Jack had.

She already missed him. She missed the dark look in his eyes when he'd gazed at her at the bottom of the stairs. That compelling mix of tenderness and need.

Yet she knew she had made the right decision. True, marriages had been built on far less than what had already developed between her and Jack. Even in recent times, it wasn't uncommon for a wife to have little more than a formal introduction to her husband before she pledged herself to him for eternity. But that wasn't for Becky.

"Thinking of Mr. Fulton?" Cecelia asked softly.

She hid her expression behind her cup of chocolate. "Well...yes."

"It is not difficult to discern your thoughts, Becky."

Cecelia nibbled at her buttered toast. "How do you feel about what happened last night?"

Lowering her cup, Becky sighed. "Confused, perhaps? I wonder whether I made the right decision, even though I am certain it's the best decision I could have made under the circumstances."

"I believe you truly shocked that bombastic father of his."

Becky frowned at her egg.

"Do not mistake me, Becky. I'm glad you shocked him. Glad you shocked them all."

"Why?"

"You place yourself in a position of power when you're unpredictable."

Becky frowned. "I suppose..."

"It's true. People don't know what to expect from you, and that makes you formidable."

Becky raised her brows. "Me?"

"Of course. You are a great beauty, and yet you are quiet and bookish. At the tender age of eighteen you ran off to Gretna with a near stranger. You spent the next four years in quiet obscurity, securing your reputation as a shy and bookish widow, but then at two-and-twenty you were caught in bed with an enigmatic scoundrel. Do you think all that hasn't provided you with an air of mystery?"

"I rather thought it provided fodder for rumor."

"Well, that, too, of course. But I daresay you are quite an intimidating woman to most."

"I'm not intimidating to Jack." She flinched, inwardly chastising herself for bringing him up again.

"I did take note of that." Cecelia's lips curled up. She

tapped her fingernails on the lacquered tabletop. "That is something, isn't it?"

It was hopeless. Like everyone else, Cecelia seemed to be an admirer of Jack Fulton, and though she didn't overtly put pressure on Becky, Becky felt the weight of it as much as she had from her family.

Why was she the only one hesitant to bind herself to this man? How had Jack Fulton so easily charmed the world? Was she the only rational, cautious person left on earth?

Cecelia took another nibble of her toast, and after she set it down, she sifted through the short pile of mail beside her plate. She glanced up at Becky over a sheet of white stationery with gilded edging. "A friend of mine, Mrs. Pionchet, has invited me to her masquerade ball Friday next."

"Really?" Becky asked, instantly intrigued. She'd heard about those wild, licentious parties, which had been so popular in the last century. They had fallen out of favor among the London *ton* due to their tendency to evoke debauchery and vice. Here was another item of proof that Becky had been far too sheltered—she hadn't suspected anyone in the world still held masquerades.

"Would you like to join me? Georgianna would be thrilled to have you in attendance."

Becky swallowed hard, then gave a firm shake of her head. "No. It's too soon. I shouldn't be seen in public. Not yet." *Not for another year, at least*, she thought.

"It's a *masquerade*." Cecelia lowered the invitation to the table. "That is the whole point. You needn't be seen at all. Only our hostess and I need to be aware of your identity."

If no one recognized her, what would be the harm? Becky gave her friend a tentative smile. "I'll think about it."

Jack left his guestroom at Stratford's fashionable townhouse after noon, because he knew by now that Stratford never showed his face to the world before midday. He went to the small dining room where a variety of meats and cheeses were laid out on the sideboard, along with a silver pot. He gave the pot an experimental sniff and sighed in appreciation. Coffee. Like him, Stratford preferred his coffee thick and strong enough to scour the gut.

He poured himself a cupful and went to the table, where a pile of newspapers lay as a centerpiece. Jack compared it to the elaborate floral design of the centerpiece at last night's disaster of a dinner and decided that a tidy pile of newspapers suited him better.

After Becky had left him, Jack had dragged himself back to Stratford's, where he sat in the front drawing room until his friend returned home from a night of carousing. He'd told him the whole sordid tale, and Stratford had listened to it all, a bemused expression on his face. At the end, he'd slapped Jack on the back and said, "Well, it's obvious now why you'd rather be a guest at my home than return to the soft bosom of your family. You can stay as long as you like, old chap."

With that, Stratford had excused himself and retired for the night, leaving Jack brooding in an armchair by the fire until the gray light of dawn nudged through the curtains.

He sank into one of the padded chairs and took the

top newspaper from the pile, nodding in approval when he saw it was today's *Times*. He had opened the paper and settled into reading the news and drinking his coffee—one of the purest simple pleasures in life, Jack thought—when Stratford strode in.

Thanks to his fastidious valet, the earl was shaved, combed, and dressed in the height of fashion, with a stiff, high collar, a patterned waistcoat, and a velvet-lapelled morning coat. He'd once expressed to Jack his pleasure that his valet had judged his shoulders broad enough and his waist narrow enough to allow him to forgo men's stays. However, the man had heartily encouraged his master to cease imbibing spirits and eating rich foods, for such habits were certain to fatten him up enough to make a tightly cinched corset a requirement of his wardrobe.

Jack had only chuckled, knowing he'd never succumb to such measures for the sake of fashion. Stratford probably would one day, but he couldn't be blamed. Stratford was an earl, and this was one of the disadvantages of being born into a life of aristocratic privilege. Style was a necessity, no matter how ridiculous or emasculating.

Perhaps Stratford would continue with his preferred sport of boxing until he was well into his dotage, maintain his fit pugilist's body, and never have to worry about wearing a gentleman's corset.

Jack smiled over the top of his paper. "Morning."

Stratford poured himself a cup of coffee and took the seat across from Jack. "Good morning."

Jack handed him a section of the *Times* and Stratford shook it open. They read in companionable silence. A footman replenished the pot, and Jack rose to fetch himself more coffee. When he returned to his seat with his steaming cup, Stratford laid his paper on the table.

"England is dull this time of year, Fulton."

Jack looked up from the article he was reading. "Is it? I hadn't noticed."

"As the weeks progress, the holiday becomes the focus. People gather round, cosseting the loved ones they've forgotten the year round, blethering about love and joy and all that nonsense. *Damn* dull, if you ask me." Shuddering, the earl took a sip of coffee. "And Maria...she's become a trifle too demanding, on the whole. Wanting more money to buy her fripperies and dresses, and frankly I am tired of bowing to her whims."

"Will you break it off?" Jack asked. Maria was Stratford's current mistress, a much-sought-after courtesan.

"Certainly." Stratford grimaced and took a hearty swallow of coffee as if to fortify himself with it. "I have no desire to do it today, however, not when I am feeling so..." After a pause, he said, "I don't belong in London this time of year."

"Where, then? Will you go home to Sussex?"

"Absolutely not. To return to that ancient pile and subject myself to the incessant naggings of my mother? Christ, Christmas in London will be a far better fate than that." He shrugged. "I've an invitation from a friend in Northumberland, William Langley, who says the hunting has been fruitful this season." He paused, his head tilted and his expression turning inward, as if he were searching for the source of his discontent. "I'm bored with hunting."

Jack met his friend's gaze, certain he wasn't speaking of hunting deer and grouse.

"And I'm in no mood to travel," Stratford continued. "Suppose this means I'm destined to suffer through another Christmas in London." His lips curled. "It would be rather convenient to close my eyes and then open them to a nice, snowy January."

"New year, new start," Jack said quietly.

Stratford gave a low, sardonic snort. "If only that were possible."

Jack understood all too well. Before he met Becky, he'd felt that unsettled, discontented feeling often. He raised his cup in a toast and then drank down his remaining coffee in one draught.

Seeming to shake himself out of his melancholy, Stratford pushed his paper aside and sat a little taller, tapping his thumbs on his coffee cup. "So now that young Lady Rebecca has proved herself quite the spit-fire and left London, what will be your course of action?"

Jack spoke quietly. "I still intend to marry her."

Stratford chuckled. "You said she made it clear she doesn't want you."

"She made it clear that she doesn't want me *immediately*. But I will change her mind."

"Oh? How?"

Shrugging, Jack gazed into the dregs in his cup, as if he were a fortune teller and the residual coffee grounds might show his future. "I don't know, exactly. But it must be done. And as you know, I haven't much time."

"The blackmailer has demanded the funds by the middle of December, correct? So you have a month."

"Yes. Just over a month." Jack had considered asking Tom for more time, but he had a sick feeling that the specified date wasn't under Tom's control, as much as the man would like him to think it. Tom wasn't talking, but

Jack had sensed his desperation. There was more to his old friend's demands than raw greed.

Jack looked up at the earl. He'd never thought to dig for more information about Becky's dead husband—he hadn't wanted anything to do with the man. Now, however, it struck him that it might be a good idea to delve into Fisk's character a bit more. He needed a better idea of what drove Becky. "What do you know about William Fisk?"

"Hm." Stratford took a thoughtful sip of coffee. "Well, when you consider Fisk, her hesitation makes perfect sense."

Jack leaned forward. "Why?"

"The lady hadn't been acquainted with Fisk long before they eloped to Gretna. I don't know the exact length of time, but I can tell you this: Fisk was a bastard. He'd swindled Calton and his family into befriending him, but it was revealed later that he wanted Lady Rebecca solely for her fortune. You know their family is incredibly private, but the rumors say that Fisk took a mistress shortly after they married, and he became involved in a smuggling scheme. The first shipment didn't turn out as lucrative as planned, and he was killed by his partners in the venture."

"Were the partners ever convicted?"

"I don't know." Stratford shrugged. "I don't think so. These events took place in Warwickshire, and from there, her family retired to Yorkshire, and they weren't seen in London for over a year."

Jack pushed out a breath through his pursed lips. Despite the similarity of their initial motivation, he was nothing like Fisk. He would not take a mistress. Why would he have need of one when he had a woman like Becky to share his bed? He was prepared to commit himself to her. Once he was committed to something, nothing could turn him away.

He was different from Fisk. Damn it. He *was*.

He tightened his hands over his empty coffee cup.

"So…" Stratford studied him. "What are you going to do?"

"Follow her wherever she has gone. Make her love me," Jack said. "I have a month in which to accomplish the feat. There is no other choice."

"Certainly there are other choices. The lady has made up her mind. In such a case, it would seem to me that it would be far easier to find a new bride than to try to chase this one across England and win her over."

Jack narrowed his eyes, then tried to soften the scowl that had formed on his lips. Stratford's point was sound enough, and he should give it due consideration. Yet when he thought of last night, of Becky's strength, of her cool determination when she turned her back on his father, he knew.

He wanted *her*. He wouldn't let her go.

Stratford waved his hand. "No one is in London right now, so you must go to the country in any case. I hear Hampshire is particularly rich with heiresses these days. Attend some of those tedious festive country affairs, and you'll find a new chit to attach yourself to within a week." He leaned closer. "Look for an old one. A spinster who believes herself on the shelf. With your looks and bloodline, it will be a simple matter to catch an aging spinster with a nice, fat dowry."

The thought of chasing another woman—any woman

but Rebecca Fisk—made the coffee gurgle in Jack's stomach. "No."

Understanding dawned in Stratford's face. "You don't wish to make this easy, do you?"

"The level of difficulty has nothing to do with it," Jack said stiffly.

"I see. It is *her* you want."

Jack was quiet, then he gritted his teeth. "No one else."

"Could it be my imagination, Fulton, or am I detecting that you possess some strong feeling for this lady?"

Jack kept his expression flat. "My only strong feeling is for my own life. And Lady Rebecca Fisk will be the one to save it."

"Mmm…" Steepling his fingers under his chin, Stratford leaned back in his chair. "So how do you intend to woo the chit?"

"Woo?" The word emerged from Jack's mouth sounding like something foreign and exotic. "What the devil are you talking about?"

Stratford raised a blond brow. "Don't tell me you've never wooed a woman."

"I've bedded women."

"You know that's not what I mean."

He tried to think back. Long ago, the concept of courting a woman wouldn't have seemed so utterly alien to him. Yet he and Anne had been friends, then lovers. He'd never *wooed* her. After she'd died, he'd fallen into bed with women, but that had been easy: whispered suggestions, coy acceptances. He'd never put forth with any other woman the effort he'd already put into Lady Rebecca.

He looked up at Stratford. "I suppose I've never courted, wooed, or pursued a woman, not for more than one night."

Shaking his head, Stratford chuckled. "I shouldn't be surprised."

Becky was a far more complicated individual than she appeared at first sight, and therefore it followed that winning her would be more complex, too. Jack's plan to lure her into marriage hadn't worked on the first attempt, but neither had he botched it completely. It could have been much worse—if she ever discovered he was the one who'd orchestrated the delivery of that letter to her brother, it would be over for him.

"Well, then. You must tell me what to do." Jack leaned forward, awaiting his instruction. "But please note, I haven't the time for a standard courtship. I'll need to speed things along. Significantly."

Stratford tapped the tips of his fingers together under his chin. "Then you must bombard her. Accelerated courting, we'll call it."

"Tell me how."

"First, you must pretend to listen to every bit of her prattle."

"Lady Rebecca doesn't prattle."

Giving him a dubious look, Stratford lowered his hands to his coffee cup. "Every lady prattles," he said patiently. "Unless she is mute, and I know that one is not—I've heard her speak."

"She speaks," Jack said. "She converses. She does *not* prattle."

Stratford shrugged. "Very well, if you say so. Whenever she speaks, you must pretend to listen. Wholeheartedly."

Jack thought back on their conversations, how he'd lapped up her every word like a voracious wolf, and shrugged. "Easily done."

"You must compliment her. Incessantly. Wax poetic about her flaxen hair, her dewy skin, her exquisite form—"

"Her flaxen hair?"

"Well, make it believable, of course. Silken ebony locks? I don't know." The earl waved a dismissive hand. "And you must tell her how utterly valuable she is to you." He broke off and winked at him. "Well, that's the truth, eh? Her forty thousand *is* valuable to you."

Suddenly and vehemently, Jack wished Stratford didn't know the truth. He stared at his friend without answering.

Stratford chuckled. "I was correct," he said under his breath.

Jack refused to take the bait.

Sobering quickly, Stratford locked his eyes on Jack's. "You needn't worry, Fulton. The truth about you and Lady Rebecca will die with me."

"I know." Jack did trust Stratford. As much as the man teased and tested him, Jack knew he understood.

Stratford broke the tension by continuing his instruction. "Ask, 'What is light, if Lady Rebecca be not seen? What is joy if she be not by?' And you must compare her to a summer's day."

Or a winter's day, Jack thought. He cast a wry look at his friend. "So I must quote Shakespeare."

"Oh, yes. Byron, Shakespeare, Milton—all of them. Even better, write poetry of your own. Send her flowers, jewels, expensive gifts."

Jack sighed. "All this sounds rather dull." Not to mention that she was a duke's sister and no doubt accustomed to expensive things. He didn't have the money to buy anything expensive for her.

"You're right—it's utterly tedious." Stratford grinned. "But I assure you, it is most effective."

He stared at Stratford in silence, a plan taking shape in his mind. Effective for most women, perhaps. But Becky was not most women.

Chapter Eight

The following afternoon, Jack paced the entry hall at Devore House. He snapped a chrysanthemum and daisy bouquet against his thigh with every stride. What the devil was taking so long?

He was nervous, he admitted to himself. What if she didn't like the flowers? What if she didn't like the small token he'd agonized over tying to the stems?

He stared at the door leading to the front drawing room and paused for an instant, debating whether to intrude without invitation.

No. He was here to formally ask Becky if he might be allowed to court her, not to act like a savage heathen. He smiled a little, remembering the natives he'd met in the Sandwich Islands. A friendlier, more open sort he'd never encountered. The British, with all their rules and genteel conventions, could learn a lesson or two from the Hawaiians.

Finally, he heard the swish of skirts. He reeled to a halt, clenching the flower stems in his fist, and spun around.

It wasn't Becky.

Sighing, he pulled off his hat. "Lady Devore."

She inclined her head, her gaze flicking from the bouquet he gripped tightly in one hand to his face. "Mr. Fulton."

"I've come to see Becky."

Her thin, dark brows arched, and she gestured at the doorway behind her. "We should talk, Mr. Fulton. Would you care to join me in my drawing room?"

He followed her in and sat in the wicker-backed chair she gestured at. She sat in the settee across from him. A servant brought in tea, and she offered him some. He declined, and she waved the servant away.

When the woman left, she asked, "How did you know she was here?"

Realizing he was apt to break the delicate flower stems, Jack laid the bouquet across his lap and clenched his fist in his lap. "I visited the duke and duchess earlier. They wouldn't break Lady Rebecca's confidence, of course, but they provided enough hints to leave me with no doubt she must be here." He'd been vastly relieved to discover she hadn't left London after all.

Lady Devore chuckled. "It wasn't meant to be a state secret, but I don't think the lady will be ecstatic about you so easily discovering her place of escape."

Jack didn't respond. She'd misjudged him if she didn't think he would find her here.

"I should get to the point," Lady Devore said. "She doesn't wish to see you. She is understandably distraught about what happened last night, but she thinks you will want to move forward now after she gave you and your family such a thorough set-down. She believes you are eager to marry and expects you will soon begin the hunt for another bride."

Jack took a deep breath. When he spoke, his voice was quiet and controlled. "Can she believe I am so fickle?"

Lady Devore sighed. "Truly, I don't know. She needs time, Mr. Fulton. Apparently more time than you are willing to give."

He met the woman's cool, dark eyes. "I'd like to speak to her."

"I'll tell her that is your wish."

"I'll wait."

"No. Not today. I shall speak to her about this—perhaps I shall engage in some convincing. You look as if you haven't slept a wink. Go home, get a good night's sleep, and return tomorrow."

"I could walk right past you," he said in a quiet voice. "I could force my way to her and demand she speak with me now."

"You could do that," Lady Devore agreed mildly. "But you're a gentleman, and you won't."

Lady Devore was right—he couldn't risk pushing Becky farther away. For the moment, he must take small, tentative steps, but he'd see her again. Soon. There was one important thing he'd learned in the past few minutes, and it was somewhat of a surprise: Lady Devore appeared to be firmly on his side.

Rising, Jack held out the bouquet. "Will you give her these?"

Lady Devore inclined her head and took the bouquet from him. "Of course."

Jack bowed, turned on his heel, and strode out.

• • •

A week later, a footman knocked on Becky's door bearing a small package that had just been delivered for her. Cecelia, who was sitting in the corner embroidering a gown for one of her young nephews, chuckled when the man left.

"What has Mr. Fulton sent you today?"

Becky sat on the edge of the bed and slid her finger beneath the seal holding the package closed. She opened the paper wrapping. Lying inside was a folded piece of material. Stroking the coarse fabric, Becky sighed with pleasure. "It is a shawl made from tapa, I believe."

"From what?"

"Tapa." She ran her fingers over the bold geometric pattern. "It's a cloth from the bark of breadfruit, made by the natives of the South Pacific islands."

Cecelia shook her head. "Another oddity to add to your collection."

"Yes." Becky smiled at her dressing table, her gaze skimming over the items Jack had sent her in the past few days. There was the bouquet he'd sent the day after the dinner, still fresh in a vase. Tied around the bouquet had been a little carved man with a stocky build and wide, round eyes—the paper tucked into the curve of its arm had said it was a very old carved sperm whale ivory pendant from Fiji. She'd set the man up on her dressing table, thinking he looked rather appalled to be resident with her silver dishes and bottles of cosmetics.

On the opposite side of the dressing table was the bouquet Jack had sent her the following day—a black calabash, a smooth, rounded gourd from the island of

Hawaii. Sleek lines and triangles painted in an earthy red dye covered its smooth, black surface. According to Jack's note, gourds served multiple purposes for the Hawaiians—they used them for everything from water basins to drums for their native dances. He added that he'd found the item useful during his sailing days. But now Jack had used it as a vase. A pair of tall amaryllises sprang up from its spout. Dark pink burst from the flowers' centers and speckled their smooth white pointed petals.

Becky wondered if he knew pink was her favorite color.

Probably. He seemed to have read her mind. How else could he know that the Indian arrowhead he'd found on a hunting expedition outside Boston held so much more meaning for her than any gaudy bauble?

With a wistful sigh, she turned back to the tapa, admiring the design on the fabric as she unfolded it. She frowned when it lay open on her bed, for there was a large slit in its center. She took up the note that Jack had tucked into its folds. As she read it, she sat down hard on the edge of the bed.

She stared at Jack's words in rising excitement. "Not a shawl."

"What on earth is it then?" Cecelia asked, focused on her embroidery.

"He says it is a 'tiputa,' a mantle of sorts, from Pitcairn Island."

"Ah."

"From Pitcairn Island," Becky repeated emphatically. "You know, where some of Captain Bligh's men settled after the infamous mutiny. Jack has been to Pitcairn Island!"

"Is that so?"

Oh, goodness. Cecelia didn't understand. Becky flattened her hand over the rough fabric. Jack had written that a young man had given it to him as a gesture of friendship—though he'd been wearing only a loincloth and shell jewelry, the man had spoken English and he'd been of lighter complexion and skin than the Polynesians; clearly he had been a grandson of one of the mutineers.

"Cecelia," she said, managing to keep most of the censure from her voice, "have you never read about William Bligh and the *Bounty*?"

A groove deepened between Cecelia's brows as she looked up. "I believe I recall hearing about it." She gave a dismissive shrug of one thin shoulder. "It all happened before we were born, though."

"Yes, but Jack has met the descendants of one of those famous outlaws. Those men will be remembered forever, and Jack has met them! He's seen them!"

"I see." Clearly Cecelia did not comprehend her excitement. Sighing, Becky looked down at the *tiputa*. How incredible that Jack had seen this, that one of the family members of the famous mutineers had made it.

She'd treasure this forever, along with all the other fascinating objects he'd given her. A part of her knew she should return them, that she was encouraging him by accepting them. But she couldn't help it. They were too utterly wonderful to give up.

She opened Jack's note again and let her eyes linger on the final line, written in his tight, compact script: *When will I see you?*

Taking a deep breath, she said, "I think I'll write a letter."

She'd finally snared Cecelia's attention. Her friend's gaze snapped up. "Oh? To Mr. Fulton?"

"Yes. To thank him for...everything."

A sly smile curved Cecelia's lips. "Seems to me you don't intend to return them after all."

For the past few days, Becky had been torn between sending back the gifts and keeping them. Now, she couldn't help the soft smile that tipped up her own lips when she looked at them again. "To be truthful, I don't believe I can."

"He has charmed you with oddities."

"Yes." Becky turned to Cecelia. "But I should not be so easily swayed, Cecelia. My husband charmed me, too, at first."

Cecelia shook her head. "I do regret encouraging your involvement with Mr. Fulton, Becky, but I cannot help but to think that you and he have the possibility of forging a true affection for each other."

"Do you think so?"

"Yes, I do." Cecelia hesitated, and when she raised her eyes to Becky's again, concern shaded them. "But I know you will be cautious."

"I will." Becky's gaze wandered back to the intriguing gifts Jack had sent her. "I must be."

The following morning, Becky awakened early and couldn't get back to sleep. Jack was coming to call today, and she was more confused than ever about how to approach him. If her heart had warred with her mind before, it did so doubly now. Her nerves jangled with a mixture of eager anticipation and curdling dread.

She'd struggled all night long with what she should say to him. She'd written a speech in her mind, but didn't know whether she'd be able to follow it. It depended on his reactions, she supposed.

By the time the footman entered the drawing room to inform her and Cecelia that Jack had arrived, it was all she could do to contain her nerves.

Both ladies rose, and Cecelia gave her a quick hug. "He's just a man. Never forget, men are simple creatures."

With that, she slipped out of the drawing room. Becky waited, hands clenched before her, and a few moments later, the door opened, and Jack stepped inside.

She sucked in a breath, for he was as handsome as always, but today he'd done nothing to rein in his roguish edge. He wore sleek black trousers tucked into black Wellington boots, with matching black waistcoat and tailcoat. In one hand he clasped a heavy, tattered book.

Becky swallowed as he snapped the door shut and turned to her. His brown eyes flashed with a predatory mix of possessiveness and desire, but he held himself aloof and comported himself like a gentleman.

His gaze roved over her before coming to rest on her face. "Becky."

Pressing a nervous hand to the dark green silk of her bodice, she curtsied. "Mr. Fulton."

He raised a brow. "Not Jack?"

"I...don't know."

He took a step toward her. She felt hot. Hot all over. Burning heat crept up her spine, across her cheeks, down her chest.

"Thank you for all the gifts," she said in a near whisper.

His sudden smile reached his eyes, making them crinkle at their corners. "Did you like them?"

"Oh, very much. They're wonderful."

His smile melted her. She wanted to know everything about the gifts he'd sent her. She wanted to sit with him and listen all through the day and night as he told her about all the places he had gone.

"I brought you something." He held out the book. "It isn't much, but…"

She took it from him, weighing the heavy volume in both hands. It was a battered, dog-eared book entitled *A Dictionary of Practical Surgery*. Grease spots covered the tome and the salty, musty smell of the ocean drifted from its warped pages.

"It belonged to Smith, the ship's surgeon on the *Gloriana*."

She gripped the book tightly, staring down at the scratched, gilt-embossed title. She'd never received such a gift. She'd read many books about medicine and surgery, but she'd borrowed those volumes from the libraries at Calton House and the London house and used her own funds to purchase various journals. No one would ever dream of giving such a book to her. No one but Jack.

"Smith died about a year ago, and he left this book to me in his will."

Before she could protest his giving her such a personally valuable gift, Jack's lips twisted. "It was his last joke on me. The crew thought it very amusing. They all knew I possess no desire to read about hernias, concussions, and amputations. But…" He hesitated. "I thought you might."

"Yes, I would," she breathed. She clasped the book to her breast. "Thank you, Jack."

His smile was devastating, carving those deep grooves in his cheeks and sending a bright glitter to his eyes. He motioned toward the chairs, gesturing for her to sit. She complied, lowering herself into the velvet settee across from the pair of matching wicker chairs. The cushions were hard, the seat not nearly as comfortable as her favorite chair in Garrett's salon. She sat stiffly, her fingers curved around the upholstered armrest.

Instead of taking one of the chairs across from her, Jack sat on the narrow cushion beside her. These seats weren't meant for two, Becky thought, unless the two were lovers.

Not so long ago, she'd thought of Jack as her lover.

She clenched the armrest harder. She was an intelligent woman. She was a thoughtful person, well educated and well read. Yet she wanted to be a strong, confident woman. Like Cecelia was. Like Sophie and Kate were.

"I should return all your gifts." She fixed her gaze on his face, forcing her hip against the armrest so her thigh wouldn't touch his. She pressed her free hand over the book in her lap.

His brows crept upward. "Oh?"

"Yes." Her voice was somber, but one corner of her mouth quirked up into the beginnings of a smile. "But I cannot. They are special, one-of-a-kind, and I am too selfish."

"Good. I want you to keep them."

"Why are you here, Mr. Fulton?" She searched his face for a clue. She didn't understand why he seemed so intent on giving her such special, unusual gifts, on seeing her…on continuing along this mad course.

"I wished to formally ask if I might court you."

"Court me?" she repeated in confusion. Hadn't they already gone far beyond courtship?

"I went about it wrong. I never thought..." He paused, took a breath, and continued. "I never thought you wanted anything more than..."

"I don't," she said quickly.

"And I didn't either," he continued, "but now there is more to it. More I'd like to explore." He looked down at his lap, then up at her. "I know I'm far beneath you, socially and financially—"

She coughed out a horrified laugh. "Please tell me you don't believe my refusal has anything to do with that!"

"No, I don't. I learned quickly that your family isn't characteristic of the aristocracy." He paused. "Becky, the time we spent together...those were some of the finest moments of my life."

Mine, too, she wanted to say. And she wanted to be alone with him again in such a way. Talking, naked and in bed, after they'd made passionate love and were sated and comfortable. She wanted to wrap her arms around his bare chest and talk and talk about the world until they were too tired to say any more. She wanted to fall asleep beside him, then wake up, make love, and talk some more.

These thoughts were dangerous. "This has nothing to do with the scandal? With my family?"

"No. It has only to do with you and with me."

Becky clasped her hands firmly over the book in her lap. "Mr. Fulton, I do believe it's possible that it might work out between us in time, but my first priority is to alleviate the strain this scandal has caused to my family. I should very much like to see you again, but only when the gossip has been long forgotten. If you decide you don't want to wait—" She broke off, swallowed hard, then continued. "I will understand. And please forgive me for being rude to your father. It was not well done of me, not at all. I regret any inconvenience it might have caused you."

"It wasn't an inconvenience." He took her hand and cradled it in his own. "You made me proud."

"What?"

"You were magnificent." He raised her hand to his mouth and pressed his lips against it.

"I allowed my temper to get the better of me. I rarely do that."

He lowered her hand and met her gaze head-on. "I am glad you did. My father deserved it."

His eyes looked deep into her, as if they saw her, not her outside shell, not her twisted arm, but *her*. She shifted on the hard cushion, trying to regain her equilibrium.

"Becky...I want you."

It took her a moment to recapture her breath before she spoke again. "You must understand that I cannot allow the outcome of my entire life to depend on an ephemeral 'want.'"

"No. Not ephemeral."

She ignored that statement. "I cannot base my future on a corporeal feeling. I cannot promise to spend the whole of my life with a man I don't know."

"I am a man. Who wants you. *You*, and no one else. What more is there to it than that?"

She clasped her hands in front of her. "There is far more to it, Jack."

He thrust his fingers over his scalp, then closed his fist

around a clump of hair, closing his eyes in defeat. "You're right. This is why I propose a formal courtship."

"That would be a farce," she said quietly, "given that it's public knowledge we were in bed together."

Jack shook his head. "Not a courtship to display to the world, Becky. One between you and me. No one else needs to know, or even be involved."

Her resolve wavered. He dropped his hand, leaving his hair tousled. The desire to try to tame it with her fingers flitted through her, but she thrust the notion aside.

He smelled so good, so salty and clean and masculine. His lips were supple and soft, she knew from experience. She wanted to touch her own lips to them, to feel them glide over her skin.

"I'm not giving up, Becky. I want to be married to you someday. Someday soon."

"There are many ladies on the marriage market who are far more qualified, and far more eager for marriage, than I am."

"I'm not interested in any of them. Wives are not horses. I won't choose a woman from a pool of eligibles only to toss her back and select another when something goes awry."

He was so different from other men. So focused, so intent on her. Why her? A soft shudder tickled up her spine.

"I've already found the woman I want."

"And if the woman you want has no desire..." She paused. She couldn't say she had no desire for him. That would be a lie. "...to be married?"

"Then I will change her mind."

She broke her gaze from his face, her own face

growing warmer by the second. "You should go," she whispered.

"Yes, I'll go." His voice was gruff. He pried the book out of her hands and set it aside. Then he leaned closer, turning a little so his breath blew softly over her cheek. "But you're coming with me."

Chapter Nine

W here are we going?"

Jack glanced at Becky. A light flush suffused her cheeks, and she had gnawed on her lower lip incessantly since he'd helped her into the carriage.

"I told you—it's a surprise. But I promise you'll enjoy it." He slid his fingers over hers, the gesture intended to comfort her. His thumb played over the fine lace on the edge of her sleeve. "We're almost there," he murmured. Their destination was only a few minutes away from Lady Devore's house, and there wasn't much traffic today, for the promise of rain was heavy in the air.

She slid him a nervous glance. "We shouldn't be seen together."

"I know." He squeezed her fingers. "I won't do anything to further damage your reputation."

At that, she released a short burst of cynical laughter.

"It doesn't matter, I suppose. My reputation is quite beyond repair."

She made her voice light, but her eyes were stark with the upset the scandal had caused her. The scandal orchestrated by him.

It had to be done, he reminded himself. The ends justified the means.

A blustery wind propelled the carriage to the bottom of Bond Street, where it stopped at the corner of Piccadilly. Jack exited and went around to Becky's side to help her out.

She glanced up as they stepped out of the carriage, then her eyes sparkled in genuine pleasure. "The Egyptian Hall."

"Mmm." He gazed up at the façade of the Hall with her. "The museum is closed this afternoon. They're adding a few final touches to their newest exhibit before it opens to the public next month."

"Their African exhibit?"

He smiled. "I thought you would have heard about it. I've arranged a private showing for us."

She didn't move for a long moment. Then, as if in slow motion, she slipped her arm through his.

He stood beside her on the pavement, gazing at the edifice of the Egyptian Hall, relishing the trust in her touch and the contentment in her expression. People brushed by on all sides, and behind them the street was thick with the sounds of traffic. He wished he were alone with her. The image of her body, bare and creamy, in the semidarkness at Sheffield's Hotel assaulted his memory, and his body hardened all over—one particular part of his anatomy in rather extreme, painful fashion.

God, he wanted her. He wondered whether anything would be able to coerce him to leave their bed once they were married.

He'd best focus on the present lest his carnal recollections run away with him and his state become obvious. He was thankful that the day was frigid, and he wore a heavy woolen coat. He pressed his free hand over hers, the black of his glove a sharp contrast to the bright white of hers.

"Do you know what it says?" He gestured up at the symbols carved into the architrave of the building.

"I think the hieroglyphs are nonsensical. The architect claimed the design of this place was taken from the temple at Dendera, but…" She frowned. "It possesses certain Egyptian qualities, I believe, but it is not an accurate representation."

"But you have never been to Egypt."

"No, I haven't." She shrugged. "I might be wrong, of course."

He studied her from the corner of his eye. It was clear that she didn't really think she was wrong. He didn't think she was wrong, either. She read profusely and with impeccable attention to detail.

They entered the Hall, and the curator hurried up to welcome them. It was thanks to Stratford's acquaintance with the man that they'd been allowed to explore the museum today. After shaking Jack's hand vigorously and bowing to Lady Rebecca, the man took their coats and excused himself, saying he had much work to do with the forthcoming opening, and he hoped they'd make themselves at home. This had been planned, too. Jack had wanted their private showing to be completely private.

After the man vanished into one of the side rooms, Jack led Becky through the silent entry hall toward the natural history collection from southern Africa. They entered the Great Room of the Hall. The place had been redecorated since he'd last come here as a boy, in an ostentatious permutation of modern and Egyptian styles. Columns painted in earthy colors and encircled at their tops by the carved visage of an Egyptian goddess lined the walls. To Jack and Becky's left, tucked between two of the outlandish columns, lay two live dogs sleeping in a cage. Becky hurried up to them and he read the plaque attached to the cage: "African Canines: Specimens from the Cape." The dogs inside were smallish, with wolflike features and random patterns of black, red, yellow, and white in their fur.

As Becky studied the animals, Jack's gaze wandered to the center of the room, where a bevy of stuffed ducks, geese, and birds stood round a large swatch of blue fabric meant to resemble a pond. In the center of the pond stood a monstrously fat creature he didn't recognize. "I suppose they couldn't acquire a live specimen of one of those," he murmured.

"Mm," Becky said as they approached. "A hippopotamus. It's enormous, isn't it?"

"I wouldn't like to be attacked by one," he said. "Looks like he could eat an entire ship."

"They're known to become quite aggressive," Becky agreed. "They'll occasionally attack Nile boats."

"I suppose we should be happy we don't reside in Africa. No chance of encountering such ferocious beasts."

"Oh, I don't know." Wryness edged Becky's voice.

"There are ferocious beasts aplenty in England. Mostly of the human variety."

He chuckled, but at the same time he acknowledged there was some truth to her joke. More truth than he was comfortable admitting.

A movement caught his eye, and he looked across the room. A cage was tucked into the corner, no bigger than the cage holding the dogs, but the animal inside was much larger. The horned creature gazed at them between the bars with dark, watering eyes. It was incredibly ugly—a little smaller than a cow, with black fur, skinny legs, a mat of tangled shaggy hair for a mane, and a long, pointed beard. Horns curled up from its ears, and its nostrils flared.

"What is that?" he asked, equally appalled and intrigued.

"I believe it's a gnu," Becky murmured. "Poor thing, it can hardly move."

He gazed at her, at the compassion in her face and stance as she reached through the bars and stroked the animal's woebegone muzzle, and something inside him went soft.

She was so different. So unlike any woman he'd ever known. She was *special*.

"Look at him," she murmured. "Once he ran free on the African plains with his herd, and now...he is alone and trapped. You can almost see his spirit seeping out of him." She looked up at Jack with shining eyes.

"Shall we set him free?" he whispered, gazing at Becky rather than the gnu.

"I wish we could." She blinked hard. "But what good will it do? He would die in London. He would be caught again, or shot…" She drew in a ragged breath. "There is no freedom here."

"You possess a great deal of compassion toward a creature you know nothing of."

"I do know a few things about gnus," she said. "I've read about them."

"Of course you have."

"Despite their wild appearance, they're more mild-tempered than many of God's creatures. They live in tight herds, and they protect one another. None of them deserves to be caught, caged, and taken from everything he knows."

"That's probably true." He studied her. She looked beautiful, with dark curling tendrils of hair peeking from the brim of her green velvet-trimmed bonnet, with the matching lapels of her moss green silk redingote, and her shining midnight-blue eyes, so expressive and rich with feeling. Her dark gaze, so sad, so full of the life she'd lived and of the experiences she'd had, smacked him in the chest.

She'd been beaten down by her husband, and that made her tentative and hesitant, fearful of setting herself free, of opening her heart. She believed she couldn't survive being hurt again. Jack understood completely. He'd been in that same place for many years after Anne's death.

Jack wanted her to stop hurting. He wanted to protect her, cosset and spoil her, until she was confident enough to set herself free. Until she was confident enough to allow herself to be happy.

He wouldn't let anyone hurt her. Never again.

"Come." Becky smiled, but the look of sadness lingered in her eyes. Sighing, she threaded her arm through his again and turned him away from the gnu. "Let us walk awhile."

Arm in arm, they began a slow promenade through the Hall, their heels tapping on the wood floors as they progressed through the otherwise silent rooms.

When they reached the landing on the second floor, they gazed out the front windows, watching the rain fall sideways onto the street below.

He leaned closer to her, breathing her in. She smelled sweet and fresh, like the pink amaryllis he'd sent her.

Gathering her hand in his, he tugged off her glove. She watched him with a bemused expression, but she didn't try to stop him as he tucked the glove in the inside pocket of his tailcoat.

"I once met a fortune-teller," he said, "at port in Kingston. She claimed to be able to read a person's future in his palm."

"Did she read your palm?"

"Oh, yes. She said I would have a long and prosperous life. She counted the lines coming off of this deeper line here—" he slid his fingertip across the top line beneath her little finger, "—and said I'd father three children."

She frowned at her hand. "How many children shall I have by her method?"

"Three."

She sucked in a breath. "It means nothing."

"True," he said easily.

"I... You see, I have reason to believe I am barren."

"What makes you think so?"

"I was married for four months and did not conceive."

"Conception can take longer than four months."

She swallowed and nodded. "I hoped...I hoped that if I conceived, William would stop ignoring me. That he would grow to love me again."

Four months. How quickly her first husband had proved to be a bastard.

"People have little control over such things. Perhaps a higher power determined it wasn't your time."

She grew even more somber. "Perhaps. If I'd had a child by William, he wouldn't have a father, and I would know his true father was..." Her voice dwindled.

He closed his hand over hers, so that her fingers folded into a small fist encompassed by his own. The fortune-teller had also told him that he would experience great love in his life, and that if he wasn't careful, he'd lose that love.

He'd known—just known—there was something of truth in what the old crone had told him. She was speaking of Anne. But it was too late for him—he'd already lost her.

Yet maybe she'd been speaking of Becky.

Beautiful Lady Rebecca Fisk, daughter of a duke, wounded soul, and oh so rich. Could he love this woman? He certainly liked her. He'd liked her from the beginning, and that feeling grew each time he saw her, witnessed the quirks of her personality, learned more about her.

"Trust," he said quietly, "is a leap of faith. One must make a decision to abandon doubt and release all misgivings. One must hold on to the conviction that the soul upon whom you've bestowed the gift will hold it close and never destroy it."

"I gave William my trust so easily." Her expression darkened. "Far too easily."

"Yes, you gave it generously, and in all innocence. But no longer."

"No." She squeezed her eyes shut.

"I understand."

"Then you should understand why I cannot trust anyone ever again."

"I understand it, Becky. But there is no way for me to prove beyond a shadow of a doubt that I will not hurt you. I can tell you I won't, over and over again, but that isn't proof."

"No, it isn't."

"Words are meaningless; only actions will provide you with the proof you need."

"Yes."

He shrugged, then brought her fist to his lips, opening her fingers and brushing small kisses over each of her knuckles. "Then all I can do is attempt to show you how I feel for you. How much I wish to see you content and happy. What a life with me would be like."

"You could do that." She opened her eyes and looked at him with something akin to desperation. "But what would it prove? William—" Her voice cracked and she tried again. "William was so kind, so loving—passionate, even—before we ran away together. And then, as soon as we were married—" Her eyes turned glassy and she looked away.

"That is where the leap of faith comes in."

"But," she whispered, "what if I cannot make that leap?"

"You will," he promised. He wanted her lips. Badly. He tightened his grip on her, effectively trapping her against him.

Her gaze shot to his, pupils flaring a bit, whether with excitement or alarm, he couldn't quite tell.

"Your bonnet is in the way," he said in a low voice. He moved his hand to the ribbon tied around her chin and with a flick of his fingers, loosened the bow. He removed the bonnet carefully, making sure none of the straw strands caught on her hair. He set it on the window ledge and turned back to her.

The traffic had increased on Piccadilly below. If anyone chanced to gaze up at the Egyptian Hall's window, he would see Jack gripping Becky's upper arms. Jack didn't care.

Pressing a finger to her chin, he tipped her face up. She didn't resist. Ever so softly, he pressed his lips to hers.

His eyelids sank shut as every nerve in his body flared into high alert. But he schooled himself to gentleness, gliding his lips over hers in a delicate caress. She tasted so sweet.

She didn't fight him. She didn't draw away. Her lips moved tentatively over his, her hands slid hesitantly up his arms. Slipping his arm around her waist, he drew her tightly against him, showing her just how much he wanted her.

Her arms tightened over his shoulders and closed around his neck. Her mouth opened and her lips moved more boldly over his. He cradled her face in his palm. There was nothing softer, warmer, sweeter than the curve of her cheek.

And her taste, God…He touched his tongue to hers, certain he could never get enough of her taste. She whimpered softly into his mouth, her fingertips playing in the strands of hair at the base of his skull, tickling and teasing him in a place he'd never known could affect him.

Gently, he pulled away, staying close enough to feel her warm, ragged breaths dance over his cheek.

He ran his hands up her face and down her arms, feeling the crookedly set bones in her right arm before pulling her hands down between them, entwining his fingers with hers.

He gave her a questioning smile. "I've never courted a woman."

"Why?"

He shrugged. "Never wished to."

"Until now?"

"Until now."

"Why me, Jack?"

"I like you," he said.

After he'd spoken, he remembered the true reason he was courting her, and his gut clenched tight.

But he hadn't lied. He did like her. He wasn't going to spout Shakespeare or write a sonnet about it, because it was a simple fact. Furthermore, Shakespeare didn't appear to be necessary—from her expression it was clear that she understood the significance of his simple words.

"I...like you, too." She didn't appear at all happy about that revelation. "I am trying very hard not to, but I can't seem to help it."

She was teetering on the edge of a chasm of self-doubt. He had to divert her. Squeezing her hands, he said, "Let's explore the rest of the rooms."

She sighed in relief and nodded. "Yes."

He returned her glove and bonnet to her, and she pulled on the glove, then retied the bonnet's ribbons under her chin as they left the landing. In the Roman Gallery, they gazed at the painting taking up the greater portion of the wall at the far end of the room. The work was labeled *The Death of Virginia.*

"I vaguely remember this story," he murmured. "Virginia...she was about to be carted off by the tyrant—" He pointed at the man who stood at the tribunal in the midst of the Roman Forum.

"Appius Claudius."

"Yes. That's his name."

"There's her father—" Becky gestured at the man raising a bloodied knife toward the figure who stood at the tribunal. At the man's feet lay the fallen girl crumpled in a heap. "Virginius. He slew his own daughter to save her from a life of misery with Appius Claudius."

Becky continued to talk of the painting, naming the landmarks of Rome depicted in the painting: the Forum, the Tarpeian Rock, the Temple of Jupiter, the Temple of Venus Cloacina. Catching him staring at her, she stopped speaking abruptly and flushed pink all the way to the tips of her ears. "I'm sorry."

He grinned. "I've never known a bluestocking. It's fascinating."

"Perhaps that is why you are so tenacious," she said stiffly, turning away from the painting. "All that most of my suitors require is the statement that I am a bluestocking, and they run without a backward glance."

"Have you had many suitors?" He fell into step beside her as she headed toward the door of the Roman Room.

"No. Not many."

"Why would they run upon learning that you are a bluestocking?" Jack pressed.

"Because we are, 'without being positively criminal, the most odious characters in society.'"

"Who said that?"

"It's from an article in *The British Critic* I read a few years ago."

"I think he who finds bluestockings 'odious,' as you say, is merely jealous that a woman can be more intelligent and more literate than himself."

The edges of her lips twitched upward.

"I have always held the impression, however," he continued, "that bluestockings are pompous, affected braggarts brimming with conceit." He smiled as they began to descend the stairs. "Hence my surprise when you labeled yourself as one."

"So you concur with the assessment that we are 'odious.'"

"If I did once, I don't anymore."

She sniffed. "You've latched on to the preconceived and oversimplified notion of what being a bluestocking entails."

"Perhaps you are right. I insist you define the term properly to set me straight."

"I imagine it means different things to different people, but to me, it is a woman who is interested in the acquisition and applications of knowledge."

"I see."

"While some ladies might take an interest in drawing or singing or the pianoforte, I prefer books and the knowledge contained in them." She shrugged. "It is a matter of preference, nothing more."

They'd arrived at the bottom of the stairs. From the corner of his eye, Jack saw a door opening and the dark figure of the curator approaching them. "You play the pianoforte."

"I am, and will always be, a novice at the pianoforte."

The curator thanked them for coming and gave them their coats. Jack held Becky's coat as she slipped her arms into it. Outside, the coachman met them with a large umbrella, and they hunched beneath it and hurried toward Stratford's carriage.

He held her hand as they rode to Mayfair, images of stealing her away and dragging her to the altar cascading through his head.

But by the time they arrived at Lady Devore's door, he had recalled himself and was a gentleman. He bade her farewell, tipped his hat, kissed the back of her hand, and said he sincerely hoped to see her again very soon.

He hated watching her turn away from him, though. And when the door closed behind her, he felt utterly alone.

Chapter Ten

The next evening, Jack relaxed before a cheerful, crackling fire, sharing a fine brandy with Stratford in his drawing room.

"So..." Leaning back in his sleek leather armchair, the earl crossed his feet at the ankles. He was dressed for going out, in a nondescript but finely tailored gray striped waistcoat and double-breasted cutaway tailcoat with smooth dark satin lapels. "What next?"

Jack took a swallow of brandy and savored the burn down his throat. "She is thawing."

"Is she really?" Stratford shook his head, musing. "Shocking, really, considering the company she keeps."

"What do you mean?"

Stratford's face bore no expression. "Lady Devore. I know that woman, Fulton. She is an icicle, and she holds a grudge forever. I am surprised she hasn't turned the lady against you completely."

"She has been quite generous toward me," Jack said, and then he pointed out, "You had an affair with her, and yet she treats you with civility."

"She treats me with far more civility than is warranted, but she simmers on the inside. She hates me—I see it in her eyes." Stratford flicked a piece of dust from his sleeve. He didn't seem at all perturbed by his admission. He said the words in a flat, confident tone that made Jack slightly uneasy. Perhaps his friend was even more world-weary than he was.

"The clock is ticking, Fulton." Stratford settled back in his chair. "Less than a month remains. Hardly enough time to plan a wedding, much less marry the girl properly, withdraw her funds, and dispense them without evoking suspicion."

"True enough," Jack said easily. "But I have resolved to take this day by day. I'm happy with my progress. As I told you, she is thawing."

"Your accelerated courting technique might not be accelerated enough." Stratford frowned. "What will you do if you run out of time? Resort to whisking an heiress spinster off to Gretna? Or perhaps give up on the scheme altogether and escape to the Continent?"

"If I escape to the Continent, or anywhere else, I will never be able to return to England." Jack stared moodily into the fire, rubbing his near-empty glass along his lips. He wasn't afraid of losing Becky, but Stratford was right—he *was* running out of time. Yet he couldn't—he *wouldn't*—force her to go any faster than she was willing to go. If he forced her, he might lose her.

Nevertheless, if he was too late, if he didn't pay on

time, Tom would expose the incriminating evidence, and Jack would either hang or be forced to leave England forever. Jack would accept neither option.

"An heiress, then?" Stratford asked, more lightly than the situation warranted.

"No, damn it. I don't want an heiress, and you know it."

A knock sounded at the door, and both men turned toward it. "Yes?" Stratford asked.

A harried footman entered and looked to Jack. "A gentleman is here asking to see you, sir."

Jack frowned. "Someone for me? At this hour? Who—"

That someone pushed past the footman, and Jack groaned aloud when the man's tall, willowy frame came into view. It was the man he least wanted to see in this world, who had followed him constantly when they were youths and who had pursued him incessantly since his return to England. It was the one man certain to know Jack's every move. This was the man who aimed to extort money from him. Thomas Wortingham, the vicar's son and Jack's boyhood friend from Hambly.

Stratford looked from Tom to Jack, one blond brow raised. When he saw the look on Jack's face, understanding dawned in his expression.

"Ah," he said softly. He rose and held out his hand. "Stratford."

The man swept into a low bow, all foppish propriety, and Jack's stomach twisted. "Tom Wortingham, my lord. A pleasure to meet you, a true pleasure indeed. What a fine home you have here."

Jack had held on to his friendship with Tom during the years he'd been away from Hambly at school. Whenever he returned home on holiday, he'd split his time between

Tom and Anne. Often, the three of them had spent their days together. Later, Tom had frequently accompanied Jack to London.

Tom knew everything. *Everything*. Just that truth was frustrating enough. The fact that Jack's one-time closest friend had now betrayed him made it much worse.

He slid a glance at the earl. Stratford already knew too much, but he didn't know the whole story, and Jack didn't want him to. Hell, he didn't want anyone to know anything. It was bad enough that Tom was privy to that information.

Doubtless the man had lurked at the window all evening, watching Jack and Stratford as they'd settled in the drawing room. Deciding to pay them a visit, he'd probably attempted to use his oily charm on the butler, and then when his efforts had no effect on the man, had sauntered into the house uninvited.

"Tom, this isn't a good time—"

Stratford gave a friendly flick of his wrist. "Nonsense. I'm going out, but please stay as long as you like, Wortingham. Enjoy the brandy." He grinned at Jack. "See you tomorrow?"

"Yes," Jack said, unsettled, half wishing Stratford had thrown Tom out. "Of course."

Tom didn't belong here, and Jack wanted him gone. His desire for him to disappear, however, was overruled by curiosity about what he had come to say—and a wild, unreasonable hope his old friend would call off the entire scheme.

With a pleasant "good evening," Stratford left them alone, closing the door carefully behind him.

Taking the earl's offer to heart, Tom went to the sidebar and poured himself a generous glass of brandy. He took a long drink, then lowered the glass, studying Jack over its rim, his gray eyes calculating. "What does he know of our arrangement?"

"Very little. Too much."

Always very pale, Tom looked ghostlike in the flickering firelight. He had a long face and was tall and too slender for his height, and his worn clothes draped loosely over his gaunt frame. He'd never grown out of his days of gawky youth. He smiled, his pale lips stretching wide and thin.

"Still so secretive," he said, "even with your powerful friends. An earl, eh?"

Jack didn't mention that Stratford was a second son who'd never expected to inherit an earldom. "There are some things it will do the world no good to know."

Tom studied his hands. They were long and pale like the rest of him, and the shadows of his fingers stretched even longer across the ivory-wallpapered wall behind him. "You know I might disagree with that, Jack."

"I know." Jack could kill this man right here, right now, despite the fact that Tom had warned him that if any harm should come to him, his agent would simply hand the evidence over to the authorities.

It didn't matter. Jack was no murderer. Not anymore. He just wanted this to be over.

"What do you want? Why have you followed me here?"

Tom shrugged. "You know I've been watching you. I've come because I'm worried, Jack. I'm worried that you won't pull through. I'm still hoping you will, for your sake and for mine, but nevertheless, I am deeply concerned."

"You'll get your damned blood money."

"Will I?" Tom's pale eyes focused on him. "I don't know, Jack. The woman has refused you. I know she has more than enough, but it's crystal clear that she doesn't want you."

"She will."

"Are you certain this is the best way to deliver me my fifteen thousand pounds? Because I need it, Jack. And so do you."

Tom turned slightly, and Jack saw the bulge in his oversized coat pocket. The man carried a gun. Had he expected Jack to try to kill him? Or did he carry it for self-defense from those who truly meant him harm?

Jack had a strong suspicion that there were some far less savory characters than himself after Tom Wortingham. He didn't want to know who or why. He didn't want to know anything about Tom. He just wanted to give him the damned money and wash his hands of the matter.

It had become almost symbolic to him. The handing over of the fifteen thousand pounds would close this chapter in Jack's life. He could begin to live again, without all the damn regrets and guilt from the past that had plagued him for so many years.

The pale gray stare focused unerringly on him. "Perhaps if you can't get it from her, I can."

Every muscle in Jack's body went hard and brittle as ice. "You will not touch her."

Tom shrugged. "You must know that I will go to whatever lengths necessary. I won't hesitate to use her to achieve my ends. I must have that money, Jack. Your life is at stake, and..."

His voice dwindled, but Jack knew what he'd been about to say. *"...and mine is, too."*

"Look," Jack said through his teeth. "I am aware of the date you require the funds, but if you touch the lady in the interim..." He paused, knowing he could not be responsible for his actions if Tom went after Becky. When he continued, his words were chillingly quiet. "If you go near her, if you speak to her, communicate with her in any way, you will regret it."

Tom waved his hand dismissively. "You have less than four weeks."

"I will hand over the funds in time," Jack said, his voice cold. "Now leave."

"Are you sure? Because everything is in place, Jack. You know I hate to do this to you—"

"There is no need to lie to me."

Tom hesitated and then nodded, his eyes flat, almost reptilian, in their coldness. "Very well. I just came to warn you. I'll be watching you, Jack. Don't do anything stupid."

Jack, Jack, Jack. Why did Tom say his name over and over? It was as if he was trying to reiterate the fact that they had once been—and would always be—close enough to call each other by their Christian names.

Jack raised his hand. He wasn't going to overcomplicate this by dragging his own guilt into it. Nor was he going to dwell on Tom's belief that Jack owed him not only for his years of silence, but for stealing Anne from him.

Only one thing mattered: If he did not give Tom the blackmail money, Tom would take his damning evidence to the authorities, and Jack would hang.

He wanted to live. He wanted a life in England. With Becky.

He'd known Tom since they were in swaddling clothes. Tom often lacked common sense, but he wasn't a fool, and he would have thought of every contingency. The incriminating evidence was in the form of signed, witnessed statements, stored in a secret location. Nobody knew where it was but Tom and his agent—a man whose identity Tom had kept secret. And if Tom was hurt or killed, or if Jack didn't deliver the money on time, the agent would reveal everything.

"Go away," Jack said. "I don't need your distraction here. Get out of my life. Your funds will be delivered on the fifteenth of December, as promised."

Fifteen thousand on the fifteenth.

Tom's lips flattened. "You should pursue someone else."

"No," Jack bit out.

"What's so special about her? She's nothing like Anne. Anne was a voluptuous beauty. That lady is skinny and insipid, with nothing in the way of titties—"

"Get the hell out of here, Tom," Jack growled. His hands shook. Suddenly glass exploded, and a sharp, stinging pain sliced through his palm. He opened his hand, releasing shards of his brandy glass onto the carpet.

Tom eyed the cut on Jack's hand and took a wary step backward. He knew all about Jack's weakness when it came to blood, but Jack ground his teeth and stood firm.

"Very well, then. But I'll be close, Jack. To make sure you don't bungle it. Like you have everything else."

He hurried out of the room, leaving Jack dripping blood onto the carpet. Jack's head reeled, and he steeled himself, diligently keeping his gaze off his cut hand. The sight of blood always made him faint. The crew of the *Gloriana* joked that once Jack had completed his first voyage, nothing could ruffle his feathers except for a "sight o' the red stuff." He'd suffered a hazing or two in which the sailors had dragged him to the infirmary to view someone's broken head or cut-up arm. The *Gloriana*'s surgeon had revived him from a dead faint more than once. Even on the last voyage they'd made from Jamaica, a midshipman had knocked at the door to his cabin one night, and when he'd opened it the man's face had split into a wide grin. "Cap'n Calow's got 'imself a scratched knee," he'd said, "would yer like to come up to see it, Mister Fulton?"

Jack took out his handkerchief, and cursing the day he'd befriended Tom Wortingham, he stared at the dying fire while he wrapped the cloth around the stinging cut in his hand.

Chapter Eleven

The masquerade was not an event attended by those whom most persons would consider at the pinnacle of society, but the attendees were nevertheless a fashionable set. The bulk of the guests had been scraped together from genteel society remaining in Town, but some had traveled from as far as Devonshire to attend Mrs. Pionchet's annual event.

Cecelia had explained that the masquerade party consisted of gentlemen and ladies willing to tread on the cusp of scandal but unwilling to overtly flaunt their adventurousness to the world. The failure to disguise oneself could lead to disparaging gossip, but those whose identities remained a mystery could be topics of intrigue, sometimes for months.

Cecelia described the costume as a fairly simple affair. There was no need to spend a fortune designing the perfect sultana or Grecian goddess costume, she said.

Instead, most of the attendees wore evening wear with complementing dominos and hats to disguise themselves. The most important accessory was the mask, which hid a person's features and kept everyone guessing. Cecelia explained that the different levels of anonymity provided the bulk of the evening's entertainment, though she warned that Becky might be shocked by some of the behavior she witnessed.

The masquerade took place on the twenty-third of November, two days after Becky and Jack's visit to the Egyptian Hall. Cecelia wore a dress of amber silk trimmed with dozens of bows, and Becky wore a tulle dress over a satin slip of soft blue. A wide sash was clasped about her waist with an offset bow with long ribbons that fell all the way to her shins. Silk buttons adorned the dress's long, full sleeves, and brilliant white kidskin gloves covered her arms. She wore two golden bracelets around her wrists, a necklace of Egyptian pebbles, and a black velvet hat festooned with gold feathers sat jauntily askew atop her head. Matching black velvet lined her blue silk domino.

The party was held in a sprawling mansion outside London. As Cecelia's carriage rattled along in the dark—the days were so short this time of year—Cecelia explained that Georgianna Pionchet was the widow of a French diplomat. She had been born into a distinguished British family and had resided with her father, one of Wellington's officers, in Brussels during the Hundred Days. In the midst of the war, she'd eloped with a Frenchman. Her family had disowned her in the ensuing scandal, but she and her husband had thrived beyond the war's end, and he was soon assigned to service in London.

Since her husband had died five years ago, their home had become the site of some of the most exciting and anticipated parties in England.

"Why is it that I have never heard of her?" Becky asked.

Cecelia chuckled. "You've been too young and sheltered to have heard of her, but I assure you, she becomes known to everyone sooner or later. Her masquerade is the most wickedly intriguing event of the season. You'll soon see why."

The coach lumbered down a long drive and finally halted in a brightly lit clearing cluttered with other conveyances. Seeing a footman approach, Becky prepared to exit the carriage, but Cecelia laid a hand on her arm. "Wait," she whispered. "Your mask."

"Oh, yes." Becky reached for her half-mask, which lay with Cecelia's on the seat across from them. The mask was made of stiff silk the same color as her dress, trimmed in black velvet. Sapphire chips encircled the whole, and the almond-shaped eye cutouts tilted up strongly at their edges. *Cat's eyes*, Becky had thought when she'd first seen it.

Cecelia tied the ribbons behind Becky's head, and then Becky returned the favor. Cecelia's mask was a ghostly white abomination that completely covered her face, but Cecelia adored it—when they'd seen it in the shop, she'd exclaimed with glee that no one could possibly identify her when she wore it.

A footman met them at the door and led them down a carpeted corridor lined with blazing gilt wall sconces. He opened a door and bowed as they slipped into the ballroom unannounced.

Guests thronged the cavernous room, the majority dressed as Cecelia had described—in colorful, flowing capes with complementing hats or hoods. All wore masks. Many were plain half-masks dyed black or in colors complementing their clothing, but others were far more elaborate than Becky's: gilded, painted, and encrusted with jewels. People stood in groups, where they chatted and laughed, and the noise level was very high. This was certainly no subdued *ton* party.

Scattered elaborate gold wall sconces and an enormous chandelier in the center of the room provided the light, but the room was not well lit at all. In fact, Becky found it rather gloomy and shadowy, more like a theater box during an opera than a ballroom. The thick, pungent smell of warm bodies in close proximity steamed from the dense crowd. Servants wearing stiff black and white clothing and simple black half-masks slipped through the mass of bodies, balancing trays of wine and champagne. Through the noises of revelry, Becky discerned the strains of music drifting across the vast space.

Cecelia squeezed her hand. "Well, let's find Georgianna, shall we?"

"How on earth will we find anyone in this crowd?"

She hadn't expected Cecelia to hear her over the din, so she was surprised when her friend answered with a chuckle, "Oh, we'll find her."

A giggling woman in a flowing cape pushed past them, nearly trampling Becky. As Becky struggled to regain her balance, a masked gentleman wearing a puce domino brushed past her, in hot pursuit of the woman.

"Goodness," Becky murmured.

Cecelia gave her a knowing smile. "Oh, it hasn't even begun. You'll see."

Becky had never been in the midst of such boisterous cheerfulness before and found it all rather overwhelming. She allowed Cecelia to tug her along, and they weaved through the crowd together, hand in hand.

Suddenly, Cecelia came to such an abrupt halt that Becky nearly slammed into her from behind. A man stood a few feet in front of them—a tall, dark-haired man wearing a black half-mask over a straight Roman nose. He was staring directly at Cecelia.

"Oh, drat," Cecelia muttered.

The man's lush lips curled into a sinful smile, and his dark eyes flared with recognition. The three of them gazed at one another for a protracted moment, and then the man gave a mocking bow before returning his attention to his companions.

Cecelia blew out a breath through pursed lips. Grasping Becky's hand again, she pulled her forward. "Isn't it lovely," she said with more than a hint of sarcasm, "that *he* should be the one to recognize me in this mask."

"Who is he?" Becky asked.

"Oh, I dare not say his name aloud here. You wouldn't know him, in any case. Over the summer we had a liaison. It is quite over, but he hasn't acknowledged that yet. Ah, there is our esteemed hostess. Come, let us go pay our respects."

They came to a halt before a tall and generously proportioned woman wearing rust-colored silk and a matching mask bedecked with rubies. Her hat was at least two feet tall, with plumes of dark red feathers bursting from the brim. No wonder she'd been easy to find—with her height and the hat combined, she towered over everyone here.

The woman turned to them, smiling through a wide, generous mouth. Behind the mask, dancing eyes observed them, and Becky instantly realized that the woman had already perceived her identity. Becky curtsied, and Mrs. Pionchet returned the gesture.

"Good evening," their hostess said, her voice low, rich, and husky.

"Good evening," Cecelia said. "I'd like to introduce my good friend."

The dark eyes glinted at her. "Welcome, my dear."

"Thank you," Becky said. The fact that none of them used names made her feel slightly disoriented.

The woman flicked out a hand. A tray of champagne appeared beneath it, and she plucked up a glass and handed it to Becky. She took another and handed it to Cecelia.

"Have you met the comte, viscountess?" Mrs. Pionchet inquired of Cecelia.

"Why, no. I haven't."

"Come, then," she said, beckoning at them, curling her long, black-gloved fingers in an inviting gesture. "I shall introduce you."

The comte was a short, balding man with a thick French accent, and again, no names were exchanged. Mrs. Pionchet referred to Becky as "the lady" and Cecelia as "the viscountess." It was all very odd indeed, Becky thought. And she didn't miss that the comte stared hard at Cecelia, licking his lips as they walked away from him.

Mrs. Pionchet introduced them to several more people.

Becky was silent, speaking only when spoken to, fascinated by the costumes and attitudes of the people surrounding her. It was a different world.

She and Cecelia found some space to stand at one side of the room. Elaborately painted Chinese screens stood at intervals along the walls, and when Becky peeked behind one of them, she jerked her head back, heat rushing to her face. A man and a woman, her dress sleeves pulled down low on her arms and the tops of her breasts exposed, had been embracing—*emphatically* embracing—on a couch set in an alcove.

Seeing the look on Becky's face, Cecelia laughed. "Don't tell me."

"Very well, I won't," Becky said primly.

"Becky, for goodness' sakes. Don't be missish."

Cecelia was right—she shouldn't be feeling appalled, or even surprised. She had embraced a man—*men*—before. Yet the flagrant decadence of this display was beginning to make her uncomfortable.

She didn't judge anyone here—how could she? She'd done far more with Jack, a man to whom she wasn't married, than the man and woman behind the screen. Still, she didn't belong here. All around them, men and women flirted, the men aggressive, the women coquettish. Becky didn't want to flirt with anyone...not anyone here.

Cecelia had leaned away from her, and Becky saw that a slight, black-clad man was whispering into her ear. When he finished, Cecelia gave a murmured response, and he walked away as Cecelia turned back to Becky.

"Becky..." She hesitated, glancing in the direction the man had gone.

"What is it?"

"George—the man we encountered earlier. He has told several people I am here…with him." Her lips thinned in annoyance. "He has asked me to meet him on the terrace. I've no idea as to his intentions, but I feel I must explain to him in no uncertain terms—"

"Of course you must," Becky said.

"I don't like to leave you alone."

"I can see that this is distressing you, Cecelia, so I think you should speak to him. In any case, I'll not be alone," she assured her friend, and then, spotting Mrs. Pionchet, "Look, our hostess is approaching."

Mrs. Pionchet arrived on the arm of a masked gentleman, whom she introduced as "the baronet." Cecelia curtsied politely and then made her excuses. With a final squeeze of Becky's hand, she took her leave.

Mrs. Pionchet and the gentleman led her about and introduced her to a string of people, but they had all begun to look alike to Becky. Her head felt fuzzy from the champagne, and she didn't like the way every man she was introduced to studied her as if to determine whether she was a piece of meat worthy of sticking a fork into.

Spotting an empty velvet-cushioned chair tucked between one of the Chinese screens and a terrace door, Becky said, "Oh, you go ahead, Mrs. Pionchet. I believe I should like to sit for a while."

Mrs. Pionchet didn't argue. Pressing another glass of champagne into Becky's hand, she and the baronet swept away, cutting a swathe through the crowd.

Becky sipped at the champagne and watched people come and go. She saw a man proposition a woman, saw the woman's chest flush pink in response before she wrapped her arms around the man's neck, drew him in, and whispered in his ear—probably an affirmative response, because within a matter of seconds, they had slipped away.

Another couple toasted each other, drank their full glasses of champagne in one draught, and then threw back their heads and laughed full, throaty, uninhibited laughs. Their obvious joy made tears of envy sting at Becky's eyes.

She shook herself slightly. Why did she feel so melancholy? An empty, hollow feeling had settled in her stomach. Loneliness, that was it. Yet she had no desire to carouse with these strangers. Nobody here interested her.

Nothing had changed, she thought ruefully. She'd never been one for social gatherings. She was too shy, too bookish. Too much of a bluestocking.

A high-pitched laugh sounded from beyond the screen, and Becky tilted her head. She'd heard that laugh before.

"Did you see that pamphlet showing the two of them in bed?" The person who spoke was a woman, her voice unfamiliar. "With the duke and that enormous scar looking on in rage? I nearly burst my seams for laughing!"

Becky went very still. She'd assumed she was a topic at parties and in drawing rooms, but she'd thought they'd be whispering about her disgrace and shame. She hadn't expected anyone would be laughing at her.

"Mr. Fulton is such a handsome man." The tone matched the sound of the first laugh Becky had heard, and from the high-pitched nasality of the speaking voice, she knew who it was: Lady Borrill, the woman who'd passed her on the stairs at Sheffield's Hotel, had informed Garrett, and had been one of the crowd to storm in on her and Jack.

The other lady made a disparaging noise through her nose. "Indeed. And he could have any woman in London in his bed, and he chose her. Can you imagine?" She paused briefly, and then added in a disgusted tone, "She is such a mouse, so bookish. And a cripple, to boot!"

Becky sat very still, her face a frozen mask. She would not react. She knew people judged her and disparaged her scarred elbow. She knew people were gossiping about her, and she knew Lady Borrill was the instigator of the entire scandal. None of this was a surprise.

"That family grows more disgraceful by the year," Lady Borrill said. "It is only due to Viscount Westcliff's influence that they are not shunned by every soul in London."

"Surely even his good reputation will not survive a breach this reprehensible!"

Lady Borrill sighed loudly. "I doubt it. I know I shall never speak with any of them again. And neither should you. Think of what it would do to your own reputation should you be linked to one of the Jameses."

"My daughter is a friend to the duke's daughter."

"You must call an end to their acquaintance. Immediately."

"Oh, of course. I certainly will," the other woman, whom Becky still had not recognized, said, a note of finality in her voice. "I will order all communication between them to cease this very instant."

"What's a beautiful lady like you doing all alone here on zees lonely sofa?"

Becky snapped to attention as clammy fingers stroked her neck. She jumped up out of the chair, spinning to look at the person who'd touched her. Blinking in surprise, she studied the stranger. Beyond him, the party continued. She'd been so engrossed in the horrid conversation behind the screen that she had forgotten where she was.

The Frenchman wore a mustard-colored domino, a simple brown half-mask, and a felt cap, and he didn't look familiar at all. Obviously deep in his cups, he reeked of spirits. She racked her brain, trying to recall if Mrs. Pionchet had introduced her to this man. For the life of her, she couldn't remember. There were many Frenchmen in this crowd, and Becky's attention had waned after the first dozen nameless introductions.

"Just resting...er...monsieur," she responded, trying to be polite even as the skin on the back of her neck crawled from his touch.

He reached up a finger to trace her collarbone. It was an attempt at a seductive gesture, but Becky yanked herself away, feeling unconscionably soiled. Appalled, she gazed into his bleary eyes. A hazy recollection of the rules of propriety came to her, insisting she slap him across the face and march away. But that awareness came too late. His fingers wrapped around her neck, and he heaved her against him.

"Just one leetle kiss, eh?" he murmured down at her, his acrid alcoholic breath washing over her face.

Panic surged through Becky. They were surrounded by people, but no one paid them any heed—not here. His arms wrapped around her, solid bands of iron, pinning her against him.

A pair of thin, shiny lips descended toward hers.

No. This was *not* going to happen. She was going to severely damage his ballocks. She nudged her knee between his legs, as if she were snuggling closer. He sighed in pleasure, clearly thinking she'd submitted to his irresistible amorous advances.

And then he jerked away from her, his hands wrenched from her body so forcefully she could feel the strain on her buttons. She gasped from shock at the sudden movement, and looking up, she saw a suntanned hand gripping the man's mustard-silk-covered shoulder.

"Jack." She said it in an almost-whisper, her voice replete with relief, happiness, true pleasure. She gazed up at him, but he didn't look at her. Instead, he gazed down at the stranger from behind a plain black mask, his features implacable.

"Go away." His voice was pleasant, but there was an edge to it that sharpened each word to a dagger point. "And you will never approach this lady again, do you understand?"

"Ah," said the Frenchman with a bleary smile. "You tink she ees yours?"

Jack's dark eyes slid for the briefest of seconds to Becky and then returned to focus on the stranger. "Yes," he said, quiet but very certain of himself. "She is mine."

And then he shoved him away. The Frenchman stumbled backward into a group of revelers, who seemed to think a man literally crashing into their group was the funniest thing they'd ever seen. They helped him up as one, then saw him off with multiple pats to the back, no one sparing a glance at either Becky or Jack.

"Oh, Jack. I'm so glad you're here."

His features didn't soften. He stared at her. "You were kissing that man."

His eyes flashed with hurt. He thought...oh, God! She shook her head vehemently. "No! He grabbed me. I was trying to defend myself—"

Jack made a scoffing noise. "Didn't look like it to me."

She closed her eyes to stave off a sudden onslaught of tears. Her hands shook at her sides. Now that it was over, the horror of what had just happened surged through her. The man could have dragged her out of this place screaming, and no one would have done a thing.

Her knees softening, she sank back onto the chair.

"He was going to kiss me," she said, trying desperately to keep her voice level. "At first I panicked, but then I just wanted to get away. I was going to knee him in the...in the..." She looked up at him, unable to finish.

Jack studied her for a long moment, and then his lips tightened. His entire expression transformed to a different sort of anger. Becky knew he believed her.

"Did he hurt you?"

"He grabbed me very hard—"

Jack's eyes narrowed to slits and his hands curled into fists. He turned, obviously searching for the Frenchman, but she grabbed his arm.

"But no, he didn't hurt me." She gave him a shaky smile. "I am all right, truly. Just a little frightened, I suppose. Nothing like that has ever happened to me before."

Appearing somewhat mollified, Jack glanced around them. The guests grew more intoxicated by the minute, it seemed, and people touched and embraced in full view of everyone in the room. Becky no longer heard the voices of the two ladies beyond the screen—they'd probably gone off to make their own conquests. *The hypocrites*, she thought bitterly.

"Why are you here?" Jack asked.

"Cecelia brought me. I was curious." At this moment, that seemed like a very weak reason to come. "People haven't recognized me—I heard them talking about me, about my family. And then that man... Oh, Jack, I want to leave."

He gave a sharp nod. "Of course."

"I mean... I just want to get away. Not only from this, but from everything." She should return to Calton House as she'd originally planned...but she couldn't abandon Kate.

"I understand," Jack said.

Wrapping her arms around her body, she stared up at him. "I wish I could leave London. Leave the judgment of others far behind. Go someplace where none of it exists."

Even in Yorkshire, this scandal would exist. The insults would not be as overt as they were in London; instead, they'd be brutal in their subtlety.

"Come." Jack reached for her hand. "I'll take you away."

He helped her from the chair and they slipped out of the enormous ballroom. Jack led her to a carriage—Lord Stratford's, she assumed—and when Jack began to tuck a heavy fur over her, she remembered her friend. "Oh, dear. Cecelia is on the terrace. She won't know where I have gone."

"I'll take care of it. Stay right here." Leaving her in the warmth of the carriage, Jack returned to the house. After a few short minutes, he returned. "I informed Lady Devore that you're with me."

She smiled gratefully at him. Jack went to speak with the coachman, and Becky untied her mask and set it aside before settling against the violet velvet squabs, allowing herself to relax for the first time in hours. Finally, Jack sat on the cushion beside her. He tossed his mask to the opposite bench and leaned back. When the carriage lurched into motion, he took her hand. "I'm sorry. I should have come earlier."

"I hadn't expected you to come at all, and I'm so glad you did," she said with heartfelt sincerity.

"I wasn't certain you would be here, but Stratford had mentioned Lady Devore had been invited, and he told me exactly what kind of gathering it was. If you had come with her—well, I decided to make an appearance, just to make sure you were all right."

She gave him a quizzical look. "*That* was why you came? To be certain I was all right?"

His eyes didn't stray from hers. "Yes."

For some reason, her throat felt thick, and tears burned at her eyes. Perhaps she was just tired.

"Thank you," she whispered.

Chapter Twelve

It took longer than Jack had predicted before she suspected anything. She'd scooted away from him, drawing the curtain shut as if in an attempt to block out the world, and she'd leaned against the carriage door and closed her eyes.

Eventually, she straightened and turned to him. "Shouldn't we be in Mayfair by now? Or at least deeper in Town..."

He chose his words carefully. "I'm not returning you to Lady Devore's house."

Her eyes widened. "What?"

"You said you wanted to go away. So I'm taking you away."

"But I can't leave London! Kate is nearing her—"

Raising his hand, he pressed two gloved fingers to her lips. "Ssh. I told Lady Devore where we're going. If anything should happen to your sister-in-law, she'll make certain we're informed immediately."

Her mouth opened as if in protest, then she snapped it shut. Then she opened it again. "But—if anyone . . . we'll be the laughingstock of the *ton*."

"Nonsense." He took her hand in his own and traced his finger over the soft, delicate flesh of the back of her hand. "No one but Lady Devore—and Stratford, when I send the carriage back to him—will know. We'll be completely alone."

She stared at him. Shock, fear, denial, anticipation—all of it passed over her expression in waves.

"And if people do find out—well, weren't you the one who said scandal didn't touch you?"

"Yes. But I was wrong. When it affects my whole family's reputation—" she hesitated, then finished, "—it hurts."

He tried not to grimace. He hated that she'd been hurt. He hated that people spoke ill of her. How could they? She was the most beautiful, sweetest, most intelligent, most fascinating woman he'd ever encountered.

Frustration tugged at his nerves. He wished he could approach all the busybody gossips in London and wring the cruelty from the marrow of their bones. He couldn't, of course, but he could provide her some peace.

"We're going to the house I've let near Richmond. We'll be away from London, yet close enough to return on a moment's notice." He curled his fingers around her hand and squeezed. "You need freedom from the city right now. I can give that to you. Let me."

"My brother would never approve of this," she murmured.

"It is your life, not his."

"He will find us. He nearly killed you once already."

Jack raised a cynical brow. "What gives you the idea that he nearly killed me?"

"There was murder in his eyes when he found us at Sheffield's Hotel."

"Murder in his eyes does not equate to my death."

"You don't know my brother. What he..." Her voice dwindled, and she looked away. "When Garrett is determined to follow a certain course, nothing can deter him."

"I could."

For long moments, she stared out the window in silence. They drove along the river's edge, a full moon casting a dim glow over the road. In the distance, the black water of the Thames peeped out from between the dry branches of the brush.

Finally, she turned back to him. "Do you still wish to marry me?"

"Yes."

The muscles across his back tensed as he waited for her to respond, wondering if she'd order him to return her to Lady Devore's this instant or whether she'd agree to wed him right here, right now.

"This is an attempt...a ruse intended to coerce me into agreeing to becoming your wife."

That staggered him into silence. Not so very long ago it would have been a Machiavellian tactic he'd approve of.

But since witnessing her vulnerable reaction to that stranger's amorous embrace, he'd wanted nothing more than to take her far away. To shelter her from the lecherous gazes and the prying eyes and the harsh tongues that surrounded her. To hold her, to protect her from all of it. To keep her safe. And he knew the perfect place to do that—the house he'd planned for them to live in after their marriage.

He gazed into her eyes and said with complete honesty, "It's not a ruse. I wasn't thinking about marrying you when I told Cecelia about it, or when I instructed the coachman where to drive. I was thinking only of your desire to get away."

Long minutes of silence passed before she spoke again. "What if you succeed, Jack? You convince me that you will make me a good husband. You make me believe that we will be happy together. And then I marry you." Her eyes shone indigo in the murky gloom inside the carriage. "But what if you don't? What if you rip it all away the moment we are married? What if it is impossible for me to attain happiness? What if it is impossible for me to ever be happy again?"

"It's not impossible."

"How can you know that?"

Because he'd once thought the same of himself.

"I just know," he said.

He'd been wrong when he'd so flippantly implied to Stratford that she was worth nothing to him beyond her money. No, she was worth far, far more than the money. Then, he knew she could save his skin, but in the days since she'd left him staring after her at that dinner with their families, something had shifted, and understanding had unfurled like a bloom in his chest.

He'd lied to Stratford about it. He'd been confused and uncertain, and trying to convince himself otherwise, scrabbling to hold on to the youthful vow he'd made to himself twelve years ago—that he'd never love another woman after Anne.

Becky turned away from him to once again gaze out the window. "You're a trader, Jack, so you should understand it when I tell you that I am damaged goods."

"So am I," he said. For more reasons that she would ever know.

"Why wouldn't you choose someone else, then? Someone easier than me? Someone *better*?"

Lady Rebecca Fisk was the only woman he wanted. The only woman for him.

"No one is better."

The cottage was a charming, cozy affair situated on the banks of the Thames. As they drove up. Jack explained that this was the house he'd rented on the morning of his proposal, and that he'd intended for them to live here once they were married. Apparently there were no servants, but Jack told Becky he would arrange to have food delivered to them in the morning.

Inside, Jack lifted her domino from her shoulders, and he sat her on a sofa in the dim front parlor. She realized she'd forgotten one argument against coming here— she'd brought no clothes with her.

She gazed up at him, and heat flared, subtly cracking between them. Perhaps there was no need for clothes. A blush warmed her cheeks at the thought.

"Stay here," Jack instructed.

She didn't move as he lit a lantern and started a fire. As he worked, she studied him surreptitiously while removing her gloves. For such a large man, he was graceful. Each movement was executed with precise dexterity.

When the fire crackled cheerfully, he took up the

lantern with one hand, grasped her fingers with the other, and pulled her up.

"Come. I'll show you the house."

He led her from the parlor through a small dining area into a kitchen. They mounted the narrow stairs, which led to a landing and three bedrooms upstairs—two of them tiny and one quite large. On the whole, it was a simple but tidy dwelling, clean and comfortable.

In the largest bedroom, he paused and turned to her, brushing her cheek with a rough finger. She tilted her head toward him, instinctively seeking more of his touch. He stared at her for a moment, his eyes so dark and so compelling her fingertips tingled with the urge to touch him.

At that moment, her stomach chose to growl.

He dropped his hand and closed it around hers. "Are you hungry?"

She gave him a rueful smile. "I suppose the night's adventures have increased my appetite."

"Well, there won't be anything fresh, but I think I saw some nice-looking apples in the larder when I was here last."

He took her through the dim kitchen and into the larder, where there was indeed a basket of apples. He took it, along with a bottle of wine and two glasses, and they returned to the parlor, where the wood fire crackled cheerfully in the hearth. She sat on the sofa, tucking her legs beneath her. He placed the basket on the cushion beside her, sat on the other side of the basket, and chose two apples, one of which he handed to her.

"Thank you."

Heat from the fire licked over Becky's cheeks and

filtered through the thick, stiff material of her dress. Taking a bite of the apple, she inhaled, its fresh, crisp scent mingling with the wood smoke, and she sighed in contentment.

She admired his profile as he opened the bottle of wine and poured it into the glasses. Strong chin, high forehead, blade of a nose, and, Lord, those wicked lips...

He looked up and captured her eyes in his own. "I miss you," he said quietly. "I've missed touching you. I still want you, Becky." He paused briefly before lowering his voice to ask, "Do you still want me?"

She hesitated. "Wanting you was different...before."

A shadow crossed his face as he handed her a glass. "How?"

"I'd assigned less importance to it." She took a healthy swallow of wine. It was full and rich, its flavor mingling nicely with the tartness of the apple.

"You thought to be a merry widow like Lady Devore. I thought you were like her, at first. But you surprised me. You're nothing like her."

She sucked in a breath. "What do you know of Lady Devore?"

"She is cynical."

"So am I."

"No. Not like her. She has given up. You—hope still shines in your eyes. Sometimes you try to hide it behind a wintry mask, but it's there, begging to be set free."

"I don't think so." Becky closed her eyes and then opened them slowly, hoping to erase whatever Jack thought he saw there.

She'd abandoned hope four years ago. She could place

her finger on the exact moment. It was the night before William died. She'd followed him downstairs in the middle of the night and hidden on the stairs while he talked to his servant, and she'd heard the truth. William cared nothing for her—he'd married her only so he could steal her money, money he meant to use to take his mistress to France. After he murdered Becky.

She focused on her apple, and for a while, both of them ate and drank, the silence broken only by the sounds of crunching fruit and the pops and crackles of the fire.

Jack set his apple core aside. "Don't be afraid of me."

How could she not be afraid? She wanted him as she had never wanted anything in her life, and she was scared to death of the feelings he evoked in her.

He moved his hand to her knee, his fingers playing over the tulle overdress and the layers of her skirts and petticoats.

Becky cocked her head. "What's that?"

"What's what?"

She lifted his hand and turned it over in her own. A long scab slashed across his palm. "You've been cut. What happened?"

He shook his head and gave her a rueful smile. "I broke a tumbler of brandy in my hand. I suppose we didn't have anything as delicate as Stratford's fine crystal aboard the *Gloriana*." He shrugged. "It is healing."

Finishing the last of his glass of wine, he glanced at the clock on the mantel. She followed his gaze and saw that it was after one o'clock in the morning.

"It's late," she said.

"Are you tired?"

"Yes. I should go to bed, but..." Chagrined, she kept

her gaze on the mantel. "I cannot undo the buttons on my dress."

"I'll help you." His voice was low, devoid of undertone.

In an abrupt motion, she rose and turned her back to him. When he didn't move or speak, she looked at him over her shoulder, her brows raised in question.

He rose, unfolding his body until his presence seemed to overwhelm the small parlor.

He smelled of apples and wine, his scent intoxicating. It made her so dizzy she shifted her stance to prevent herself from swaying.

His hands rested on her shoulders, big and heavy, stabilizing her, his palms covering the entire width of her upper back. His hands passed over the puffs of her sleeves, then smoothed down her wrists before traveling all the way back up again and meeting at her nape.

Brushing his fingertips over the back of her neck, he undid the top button. He took his time, working each cloth-covered button as if the process of undressing her fascinated him.

When he finally finished, he pushed the sleeves of the gown from her shoulders down her arms. She helped him by pulling the sleeves all the way off. Fabric pooled around her knees, and he went to work on the buttons of her petticoats. When her petticoats dropped over her dress, she stepped out of the pile of clothing.

"Well done." She laid the dress and petticoats over a chair. "You've obviously undressed many women."

She regretted saying that instantly. It was none of her business how many women he'd undressed.

"I've never undressed you." His voice was quiet, yet rough as gravel.

She ran her hands down the front of her stays and looked up at him nervously. "Will you——?"

"Of course. Turn around."

She obeyed, holding her palms flat against the stiff boning of her stays. He untied the knot Josie had tied yesterday morning and tugged at the crisscrossed lacings, pulling them loose. When the stays gaped open, he lifted them over her head, leaving her clad in nothing but her chemise. She turned and took the stays from him, clasping them to her body.

"Better?"

"Yes. Thank you." She bit her lip and looked away, still clutching her stays to her chest.

He gently pried them out of her hands and laid them on the chair. "You shouldn't be shy with me."

"I don't often find myself in the presence of a man in nothing but my chemise."

"Remember what you wore on that night?"

"Yes." Becky fought the flush creeping up to her cheeks.

"It was more transparent than what you're wearing now."

Her feelings about Jack had been different then, though, and while she'd felt shy about that dress, it was nothing to how she felt now. She gave him a half smile. "You're right."

He tugged her gently against him and slid his arm around her waist.

"Come, I'll take you upstairs."

They walked out into the tiny entryway and turned to go up the stairs. The steps were too narrow to ascend side by side, so he took her hand and led her up, pulling her against his side again as they reached the landing.

Once they were inside the largest bedroom, he turned away, leaving her standing in the center of the room, and went to set down the lamp on an empty table. He strode to the window, gazed out for a moment as if checking to see whether anyone lurked in the darkness, and then drew the curtains tightly shut.

He evoked such strong, conflicting emotions in her. He made her feel weak and delicate, and utterly breakable. How could she not feel fear when just a look from him made her as wobbly as a newborn foal and as uncertain as if she were poised on the edge of a deadly precipice?

He took her hand and led her to the chair that stood before a small dressing table topped by a square, wood-framed looking glass. "Sit."

Warily, she obeyed, glancing up at him in question, but he was looking at her hair, not her face. His hands moved deftly over her head, his fingers pressing gently into her scalp, as he unpinned and unbraided her hair and let it fall to her waist.

He took up the brush from the dressing table and brushed through the tangles, strand by strand, his strokes so gentle it was an exercise in pleasure rather than pain. She closed her eyes and nearly purred as the bristles stroked over her scalp and through the strands until they were smooth.

"It is just as I thought," he murmured.

Her eyes popped open, and she stared at him to see that his focus remained on her hair. "What is?"

"Your hair. Smooth and sleek and so black as to nearly be indigo. Like your eyes."

"My eyes are blue. Dark blue."

"Sometimes they look dark purple. And in this light, your hair has that same sheen. I have never seen the likes of it. So beautiful."

He set the brush on the table and plunged his hands into her hair, sifting his fingers through the strands. Then he smiled at her in the mirror, his hands pressing on the base of her skull.

"Oh," she whispered. "That feels good." She fought against the urge to close her eyes and groan with pleasure, for his fingers pushed hard against the tight cords of muscle in her neck.

He moved over her neck and shoulders until they felt warm and languid. She sagged in the chair as he rubbed and kneaded, working away what felt like years' worth of tension.

Finally, he curled his palms over her shoulders. "I'll take you to bed now."

He slid his arm beneath her knees and scooped her from the chair. In a few steps, he stopped at the edge of the bed. He laid her down, and he slipped his hand up her leg, his fingers brushing over her stocking, to her garter. He untied her garter and set it aside, then rolled her stocking down, taking his time, his fingers a rough heaven over the exposed skin of her calf and shin as he progressed downward.

She wanted him hopelessly. Desperately. She'd wanted him in London, and she wanted him now. Yet as much as her body yearned to be his, her mind struggled against it. It wouldn't be wise, logic told her. This was different from those nights in the hotel. Now, she was drawn to him in a deeper way, which made him far more dangerous.

He went to work on her second stocking, the feathering brushes of his fingertips sending her senses into a pleasurable spin.

He walked away to lay her stockings on the dressing table and returned seconds later.

His broad body loomed over her. He reached out, stroked a fingertip down her arm, pausing at her twisted elbow. He cupped it in his palm and bent his head. She stared at his square, masculine jaw, shadowed by the beginnings of a beard, and the sharp angles of his cheekbones. His lips, supple, full, the softest, most masculine pink, descended inexorably toward hers.

His mouth brushed hers. She reached up with her good arm, filtering her fingers through the softness of his hair, holding him but resisting the urge to yank him against her. His lips pressed against hers, his tongue swiped along her upper lip.

Their breaths collided, mingled, and brushed over her mouth, tantalizing, feather-light. He tasted of wine, but his salty masculine essence was far more intoxicating. His hand left her elbow and clasped her around the dip at the side of her waist, traveling lower to her hip, then her thigh, then sliding back up and slipping over her bottom.

Her breasts tingled, the nipples brushing against the fabric of her chemise, aching for something—to be touched, that was it. They ached for his touch.

She wiggled and arched, pressed her legs together to quell the throb building there.

Then she did tug him closer, pressing her palms to his neck and pulling him tight against her. She opened to him, exchanged brushes of tongues and lips, nipped and licked, her need and pleasure building with every taste, every breath they shared.

"Jack," she whispered. The ache grew bolder, the desperation to be close to somebody—no, to *him*. The desire to lose herself, to lose all awareness of where she ended and he began.

His hand traveled from her body over her stomach and up, brushing her tightly beaded nipple. She whimpered as an electric sensation whipped through her, straight between her legs.

His hand didn't linger on her breast. It moved up, over her collarbones and shoulder, up her neck, over her jaw until he cupped her cheek. Energy simmered between his fingers and her skin, a subtle buzzing that resonated through her veins.

"Do you trust me?" he murmured against her mouth.

"I…" She closed her eyes. "I don't know."

He pressed a kiss to her lips then gently pulled himself free of her grip. "Good night, Becky."

He swept up the lantern and he was gone, leaving her alone in the dark.

Chapter Thirteen

Jack lay wide awake in the small bedroom, staring at the ceiling. It had taken what seemed like hours to calm the raging need that had roared through his blood before he'd left her. The struggle to remain in control had taken more power than he'd known he possessed. After he'd shut the door behind him, he'd stood in the corridor for long minutes, pressing his forehead against the cool plaster of the wall.

Patience. He could not sacrifice the fragile bond developing between them; could not let base desire overrun common sense.

Becky required time to sort through her feelings, to pry off the stranglehold her dead husband held on her heart. If Jack had six months, he could seduce her into loving him completely, honestly. Hell, he could seduce her into begging him to marry him.

He didn't have that luxury. The fifteenth of December

was three weeks away. Tom was near. Jack wouldn't be surprised if he lingered outside the cottage on this frosty night. The man was wily, and he was experienced at tracking Jack.

When Jack was sixteen years old, a school friend had invited him to spend the winter holidays at his family's home in Somersetshire. One night, Jack had looked out the window to watch the first snowfall of the season only to see Tom Wortingham standing on the lawn, smiling and waving at him. Too shocked to think clearly, Jack had told his friend, and his family had invited him in for the night. Tom had invented some story about visiting relatives in Somerset. But Jack knew Tom had pursued him all the way from Kent. It had made him uneasy at the time, but those had been his days of carefree youth, and he'd shrugged away his friend's strange behavior.

Now, years later, Jack had no doubt that Tom Wortingham was still capable of such actions. Not only that, Tom now had a vested interest in knowing his whereabouts. Until the fifteen thousand was safely in his hands, Tom would be close.

Sighing, Jack squeezed his eyes shut. He'd realized many years ago that Tom Wortingham was not quite right in the head. The man had spent so long hiding that raw edge of insanity behind his guileless manner and bookish intelligence that the truth hadn't struck Jack until Anne had died. He would never forget Tom's primal scream when he'd told him what had happened to her. Her death had been enough to erase any impulse Tom ever had to pretend at being an upstanding member of society.

From the beginning, Tom had insisted that Anne's death was Jack's fault. Along with squandering what little money his father had left him, Tom had probably spent the past years planning his vengeance on Jack.

At times, Jack believed himself responsible, too. Not a day passed that he didn't feel the twinges of guilt and regret. It was only the soul-deep knowledge that he'd done what he could for her, that he'd tried his damndest to save her, that kept him holding his head high.

Despite all that had happened, Jack had known Tom Wortingham since they were children, and he knew what to expect from him. If Tom could be trusted in anything, it was staying true to his word. His threats weren't empty. If Jack didn't deliver the money, Tom wouldn't hesitate to take his damning evidence to the authorities. If Jack did hand over the fifteen thousand, however, Tom would relinquish the evidence to him and leave him alone. The man always kept his word. He was a vicar's son, after all.

Ultimately, it didn't matter how close Tom was tonight. Jack wanted to stay in England, damn it, and he didn't want to die a wanted criminal on the run from the noose. Tom would have his money in time. And then, as promised, he'd be out of Jack's life forever.

Jack turned onto his side and stared at the closed door to the tiny bedchamber. The bed was hard and narrow, unlike the bed Becky slept on, which was soft and more than double the size of this one. Perfect for two.

It had been necessary for him to leave her, but it had nearly killed him. She'd wanted him tonight. She'd sighed sweetly into his mouth, kissed him with abandoned passion, her fingers tight around his neck, locking him in place against her. She'd still been gasping when he'd walked away.

What was she doing now? Did she lie awake as he did? Was she thinking of him? Of that kiss? Was she touching herself, imagining his hands stroking her in those places his fingers ached to explore again?

Desire rose in his veins once more, and he hardened, thinking of her slender, delicate hand roaming over her body, her lips parted but her eyes closed as she imagined it was him who pleasured her.

He was burning hot, stiff as a pike, pulsing angrily. And it was damned painful.

"Hell," he said through clenched teeth. *Focus on something else!* But he couldn't. All he could think about was Becky. Her sweet, soft, willing flesh. Her sighs of pleasure as he sank into her and she closed tightly around him.

Just Becky.

Becky turned restlessly, first one way and then the other. Though the bed was soft, she could find no comfort. The sheets felt scratchy against her, her chemise bunched at her waist, she was cold, and the weight of the blankets did nothing to warm her.

Worst of all, she couldn't stop thinking about Jack. About the heated press of his lips on hers, the way his hand had cupped her deformed elbow. Not as if it repulsed him, but as if he wanted to protect it from further harm.

Perhaps it was a delusion; perhaps he had no such thoughts when he touched her there. Yet one thing was blatantly clear—he wanted her. She'd seen the shadowy bulge in his trousers as he'd walked away. He'd wanted her badly, and yet he had not taken advantage of his power over her. He was waiting for her to trust him.

Could she make that leap for him? As she lay there, cold and lonely, the compulsion to try grew stronger with every minute.

He'd made it clear he still wished to marry her, despite how she'd tried to push him away. He still wanted her. He seemed to enjoy her presence. He took pleasure in conversing with her. He found her beautiful on the outside—and possibly on the inside as well.

She rubbed her twisted elbow and flexed her tingling fingers. She wanted to trust him. If she was going to trust anyone beyond the closest members of her family, she wanted it to be Jack.

Oh, God. She clutched the blanket to her chest and stared up at the shadowy ceiling. She was falling in love with him.

No . . . no, it couldn't be. She had believed herself incapable of loving anyone after what William had done to her. But how else to explain this restless feeling, these feelings of need, of desire, of *hope*? These feelings were so different from the fluttering excitement she'd felt when she'd agreed to run to Gretna with William. The feelings were deep, intense, so powerful they almost hurt.

Her position was very precarious indeed. Yet Jack professed to care for her. He wanted to marry her. He wanted to make her his. His actions had proved he cared for her. They also proved he understood her in a way no one ever had.

All she needed to do was believe. Release the shields she'd spent so long building around her and trust him. That was the difficult part.

There was no reason for him to pretend to admire her if he didn't. He was so very different from William. She'd been stubbornly cautious ever since she met Jack, but she'd failed to take into account the fact that she was older now—she was wiser than when she'd so stupidly believed William's protestations of never-ending passion. Now, if William came to her and sobbed his undying adoration for her, she would know it as deception and false flattery. She would smell it, sniff it out like a hound.

When Jack professed his admiration for her, she saw the truth of it in his dark eyes, and the eyes were the windows to the soul.

Was he lying awake in one of those rooms across the corridor? Was he thinking of her as she was thinking of him?

She was still so very afraid. But Jack was right—there would be no peace for her until she conquered her fear and allowed instinct to prevail. Instinct told her to trust Jack Fulton. And her heart told her she wanted him, perhaps even more than he wanted her.

Since she was a little girl, she'd desired only one thing: to be happy. She'd always been lonely, always by herself, always withdrawn into a distant world of fantasies and imaginings. Then, four years ago, she thought she'd found what she'd longed for. Someone who loved her desperately, who would fulfill her every need. For a few fleeting days, she'd been in true bliss. But then William had yanked that away from her, thoroughly and cruelly, and with it he'd stolen every one of her dreams. She'd spent the past four years believing happiness was just another impossible fantasy. Yet in the past weeks, Jack had offered her fleeting glimpses of it.

She kicked off the blankets and slipped out of bed.

The air was frigid, and she wrapped her arms around her as she padded on bare feet over the cool planks of the floor. Across the passageway, both bedroom doors were closed. Jack could be beyond one of those doors, asleep or awake, or he could be downstairs. No light or sound emanated from any of those places.

The first door creaked loudly as she opened it. Grimacing, she scanned the little room and found it empty. She backed out and went to the second door, opening it more slowly than the first. The door glided open without a sound.

A figure sat in the gloom provided by the scant moonlight that filtered through the curtain. He sat at the edge of the bed, his face turned to the door.

"Becky?" His voice was a gruff whisper.

She stepped into the room. "Yes."

"What is it?" he asked. "Can't you sleep?"

"I—no. I couldn't." She sucked in a breath. "I was thinking about trust."

He cocked his head as she came to stand before him.

"I'm still so afraid," she said.

He reached out, finding her hand and grasping it in his own.

"I know."

"I don't want to hurt anymore, Jack. I—I want to be happy."

"Becky..." He surged upward and pulled her hard against him. "I want to make you happy. More than anything."

She shook from head to toe, shuddered too violently to hold on to him. And suddenly, his hands were all over her, stroking her through the silk of her chemise, heating her chilled skin, and he whispered soft, calming words. "Shh. It's going to be all right. You'll see. We'll make it work, sweetheart. We'll be happy together."

She pressed her body against him. He was bare-chested, wearing only his drawers. His skin was smooth, warm, and comforting, and she could feel his growing arousal behind the layers of fabric separating them.

She managed to raise her trembling hand to cup his cheek, the bristles of his new beard rough against her skin.

"I trust you, Jack."

He sucked in a breath, and even in the darkness, she could see the raw vulnerability in his expression, shining in his eyes. He bowed his head. "I won't fail you."

"Will you be honest with me? Always?"

After an infinitesimal pause, "Yes."

"And I will be honest with you. I promise."

He closed his eyes, squeezed them, and then opened them again. The look of vulnerability that had darkened his face seconds ago was gone.

"Let me make you mine. Let me love you."

"Yes," she whispered, unable to keep the tremor out of her voice.

She wrapped her arms around his neck. Easily lifting her, he carried her into the larger bedroom and laid her once again on the bed. This time he settled beside her, bending his arm and resting his head on his hand as he lay on his side, looking down at her in the dimness.

"This is…" His Adam's apple moved in his throat as he swallowed.

"What…?"

He closed his eyes in a long blink. "I've wanted you

for a long time, Becky. I don't know... I might not... I want to give you pleasure, but..."

She pushed on his shoulder until he lay on his back, then she pulled her chemise to her thighs and straddled him. She stared down at him, speechless, for her own action had made the lips of her sex cradle the long, solid length of his, the touch of their skin separated only by the thin linen of his drawers.

"God," he choked. He stared up at her, the stricken look in his eyes mirroring hers. He was shaking, too, she realized.

Her lungs constricted, compressed in her chest, and she could hardly suck in enough air.

"I want you," she managed to say in a tight voice.

With her hands flat on the hot, tight skin of his shoulders, she slid her body up and down the length of him, biting the inside of her cheek to prevent herself from groaning.

She moved her hands down his chest, feeling the fine points of his nipples against her palms, then moving downward, her fingers flowing over the compelling dips and curves of his muscles, using her sense of touch in the dimness. She reached his navel, skimmed the bunched muscles around it, and traveled lower, down the trail of hair that led to the waistband of his drawers.

She moved backward, still straddling his legs, until she touched the ties on his drawers. She pulled the loosened waistband carefully over his sex, revealing him in full arousal. She wished there was more light, for she could see nothing but the shadow of his shape.

As he kicked his drawers away, she tentatively skimmed her fingertips down his sex. Encouraged by his sharp intake of breath, she took him into her hand, curling her fingers around his length.

She'd never been so bold with William. She glanced at him. "Do...do you like this?"

"Yes," he said in a strangled voice.

She moved her fist over him, stroking up the silky, solid length. It fascinated her. She moved again, this time downward.

"Becky," he groaned. "Stop."

Instantly, she let go. "I'm sorry."

He grabbed her beneath her arms and hauled her up over him so she straddled him again. But this time there was nothing between them, and the feel of the hot length of him between her legs made her gasp out loud.

"No," he grated out. "I'm the one who is sorry. I—God, just your touch is so close to making me explode."

"Why?" She was truly curious. Even as she asked the question, though, she fidgeted over him, every move of his flesh against hers sending tiny tremors of pleasure sparking through her.

"Because it feels good. Too good."

She smiled at him. It was a smile of conquest, a smile of power. She could bring this man to the edge of fulfillment with a simple touch.

"Kiss me," he commanded.

She knelt to drop a kiss on his lips. As soon as their lips connected, a pulse of energy ran through them both, connecting them, and Jack took control. One hand pressed on the small of her back; the other fisted in her hair, locking her to him. She couldn't move. She had no desire to move.

His mouth took possession of hers, his tongue exploring greedily, sensuously, and his taste exploded through her—hot, salty, commandingly male.

He nipped at her lip, then soothed the area with soft, warm kisses, leaving a trail of white-hot pleasure in the path of the pain. All the while, the length of his sex slid over the most sensitive parts of her.

Still kissing her, he turned her onto her back. He loomed over her, his body seeming twice as wide, twice as large, as her own.

The rough pad of his thumb stroked across her cheekbone, and his kiss traveled away from her mouth. He sampled her flesh, her jaw, her nose, her eyelids, and then he moved lower. He untied the neckline of her chemise to access her breasts, then used his mouth and hands to work the plump flesh and her nipples until every touch made her gasp and squirm, seeking more of him, seeking the fulfillment he could offer, the satisfaction only he could give.

"Please, Jack, please..."

He drowned her words in another of his overwhelming, hot kisses. She clutched his shoulders as he reached down, adjusting himself at her entrance. With his hand still tangled in her hair, he thrust into her.

Becky cried out. Her body arched convulsively.

"Oh, God. Am I hurting you?"

"No." She writhed, moving against him, away from him. He drew out, and she whimpered at the sensation of his hot, hard flesh sliding against her inner walls.

"So sweet," he murmured against her mouth. "So tight."

Closing her eyes, she sighed in an agony of pleasure.

She allowed the sheer power of her desire and her love to rise, to burn her distrust and fear to ashes. They fluttered away on the wind, and without all that fear blinding her, she could see clearly again.

He would be—no he *was*—hers. Her lover. Soon, her husband. She was his.

She loved this man. Loved how he made her feel. But now, so close, so connected, she could not fathom a life, another moment, without him.

She was so in love with him. And that didn't bring her pain. It didn't even evoke fear. Instead it made her feel powerful. Invincible. He was beauty incarnate. Intelligent and worldly. Affectionate, and possessive. And she was worthy of all of those things.

He saw reciprocal qualities in her. He wanted her as much as she wanted him.

"Jack," she said as he moved within her, a rhythm of pleasure. "Jack."

The pleasure built, dark clouds gathering into a gale, beautiful and powerful at the same time.

"I can't stop it," he gasped.

She could hardly speak for the storm building within her. "Don't stop."

His strong body moved with quick, deep thrusts. He moved faster, harder, each of his exhalations a sharp explosion of breath. And then his fingers tightened in her hair, and the storm burst in a violent shower of pleasure that shuddered all the way through her, curling her toes and her fingers. Her nails dug into his shoulder blades.

"Becky." It was a half-whisper, half-groan. He stiffened and stilled, and through her own pulsing pleasure, she felt his, contracting deep and hard inside her.

She lost awareness of everything except the point where they were connected, only returning to the world when the pulsing subsided and the tension in the body over her relaxed.

He touched his forehead to her shoulder. "I'm sorry."

She blinked. "What?"

"That was too fast. I did not give you pleasure. It was selfish of me." She heard him grinding his teeth. "Damned inconsiderate."

Reaching up, she pressed her hand against his cheek, turning his face so he could see her—or at least the shadowy outline of her face. "No. You gave me pleasure. So much pleasure."

He released a harsh breath. "Come here, sweetheart."

He rolled onto his side, bringing her along with him and tucking her backside against his body.

They lay pressed together for long, delicious minutes. This bed had seemed cold before he had joined her in it, but now a thin sheen of sweat covered her body, and she wiggled.

"Are you too warm?"

"A little."

He pulled back and lifted her chemise over her head, leaving her completely bare. He tossed away the offending material and once again pulled her close.

"You fit here," he murmured. "Perfectly."

Yes, she did. She gave a drowsy murmur of agreement and snuggled against him, his warmth a lure, a promise of contentment. Of happiness.

Jack lay awake a long while after Becky's breaths deepened and her body went slack against his. Still he kept his arms wrapped around her, unwilling to let her go.

He'd promised her honesty. Yet there were two things he could never reveal to her. The first was the truth about the night the Marquis of Haredowne had died. The second was his initial reason for wanting to marry her.

He was falling in love with the precious woman in his arms. Both of those truths would hurt her, abolish the trust she'd so generously extended to him, sever the connection they had built.

He couldn't do that to her. Worse—he couldn't do it to himself. He needed her too much. He was too selfish.

Full of self-loathing, he closed his eyes. And offered a prayer up to God that she would never put him in a position to lie to her. He would be honest about everything but those two things, and God must know that his intentions toward Lady Rebecca Fisk were now nothing but honorable and pure.

Please, God, don't let me hurt her.

Still holding her tightly against him, he dropped into a fitful slumber.

Chapter Fourteen

She came downstairs in the late morning, just after Jack had returned from fetching their breakfast from their landlady in the village. Since he'd let the house, he'd communicated with the woman—a stolid, even-tempered widow with a puff of brownish-red hair and a deeply lined face—and he'd prepared her for his and Becky's possible arrival at the house without notice. He'd already warned her about their need for board, and she obligingly provided him with a simple repast for breakfast and a promise of hot stewed beef for their luncheon.

Becky hesitated in the doorway to the kitchen, and Jack turned from the stove. His chest tightened at the sight of her. So beautiful, in her rumpled chemise. She'd brushed her hair and it hung in a sleek black fall down her back. His eyes lingered on the suggestion of creamy mounds rising from the neckline of her shift.

"Good morning," he murmured, dragging his gaze to her face. "Coffee?"

"Oh. Well, yes. Thank you."

"Have a seat. I'll bring you some. There's also fresh hot cross buns and some boiled eggs."

She nodded and sat at the table. He lowered a plate and a cup of steaming coffee in front of her and then took the chair beside her with his own food. She took a tentative sip of coffee. From the way she grimaced, it seemed she didn't drink coffee often.

They ate their breakfast in comfortable silence, and though the table lacked Stratford's ever-present stack of newspapers. Jack found himself more content to be drinking his coffee beside Becky.

When they finished eating, he took the dishes into the scullery, rolled up his sleeves, and washed them. She trailed after him and watched him with a bemused expression on her face.

"How odd."

Up to his elbows in water, he raised his brows at her. "What's odd?"

"You're washing."

"Yes...?"

"I never knew a gentleman who cleaned dishes before."

"You haven't known very many gentlemen."

"True."

"And we haven't any servants to perform the task for us." He reached a soapy hand out to her, and asked, "Would you like to help?"

Her lips twitched. "I haven't the first idea what to do."

"Tell me you've never in your life washed a dish."

"I've never in my life washed a dish."

"Not even when you were a child scampering after the servants and their children?"

"No. I never scampered."

"Ah," he said. "Did you frolic? Cavort? Romp? Play?"

"No." She leaned against the doorframe, perfectly relaxed. "My father died when I was four years old, you see, and my mother when I was six. Garrett purchased his commission in the army when I was very young and was absent for most of my childhood. My aunt Bertrice made certain I was safe and well, but she wasn't the most maternal of guardians, and she discouraged childish behavior."

The wistful expression on her face pulled at his chest. She'd been lonely even as a child. He held out a cloth. "Well, then, I'll help you. Use this rag and rub it round the plate. When it's clean, rinse it in the tub here."

She pushed up her sleeves and followed his directions. He nodded in approval after she pulled the clean plate from the rinse water, and he directed her how to place it on the drying rack.

"What happened to your parents?" he asked as he handed her another plate.

"My father died of an apoplexy. My mother of consumption."

"Do you remember them well?"

She dipped the plate in the rinse water. "Not my father. I recall a very stern, scowling man, but I cannot say for certain whether my memory of him is accurate. My mother I remember a little better. She was always very frail, and she seemed unhappy. I was never to raise my voice or become boisterous in her presence, for such behavior agitated her. I always thought she was so sad because of something I did wrong, but now that I think back on it, I cannot imagine what it was."

"I doubt she was sad because of something you did, Becky."

They finished cleaning the dishes in silence, and then they went into the parlor, where Jack built a fire and then sat beside her on the sofa. He drew her head against his chest and played with the soft, silky strands of her hair while they gazed at the flickering orange flames.

"It is so peaceful here," she murmured. "It's like a dream. When we leave, we'll wake up in a completely different world."

"The harshness of that world cannot diminish what we've shared here." What he hoped they could continue to share. He was unaccountably, oddly nervous. They both knew he'd ask her to marry him again, but the question was when. He wanted to choose the right time.

"I hope you're right."

He kissed the top of her head. "I know I am."

"Did the harsh outside world diminish what you and Anne shared?" she whispered some moments later.

Against his will, he stiffened. Then he forced himself to relax. "I told you the rumors weren't true. We weren't lovers after her marriage."

She was very still beneath his arm. "But you were before she was married."

"Yes."

She sighed.

"That was many years ago. I was a boy of seventeen."

"I know."

"I don't like talking about her," he admitted. "I don't speak of her to anyone."

"I understand." She paused. "I don't like talking about William, either. But you can tell me now...if you will. I know you don't like to speak of it, but..." Her voice trailed off, and then she added, "Perhaps I should know."

She was right. Nevertheless, sickness churned in his gut. He had to be so careful. Careful not to lie to her, and yet he couldn't reveal the truth. "What would you like to know?"

"Tell me about her."

He was quiet for a long moment. "We were friends," he finally said. "Her father's lands bordered Hambly, my father's estate in Kent. We were of an age—well, she was half a year older than I was. She seemed infinitely older than me when we were young."

He tried to keep the facts on the surface, but as he said them aloud, they dug under his skin and burrowed deep. Anne, with her joyful smile and yellow hair and her snapping cornflower blue eyes. She was a bright, lively daisy.

"Did you love her?" Becky whispered.

He looked down into her ocean-blue eyes. So different from Anne's. She was different all over. Older than Anne ever was.

This one, he wouldn't let go.

"I loved her. Yes."

Becky looked away from him, and he took her jaw in his hand, turning her back to him. "You asked for the truth."

"Sometimes the truth hurts. I know it shouldn't. But it does."

"I won't lie to you, Becky. You don't want to hear my lies."

"True." She clenched her fists in her lap. "It is unfair of me. But I wish you didn't love her."

"I don't love her anymore." He pulled her close and kissed the corners of her eyes, tasting the salt of her unshed tears. "It was a long time ago. I was young. The young love violently."

"Yes, they do."

Jack realized that Becky was only three years older than Anne had been when she'd died. Older, yes, but still so young. And yet she'd eloped four years ago. Before her husband had destroyed her, she must have loved him as he'd loved Anne.

"There's something about love that I always wondered," Becky murmured.

"What is that?"

She licked her lips, stared up at him with eyes that had darkened to indigo. "Once you love someone so powerfully, is it possible to love again?"

He didn't answer her; just stared down at her beautiful oval face.

"I have thought often that I could never love anyone after what happened with William," she murmured. "Then again, there is my brother..."

"What about him?" Jack had heard the basic facts surrounding the divorce of the Duke of Calton and Sophie, the current Viscountess Westcliff, but Jack had only been back in England for a short time, and the complexities of the duke's marriages and offspring had been difficult for him to follow.

"When I was a little girl, Garrett was madly in love

with Sophie. He married her when I was six years old. They were very happy together, and when he went away to Waterloo, she was pregnant with his child. He didn't return for eight years. He was presumed dead, and by the time he finally came home, I was eighteen, his daughter was seven years old, and Sophie had married Tristan, his cousin and heir, who had also assumed the title of Duke of Calton."

"Good God," Jack said. "What did he do?"

"He took possession of his title and lands and tried to win Sophie back. In many ways, he still loved her, and she still loved him. But they had both changed too much in all those years away from each other, and Sophie loves Tristan beyond measure. She couldn't let him go. Finally, Garrett understood that Sophie would never fully come back to him. So he gave her up. He divorced her, and they share custody of their child."

"Incredible," Jack murmured.

"You've seen Tristan and Garrett together. On the whole, it is amicable, oddly and uncomfortably so for most. My family is one of the oddest families you shall ever meet, I'm certain of it. Yet they are also the most loving and generous people in the world. Any one of us would sacrifice anything for any one of the others."

Despite their twisted relations, Becky's family sounded far superior to his own. "You should feel proud to be part of such a family."

"I am," she said quietly. "I am very proud." She gazed up at him. "Perhaps you have seen how deeply my brother loves his wife. Kate is my dearest friend, and they fought with such violent passion to be with each other. Yet Garrett is in his thirty-ninth year. He still loves passionately, even though he is no longer young, and even though Kate was not the first woman he loved."

He gazed at Becky, rubbing his thumb back and forth over her plump lower lip. "So your brother has proven it is possible to love again. But I didn't require evidence."

"Can you really love again, Jack? Love as powerfully and as violently as you did the first time?"

"Yes," he murmured as he bent down to kiss her. "Perhaps I already do."

She flung her arms round his neck, kissing him back and thrusting her breasts against his chest with an urgent, brazen need that made his cock flare to life. Lady Rebecca, so reserved, so bookish, so melancholy and quiet, had proven herself to be a vixen in bed. And he loved it.

He ran his hands from the flare of her hips up over her narrow waist and pressed between them, insinuating his palms over her breasts, cupping them over her chemise.

He lowered one hand to the hem of her chemise and dragged it up her leg, trailing his fingertips over the smooth skin of her calf and then her thigh. She was all soft, eager woman, panting under his touch. Damned if he didn't want her every second of the day.

He pressed his hand between her legs, sliding through the already slick folds of her sex, and she arched into his hand.

He slid his fingers over her again and again, circling her clitoris and finally burying a finger deep inside her.

"Ahhhh..." She shuddered over his hand, clutched wildly at his shirt. Still in a seated position beside him on the sofa, she twisted restlessly this way and that, her face flushed, her eyes half-lidded and glazed with passion.

He pumped his finger inside her, then added a second finger, grazing along that spot deep inside her that made her shudder and whimper, made her body tighten around him. If he kept stroking, it would bring her to release.

He never took his eyes off her, because every breath, every pant, every cry of pleasure she made added to his own. Made him want her more. Made him love her more.

"Jack," she whispered, her eyes locked on his. "Jack... please..."

Without removing his hand from between her legs, he slid off the sofa and knelt on the floor before her, gently pressing her knees apart and tugging her forward so she sat perched on the edge of the sofa completely exposed to him.

She braced her hands on the cushions at her sides, staring down at him with wide eyes.

"What are you...?"

But her words were cut off when he leaned forward and pressed a kiss against her sex. Then he swiped his tongue over her slick inner lips.

"Jack!"

He backed away, licking her spring-flower taste from his lips and looking up at her.

"Wha-what are you...?"

"Tasting you." He moved his fingers, still lodged deeply inside her, and he could see her struggle to maintain her focus on him.

"Why?"

"Because I want to." He gave her a crooked smile and moved forward again, starting a slow rhythm with his fingers and his tongue, pushing deep into her and stroking along her inner walls while he swiped his tongue over her sex, focusing on the small nub of her clitoris. He circled it, feeling it grow taut beneath his tongue, and then he sucked it gently, bending his fingers inside her so they'd stroke along the spot that drove her to the brink.

She came instantly, surprising him. Her thighs tensed around his ears and her hands fisted in his hair as she called out his name. Her body pulsed over his fingers, against his lips, and her sweet, musky taste flooded his tongue.

He stroked her through it gently, and as soon as it ended, he pulled away. He made short work of his trousers, shoving them down over his hips, and his shirt, yanking it over his head. Then he reached down to adjust her, laying her on her back on the sofa. As soon as she was in place, he moved over her.

He couldn't wait another second. He had to have her.

Positioning himself quickly, he pushed into her hot, wet, willing body. The pleasure hit him with such intensity that white lights blinked behind his eyes. He stopped, lodged deep inside her, his fingers tangled in her hair, while he struggled to regain a semblance of sanity.

She stared up at him, her gaze rapt, filled with pleasure. Her hands slid over his ribs, then smoothed down his back, and she wrapped her legs around him, her heels pushing the area just below his arse.

Gritting his teeth against the urge to pound into her relentlessly, to chase his release at a full run until he conquered it, he began a slow rhythm, each push into her infinitesimally deeper, infinitesimally harder. This connection was something for both of them to savor, a slow ramp up to heaven.

His muscles grew tenser over her. His ballocks drew up taut against his body. His cock grew longer and stiffer, and his jaw clenched so hard it felt close to snapping. She traveled the same path he did, her muscles making a slow transformation from languidness to stiffness. Her hands went from smoothing over his body, to moving restlessly and without direction, to gripping him for all she was worth. Her eyelids sank and then her eyes squeezed tightly shut, and whimpers of pleasure emerged from her mouth even though her lips pressed together in a thin line.

He watched her. His muscles and jaw stiff, his release so close, he kept his eyes pried open and focused on the woman he loved, so beautiful in rapture.

Finally, she let go, shuddering, shaking, pulsing around him. Her lips parted and her body arched in the throes of a magnificent orgasm. Her body clutched him hard, growing tight as a vise all around him.

He rose to the top of the wave, cresting it. With a groan and a deep thrust, he toppled over into the churning water below. His shuddering in time to hers, pumping his seed, his heart, his soul, deep into her.

"Becky," he whispered as her body milked him of the remaining drops.

He squeezed himself between her and the sofa back, turning toward the fire, wrapping his arms around her chest and resting his chin on the top of her head. She snuggled against him. Even in this position, they fit together perfectly.

He stared into the fire, his eyes half-lidded, comfortable in silence.

A while later, she murmured, "Do you really think it will work?"

"Do I think what will work?"

"Us."

"Yes." He said the word with a definitive finality. Despite how differently they'd spent the past years, they were far more compatible than he had ever guessed. Long ago, they had traveled the same path, but each of them had taken a fork onto a divergent course—Jack when he'd been accused of murder and Becky when her husband had died. Yet something had thrown them together, and now they traveled as one again. On a path of healing, leading toward a far brighter future than the dull purgatory in which both of them had subsisted.

She pressed her body more firmly against him, her hand reaching back to stroke his hip. "Me, too."

"Marry me, Becky."

She hesitated, and under his arm her torso rose and fell as she took deep breaths. Finally, she whispered, "Yes, Jack. I'll marry you."

Jack's whole body resonated with the force of those few words. He squeezed his eyes shut as emotion poured through him. Holding her tightly, he vowed to himself that no matter what, he'd do right by her.

Chapter Fifteen

Sometime later, Jack shifted behind her, adjusting his body to a more comfortable position.

"Do you want to go upstairs?" Her voice sounded loud in the quiet of the room. Even the fire was almost silent, just a quiet whisper in the hearth. The wood had apparently exhausted its supply of crackling sap.

"In a while."

She nodded.

"Will you tell me about William Fisk?" he asked. "I should know exactly what happened between you and him."

She drew in a slow breath. "I was eighteen. A very young eighteen, too. I'd come into Town for my first Season and for my presentation to the king. Neither ever happened."

"What did happen?"

"I met William."

"Who was he? Where did he come from?"

"He'd returned from the Continent with Garrett. They were good friends—or so my brother thought." She closed her eyes. "I was taken by him instantly. He was so kind, so handsome. It was a very difficult time for Garrett, and William was the only person who could manage my brother. Garrett trusted him when he trusted no one else, so I did, too.

"He was a guest at our house, and he began to secretly visit my room at night. At first we only talked, but then he would kiss me. Caress me." She sighed. "He so easily fooled me. I was utterly besotted."

Behind her, Jack was silent. His arms remained banded over her chest, and she slid her fingers over his hand.

"He asked me to be his wife, and by then—only a few weeks had passed since I first met him, mind—I was so enamored of him I said yes, of course. Nothing in the world could bring me more happiness." She gave a bitter laugh. "He asked my brother, who was thrilled with the match, but Sophie never liked him."

"Why?" Jack asked.

"She didn't trust him. Out of all of us, she was the first to see through him. She and Tristan."

"I see," Jack murmured.

"One night, William came into my room. He said Garrett and Sophie wanted to delay the wedding, but he loved me and couldn't wait another moment to make me his. He said he wanted to marry me as soon as possible. He wanted us to run to Gretna so we could be joined right away."

Jack made a noncommittal noise behind her.

"I agreed, and we left in the middle of the night. Sophie, Garrett, and Tristan pursued us and tried to stop

us, but we escaped from them. We married the moment
we arrived at Gretna."

She paused. "It grew bad after that, Jack. It is difficult
to speak of it."

"It's all right, sweetheart." His breath was a low
murmur against her ear. "It's over."

Sometimes it seemed that it was still happening, that
she was still mired in that misery—the loneliness of
those first days of her marriage descending over her like
a shroud. But not with Jack. When she was with Jack,
loneliness was the farthest thing from her mind.

"He grew distant. We moved from place to place until
we ended at Kenilworth in Warwickshire. He grew even
colder there. I knew something was wrong, and I was
beginning to realize I'd made a horrible mistake.

"One night I woke and he was gone. I wanted so desperately to win back his love—I thought I would go
downstairs and search for him, and if I found him I might
offer to make him a drink or rub his feet, show him I
could still be a good wife. All I wanted was to make him
happy."

"Whatever happened," Jack said in a low, rasping
voice, "it wasn't your fault."

She closed her eyes. "I went downstairs and found him
talking with his manservant. They didn't hear me.
William called me insipid and dull, and said it was to his
great misfortune he'd ever met me." Her voice descended
to a dry whisper. "He planned to murder Garrett and me,
and then he planned to take my money to Paris and live
like a prince with his mistress."

Jack's body tightened behind her. "Good God."

"He hated Garrett. He blamed Garrett for his own

brother's death in the war. This plan—it was his vengeance."

"He must have been insane."

"Yes. Yes, I am afraid he was."

"What happened?"

"Garrett shot him."

"The common knowledge is that your husband was murdered by a band of smugglers."

"Yes. That is common knowledge. Common knowledge is often inaccurate, and in this case, it is a fiction created to protect the Duke of Calton. My brother was the man who killed my husband."

"God, Becky." Jack sounded shaken.

She scrambled to turn over to face him. She wanted to see the look on his face.

To her surprise, his eyes shone with tears. He gripped her shoulder, hard. "He was mad, Becky. Only a madman would knowingly cause you harm."

She stared at him.

"Only an idiot and a fool would think you were insipid or dull. You're beautiful. Intelligent, and full of life. He tried to suck it out of you, but he did not succeed."

"Sometimes I think he did."

"No." His voice shook with his conviction. She sighed, and he pulled her closer. "Thank you."

"For what?"

"For telling me your story, first of all. But mostly—" his hand trailed down her waist and then slid behind it, "—thank you for giving me your trust. Now I can understand how difficult that must have been."

Her lips wobbled as she tried to smile at him. "It is done, though. It is no longer difficult." Leaning forward, she pressed a hard kiss against the corner of his lips. "You don't think I was a stupid fool for what I did?" she whispered against his skin. "For being so naïve?"

"No. You were young. You were innocent. He manipulated you into believing he loved you when you were vulnerable and needed to be loved by someone."

"I hurt my family. I led them into danger. I was nearly responsible for my own brother's death."

"He fooled you thoroughly. Even if he had succeeded in murdering your brother, it wouldn't have been your fault. Far from it."

"Do you truly believe that?"

"Yes. He hurt you." He bowed his head, touched his forehead to hers, and closed his eyes. "I can't bear to see you hurt."

The next morning, Becky and Jack awakened early, and after lingering in bed for an hour of talking and love-making they rose and dressed. They planned to walk to Richmond, hire a carriage, and arrive in London before noon.

They ate a quick breakfast of bread dipped in cream, and Jack scrawled a letter to the landlady, thanking her for her hospitality and saying that he had no further need of her services for the time being. Becky combed and braided her hair in the simplest style, for she could manage no other on her own.

He watched her, a smile twitching at his lips, as she struggled to fasten the pearl buttons of her gloves.

"Let me guess," he murmured. "You've never before buttoned your own gloves."

"Not these," she admitted. "They are more difficult than most."

He held out his hand. "Come. I'll help you."

He had to remove his own gloves to tackle the buttons, and she was choking on silent laughter by the time he finished, grumbling that with so many tiny buttons on her gloves, it would be noon before they left.

"It usually doesn't take this long," she murmured. "I am one-handed and your fingers are too big. We need servants."

"Or we need to get rid of these damn gloves."

A chuckle burst from her lips, but it died away as he brought her fully gloved hand to his mouth. He pressed his lips against the buttery kidskin. "There."

She tore her hand out of his grip and threw her arms around him, planting her lips on his. "I cannot do this in public." She kissed him again. "So I wanted to kiss and hug you one last time…"

"Nonsense." That wicked smile curled his lips. "There's tonight, in your brother's house—"

"My brother's house!" she gasped, widening her eyes at him.

"—and many, many more nights to come."

Their lips met again, in a fiery clash that left her breathless. He finally pulled away, his gaze raking her body, finally lingering at her gloved hands.

"Hell," he muttered. "As much as I want to strip all those clothes off you and take you on the floor, it really will be noon before we leave. The damnable gloves alone take a quarter of an hour to button."

Smiling, she slipped her hand between them, running her fingers up the length of his erection. Then, on, impulse, she dropped to her knees and kissed him through the fabric of his trousers.

"Becky, what are you—?"

She was already undoing his buttons. Making short work of them, she slid his trousers down his narrow hips, taking his drawers down with them.

She looked up at him from beneath her lashes. "There's time."

By the time she was finished, he'd appreciate these "damnable" gloves as much as she did. They were made of the softest, finest kid, and not only were they the most beautiful gloves she owned, they were also the most comfortable.

She took him, already brick-hard, into her hands, cradling him in her fingers. Then she began a rhythmic stroke, moving the soft kid up and down his shaft. After just a few seconds, his hands rested heavily on her shoulders. "Becky..."

"Mmm?"

"I—"

But she'd pressed her lips to the crown of his organ, and he gasped, his hips jerking toward her.

She pulled away, biting her lip. Did he want...? Could she...?

Sliding her fingers down his shaft, she kissed him again, then tentatively opened her mouth over him.

He groaned, long and low. His fingers pressed behind her neck, encouraging her to take him deeper.

She did. She took him as deep as she could into her mouth, his silky-hard skin gliding beneath her lips. He tasted salty, musky, masculine. She held him there until he moved his hips back, pulling himself from her mouth.

When she began to move away, however, his fingers
tightened on her neck, and she obediently pressed forward
once more, allowing her kidskin-covered fingers to slide
over him, leading the way for her lips.

He pulled out a little, and it struck her that the movements they'd made imitated sexual congress. Was that
what he wanted? Testing her theory, she did it again,
retreating again until she nearly released him, and then
when his fingers tightened over her neck, she pressed
forward, swallowing him as deeply as she could.

He made a small noise. Under her fingertips and the
sensitive skin of her lips, he grew tighter, harder.

Yes.

She tried it again, this time without any urging from
him. She withdrew and then, even before he applied pressure on her neck, took him in, swirling her tongue around
the silken skin of his shaft as she did so.

"Yes, Becky," he said, his voice a near-moan. "Yes."

She did it again and again, sinking into the rhythm of
it, working her lips over him, experimenting with the pressure and the depth of her caresses, learning quickly that
the deeper she took him, the more he trembled. And when
she withdrew, if she swirled her tongue around his crown,
his fingers would curl into her hair, and he would groan.

His texture and his shape. His taste and his touch. She
learned it all, and mimicking the way he moved inside
her, she moved over him.

Suddenly, his fists tightened in her hair, and his thigh
tightened under her palm. "I'm going to—"

Whatever he was going to say, he didn't finish. He
froze, holding her locked against him. She couldn't
continue—she couldn't even move. His shaft contracted

under her fingertips, under her lips, over her tongue. And his seed spilled deep into her mouth.

She closed her eyes and swallowed convulsively, then again.

Finally he stilled. His hands loosened from her hair, and he pulled away from her. She remained there, dazed, as he fell to his knees before her and took her into his arms, his lips pressing into her hair.

He was shaking, she realized. "God, Becky. You didn't have to do that. I didn't mean to force you—"

"But...I wanted to. Didn't you like it?"

"Like...?" He pulled away. Gripping her by the shoulders, he shook her a little. "I loved it, woman. No one...well..." He broke off, shaking his head. "Never mind."

She brought her gloved hands to his face, turning it so he looked at her. She was so confused. "What? What are you talking about?"

"No other woman has ever done that for me." He sucked in a breath. "Without...compensation."

She frowned. "Why not?"

"Women generally...well, they don't seem to be fond of that particular act."

She ran her tongue over her lips, still tasting his salty, tangy flavor. His expression darkened, and he groaned softly.

"Would it be very debauched of me, then, if I told you I enjoyed it?"

He laughed outright, and gathered her close. "I'm more inclined to think I'm the luckiest man on earth."

"We should go," she whispered against his shoulder, though her body ached for him to keep holding her.

Sighing, he rose and helped her up, too. He dressed, then pulled on his own gloves as she tied on her velvet hat, took her hand, and led her to the door. When he opened it, they both reeled to a halt, gawking in surprise at the figure standing on the threshold.

A blast of cold autumn air swept over their faces.

And Garrett's brawny fist shot out and slammed into Jack's face.

Chapter Sixteen

The blow tore Jack's grip from Becky's arm. He careened backward, and Garrett stalked after him into the tiny entry hall, aiming another punch at Jack's face.

Jack was ready this time. He twisted away, dodging the blow, and followed up with a low fist to Garrett's stomach.

"Stop!" Becky shouted. "Stop this instant!"

She grabbed her brother's arm as he raised it to aim once again at her lover. She dug in her heels and yanked him back—away. "What are you doing, Garrett? Stop it!"

He turned, gazed at her for an instant, then whipped back round to Jack, who snarled at him and raised his fists.

"Wait outside for me, Rebecca," Garrett growled, shaking off her arm.

"No!"

He didn't look at her again. Instead he adopted a

fighting stance. "I'll take you home when I'm finished with him."

Becky hissed out a breath. "You certainly will not! If I go anywhere, it will be with Jack."

Garrett aimed another punch at Jack's face. Jack dodged it.

Grabbing Garrett's arm again, Becky pulled back with all her might. She might as well have tried to move a tree trunk. He didn't budge, but her efforts did gain his attention. He glanced over his shoulder at her, his brow wrinkled, the scar above it bulging and red.

"No more fighting, Garrett! It's over. I've decided to marry him. We were going home this morning."

Garrett was stiff and solid beneath her arms. He went back to staring down Jack, who stood with his fists up, ready for the next onslaught. "He abducted you from Lady Devore. She came to me—"

"Jack told her he was with me. I wanted to go. I asked him to take me away."

"She said she knew you were with him, but that she'd expected you to return to her house later that night. You'd been gone for longer than a day, and she was growing concerned."

"I told her—" Jack began. Then, gritting his teeth, he shook his head. "She was...with someone. She was distracted."

"There was no reason to be concerned, Garrett," Becky said. "I wanted to be here with him. We were coming home."

Garrett turned to stare down at her face. He gripped her shoulders. "Is that true, Rebecca? Because if he is coercing you in any way, if he has threatened you...you would say something, wouldn't you? Tell me the truth—I won't let him harm you. Is this what you want?"

Becky glanced at Jack. A thin line of blood trailed down from his nose from Garrett's first punch. "Yes. It is." She smiled at Jack. His stance relaxed, and he managed a small smile back at her when their eyes met. "I want to marry him," she whispered. "More than anything in this world."

A short time later, the three of them were on their way back to London, crammed together in the carriage in rigid silence. Garrett scowled whenever Jack and Becky came within inches of touching each other, and by the time they arrived in Mayfair, Becky already missed him. Her body craved his touch, and she'd only been separated from him for a few hours.

Still, when they drove up the circling drive at Garrett's house, Becky was relieved to be home. Frigid air had permeated the carriage all the way from Richmond, and her domino wasn't meant for this weather. Her elbow ached, her fingers tingled, and she was cold to her bones. She looked forward to a cup of warm chocolate and a nice fire in the drawing room with Jack.

When she stepped out of the carriage, however, Jack gathered her hand in his, brushed his lips over it, and said good-bye. Before she had a chance to protest, he'd dropped her hand and was taking long strides down the drive.

Bemused by his abrupt departure, she watched him disappear down Curzon Street, and then she turned to question Garrett, only to find that he and the carriage had disappeared, too. She asked the footman where he had gone.

"His Grace has gone to the stables to unhitch the horses, my lady."

Shaking her head at her brother's insistence on doing everything for himself, she mounted the front stairs, working the top buttons of her gloves. The house was quiet—too quiet. How odd that Kate and Aunt Bertrice had not come down to greet her. With her fingers on the pearly buttons, Becky paused near the foot of the main staircase, tilting her head in curiosity.

Behind her, Garrett blustered in with a gust of cold air. Without bothering to close the door, he stalked past her toward the stairs. She picked up her skirts and hurried after him.

"What is it?" she asked, her heart surging to her throat.

"It's Kate," he bit out. "Sam just told me she's laboring."

"Oh, Lord." Becky's heart banged against her breastbone as she hurried after her brother, taking the stairs two at a time.

Garrett threw open the door to the bedchamber he shared with Kate, Becky at his shoulder. The group of women standing at the bedside looked up in surprise. The bed curtains were open, so Kate was clearly visible. She lay in bed on her back, her stomach heaving, and when she heard the sound of the door, she turned toward them, her face flushed.

"Oh, Garrett. Becky. I'm so happy to see you. I knew you would come."

Early that evening, Becky sat at Kate's bedside, holding her new nephew in her arms. This was Garrett's fifth child. His first two legitimate children—the first with Sophie and the second with Kate—were girls. Then there was Reginald, Kate's much-younger half-brother, and Charlotte, Garrett's illegitimate daughter, both of whom Garrett and Kate were raising as their own.

When Garrett was married to Sophie, they'd been barren for years, and he'd never thought he'd have children. Now he had five—and finally, after so very long, he had his heir. Cuddled up in Becky's arms and lightly sucking on his little fist lay her brother's tiny son.

Kate lay on the bed in a light sleep, a peaceful smile on her face. She'd wanted for years to give Garrett a son, and now she had. Garrett himself was in such a state of joy he'd been keeping both mother and child awake, and Aunt Bertrice had finally bustled him out of the room.

They'd decided to give him a simple name: Henry. Little Henry James, the Marquis of Winterburne. Born a touch on the early side, he was a tiny thing, but he was healthy—round and plump and pink, with folds of fat on his arms and legs.

Becky stroked a finger down his velvety little cheek, and he made a soft gurgling sound. A sweet kind of happiness surged in her; he was the handsomest thing she'd ever seen.

A maid peeked in. "My lady?" she whispered.

Becky glanced at Kate, who still slept, then rose and walked over to the maid so she wouldn't wake her sister-in-law. "Yes?"

"There's a gentleman come to see you."

Becky's heartbeat quickened. "Mr. Fulton?"

"Yes, ma'am."

She glanced down at Henry, who cuddled closer as if to tell her not to give him up to anyone else. "I'll take him with me. If Her Grace wakes, inform me immediately."

The maid's white cap bobbed her assent.

"Where is he?"

"In the drawing room, ma'am."

"You aren't to leave Her Grace until she wakes."

Again, the maid nodded. Becky walked slowly, careful not to jostle Henry, until she entered the drawing room. Jack glanced up. His eyes widened as he rose from his chair.

"What's that?"

She grinned. She would have thrown herself in his arms if she hadn't been holding Henry. "Kate and Garrett's baby," she said in a low voice. "Isn't he precious?"

"Er...the duchess had her baby?"

"She did. He's only a few hours old. We arrived home just in time."

"I see." He shifted his stance awkwardly. "Where is your brother?"

"He's in his study writing letters announcing the birth of his heir to the world." She grinned. "I have never seen Garrett in such high spirits."

And although she was tired and hadn't changed her clothes since she'd arrived home, she was in high spirits, too. The birth had been easy, as births go, and both Kate and Henry were healthy as could be. As with Jessica, Becky not only was honored to have been there, but was still floating from the beauty of it all. There was nothing like hearing the sound of a healthy newborn baby's cry, nothing like seeing its little eyes open to view its brand-new world. Nothing like watching the look on a mother's face when she held her child for the first time.

But Jack was a man, and he probably wouldn't understand any of that. Giving him a beatific smile, Becky made her way to one of the palm-print sofas and settled onto it, holding the babe in a position comfortable for them both.

Her smile widened as he took a seat across from her, casting doubtful glances at the bundle in her arms.

"Where did you run off to?" she asked.

He raised a brow. "Did you think I'd be staying here?"

"Of course."

"That wouldn't be prudent."

"Certainly you've no wish to stay with your family."

"No, I don't. But fortunately, my brother and father are far from London—they've retired to Kent for the remainder of the season. I went to see Stratford, and I'll be staying with him for a few days." His gaze slid once again to the baby. "You are very good with children."

He said it more as a question than a statement, and she smiled down at the little bundle in her arms.

"I enjoy my nieces and nephews very much."

"Yet you do not think you will ever be a mother."

"I don't think so." She looked up at him, her heart fluttering like a butterfly wing in her chest. "Do you...will you...will it make you very unhappy if I prove unable to conceive?"

He stared at her for a long moment. "I'd never thought of it. Before I met you, I'd hardly thought of marriage, much less of being a father."

"But if you were to never have a son...an heir..."

"What would a son of mine be heir to?" Jack shook his head. "No, that has naught to do with it. I just...I don't know. Marriage, children. These are things I haven't expected to happen to me, since..."

His voice trailed off, but Becky knew what he had almost said: "...since Anne married someone else."

A spasm of jealousy swept through her. She had to control her breathing in order to squelch it. She couldn't ask him—she couldn't even voice the thought aloud. But she wanted, so badly, for him to love her more than he had loved Anne.

It was such a selfish thought that her cheeks heated in shame. Still, awareness of her own selfishness did nothing to eradicate the thought. She wanted Jack's love. All of it. She didn't want to share it, even with a dead woman. And she wanted to keep it, not lose it years from now due to a physical shortcoming.

"What if you later decided it was important to you to have a child, a son, and I could not provide you with one?"

He rose from the chair and sat beside her. Mindful of the infant in her arms, he slid an arm over her shoulder and pulled her close, pressing his lips to her temple.

"I am not inconstant in my affections. I would never turn from you for something so trifling."

"It's not a trifling matter to many," she said, her voice rough as sand.

"It's something neither of us can control. If we have children, I will be happy, most of all because I think it will make you happy. If we cannot, there is nothing we can do about it, and neither one of us should suffer for it."

With a sudden fierceness that stole her breath, she wanted to be able to bear his child. Yet she was almost certain she would never be able to give him that gift.

"Thank you." She held baby Henry a bit tighter. "We will always have our nieces and nephews to adore, I suppose."

He cast a dubious glance at the infant. "Yes." But his voice was halting, and she laughed softly.

"I think you are afraid of him."

He straightened. "I am not. I...it is just that I see babies so infrequently, and...well, that one is more or less...squished and bruised-looking. It...*he* looks like a boxer."

She smiled down at Henry. "He looks like his papa. Would you like to hold him?"

Jack surged away from her. "No. No, I don't think so."

She chuckled. "Come, it's not so frightening."

"I'm not frightened."

"Hold out your arms."

He stared at her for a long moment, then reached out stiffly, his arms stick straight. She placed the tiny bundle in Jack's arms, then gently bent his elbows into a more comfortable position. Henry gurgled, opened his eyes, gazed at Jack, then drifted off again. Jack stared at him in bemusement.

"There, you see. It's not so bad."

He looked up at her, gave her a crooked smile, and then looked down at the baby again. For an instant, Becky imagined him gazing down at another child—their child—and her heart gave a melancholy lurch.

A knock sounded at the door, and Becky called for whoever it was to enter. It was a footman. "My lady, I am to deliver the message that Her Grace has awakened."

"Oh, thank you. You may go." When the man closed the door, Becky looked at Jack. She didn't want to leave him, but her first responsibility today was to Kate.

"I must go to her."

Jack nodded. "Of course. But before you go, I want to tell you something."

"What is it?"

"I've arranged a wedding date."

She sucked in a breath. "When?"

"The first of December at nine o'clock at St. George's." He cocked his head at her, his eyes sparking with challenge, as if he expected her to protest that it was too soon.

Instead, everything inside her went soft with pleasure at his words. The first of December was six days from now. In just six days, she would be his. "I am so glad," she murmured. For a long moment, their eyes met and held.

Henry gurgled, and the spell broke. She took the baby from him. "I'll be ready, Jack. Well, I'm ready now, but I suppose next Saturday will do."

He smiled. "Good."

"I'll see you again before then, won't I?"

"You certainly will. I couldn't wait that long to see you again."

He pressed his lips to her temple, and, smiling, she took her leave.

Ping. Ping.

Becky's eyelids flew open. There it was again.

Ping. Ping. Plunk.

The sounds were coming from the direction of her window.

She waited, taking short breaths, her eyes wide open, clutching the blankets to her chest.

Then: *Ping.*

She leapt out of bed, paying no attention to her robe,

and flew to the window, yanking open the peach-colored silk curtains.

She leaned her forehead on the windowsill, staring down through the glass, a big grin spreading her lips wide.

Jack. He'd been throwing tiny pieces of gravel from the path below at her window, occasionally missing the glass and hitting the wooden casing.

There was nobody in the world she wanted to see more. She'd ached for him since she'd left him in the drawing room yesterday. Tonight, she'd lain awake for what seemed like hours, thinking of how cold and lonely her bed was without him. How lonely *she* was without him.

He stared up at her, his hat held to his chest. He looked like a bridegroom should, brimming with eager anticipation, warmth, and desire—all for her. Her blood surged with an arousing mixture of excitement and happiness.

She hurried to unlatch and open the window.

"Come up," she whispered.

He clapped his hat on his head and wasted no time. Her bedchamber was situated at the side corner of Garrett's London house, and a climbing rose-covered trellis extended from the ground to her window like a perfectly placed ladder. Four years ago, she and William Fisk had climbed down the trellis and fled to Gretna; tonight Jack Fulton climbed it to come to her.

Within seconds, he swung his legs over the windowsill and was inside, instantly turning to close the window. "Good God, you're wearing almost nothing at all. You must be freezing."

She'd felt nothing but warmth ever since she'd laid

eyes on him. "You climb like a monkey," she returned saucily.

"Years' worth of climbing the rigging on the *Gloriana*." He latched the window and turned to her. Removing his hat, he tossed it on her peach-striped armchair. He'd never been inside her bedchamber before, but he didn't take any time to study the interior of the room. He kept his focus on her and her alone.

His gaze made a languorous journey over her body, leaving a pleasurable, prickling trail in its wake. "God—" His voice cracked, and she saw his throat move as he swallowed. "I've missed you so much."

"I missed you, too."

He reached out to her at the same moment she reached for him. His hand, cool from the outside air, hooked around her neck. His other arm banded around her lower back, drawing her tightly against him.

"I can't stand to be apart from you," he said, the warmth of his breath whispering over her earlobe. "Yesterday, in the drawing room. God. I can't tell you how...I hate nothing more than the sight of you walking away from me. I never want you to walk away from me. I want you with me. Always."

The edge of vulnerability in his tone sent a shudder through her, and with all her heart, she hoped she'd never have to walk away from him again. "I hate it, too." She stroked her fingers through the cooled strands of his hair. "I hate being separated from you."

"I need you," he whispered.

His lips warmed a path from her ear to her lips, a soft nuzzle that bloomed into a possessive kiss. Holding her locked against him with one arm, his fingers wrapped around the back of her neck, he pressed her closer as he took her mouth. She slipped her arms around him, hooked her calf over his leg, rubbed her body wantonly against him. His clothes and skin were cold, but she didn't care. She struggled with his trousers as he hitched her night-dress over her hip, his fingers grazing her thigh.

"I need you, Becky. So much."

She released him just long enough to toss her night-dress away, then went back to working his falls while he unbuttoned the collar of his shirt.

"Ah," she gasped when she finally pressed the bare skin of her chest against his. "You're frozen."

"Not for long."

She released his falls and his trousers fell, followed by his drawers. He kicked them off, along with his shoes and stockings, and lifted her in his arms, keeping her chest pressed against his. Lord, he was so strong. He didn't even seem to notice that he supported all her weight.

She wrapped her legs around his hips, wrapped her arms around his neck, and kissed him again. Oh, he was warming, and rapidly. And he tasted so good. So salty, so manly. So much like Jack.

He was walking, she realized distractedly as she nipped his lower lip. And then she felt the coolness of the wallpaper against her back.

Making a quick adjustment, he pushed her over him, entering her in a deep thrust. She gasped. He buried his face in her neck.

Overwhelmed with sensation, she could only hold on to him, grip him for all she was worth. He pushed deeper into her, pinning her against the wall. And then he drove into her body again and again, his movements frantic and urgent. Becky closed her eyes, pressed her forehead to his shoulder, and held on, emotion, lust, and power surging through her, mingling with her growing affection for this man. Her love for him.

"I need you," he whispered against her neck, pushing himself deep, so deep. She felt full, whole, complete. Unable to control her passion, she ground herself over him even as he moved inside of her.

She threaded her fingers into his hair as desire swirled within her, so forceful she bit the inside of her cheek to keep from sobbing with each of his thrusts, with each bright streaming surge of pleasure flaring deep inside.

Her fingers and legs tightened over him while his movements grew stronger, more urgent. The quiet rasp of his breath filled the room.

Becky gritted her teeth so she didn't cry out and wake the whole house, but her lips parted as the pleasure built even higher. She squeezed her eyes shut as her body vibrated under his onslaught.

And then she came apart. The ribbons of pleasure burst into colorful flames that spread like a fast-burning fuse throughout her limbs and to her extremities. Her toes curled. Her nails bit into his neck. Holding on to Jack for dear life, she closed her teeth over his shoulder to bury her scream in his flesh. The orgasm shuddered through her, overtaking every one of her senses with spasms of rapture.

As she drifted down, she realized Jack had reached his pinnacle as well, for he held himself rigid except for the subtle contractions as he released the last of his seed deep inside her.

Holding him tight, she smoothed her fingertips over the places on his neck where her nails had dug into his skin seconds ago. She feathered her lips over the bite marks on his shoulder and gave a deep sigh of contentment.

Jack released her gently, allowing her slight body to slide down his. She kept her hands linked around his neck and stared up at him, her eyes shining.

"Did I hurt you?" she whispered.

Jack gave her a lopsided smile and shook his head. It *had* hurt when she'd bitten his shoulder, but it had also sent a jolt of pleasure through him so powerful that he'd lost his ability to do anything but yield to the most powerful orgasm of his life.

He pulled her against him. He took such surprising comfort from the feel of her skin pressed against his. "I like it when you bite."

Her brows peaked. "Do you?"

"Mmm." He bent toward her, close enough to kiss, and their breaths danced between them as they shared a chuckle. Her fingertips pressed over the small stinging area on the back of his neck, and she sobered.

"I believe I might have drawn blood, Jack. I'm so sorry."

He released her quickly enough to pass his hand over the area before taking her up in his arms again.

"I couldn't...I wasn't thinking..."

"I wasn't thinking either," he murmured. "Yet for some reason I cannot regret taking you up against the wall like a barbarian." He soothed his fingertips over her temple. "I believe you enjoyed it."

He could feel the shudder racing through her as her luxurious, dark-fringed blue eyes blinked at him. "I...did," she breathed. "Does that make *me* a barbarian?"

He laughed. "Yes. It also makes me a fortunate man. Doubly fortunate," he added, recalling how she'd taken him into her mouth yesterday morning. His wayward cock, only recently satisfied, jerked with renewed interest at the memory.

"I like very much that I can make you feel...doubly fortunate."

He stilled, momentarily unable to breathe. That this beautiful woman enjoyed bringing him such pleasure—it was more than he could ever have hoped for.

It was more than he deserved.

For the last several days he'd focused only on Becky. On winning her, and on keeping her. On falling in love with her. He tried wholeheartedly to ignore the ignominious nature of his original intentions, but they kept coming back to haunt him. The fact that he'd pursued her with such ardor—it was true that there had been more than just her money that lured him, for from the start he'd felt something deeper for her. Yet the source of his immediate and unwavering attention had been her fortune.

And then he'd tricked her...arranged their discovery...

God, he was low.

"Becky." He closed his eyes and bowed his head. Guilt surged through him, overwhelmed him. How would she ever forgive him? How could he forgive himself? And now he was stuck in the quicksand of his lies and sinking deeper by the day. He couldn't tell her, because if he did, he'd destroy her, destroy them both. But if he didn't tell her, he'd be living a lie. The secret had begun to eat away at his gut.

He didn't care about the money anymore. He didn't care about Tom Wortingham and his damn demands. He cared about nothing more than keeping this woman, than holding on to her and never letting her go.

Her arm slipped down to his hand, and her fingers laced through his. Her palm pressed against the still-healing scab on his. "Come. Let's lie in my bed."

"I can't sleep here," he said with more than a little regret.

She sighed. "I know. But you can stay a little while, can't you?"

"Yes."

They went to the bed and lay on their sides, face-to-face. Keeping their hands linked, they spoke of their marriage. Of the future. They spoke of traveling to exotic places someday, of some of the places he'd already seen, and they spoke of her family.

And, in what seemed like mere minutes later, the sky began to gray, and Jack knew he must go before he was discovered.

Leaning forward, he kissed her good-bye. She ran her slender fingers up his side, then down over his nipples, sending a shudder through him. He caressed her breasts, cupped them and kissed them, and slipped his hand between her legs to find her wet and ready. And then he pulled her leg over his hip and entered her, watching her sweet expressions of pleasure as he slid through her willing flesh.

After they both had come, shuddering in each other's arms, he gave her a long, lingering kiss and said good-bye.

Jack left his lover's bed, dressed, and slipped out her window. Though he passed the kitchen, where the morning bustle had already begun and the smells of frying ham and eggs wafted through the window, he slipped away undetected by anyone at the Duke of Calton's house.

Chapter Seventeen

Becky stood at the drawing room window gazing out at a mild autumn evening, a smile tugging at the edges of her lips. Tomorrow she was going to do it. She was going to marry Jack Fulton.

She'd never been happier. She'd given her trust to Jack, and every time she saw him, he proved himself more worthy of her trust. He'd come to her every night for the past four nights, and he visited her on a more formal basis during the day. Tonight at dinner, he'd been charming, thoughtful, and particularly attentive to her, and she'd seen the approval in her own family's eyes. Everyone, from Aunt Bertrice to Kate and Garrett, liked Jack. They supported both him and their marriage. That meant so much to her.

She turned to watch the other women. Kate was still recovering from Henry's birth, but she had come down for the occasion, and she and Aunt Bertrice had partnered against Sophie and Cecelia to play at whist.

Cecelia had come to visit with her yesterday, and Becky had described everything that had passed between her and Jack. She'd asked Cecelia about the dark-haired man at the masquerade, and in her usual unconcerned fashion, Cecelia had chuckled and said, "Oh, I took care of him. Rest assured he'll not be trifling with me anymore."

Becky was too agitated to play at cards, but she'd convinced the other women to enjoy the game. She wouldn't have them sacrifice their fun on account of her, and she really preferred to alternate between watching, sitting at the pianoforte, and wandering off on her own. In any case, the gentlemen were currently drinking their port and would join them in the drawing room soon.

Jack would be here. She could hardly think of anything but him. After their talk the other night about the pain it caused him when she left him, it had been difficult to walk away from the dinner table tonight. It would be even more difficult to leave him later this evening.

But starting tomorrow, they'd be together forever.

Sighing, she turned back to the window. Parting the silky green curtains, she stared into the darkness.

Fog blanketed the ground, and she could only see a few prongs of the wrought-iron gate in the distance. A full moon struggled to burn through the fog but succeeded only in casting a sullen gloom over the driveway below.

Movement caught her eye, and she glanced down. The drawing room was just above the front entrance of Garrett's London house, and she watched Jack and Lord Stratford descend the stairs, their coats pulled tightly around them.

Her heart leapt into her chest. Surely they couldn't be leaving!

But they stopped at the bottom of the stairs, deep in conversation. Jack looked annoyed—no, he looked angry, and Stratford laid a hand on his shoulder to calm him.

Becky turned toward the women who sat at the card table. "I must step away for a few moments. Will you excuse me?"

Kate, the mistress of the house, and the one expected to give her permission, raised her eyes from her cards, concern creasing her forehead. "Is something wrong?"

"Oh, no," Becky lied, her voice slightly rushed. "Not at all. I just wanted to speak with the housekeeper about a detail for tomorrow. It is truly of little importance. I don't wish to disturb your game."

"Of course you may go speak with Mrs. Krum, but return as quickly as you can, won't you? I expect the gentlemen to arrive soon."

Becky inclined her head at her sister-in-law and smiled. "Of course, Kate. I'll rush back, I promise."

With that, she fled from the room.

There had been an odd occurrence during dinner. Jack had received a note. A footman had entered and said an urgent missive had been delivered for Mr. Fulton. Jack had glanced at the handwriting and then shrugged dismissively and tucked it into his tailcoat. When Cecelia questioned him about the note, he said it was nothing, and the conversation had turned to other topics.

Yet Becky had wondered. What could have been in that letter? Who had sent it? Was that why Jack was so angry now?

It could be a mistress, she realized. A jealous woman, furious that he was marrying tomorrow and trying to rouse Becky's ire by delivering a note during dinner with her family. But she hadn't thought Jack had kept a mistress in London. Then again, they'd never really discussed it. She'd never asked him. Perhaps she should have.

Without taking the time to fetch a coat, she hurried downstairs and out the servants' entrance, moving at a near run. As soon as she opened the door, the cold pierced through her dusty pink silk evening dress, but she ignored it. Staying off the crunching gravel of the path, she kept on the dirt, and tiptoeing in her silk slippers, she inched along the side of the house, ducking beneath the trellis that led to her bedroom window.

"The bastard!" Jack growled from the front landing.

Careful not to tear her silk on the barren branches of the creeping rose, Becky tucked her body between the arbor and the edge of the house. She leaned against the siding and listened to Lord Stratford hush Jack.

"Shh. What does he say?"

"He wants more money."

"Devious cur." Stratford's voice dripped with derision.

"Here. Read it." Paper crackled as Jack thrust the letter at Lord Stratford.

Becky closed her eyes and listened to Jack's friend read, his voice growing louder and more incredulous as he progressed.

"Dear Jack, etcetera. Felicitations on your upcoming marriage, etcetera, etcetera. I have recently learned that Lady R. possesses a far greater fortune than I was led to believe. It was unkind of you not to be forthcoming with me, Jack. Dare I believe you wished to hoard all the lady's money for yourself?

"In light of these revelations, I have, just now, determined that the previously requested amount of fifteen thousand pounds is too low. I now require twenty-five thousand pounds."

Becky's mouth went dry. She clenched her fists at her sides.

No.

Stratford continued. "Of course you will understand my urgency in delivering you this message, as I wanted you to be aware of the changes in the terms of our agreement prior to your nuptials. Yours, etcetera, T.W."

No, no, no.

"What a damned idiot," Stratford said in a low voice. Jack was silent, and the earl sighed. "Just pay him. Give him the money as soon as you have access to it, and be done with it."

"Twenty-five thousand pounds?" Jack's voice was harsh. "It is the better part of her fortune."

Her fists still clenched at her sides, Becky turned away. She could hardly see the ground for the blur in her eyes.

"I take it you've informed her of none of this business."

"None," Jack confirmed.

"You must tell her. Surely she'll discover it eventually, whether it's fifteen thousand pounds or twenty-five. She's not an idiot."

Jack made a low noise of frustration.

Stratford sighed. "Not exactly how you'd planned it to play out when you informed her family of your meeting that night at Sheffield's, eh?"

Becky stifled a gasp. She could hardly hear what they said next over the screaming roar of denial in her ears.

Jack had planned for them to be caught that night? That entire night had been staged?

Pushing off from the side of the house, Becky fisted her hands in her skirts. She was shaking so hard her teeth threatened to rattle, but she clamped her jaw tight.

"Twenty-five thousand pounds." Gravel crunched as Jack paced restlessly.

Stratford sighed. "Well, whether you tell her now or later, it won't make a difference."

Oh, yes it will, Becky thought bitterly.

"But for God's sake, wait till after you are legally wed," Stratford added. He laughed humorlessly. "The last thing you need is to have her change her mind about marrying you now."

Again, Jack was silent.

"Listen to me," Stratford said. "Wortingham is a fool. He's a stupid fool, completely lacking in common sense. He wants you to marry—he wants his damned money, and yet he placed everything in jeopardy tonight by sending you that note while you were dining with her and her family. Mark my words, she'll be asking you about that later."

No, she wouldn't. She didn't need to. She already possessed all the information she required.

Jack grunted.

"You can outwit him."

"How?" Jack said furiously. "Short of murdering the scheming bastard, there is nothing I can do." The paper made a crumpling noise as he crushed it in his fist. "Murdering him wouldn't even work."

Becky couldn't listen to any more of this. Only one thing was clear: Just like William, Jack had seduced her for one thing only. For her money. It was her damnable fortune he loved. Not her.

She'd been fooled once again. She'd given her trust to
a man. She'd given him her love and her body, and all he
wanted her for was her forty thousand pounds.

A deep shudder rolled through her. It was cold out
here and she wasn't wearing a coat. Already her fingers
were numb.

She strode toward the door, taking painful but resolute
steps through the chill.

No. This wouldn't happen. Not again. She wasn't
allowing it.

Jack pushed a frustrated hand over his scalp. His hair
was so cold, it chilled his fingers through his gloves.

Stratford couldn't understand why Jack couldn't tell
her. It was bad enough that he'd pursued her with the
intention of using her money to pay off a man who was
trying to extort money from him. What made it so much
worse was that he pursued her for the same reasons her
first husband had. The husband who had cheated, lied,
tried to kill the duke and Becky herself.

If Becky discovered Jack's treachery, she would never
trust him again. She would leave him.

Stratford still hadn't asked why Tom had demanded
the money. Stratford had probably guessed. He probably
didn't want to know.

The earl turned piercing blue eyes on him. "I'd not
advise murder. There must be a better way. He's proven
he's not the smartest fellow in the world." He gestured
at the note Jack held crumpled in his fist. "The choice
of this time to deliver that letter proves it. Tell him
you only have access to a thousand pounds at once.
Tell him the money is unavailable; that it's engaged in

investments." Stratford shrugged. "There must be something you can do."

Jack stared at his friend, trying to tamp down his rage, his panic. He'd buried himself in this disaster, and he didn't know how to dig himself out.

He couldn't lose her.

Stratford sighed. "You shouldn't be thinking of this now."

"No," he pushed out. "I shouldn't."

"You should be thinking of your pretty wife-to-be, warm and awaiting you inside." Stratford gestured at the house, and then he stepped closer to Jack, an inquisitive look on his face. "You have grown to care for this woman, correct?"

Jack closed his eyes. Hell, yes, he cared for her.

"And she cares for you as well. She glows when she looks at you."

He groaned, long and low. "It's a damn poor thing, what I've done."

Stratford clapped him on the shoulder. "A woman in love will forgive anything, Fulton. Just remember that. Now let's go inside and try to enjoy the remainder of the evening. Tomorrow, suffer through your wedding, and then you may have leave to think of how you're going to tell your wife about the money."

Jack opened his eyes. He gazed off down the driveway, at the gate that led to Curzon Street. A thick soup of fog diffused the light from the gas streetlamps, leaving only a meager glow to straggle across the street, and Jack couldn't see much farther than the iron gate and the occasional shadow of a horse or carriage rumbling down the street beyond.

Tom lurked somewhere out there. Jack could feel him. "I'm not going to do it."

"Not going to tell her about the money?"

"No." He was finished with threats, with Tom, with being selfish and trying to save his own hide. None of that mattered. His deception had come to an end. He wouldn't betray the woman he loved. He was going to end it with Tom, and then he was going to tell her everything.

"To hell with the money. Tom Wortingham can go to the devil. Whether it be five pounds or fifty thousand, he'll not be getting a single penny from me."

Becky dragged her body upstairs and went through the motions of the happy bride-to-be for the remainder of the night. She should be an actress, she played the part so well. She cuddled up with Jack. She gazed at him with stars in her eyes. She played a rousing round of piquet with him.

Just after midnight, Jack, Lord Stratford, Cecelia, and Tristan and Sophie went home. As soon as everyone left, Kate, who'd come and gone from the party several times to tend to her infant, slipped her hand into Becky's.

"What's wrong, Becky?" Her voice was low enough so Garrett, who was talking to one of the servants, couldn't hear.

Becky turned to her sister-in-law in surprise. "Nothing, Kate. Why do you ask?"

"It's something in your eyes. You look sad."

"Nonsense." Becky laughed lightly. "I'm not sad at all. I've never been happier, in fact."

"Are you sure?"

"Of course. It's just nerves about tomorrow."

Kate frowned. She looked tired, and older, even though she was only four years older than Becky. "Have I been a poor friend to you, Becky?"

Becky gasped. "No! Of course not."

"I feel that I haven't been spending the time with you that I should." She squeezed her hand. "I miss you."

"You've been busy with the children. I understand." Becky took a breath. "And I've felt…" *Not smothered…* "I think I've been hiding too much behind you and Garrett. After all these years, I feel I must finally emerge from under the wing of your protection. I still love you, Kate. You're still my dearest friend and sister."

Even though she was lying to her. Out of necessity. Someday Kate would understand. Becky could not involve her in this, not with a days-old infant. Plus, Becky needed her to stay calm and manage Garrett, because he was going to be furious.

Kate's dark eyes glistened. "Then you still know that I am here for you, as a friend and as a sister. You can tell me anything."

Becky nodded soberly. "I know."

She left Kate before the deep surge of sadness could well over her. Josie met her in her bedchamber, and Becky allowed her to help her out of her dinner dress, but she shooed the maid out before she took down her hair.

After Josie went away, Becky turned to gather a few garments that would sustain her for the duration of her journey. She collected them in a small satchel, gathered all the money she had on hand, and then she opened the small lacquered cabinet that held her pistol.

After William's death, she'd spent a few months mor-
bidly fascinated by guns. She'd read all she could about
weapons and had convinced Garrett to teach her how to
shoot. At the height of this interest, she'd ordered this gun
custom made for her from London. By the time it had
arrived, she'd realized her chances of needing to protect
herself had diminished greatly when William died, and
her interest in guns and shooting had waned to be
replaced by other pursuits.

In silence she opened the box and removed the gun
from its velvet case. With slow, precise movements, she
cleaned the weapon. When she'd finished, she tested
its weight in her hand, staring at the gifts Jack had
given her. The gifts he'd used to manipulate her into
loving him.

She would leave them behind. All of them. She didn't
need them. But she would take her pistol. From now on,
she would protect herself at all costs.

She sat on the edge of the bed and waited for the house
to grow quiet.

An hour later, the shuffling noises in the corridor
ceased, signifying that the staff had gone to bed. Shrugging into an old coat, she took a lantern and went to
Garrett's study, where she filled her powder horn with
fresh, dry powder and loaded the pistol.

Exiting from the servants' entrance, she headed to
the stables, mounted the stairs beside the stall doors,
and slipped into the apartment of Sam Johnson, Garrett's
head coachman.

"Sam," she whispered, shaking his shoulder. She
didn't want to wake the groomsmen, and the walls of the
stable were thin. "Sam, wake up."

"Huh?" The man's eyes popped open, and he squinted at her in the lantern light. "Lady Rebecca?"

"Yes, it's me. I need you to help me with something."

He surged up in the bed. "Of course, my lady." Then, remembering he only wore a plain white nightshirt, he yanked up the blankets to cover himself.

She waved a hand at him—this was no time for modesty. "Don't worry about that. I need you to give me some clothes. Two pairs of trousers and a few shirts. And your best coat, if you don't mind." Sam was a small man, unnaturally so. He was two years younger than her, but for some reason his growth had been stunted, and though Becky was a petite woman, Sam had never surpassed her in size.

She held out a small purse. "This is all I can spare at the moment, but I can promise you more in January."

His eyes widened. "My lady, I—"

"Please. You know I would never deceive you, nor do anything to cause you harm. It is imperative I leave London tonight. Alone. My reasoning will probably become clear to everyone at a later date, but right now, all I can ask is for you to trust me. We've known each other all our lives, Sam Johnson. I wouldn't lie to you."

She and Sam had been raised at Calton House in Yorkshire, and he'd often traveled with the family when they came to London. Now, as the head coachman, he went wherever they did.

Sam's eyes widened even more. "My lady! You mustn't leave London all by yourself. A woman, alone on the road in the middle of the night?" He gave a definitive shake of his head. "No, my lady, my conscience won't allow it."

Oh, God. Becky sucked back a panicked sob. "Please, Sam. You don't understand the importance of this. Please, do this for me. You must know I would never ask such a thing of you if it wasn't important." There was a tremulous edge of desperation in her voice, but she didn't care. She wouldn't be trapped here in London and forced to either marry Jack Fulton or reveal his treacherous intentions to the world. She had to get away.

Sam hesitated. Finally, he said, "I cannot let you go alone, my lady. Therefore... well..." He took a deep, resolute breath. "Therefore, I must go with you."

Becky nearly launched herself into his arms. Instead, she gathered herself and spoke quietly. "Thank you. Once I reach my destination, you can return to London right away. You shouldn't be absent longer than a week."

Sam would certainly be missed, and Garrett would realize right away that he'd gone with her. She'd think about that later. She continued. "We must travel on horseback. I'll ride astride. We can move faster that way, and it's the only way for me to travel anonymously."

Disapproval darkened Sam's round face, but she didn't acknowledge it, and he didn't openly try to dissuade her. Speed was more important than anything right now. She had to leave here, quickly. She didn't want to take a stagecoach or go post, because then she'd be too easily pursued. As soon as she was far away, she could think more about what she must do and how she could ask her family for forgiveness. Eventually, they would understand everything. They would forgive her, as they always did. But for now, she had to get away. Nothing was more important. *Nothing*.

Sam's chest rose and fell. "This is why you wish to have the use of my clothes?"

"Yes." She took a breath. "We'll be brothers. Traveling west to Cornwall."

Her destination was Seawood, the small house in Cornwall that had belonged to her mother. No one had spoken of it in years—it seemed everyone had forgotten about the place. But Becky hadn't. She'd never been to Seawood, but it was hers. Her own house. After William had died, she'd often thought that one day the rest of her family would tire of her, and she would make it her home. She'd maintained a frequent correspondence with the steward of the place, a Mr. Jennings, who seemed like a friendly man. Now she'd surprise him with her arrival. The surprise was unavoidable, but if Mr. Jennings's letters were accurate, the place was in good repair and fit for habitation.

Sam stared at her, aghast. "That's much too far for you to travel on horseback, my lady. Such a journey would take a toll on any man, and you're just a—"

"I'm doing this, Sam. If you don't help me, I'll find someone who will."

"Perhaps use one of His Grace's carriages."

"No." She wouldn't take anything of Garrett's.

"You could go post or perhaps hire a coach?"

"No, Sam. I don't wish to be recognized." And those methods would force her to stay in London at least until morning. She wanted to be gone *now*.

Sam sighed. Clearly, he still didn't approve of the plan, but he knew he had no choice but to go along with it. "My clothes are over there, my lady." He gestured with his chin at a row of shelves set in an alcove. "Just open the door when you're done. I'll be waiting for you on the stairs."

Modestly wrapping the blanket over his shoulders, he stepped out of the room. As soon as the door closed, Becky scanned the sparsely populated shelf of clothing. She yanked out a pair of trousers and a shirt and quickly donned them. She pulled on three layers of stockings and tucked two sets of mittens into the pockets of the trousers. With an extra pair of trousers and two extra shirts in her arms, she opened the door to allow Sam back in. He held out a heavy woolen garment. "A coat for you, my lady."

"Thank you." She glanced back at his shelves. "I only saw one pair of boots."

"They're the only ones I have," he said. "You wear those. I'll fetch some of Pip's. He's an extra pair."

Pip was Sam's younger brother and second in command of the stables. Nodding, she pulled on the boots—they were a little large but comfortable enough given the layers of stockings she wore. Sam went to fetch his brother's boots, which were surely larger for him than his boots were for her, for Pip didn't suffer from Sam's disability in height.

When Sam returned, he held the boots draped over his arm. "Pip's dead asleep and I thought it best not to wake him and listen to him—" He broke off, his eyes shifting away, and she knew exactly what he wouldn't say. Pip would have fought them—even her—on this. He would have tried to prevent them from going. He might even have tried to wake Garrett. This was why she'd chosen Sam for this task and not his brother.

"I ought to write a letter to him, though, so he doesn't worry about my disappearance."

"Of course," she agreed. "I'll tend to the horses while you write it."

Down in the stalls, she chose a saddle and saddlebags and managed—clumsily—to saddle her mare. She'd never saddled a horse by herself before. She slipped her money and garments into the saddlebags, keeping some of the money and her pistol tucked in the pockets of Sam's coat.

How practical she could be, she thought wryly. Even as she escaped from London dressed as a boy. Even as her heart was breaking.

She wouldn't think of that. Self-preservation was more important than anything right now. And she could not bear being in London. Not when Jack Fulton was here.

Sam arrived with a bundle of clothes, food, and a flask full of watered-down wine. She was already thankful he'd insisted on coming with her—she hadn't had the strength of mind to think of food and drink. He was fully dressed now, and as she'd expected, Pip's regular-sized boots looked clownish on Sam's undersized feet. She'd buy him a new pair in the first village they passed through in the morning.

He checked her mare's saddle, cinched the buckles, then chose a horse for himself and saddled it with alacrity.

A half-hour later, they were riding out of London.

Chapter Eighteen

Jack had gone through the motions of the night, but that damnable letter had sapped his ability to enjoy his bride as he should on the eve of his wedding.

As they drove to Stratford's townhouse in St. James's Square, Jack simmered quietly. When they arrived, he took leave of his friend and pretended to head off to bed.

But he didn't sleep. He lay in bed until the sounds of the house diminished, and then he foraged through his trunk for two slender metal files. Then he slipped out into the foggy predawn.

Tom Wortingham lived in Wapping, where he rented a room in a squalid boarding house. Jack had come here once before, when he'd made the mistake of visiting Tom upon his return to London in August.

Stepping around a filthy gutter, Jack stared up at the peeling paint and grime-streaked walls. Tom could have done so much better for himself. He was a vicar's son, a gentleman's son, but since depleting the funds his father had left him, he had scraped by on nothing at all.

Jack slipped into the alley that led behind the house and gazed up at the top story of the building. A row of seven tiny square windows delineated the separate rooms. Tom's was at the far corner—the only illuminated window.

Jack walked back round to the front door, a narrow slab of wood, and found it locked. He remedied that by picking the lock using his files, and the door groaned on rusty hinges as he opened it. The inside corridor wasn't illuminated, so Jack felt his way to the stairs and ascended the two flights to Tom's floor.

He hesitated at Tom's door, considering.

To hell with it.

He stepped back, then turned and lunged forward, slamming his shoulder into the door. The weak, thin wood shattered with a loud crack that resonated through the entire building. Jack didn't doubt that every single resident had heard. He did doubt they'd come running to assist their neighbor. People who lived in places like this didn't go searching for trouble.

The door swung open. Tom had been sitting at a small desk, his back to the door. He wore a frayed gray robe over a long, striped nightshirt. At the explosion of shattering wood, he leapt up and spun around, his hands clapped to his chest in horror.

A moment of stillness passed. Tom stared at Jack, his pale gray eyes wide with shock. Jack paused at the threshold, his rage building, surging.

Then it burst through him, as powerful as a tidal wave. He shoved his way across the threshold, raised his fist, and punched. Tom's head snapped to the side, and he reeled backward until his body slapped against the wall, rattling the windowpane. Chunks of dirty plaster rained down from the ceiling.

Cowering, Tom held his hands over his head. "Stop!" he cried, his voice slurring. "Don't hurt me."

Jack reached into his coat pocket and dug out the crumpled note. He threw it to Tom's feet. It landed between his bare, gray toes. Tom stared down at it.

"No."

Tom lifted his face. His upper lip was swelling rapidly. "Jack—"

"I'm not giving you twenty-five thousand pounds."

"I know she has it—"

"You won't see a penny."

Tom took a breath and seemed to collect himself. "Well, then. You are well aware of what will happen if you refuse—"

"Don't threaten me," Jack said. It wouldn't do Tom a damn bit of good. Not anymore.

"I was doing you a favor by sending that letter, you know. By making you aware of the new terms before you married the chit."

Writing covered the sheets of yellowing stationery atop the desk. Jack saw the word "Anne" and jerked his gaze away from the black scrawl on the top sheet. Tom had always fancied himself a writer. Grimly, Jack recalled the love letters he'd written to Anne. Hundreds of pages piled high on the old desk that had once belonged to Tom's father.

Seeing Jack glancing at the writings, Tom lunged to the desk and with a sweep of his arm, sent the papers flying about them.

Rage boiled up in Jack so quickly he had to take a moment to calm himself as papers fluttered to his feet. When he'd retained a semblance of control, he said, "It's been years, Tom. *Years.* Why are you still writing to her?"

Tom spun on him, his thin lips curling in disgust. "You still don't understand, do you? So slow-witted, Jack. She loved me, damn you. She loved *me*... until you... you took it all away."

Jack stared at him. This only confirmed his suspicion that Tom was not quite sane. Anne had been fond of Tom when they were children, but later he'd frightened her. When they were fifteen, Tom had given her the first of many flowery love letters. It had proclaimed that he'd gladly kill himself for her love. She'd run to Jack, terrified. He'd soothed her, believing at the time that it was only Tom's competitive streak rearing its head. Tom had seen how close Anne and Jack had grown, and he was jealous.

"You stole her from me. It's your fault she left. You took her love and then you couldn't keep your damn fool mouth shut, and Turling married her off to that bastard..." Tom gulped, tears trickling down his jaundiced cheeks.

Jack clenched his fists. "You cannot blame me for her marriage."

"Of course I can. You forced her father's hand. You all but demanded to have her. He had no choice but to marry her to the first lord that came along." Tom swiped angrily at his tears with the frayed cuff of his robe.

It made sense, in a perverse way. Yet... God damn it, no. He wouldn't shoulder the guilt for Anne's marriage. That blame lay squarely on her parents. They were the ones, in their greed and narrow-mindedness, who'd forced the match.

Jack shook off these dour thoughts. It was no use talking about Anne, assigning blame, allowing Tom Wortingham to work him into a frenzy over it. The past was over.

"For Christ's sake, Tom. That was twelve years ago."

"I loved her." Tom's fist flailed and struck the wall, sending another shower of plaster over them both. "I love her!" His chest heaved with a sob.

Jack had loved her once, too. But it was over. She would always be a fond memory, but he had a new life now. Finally, after all these years, he cared again. He had something to fight for. Something important.

"Let her go, Tom. You must let her go."

"No!" Tom shook his head, a vigorous motion, causing the ends of his hair to whip at his cheeks. "I cannot." He leaned forward, his eyes wide and determined. "I won't."

"She's gone."

"Not to me, she's not."

Jack looked at Tom and could only feel a bone-deep sadness. Tom was all that was left of his past, the only remaining symbol of happiness from Jack's childhood, and God, he had wasted away.

"Do what you want, then. You won't be receiving any money from me, or from my wife."

"Jack—" Suddenly, Tom's eyes watered. His voice broke. "Jack, please. I—I need it."

Jack shook his head.

"I'm in trouble, Jack. I was gambling. I couldn't stop—didn't want to. I made promises. And now—"

"No."

"Please. They're threatening me. They're going to kill me. Truly, it wasn't selfishness that made me ask for money—it was need. I wouldn't have asked if I hadn't needed it. I'm not so self-seeking, you know that. But, deuce it, I'm in a terrible muddle. I owe money, Jack. Piles of money. If I don't pay…" He reached toward Jack with long, waxy fingers, beseeching. "Please help me."

Jack closed his eyes in a long blink and then opened them. Ever since the first day Tom had threatened him, he'd suspected this. It was part of what had driven him to concede to Tom's demand, some glimmer of hope that he could save his old friend from what he'd become.

"You were my friend for many years. We looked out for each other…and for Anne."

"Yes," Tom whispered. "And…I need your help now."

"If you wanted my help, you should have asked for it. I might have tried to help an old friend."

"Jack—"

"Instead, you threatened me. My place in the world. My life."

He could blame Tom for making him conspire to steal money from an innocent woman, but in the end, that particular sin wasn't Tom's to carry. It was his own.

Perhaps he was just as bad at Tom. Jack gazed at his one-time friend, at his skinny body, his gaunt face, haunted pale eyes, his robe worn so thin his elbows had poked holes through the fabric.

During those years on the *Gloriana*, he had subsisted in a brittle shell, Jack realized. Taking only the barest pleasure from living, unable to feel anything but bitterness for anything or anyone.

He'd ceased to feel after Anne and his mother had died. He'd resented his life—he'd resented *living*. Tom still resented living. Just from casting one glance on him, a person could discern his unhappiness, his lack of joy.

Jack could understand that. He'd subsisted in the same way for many years. But not anymore. One woman, one small, fragile, beautiful woman, had coaxed him back into the world of the living without either of them realizing what she was doing. With her, he'd experienced happiness and joy again. With her, he'd experienced love.

It might be too late for Tom—Jack couldn't know. All he knew was that it wasn't too late for him, and he was going to hold on to this newfound humanity for all he was worth.

Tom straightened. "I still have the evidence, you know," he said, the old threatening tone returning to his voice.

Jack shook his head. Tom was still fighting for the damn money, and all Jack could feel was the heaviness of grief for the friend he'd once had. That man was lost. Gone.

"You have until the fifteenth. If twenty-five thousand is too much—"

"A shilling is too much," Jack said.

"You think to run off with that skinny chit? I told you before, she's nothing compared to—"

Jack turned away.

"Do you really think she can make you happy? Someone like that? So frigid, Jack. So cold. So lacking in substance."

Jack stepped over the broken pieces of wood, over the

threshold, and down the dim corridor. Tom's voice rose to a screech behind him.

"There's no happiness for dead men, Jack!"

The morning of December the first dawned bright and clear, warm for the season, the sun quickly burning away all trace of last night's fog. Jack looked out the window of the guest bedchamber Stratford had provided him. It was a beautiful day for a beautiful new life, and yet trepidation tugged at his chest.

Whether he would be given the gift of a beautiful new life remained to be seen. He had risen at dawn intending to leave Stratford's house early. He would dress in his wedding clothes, and then he would ride to the duke's house. He was going to Becky, and he would tell her everything.

If she would still have him after all he'd done, he would begin his marriage with a clean conscience. He and Becky would build the rest of their lives on a foundation of honesty. He would prove to her that he was deserving of her love.

If she wouldn't have him— *No*. He wasn't going to consider that.

He would take it one step at a time. If Becky still accepted him after all that had happened, and if Tom still released his evidence to the authorities, Jack would have the backing of one of the most powerful families in England. This family had manipulated the law before. Perhaps they could do so again.

Hope was all he had to hold on to this morning, and he clung to it for dear life.

Turning from the window, he used the water a servant

had brought to shave and then he dressed in his finest waistcoat. He was reaching for his tailcoat when a scuffling noise sounded outside his door and it banged open.

Jack twisted around to see the Duke of Calton at the threshold, his face tight with concern, the scar on his forehead gleaming bright red.

"What the hell?" Jack asked.

The duke's cool blue gaze searched his bedchamber as Stratford hurried up behind him. Finally, Calton's eyes settled on Jack.

"I was going to ask you the same thing."

Becky quickly learned that spending hours without rest on a saddle was far more demanding on her body than she'd anticipated. Sam had been right—she was not accustomed to such hard riding, nor was she accustomed to riding astride, and after a full day on a horse, every muscle in her body screamed in protest.

When Sam and Becky reached Basingstoke in the afternoon of what should have been her wedding day, Sam pointed out that her mare was even more exhausted than she was, and he pleaded with Becky to stay at the posting inn to await the next mail coach to Cornwall.

Despite the compulsion to forge ahead no matter the cost, Becky agreed. She didn't want to risk the health of her mare, the chances of someone recognizing her were slimmer in this part of England, and ultimately, the post would travel faster than they ever could on horseback.

The post chaise whipped through the inn yard late that night, pausing only to exchange mail, horses, and passengers. During this part of the journey Becky forewent her masculine costume for her hooded dark-blue traveling cloak, for she knew as well as Sam that there was no way she'd fool the coachman or any of the other passengers about her sex in such close company.

About twenty-four hours after they left Basingstoke, they arrived in Cornwall, where they slept for the remainder of the night at the inn at Launceston. Early the following morning, the third of December, Becky rented a pair of horses and they set off toward the coast.

By the time they reached Seawood that afternoon, Becky's bottom was sore, her muscles ached, and she was miserably heartsick.

Jack had betrayed her. Jack was no better than William. With every heavy fall of the horses' hooves that brought her closer to Seawood, the truth of it beat through her mind.

Sleet had plagued Becky and Sam throughout the day, and they were cold and wet through despite the oilskin capes Becky had purchased on the first day of their journey. The sleet eventually stopped, but a misty cold enveloped them as they traveled into a gully and through a spindly wood. They crossed a wide, shallow stream, then the road twisted uphill, and Becky slowed her horse as the house appeared through the woods ahead.

The two-story structure stood on a flat, yellow-brown plain. Short brown weeds and twiggy bushes slapped against its battered gray stone exterior. Just beyond the house, the rocky coastline ended in a sheer drop, the cliffs descending into a wind-tossed silver sea.

Sam, who led the way down the narrow, overgrown road, glanced back at her, his forehead creased as wind whipped through his hair, standing the dark brown strands on end. "This cannot be it, my lady."

Her heart sinking, Becky shook her head. "No, it is. It must be."

Tears blurred her vision. Had Mr. Jennings lied to her? She'd pictured Seawood as a beautiful gem on the ocean, pristine and sweet, in excellent repair, and containing all the modern conveniences.

Blinking hard, she continued to follow Sam as they drew across the clearing toward the front door. She tried not to notice that the window on the ocean side of the door was covered by boards, and she tried to close her ears against the sound of a loose shutter banging repeatedly against the side of the house.

Sam stopped his horse and dismounted near the arched entryway. He turned to her, eyebrows raised, as she came up behind him, pulled her foot from the stirrup, and hopped off.

She gave him a confident smile as she handed him the reins. "Well, then. Let's see if Mr. and Mrs. Jennings are here."

Without waiting for an answer, she brushed past him and marched up to the weathered front door with more resolution than she felt. She knocked briskly. No answer. She waited, squared her shoulders and straightened her spine, and tried again.

No answer. She grasped the door handle and tried to open the door. It was locked.

Do not panic. Do not panic.

Pulling her coat tightly around her, she turned to Sam, depending on him, as she had in the past few days, to present an idea.

"Are you *certain* this is the correct house, my lady?"

Unable to speak, she simply nodded. She stepped into the clearing to survey the area. The crash of waves onto the cliffs far below was a dim roar, nearly indistinguishable over the whistle of the wind and the banging shutter. The weeds grew thickly, and though the autumn chill had thinned them somewhat, it was clear that the grounds hadn't recently been tended to.

"I don't understand." She spoke to herself more than to Sam. "This is nothing like how Mr. Jennings described it."

She looked inland, back in the direction from which they had come. Her gaze came to an abrupt halt when she saw a wisp of smoke curling over the treetops in the gully. "Sam, look. Over there."

She lifted the skirts of her traveling cloak and hurried through the grass, then down the slope onto a wet, overgrown path, her boot heels sinking into the mud.

A cottage, much smaller than Seawood, was tucked into a copse of trees beside the stream, sheltered from the weather and winds by the steep walls of the valley. A light burned in its single window and smoke emerged in white puffs from its chimney—a warm, pleasant sight.

Becky knocked on the sturdy wood-planked door, her heart racing. An elderly and thin but kindly-looking man answered it, his tufted white brows raised in question.

Becky didn't respond to his salutation. Instead, she gestured toward the coastline and the weather-beaten house on the cliff. "Is that Seawood back there?"

"Why, yes, ma'am. Indeed it is."

"Who's there, Wilfred?" asked a shaky feminine voice from deeper inside the room.

He glanced back toward the voice, whose owner was hidden behind a partition, and then looked at Becky as Sam drew up beside her.

"I'm looking for Mr. Jennings. Do you have any idea of his whereabouts?"

The man paused. "Well, that would be me, ma'am. I'm Mr. Jennings."

Fury and confusion swept through Becky in equal parts. "But you said...Forgive me," she said tightly. "I am Lady Rebecca Fisk, the owner of Seawood."

Mr. Jennings's eyebrows shot impossibly high and then snapped together. "Lady Rebecca? But you are...? Well." He looked uncomfortable as he bowed stiffly. "Forgive me, my lady. We weren't expecting you."

"I know you weren't. But I am here now."

His pale lips parted, the old man just stared at her, seemingly at a loss for words.

"I intend to stay at Seawood," she explained.

"Er..." His voice dwindled.

A woman bustled up behind Mr. Jennings. Her white crown of hair matched her husband's, but she was round as an apple where Mr. Jennings was lean. The pair of them reminded Becky of an elderly Jack Sprat and his wife.

"I asked you who—" She broke off abruptly when she saw Becky and Sam.

Becky inclined her head. "I'm Lady Rebecca Fisk. Are you Mrs. Jennings?"

The woman's mouth moved but no words emerged.

Becky released a breath. She knew she wasn't expected, but even so, this was a strange welcome to her property.

"Well," she said. "I see the house is in need of some work. I saw the broken window in the front..."

The elderly couple stared at her, their eyes round with shock. Sam stood beside her, not saying a word.

"...but I should like to see the interior, if you please. I assume you have the key?"

"We didn't expect you, my lady," the woman breathed, seeming to have lost the ability to speak with a full voice.

"I know that," Becky said impatiently. "The key?"

The woman broke out of her daze and curtsied. "Yes, ma'am." She spun around and hurried away.

Becky turned her gaze to Mr. Jennings.

He wrung his hands. "You don't intend to actually *stay* at Seawood, do you, my lady?" The thought seemed to cause him a great deal of anxiety.

"Yes, I do." Hadn't she already made that clear?

He bowed his head. "Forgive me, but we weren't expecting your arrival."

"I am aware of that." Becky struggled for patience. It was growing colder and darker by the minute and she wanted nothing more than a bath—though she now realized that might be asking too much. At the very least a warm fire. Mr. and Mrs. Jennings were keeping her out on their front stoop, and the wind had seeped all the way through her damp clothes and into her bones.

She raised a brow at the old man. "You are saying the house is not fit for my occupancy?"

"Well..." the man hedged.

"You claimed it was a lovely jewel." It took all of Becky's reserves not to crumble before these people. She was a James, she reminded herself. She must stay strong. She took a deep breath and continued. "You said in your letters that the house was in good repair, and that—"

"Oh, well, that's all true," Mr. Jennings hastened to explain. "Just a mite dusty, perhaps."

"Well..." Was that all? She heaved in a great breath of relief. "What's a little dust? We shall all spend some time dusting this afternoon." She'd never dusted anything in her life. But, honestly, how difficult could it be? She didn't care about dust. If dusting could take her mind off Jack Fulton's treachery, she'd happily do it till kingdom come.

Mr. Jennings nodded gravely. "Yes, ma'am."

Mrs. Jennings arrived with the key. Becky took it from her and turned away. The three servants followed her, keeping their distance, as she picked her way over the muddy ground back to Seawood, trying not to limp or wince as her travel-weary muscles complained with every step she made.

The key fit in the lock easily, but it took some joggling before it would turn. She opened the door to musty dimness and the semisweet smell of decay.

She stared into the dismal, dirty interior. She took several seconds to steel herself—against the despair, against the pain that slammed incessantly through her, against the hopelessness of making this place into a home—then turned back to the two men and the woman hovering behind her.

"Well, then," she said briskly. "Looks like we've some work to do if we're to make this place habitable by dinnertime."

Becky's family banded with Jack in a united effort to find her. At first they all assumed she couldn't have gone far—she'd left with only the coachman and two horses, and a survey of her personal items revealed that she'd taken very little. A woman riding sidesaddle certainly couldn't travel a great distance.

It took three full days for Jack, the duke, and Lord Westcliff to scour London for her. To no avail. Nobody had seen her.

Three full days had also passed before one of the duke's groomsmen discovered that none of the side-saddles were missing from the duke's stables. She'd been riding *astride*.

On the afternoon of December the third, Calton paced his drawing room, pushing his hand through his hair over and over. Lord and Lady Westcliff were still out roaming the city in search of Becky or anyone who'd seen her. The duchess sat on a nearby sofa with the duke's aunt, Lady Bertrice, beside her. The duchess gripped the embroidery in her lap but didn't sew. Lady Bertrice intermittently paced the room and plunked her body heavily beside the duchess and sat still, her lips pinched and her brow furrowed as if she were deep in thought.

Jack stood stiffly by one of the windows. Strictly on compulsion, he kept glancing out, as if he expected her to come riding down the drive at any moment.

But he didn't expect her.

She knew. It was a sick feeling that churned in his gut. He'd searched the four corners of London for her, damn it. Had poured his soul into the search. But all the while, he'd known they wouldn't find her.

She was gone. She knew. She must know. Somehow, she'd learned that he'd betrayed her. She'd read the letter. Or she'd heard him and Stratford talking. Or she'd encountered Tom and the bastard had exposed the entire scheme. Or...

In the end, he didn't know how she knew. But she'd trusted him. When she'd looked upon him, he'd seen true affection in her eyes. Only one thing could have destroyed that trust—she'd learned that he'd pursued her for her fortune.

He'd brought this upon himself. His motives had been rotten from the beginning, and keeping the truth from her made it a hundred times worse. He'd promised her honesty, and he'd misled her. Fed her lies.

Now, though, God knew his affection for her wasn't a lie. His need for her wasn't a lie. And long ago—he couldn't pinpoint the exact moment—his need for her had bled through his skin and now ran in his blood.

Deep grooves ran in parallel across Calton's forehead. "Damned if I understand this."

Jack didn't answer.

"I've never fully comprehended Rebecca or her motives, but never, never would I have expected her to do something like this. She was so..." He paused, thinking. "So dedicated to this venture. So determined to go through with it. To have her run away—it is the last thing I expected."

What the hell kind of response could Jack give to this? He couldn't reveal the truth, but he couldn't pretend not to understand her motivation, either. So he just remained silent, turning to once again look out the window.

"You're right," the duchess said. "Only sheer desperation could have prompted such an action on Becky's part. She behaved so strangely the night before..."

"Did she?" the duke asked. "I hadn't noticed."

"Well, she made an attempt to show the same pluck and excitement she'd been displaying for the last few days, but something had altered. Did you see it, Mr. Fulton?"

"No," Jack said. He should have paid more attention, but he'd been too agitated about that damned letter from Tom. He was disgusted with himself. If only he'd known, he would have done anything to stop her.

Becky was probably aware of that. That was why she didn't tell anyone where she was going, or why, and that was how she'd misled them into thinking she'd hidden somewhere in London.

She wasn't close. He had no idea where she was, whether she was safe or in trouble. If he didn't find her soon, he was going to lose his mind.

Straightening, he turned back to the duke. "I must find her."

Calton pierced him with those icy eyes, then gave a brusque nod. "We will find her."

"Where are the places outside of Town that she could have gone?"

The duke glanced at the women.

"She'd never return to Kenilworth," the duchess murmured.

"Calton House," Lady Bertrice said. "She's spent most of her life there, and it is the place that is home to her more than anywhere else."

Perhaps she did feel at home at Calton House, but Jack wasn't convinced that she'd choose to go there. "Where else has she been? Are there any other villages or residences she's familiar with? Where do her friends live?"

"Tristan's house is in Yorkshire as well," the duke

said. "To the east of Calton House. She knows she would be welcome there."

"When she was a girl, we did not often leave Calton House," Lady Bertrice said. "Since she was widowed, she has remained with either me or Garrett at all times. She has never ventured beyond the places she knows."

"I'll leave for Yorkshire immediately," the duke said. "If she has gone there, I will find her."

The places she knows... As Jack stared at her family, the truth crashed into him. Of course they'd assume she'd gone somewhere that was familiar to her. But Becky possessed a tethered spirit that was aching to be set free. She hadn't gone to Yorkshire.

"I believe I know where she's gone," he said quietly. All of a sudden, he was certain of it. It made perfect sense.

All eyes turned to him, questioning.

"She told me she has a house in Cornwall from her mother."

Lady Bertrice waved a hand. "Oh, that old place? I'm certain it's a crumbling ruin by now."

"She's never mentioned it to me," the duke said.

Jack met the duchess's gaze, and the woman gave him a thoughtful nod. They were thinking the same thing. Becky had gone to the one place that belonged to her. The one place that seemed as distant as China, the place that no one had thought of for years. The place she could be alone and independent for the first time in her life.

Becky had gone to Cornwall. And he was going to find her there.

Chapter Nineteen

Hard labor made Becky forget. Or at least it made her shove the pain into the background while her muscles burned with fatigue. Guided by the three servants, she washed and cleaned and even hammered when the occasion called for it.

The morning after her arrival at Seawood, she took some time to write a letter to her brother and Kate, explaining where she was and that she needed to be alone for a while. She sent Sam to the village to mail the letter, and then she went back to work.

She quickly came to understand why Mr. Jennings spoke so highly of Seawood. It wasn't a sparkling jewel, but it had stood, stubborn and stout, on the edge of this cliff for two hundred years. A recent gale had blown out the front window and had damaged the roof, but the heart of the house remained, facing the beating of the harsh weather head-on.

Mr. Jennings had lived here his entire life—his father had served as steward before him. He loved it here, as windblown and forbidding as it was. For him, there could be nowhere in the world to surpass the beauty of this place.

The house had been a childhood home of Becky's mother and grandparents, all of whom had died when Becky was very young. Here at Seawood, she found evidence of their humanity: old possessions, clothes, and letters. At Seawood, Becky's mother's family started to feel real to her for the first time in her life.

Fireplaces stood at each of the four corners of the house—a requirement for staying warm on a cold winter's day in blustery Cornwall. The interior was divided into nine rooms on two floors: five bedrooms, a drawing room, a dining room, a kitchen with a small scullery and pantry, and a study. There were three additional rooms in the attic for the servants as well.

As soon as Becky had entered the house, she'd asked Mr. Jennings to give her a tour, then she'd selected the room she intended to use as her bedchamber. She didn't choose to sleep in the largest bedroom or the adjoining chamber meant for the master's wife. Instead, she chose the room Mr. Jennings said had been her mother's.

They'd spent the remainder of the day scouring the room, removing the dust from every crevice in the carved bedposts, beating the rugs, and clearing the wardrobe of old clothes.

The room was painted a light green, and Sam had worked to remove the peeling and bubbling layer of green to reveal a yellow layer underneath, leaving the walls with a spotted effect.

Becky didn't care. When spring came, she'd have the house repainted and refurbished. For now, all that mattered was that she had a clean place to sleep. A place to mourn her loss.

No, she wouldn't mourn, she thought on the second morning at Seawood as she entered the grease-and-dust-laden kitchen, a dirty rag dangling from her fingers and her pistol comfortingly heavy hidden in the depths of her apron pocket. She hadn't lost anything. By coming here, she'd gained her freedom from a man who might have caused her more misery than William had. She could only thank God that she'd discovered his treachery before they'd wed.

She'd won. Either Jack would seduce and marry some other poor rich girl, or both he and the man who'd written the letter—Wortingham, the earl had called him—would have to do without their coveted fortune.

She didn't care either way.

The thought of Jack looking at another woman in the same way he'd looked at her, though...Oh, how it made her skin crawl. Each morning, she woke sick to her stomach and even sicker in her heart. She wished she could warn every woman in London against him. Explain how he'd lie through his teeth—offer promises of love, offer caresses that would make any woman melt...but it was all a deception.

Yet she couldn't reveal his treachery—in doing so she would only reveal herself as a besotted, gullible fool. Cecelia had told her that she was mysterious and unpredictable, and this gave her power. Well, she'd wielded that power by disappearing into the night on the eve of her wedding. She'd make her own way now. From now on, her independence would be her power.

As Sam and Mr. Jennings cleaned the fireplaces and got them in working order, Becky helped Mrs. Jennings with the kitchen. While Mrs. Jennings steeped the silver in soap leys, Becky stared in dismay at layers of years-old grease on the steel grate.

"Here, ma'am, I've boiled you some emery and soap to help with that," Mrs. Jennings said, handing her a bowl filled with a gritty paste.

Becky looked from the bowl to the rag to Mrs. Jennings. "What do I do with it?"

"Why, you're to scrub it." Stepping away from the silver, Mrs. Jennings rubbed her chapped hands on her apron, then took her rag and scooped up a bit of the gray paste with it. "There, you see?"

Becky nodded. "I...think so." She was to rub the rag over the grease and the paste would help it to come off. She wondered why, with all the books she'd devoured in her life, she'd never read one about housekeeping.

Mrs. Jennings turned back to the stove, her shoulders slumped. After watching them work yesterday, Becky had realized right away that Mr. and Mrs. Jennings were too aged to accomplish much, for they were quick to tire. It was up to Becky and Sam—whom she should have already sent back to London and her brother but couldn't bear to say good-bye to quite yet—to undertake most of the work.

Becky told Mrs. Jennings to rest her plump body at the small round table in the center of the kitchen and direct Becky on how to clean the oven. It was a dirty, nasty job, and by the time she was finished, Becky's hair hung limply around her face and her arms were covered up to the elbows in grease, but both the stove and the adjacent oven sparkled.

Just sitting for two hours had exhausted Mrs. Jennings, however, so Becky sent her back to her own cottage for an afternoon rest. Sitting at the rough-hewn kitchen table, Becky ate some bread and cheese without really tasting either, and drank a tankard of country ale. Even though she wasn't accustomed to the stuff, it satisfied her thirst. And it calmed her. It made her feel that she could face the rest of the day.

She'd have to hire workers eventually. But for now, she just wanted to work and work and work. She could see nothing in her future but work, and she could wish for nothing more.

God forbid she become as melancholy as she had been in Kenilworth, when she was married to William and learning that her marriage was a sham. She'd sat listlessly in the parlor for days on end, staring at the blurring pages of books, reading but not really absorbing the words, fear and desperation clawing at her chest, worsening with every hour that passed.

She would not turn into that woman again. She'd not wile away her days feeling sorry for herself. She'd be productive. She'd make this house her own. She'd learn about the family she'd never known. When those tasks were accomplished...she'd find something else. Something to do that would prove that she was a capable, *independent* woman.

This time, she would be strong. Even if that meant shoving her broken heart into the deep recesses of her soul and forgetting about it.

After she finished her luncheon, she went upstairs to explore the master's bedroom. This was where her grandfather, Sir Barnaby Wentworth, had slept. It was a small room, entirely masculine, decorated in dusty browns and deep reds. The bed was ornate, with lavishly carved mahogany posts and heavy velvet bed curtains. Rosewood tables flanked the bed, and matching tall cabinets stood against the opposite wall.

After a brief survey of the bed and determining that the curtains were moth-eaten and would have to be discarded, Becky went to the cabinets. She opened the doors, finding men's clothing from a previous age—yellowed linen shirts and braces, drawers, stockings, buckskin breeches, woolen pantaloons, a few waistcoats and tailcoats.

The drawer below revealed a stack of gloves and old cravats. Buried beneath them was a packet of letters. Moving to the only chair in the room, a stiff-looking wooden piece with a tall back and a brown velvet-padded seat, she untied the string that held the bundle together and saw that they were all letters from her mother to her grandparents.

She opened the top one. It was dated November 1800, just four years before Becky was born. Becky's mother had been eighteen when her daughter was born, so she must have been around fourteen years old when she'd written this letter.

> *Dear Mama and Papa,*
>
> *Please let me come home. School is wretched and I hate it immensely.*
>
> *Your miserable daughter,*
> *Mary*

The next letter, dated six months later, read,

Dear Mama and Papa,

I miss you so. I have not seen you in six months. Will you not allow me to come with you to Seawood this summer? Madame Latrisse says I am doing very well with my lessons and I will not fall at all behind if I were to go away for a few weeks.

The Season has been busy in London, but the weather has been horrid, and I do feel for all the girls who are looking for husbands and run hither and thither in the mud and downpours. I am very glad not to be one of them.

Your loving daughter,
Mary

Becky read on, her hands trembling as she read letters penned by her young mother. Her mother had obviously loved her parents dearly, and she'd missed them terribly, but they'd never allowed her to come home. No wonder all her mother's belongings in her bedchamber seemed to have belonged to a very young girl. When Becky's mother had reached a certain age, she had been sent away and never allowed to return.

Becky's grandparents, while they'd paid for a genteel lady's education and, later on, a Season for their daughter, had otherwise neglected and forgotten her. Yet they'd kept all her letters together. It was odd. They'd cared enough to keep her letters close, but had failed to bring her home. They'd kept aloof and distant, ignoring their daughter's pleas for love, and yet, by the row of portraits of her mother on the mantelpiece, it was clear they never forgot her completely.

Becky's heart lurched as she studied the sad look in her mother's eyes in the portrait at the end of the mantel. It must have been painted when she was eleven or twelve years old. Becky had grown up thinking that her mother's sadness was her fault, that her mother had been disappointed in her for some reason, but it was clear to her now that her mother's melancholy had begun long before her birth.

As she grew older, her mother became more defiant, and her letters began to speak of friends and parties, of noblemen's daughters and the eligible bachelors of the *ton*. Then the letters stopped for an entire year. There were two letters after that. The second-to-last letter was very short.

> *I hate you both, and I hate him. I don't care if he is a duke. I shall be miserable forever.*

Becky stared at the letter for a long while. Her father had died two years before her mother had, and she had few memories of him. But a feeling of dread always welled within her when she thought of him, and she knew Garrett possessed no fond memories of him.

Pressing the letter to her chest, she closed her eyes. Had her mother been like Jack's Anne Turling? Married to a man she never loved just because he was a peer?

Becky looked up at the sound of footsteps in the passageway. "Mr. Jennings!"

The old man halted and leaned inside. His arms were full of linens he was taking downstairs to wash. "Yes, ma'am?"

"You knew my mother, didn't you?"

"Why, yes, of course I did." A smile flitted over his age-thinned lips. "You are the image of her, my lady."

Becky nodded. She'd been told that often. As a rule, the Jameses were a tall, tawny breed, and Garrett was a James through and through. Becky was a product of their father's second marriage, however, and hadn't inherited the traditional strong family features.

"What was she like?"

Mr. Jennings leaned against the doorframe. The long furrows deepened across his brow as he considered for a long moment. "The last I saw her, she must've been ten or twelve years old. A scrap of a lass, she was, spoiled but sweet as could be, with a ready smile for everyone."

"And then she went away," Becky said.

"Aye, that she did. She weren't happy about it, if my recollection serves."

She gestured at the stationery in her lap. "I've just read her letters. Seems she wasn't happy at all."

"And then there was that matter with the duke, poor thing."

"What matter?"

Mr. Jennings's eyes widened. "You didn't hear of it?" Then he shook his head in self-derision. "Of course you wouldn't have. You weren't yet born. Never mind it, my lady."

"Tell me."

"'Tis of no import."

"What happened between my father and my mother? All I know is—" she stared down at the top sheet of aging parchment in her lap, "—my mother...hated him."

Mr. Jennings scratched his head. "Well, I've gone and muddled it, haven't I? Wish I hadn't brought it up at all."

"But you did," Becky said gravely. "Now you must finish it."

Mr. Jennings's gaze wandered toward the dusty curtain that covered the window. "She'd become somewhat of a flirt as a young lady, your mother did. At least, that was the rumor hereabouts. And then, well, mind I cannot guarantee the accuracy of this tale, you understand, because I am a mere servant, and sometimes we only hear a piece of the story rather than the whole."

"Of course I understand," Becky said. "Please, continue."

"Well, 'twas said she'd become a bit of a flirt. One night, during the Season of her eighteenth year, she attended a ball, and becoming drunk on punch, she..." He paused, seeming uncertain.

Becky sat very straight and very still in her chair. She'd never heard the story of her parents' meeting. "Please, Mr. Jennings, go on."

"Well, ma'am, 'twas said she made advances to the Duke of Calton. Being of a rather wild sort himself, he took these advances to heart, so to speak."

"He...seduced her?"

Reaching from the pile of linens he still carried, Mr. Jennings pulled at his collar. "Well, not exactly, my lady. 'Twas said he...took great liberties with her."

Mr. Jennings's Adam's apple bobbed. "I daresay it was a mighty fine blessing that her parents—your grandparents, my lady—rushed to London and pressed him to do right by the young lady. I believe they were married within the fortnight."

After a long silence, Becky smiled and gave a tight nod. "Thank you for telling me, Mr. Jennings. I never...well, I never knew."

"I'm sorry you heard it from me, my lady. It's a right sad tale, I suppose. Well, except for its end, of course."

"Its...end?"

"Why, yes. Of course. Miss Mary went on to become a duchess." He grinned at that. As if becoming a duchess was the highest glory to which a woman could ever aspire.

"Oh, yes," Becky said faintly. "Of course."

Mr. Jennings straightened. "Well, then." Using his chin, he gestured at the dusty linens in his hands. "I'd best get downstairs. Mrs. Jennings'll be wondering where I've got to."

Becky nodded distractedly. She hardly noticed him close the door behind him as she opened the final letter. It read as follows:

December 1804

Mama and Papa,

Thank you for your recent correspondence; I was pleased to hear from you. I thank you for your inquiries as to the welfare of His Grace. He is doing exceedingly well, I assure you. He is at present on a

*hunt in Scotland; I shall remain at Calton House
until spring. The child is nearly ready to make his
appearance in the world, I am told, and His Grace
is desirous that I remain in Yorkshire until the
blessed event takes place.*

Thank you again for your correspondence.
Yours, etc.

Mary Calton

Becky sighed. It seemed her mother had grown as
aloof as her parents had been. Then she caught sight of a
postscript scrawled at the bottom of the letter.

*Her Grace the Duchess of Calton was delivered
of a daughter in the morning hours of December 6,
1804.*

Slowly, Becky folded the letter, set it along with the
others in her lap, and raised her gaze to the faded chintz
curtains covering the window. She'd forgotten that it was
almost her birthday. She would be twenty-three years old
tomorrow.

She gathered the letters, tied them back into the
bundle, and rose, her body heavy with a nearly overwhelming sadness. Her mother had never loved her
father. Nor, apparently, had he loved her. What a sad
way to live, knowing that your husband could be
nothing but your worst enemy. Becky should know—
she'd lived with that knowledge for one full day, and
even that short amount of time had altered her
irrevocably.

She'd almost made that mistake again.

Sighing, she stood and went to return the letters to the place where she had found them. Just as she was pushing the drawer closed, the door to the bedchamber flew open and banged against the inside wall.

Jack Fulton stood at the threshold.

Chapter Twenty

Becky stared at him. Bitter, choking hatred surged into her throat.

How dare he come here? How dare he invade her home—her *sanctuary*?

His hair was windblown, and his color was high. He wore no hat, but he hadn't removed his coat. His hands clenched at his sides. "Becky. Thank God I found you. Thank God you are here."

She struggled to find her voice. When she did, it was low and firm. Strong. "Get out."

He shook his head. "Let me explain—"

"I won't listen to anything you have to say. Never again." He took a step forward, and she stiffened her stance. "Get. Out."

"Please, Becky." His voice was low. Pleading. "There is so much I must explain to you."

He was dangerous. He was capable of inflicting great

harm on her—worse than the harm William had inflicted.

Her fingers twitched, seeking a weapon. And there it was, she realized. Just beneath her fingers in her apron pocket. Plunging her hand into her pocket, she snatched the pistol out.

"Get out of my house." Her voice was low. Deadly serious.

Slowly, she raised her hand, her fingers tight around the silver inlaid grip, until the gun was aimed at his chest.

His eyes widened. "For God's sake, stop this nonsense, and let's talk."

"No."

"You won't shoot me."

"Oh, yes, I will."

He didn't know what she'd done, how she'd contributed to William's death. Everyone thought a criminal had killed William. Few knew that it was actually Garrett who'd shot him. Only two people in the world— Kate and Garrett—knew what Becky had done to her husband that day.

"You told Garrett that we were together that night. You wanted him to catch us. You wanted the world to know. You planned it all. You manipulated me into marrying you."

"Come, Becky." Jack's voice was low and seductive. That was the voice that had nearly caused her to give him everything. He'd seduced her into giving him her body...and her love, damn it. But he didn't have her name, and he didn't have her money. He never would.

He reached his hand toward her. "Sweetheart, put the

gun down. I'm so sorry—I can explain. I know you don't want to do this."

She'd protected Garrett from William. She'd protected Kate. Now she must protect herself. Raising her thumb, she pulled it down with a sharp jerk, cocking the pistol. Her hands were steady. "You have no idea what I'm capable of."

"Becky, please—"

"Don't move."

He froze.

They stood a moment in charged silence. Then, she said, "I will tell you one more time. Get out of my house."

He shook his head. "I love you, Becky. More than anything in this world, I love you."

Something surged within her and her hands trembled, but she quashed it and stilled her grip on the weapon. He lied. As he had lied to her from the beginning, he lied to her now.

"I won't leave you. You love me, too. I know you do— I've seen it in your eyes, felt it in your touch. You won't shoot me."

As if in slow motion, he stepped forward. Alarm bells clanged a warning in her head. *Save yourself, Becky!* He moved closer. He was almost on her, raising his arms to touch her. She tightened her hand over the grip of the gun and pressed hard on the trigger.

The gunshot boomed through the small room. She was vaguely aware of the window rattling, and the report of the shot jerked through her arms. Pain shot through her twisted elbow, and she stumbled back from the force of it.

Jack's jaw dropped open in amazement as he staggered

backward, looking down at himself. Blood bloomed from the hole torn through his coat. And then he sagged, crumpled to his knees, and fell with a thud to the floor.

Oh, God. His chest was on fire. Jack stared at the flat, dull plaster of the ceiling. There was nothing but the raging pain and the blood. It hurt like the fires of hell, and there was so much blood. Bright red, pulsing. His blood.

His eyes burned, watered. He gasped, unable to breathe. Had she shot through his heart? His lungs?

Her dark hair came into view, then her beautiful, pale oval face, still hard and unwavering.

Sweet, sweet Becky.

She'd shot him. He'd never thought her capable of such a thing. But the pain of death burned through him, and God, it hurt to breathe.

He deserved this. He'd deceived her. He had intended to engage her in a loveless marriage, then steal her money. There was no honor in his intentions. Only lies, deception. His eyes fluttered and then he closed them, sighing painfully.

It was better this way. He would die and she would be free of the likes of him. She deserved better than him. Because God knew, if he stayed alive, he couldn't let her go.

"I require clean cloths and hot water," someone said. It was that sweet, lilting voice he'd grown to love. Becky's voice. Maybe he'd die dreaming of her voice, maybe he'd dream about her forever. That would be heaven.

She continued emotionlessly, but her voice was like an angel's. "Those tweezers from the kitchen. Wash them and bring them to me."

Oh, God. Someone was touching him where he'd been shot. Pain sliced through his body, and he cried out weakly. But he'd lost control of his muscles, and he couldn't fight it. All he could do was lie here—was he on the floor?—like a weakling while they tortured him.

Fingers sank into his wound, and he screamed in pain. They were tearing him apart. He was on the rack, being disemboweled. He was dying.

He welcomed death. Hell couldn't bring worse pain than this, could it?

He writhed in agony, but not only did his muscles fail him, firm hands held him down. He could do nothing but succumb to the torment.

It grew worse, more painful, until every nerve in his body screamed in pained horror. And then, slowly, the pain grew dim. Dimmer and dimmer until it was fuzzy, like a dream.

Then, everything slowly faded. He embraced the blackness with open arms.

"I think he's fainted," Sam announced.

You've shot Jack. You've shot the man you love.

She hadn't wanted to hurt him; she'd wanted him to go away. If he died, she wouldn't survive it.

Her rational mind pushed away those thoughts, trampled them to dust, and took charge. This man meant nothing to her. He was a liar, as adept in deception as William was. She couldn't allow emotion to intervene. Emotions were illogical.

Yet she still couldn't allow him to bleed to death.

"Good," Becky snapped. "It'll be easier if he's unconscious."

She ran her fingers over the back of his shoulder, finding no wound. The bullet was still lodged in his shoulder somewhere. Laying him back on the floor, she gazed at the oozing wound for a moment. She tore open his coat and shirt, then quickly washed her hands using the hot water Mr. Jennings had brought and pushed a finger inside the hole the bullet had made. Right away, her fingertip skimmed the smooth, round surface of the ball. She ground her teeth when she felt the splinters of bone surrounding it.

"Give me the tweezers, please, Mrs. Jennings," she ordered when the woman hurried in from the kitchen.

Openmouthed, the woman obeyed. Becky dipped the tweezers in the hot water and carefully dried them, ensuring they were clean of any dirt or lint before she directed them to the place where she'd felt the bullet. Once she had a decent grasp on it, she yanked it out and dropped it on the wood floor with a *thunk*. It rolled for a moment, then came to a stop in the center of a whorl.

Everyone stared at the bloody ball for a long moment, and then Becky sighed and reached for the tweezers again. Inserting them into Jack's wound, she withdrew the loose splinters of bone she'd felt with her fingertip when she'd searched for the ball. She also found a round scrap of linen and several threads of wool—the pieces of his clothing that had been driven into his body by the force of the bullet.

She'd read the dictionary of surgery Jack had given to her. She'd read memoirs of surgeons during the Peninsular Wars, and she'd read treatises on medicine by renowned doctors. She knew, in a theoretical sense, what to do with a bullet wound to the shoulder. So she performed the task just as she'd read about it. She went through each step, each motion, as if she'd done it a hundred times before, bemused by her own distance from the event, her own lack of emotion.

There was no swooning or panic at the sight of blood oozing from Jack's body. She didn't question herself, her motives, or her intentions. She just did what needed to be done.

She peeled away his layers of clothing and thoroughly cleaned the wound. Then she wrapped it in strips of cloth soaked in cold water. When she finished, she took a deep breath, then rocked back on her heels, biting her lip.

She needed proper medical equipment—no, a proper *doctor*—to finish this. She glanced at Sam.

"Take a horse and go into Camelford. If necessary, go all the way to Launceston. Find a doctor and return with him. Be quick, Sam."

Tears pricked at her eyes, and she jerked her gaze away from Sam and turned to Jack. God, what had she done? He lay there, his face blanched, still as death. The thick, copper tang of his blood permeated her senses.

As Sam hurried away, she forced herself to continue with the practicalities. "Mr. Jennings, please remove those dusty bed curtains. Mrs. Jennings, if we possess anything in the way of clean linens, please fetch them, and we'll use them for the bed."

The elderly couple hurried to do her bidding, and she was left sitting beside Jack.

She suppressed the urge to take his hand. She stared down at her own hands. They were covered in his blood.

Rubbing a clean part of the back of her hand over her eyes, she fumbled to her feet. She must light a fire—if the fireplace in here was working, that was. It was important to keep him warm. His coat was wet. If she wasn't careful, he'd catch a chill.

As she passed the window, she glanced outside.

Wind whistled over the barren landscape, flattening the grass, and far in the distance, the sea frothed angrily.

Winter had arrived, tomorrow was her twenty-third birthday, and she'd just shot and possibly murdered the man she'd almost married.

She crossed the room and knelt at the basin to wash the blood off her hands.

Sam returned with the doctor two hours later. By that time, Becky and Mr. and Mrs. Jennings had made the bed, stripped Jack of his wet clothing, brought more clean water, started a warming fire in the blessedly working hearth, and tucked Jack beneath heavy blankets. Mrs. Jennings, though she was exhausted, scrubbed the floor clean of blood, but Becky couldn't do anything but stare at Jack. She'd pulled the chair close to the bed and watched him. Watched the steady rise and fall of his chest. Watched his pale face, locked in a frown. He'd hardly budged since he'd lost consciousness.

The physician, a mild-mannered young man with thick black eyebrows and a thatch of hair to match, introduced himself as Dr. Bellingham. Becky was grateful that he didn't ask how Jack had been shot. He simply unwrapped Jack's bandaged wound, studied it, and used the forceps he'd brought to search for any foreign objects that might have gone into the wound. He found nothing. He closed the wound with sutures, then asked for the largest belt in the house. Becky found one in her grandfather's cabinet, and the doctor strapped Jack's arm to his chest, cushioning his elbow with a large piece of quilted fabric. He wrapped the wound in a fresh cold-water application and fashioned a sling to support Jack's arm and elbow. Jack woke in the midst of his ministrations, and gritting his teeth in pain, he managed to answer the doctor's questions as the man poked and prodded his injury. Finally, the doctor drew Becky into the corridor.

"Unfortunately, my lady, I was unable to locate the ball."

"I removed it."

He frowned. "I...see."

"Did I do it correctly?" She thought she had, but the frown on his face suggested otherwise.

"You did nothing wrong, if that is what you are asking, my lady. You didn't damage anything. However, in the future, I would advise you to leave such exertions to someone who is more learned."

She pressed her lips together and nodded. "Will he recover?"

"There are two injuries to consider—the flesh wound from the bullet and the injured bone. If everything proceeds as expected, the flesh wound will heal in time. But he will likely always possess limited use of the arm."

"His clavicle is broken, isn't it?"

The doctor's bushy brows surged upward. "Why, yes, it is. There appear to be several small fractures in a radius around the location of impact."

She'd felt the breaks with her fingertips after she'd removed the bullet and bone splinters. "And the humerus and scapula?"

"Both appear intact."

"I think...the wound seemed far enough from his shoulder joint."

"Indeed. The joint appears unaffected."

She sighed in relief. "And the nerves of his arm?"

"He appears to have proper feeling in his fingers, and it is painful for him to move his hand, but he is capable."

Becky forced herself to nod. She'd once read about a case in which a man had been shot in a place similar to where she'd shot Jack. The shot had separated the nerves in the man's arm, and the limb had remained paralyzed and devoid of sensation for the remainder of his life.

So overwhelming was the sick feeling in her stomach, she couldn't muster the voice to thank the doctor. He rattled off instructions on how she should care for him through the night, told her he'd be back in the morning, and then he left the house.

Silence fell, and she returned to Jack's side to find him dozing. She watched him for a long while, struggling against the nausea churning in her belly. Finally, she dragged her head up to see her three servants watching her.

"You may leave," she whispered.

They obeyed, their faces grave. Last to go was Mrs. Jennings, who closed the door behind her, leaving a puff of dust in her wake.

Staring down at Jack's white face, Becky rubbed her arm absently, fingering the lumps of scar tissue and badly healed bone at her elbow.

He'd lied to her. He'd pursued her only to steal her money. He was a villain, just like William.

Then why did she feel that this was terribly wrong?

She'd experienced little remorse when she'd stabbed William, and she'd felt only relief when Garrett had shot him at the end. The guilt and second-guessing had come later.

Now, misery swelled in her chest, so tight and hard she could barely breathe.

With Jack, she'd allowed her hopes to climb even higher than she had with William. Four years ago, she'd traipsed blithely into trust and love. This time, she knew the value of her trust, and she'd vigorously guarded her love. And yet she'd bestowed both of them on this man, only to learn she'd been betrayed yet again.

For the first time since she'd discovered Jack's treachery, tears stung at her eyes, then crested over her lids and made hot streams down her cheeks.

Why had he come here, when she was so weak and vulnerable? Why couldn't he have pursued some other heiress or wealthy widow? How could she bear the pain of his betrayal? Or the guilt of what she'd done to him? Even after what he'd done, even after his admitted guilt, the fact that she'd hurt him deepened and sharpened the ache inside her.

She lowered her face into her hands.

"Becky?"

His voice was gruff. Slowly, she raised her head. Tears still streamed from her eyes, but she stared at him through the blur. He was awake, though still very pale. His lips were white and tight with pain.

"Why are you crying, sweetheart?"

"Don't call me that."

Shakily, he reached toward her with his good hand. "Don't cry."

She flinched backward, ensuring he couldn't reach her. "Don't bother to be kind to me," she whispered. "I know what you are."

Not to mention the fact that she'd shot him. They were bona fide enemies now.

He winced. "There's...more to it than whatever you think you know. Believe me."

"I don't believe anything you say. I never will believe you again. I won't make that mistake."

"Becky..." His eyelids fluttered shut, but he struggled to open them. "You shot me."

"Yes."

"Am I going to die?"

"I...don't think so."

His brown eyes fixed on her. "Do you hope I will die?"

She was silent. He kept his gaze locked with hers.

She couldn't admit the truth to him. She wanted him to heal. And then she wanted to go far away, so far she'd never have to experience the slicing pain that seeing him would cause her.

His eyes closed again, and he released a long, shuddering sigh. "I still want you."

She stiffened. "Well, you can't have me. Or my money."

"Don't...want your money," he pushed out.

She twisted her hands and pressed her lips together. She wanted to rage at him that he was a liar and ask how he dared lie to her yet again. But she glanced at his shoulder and saw blood seeping through the white bandage, and she restrained herself.

"Go to sleep, Jack."

He complied almost instantly. The lines of tension around his mouth relaxed, and his breathing deepened.

Clasping her hands tightly in her lap, she watched him sleep. She didn't realize that hours had passed until Mrs. Jennings came to the door with her dinner. Becky looked up to discover that the room was dark and the fire had reduced to embers.

She ate the bread, cheese, and dried venison without tasting it. She drank some of the brandy Mrs. Jennings had brought up.

Jack woke and she fed him sips of broth without speaking to him beyond the necessities. He needed to use the chamber pot, and though she intended to help him, he asked her to leave. She didn't argue.

It took him a very long time, and finally she heard the creaking of the bed as he sat on its edge. She opened the door.

"Do you need help getting back into bed?"

He shook his head grimly. "No."

It was obvious he was in a great deal of pain as he adjusted himself onto the mattress. He lay awkwardly, and though he'd said he didn't need her help, she fluffed the pillow beneath his head and drew the covers over him. He was shaking—from cold or from pain, she couldn't know. She didn't ask.

"The doctor brought laudanum."

"I don't want it." His eyes were glassy, and his face was blanched. He still trembled.

"All right." She turned away to build up the fire. When that task was accomplished, she took her seat beside him. He frowned at her. "You should go to bed."

"No."

She didn't elaborate, and he didn't ask her to. He stared at the ceiling, and she stared at him.

After a long silence, he said, "Her maid came to me."

"Whose maid?"

"Anne's."

She shrugged, not understanding the importance of this random comment. Why broach the topic of Anne Turling now?

Jack turned his face toward her. "Anne's maid came to me, early that night. The night...Haredowne was murdered. She knew...knew that I loved Anne. That I was a friend."

Becky was silent. The emotions conflicted so strongly within her, she couldn't conjure up a thing to say. Why would he rub his love for Anne Turling into her face? Why now?

He took a shuddering breath. "The maid—she said the marquis had struck Anne. Haredowne beat her and then wouldn't allow a doctor to come, because he didn't want the word spread that he was an abuser of women. She—the maid—said the marquis had gone out to his club, but Anne was at home, injured badly. She begged me to help.

"Nothing could have stopped me. I jumped on my horse and rode to Haredowne's house. I didn't think of fetching a doctor." Jack closed his eyes. "By the time I arrived, she was...she was nearly gone. It was as if she waited for me. As soon she laid eyes on me, she took her last breath. I believe he'd beaten her so brutally, he broke a rib and it punctured her lung."

Becky pressed her arms around her body. She stared at him.

The pain that swirled around them both was nearly palpable. It wrapped around her, tight like a cocoon. She couldn't move, couldn't break her gaze from the stark paleness of his face.

"I took my father's gun, and I went to his club. I waited outside in the alleyway for him. When he came outside, I accused him of hurting his wife, of killing Anne. When he didn't deny it, I shot him."

Jack opened his eyes. The desolation in the dark depths sucked all air from Becky's body. She struggled for a breath as he continued.

"Now you know," he whispered. "I murdered him in cold blood. I am a murderer."

"As well as a liar." The ice encrusting her voice made her grimace.

"Yes. As well as a liar."

She didn't speak. There was nothing to say. He was different from William in that he'd admitted his wrong-doings. To the bitter end, William had seen himself as the victim.

"Nobody saw me shoot him—or so I thought. Suspicion naturally turned to me, though, and I was arrested. But they dropped the charges...they released me when a whore came forward and said I was with her that night." Jack sighed shakily. "She was...she was a friend. I didn't sleep with her, though the world assumed I was the jilted lover who'd gone to the whorehouse to drown my sorrows in debauchery. Instead, I talked to her. She listened. I told her the whole story about Anne, told her what a miserable wretch I was, and she took pity on me."

Jack looked away from Becky to stare at the ceiling again. "Someone had followed me that night, though, and he saw it all. He was old friend of mine and Anne's from our childhood—the vicar's son. His name was Tom Wortingham, and he'd been following me ever since we were old enough to leave home. He was jealous of my relationship with Anne. He fancied himself in love with her.

"Tom left me alone for the twelve years I was absent from England, but he is in trouble. He's desperate for a large sum of money, and when I returned to England, he demanded I pay him fifteen thousand pounds for his twelve years of silence. If I don't procure the money, he will take indisputable evidence that I killed the marquis to the authorities. He has his own signed and witnessed testimony, along with a signed and witnessed statement from the woman—the whore—saying she lied about my being with her that night." Jack ground his teeth. "He must have promised her a tidy sum for that."

"Well, you won't obtain your fifteen thousand pounds—or twenty-five thousand—from me," Becky said quietly.

"Ah." He nodded bleakly. "You saw the note, then."

"I heard Lord Stratford reading it."

"You were outside?"

"I was. I saw you and Lord Stratford leave the house. I was curious, so I followed you. I heard him read the letter, and I...I heard him say that you had planned for us to be interrupted during...while we were...that night." Her lower lip began to tremble, and she turned away from him. "You seduced me, knowing we would be caught. Knowing that we would be expected to marry. How could you?" There wasn't any rage in her voice, just an infinite sadness.

"I was wrong. I didn't know how wrong it was then, but now I do." His chest rose and fell in a sigh. "It's all right, Becky. I have reaped what I've sowed. I could no more take your money from you than I could cause you bodily harm. But I will pay for what I've done. Tom Wortingham will take his eyewitness account to the authorities, and I will hang."

She stared out the window, crossing her arms over her chest. "That is no concern of mine."

"Good. It shouldn't be. I deserved this."

Inexplicably, Becky's eyes filled with tears again. "Yes. You did."

"I don't want your pity."

"What do you want from me, then? Besides my fortune?"

"Your love." He paused. "But I have destroyed all hope of that, haven't I?"

"Yes," she said through clenched teeth. Her heart pattered in her chest. Unable to look at him, she squeezed her arms tightly, her fingers digging into the odd lumps of bone and tissue on her elbow.

"I'm sorry, Becky," he said softly. "I'm so sorry."

Chapter Twenty-one

The following morning, Becky pressed her palm to Jack's flushed cheek and discovered him feverish.

Thus began the longest seven days of her life. Vaguely, Becky remembered that Christmas drew nearer, but she couldn't drag herself from Jack's side even to write to her family. Sam always lingered nearby, concerned, flatly refusing when she told him to return to London. Mr. and Mrs. Jennings hovered in the background, ready to help whenever she asked.

The likelihood that Jack wouldn't recover increased daily. Nothing anyone did could reduce his temperature, and he'd begun to experience fits of fevered delirium.

Becky did what she could for him. She fed him, changed his bedclothes, placed soothing, cool cloths over his brow, gave him his medicines, followed to the letter every instruction the doctor gave.

The only thing she couldn't bring herself to do was talk to him. God help her, but she couldn't bring herself to beg him to get better.

Today, she sat in her chair waiting for the doctor. Jack was calm for the time being, in a state of uncommunicative half-sleep, and Becky stared down at her hands.

She could still see the blood on them. Would she ever be able to wash it off completely? Her logical mind told her that the blood was a wild invention of her imagination, that she'd washed it away that first day. But she could still see it. Slippery and slick, and such a bright red, it hurt her eyes.

The door opened, and she glanced up to see Dr. Bellingham at the door.

The doctor bowed in greeting, then approached his patient's bedside. "How is he?"

"No change," she said.

Dr. Bellingham went through his usual routine, checking Jack's temperature, his pulse, his pupils, and his wound. From the second day, the doctor had tolerated her presence in the sickroom and spoken to her as an equal. He'd realized quickly that she was knowledgeable in anatomy, healing, surgery, and all the treatments he recommended, so he spoke to her plainly, without mincing words.

"His fever is higher," he said. "The area below the wound looks to me to be in the early stages of gangrene, and the swelling in his shoulder and liver have increased to an unhealthy level."

Becky had assessed the wound herself earlier and come to a similar conclusion. She'd hoped the doctor's prognosis would be better. "What can we do?"

"I could bleed him again." He paused. "There is another option..."

Becky spoke automatically. "Amputate his arm."

"Yes." The doctor sighed. "I'm not entirely convinced it will help."

Becky stared at Jack for a long moment, remembering how he'd climbed the trellis to her room and told her that he'd often climbed the rigging of the *Gloriana*. He'd no longer be able to do such a thing. Without his right arm, he'd be a cripple, far worse off than she was with her mangled elbow.

She met Dr. Bellingham's serious gaze. "Is it our only hope?"

"It might be."

She swallowed hard. If she must choose between Jack's arm and Jack's life, the choice was obvious.

"Then do it."

Dr. Bellingham scheduled the surgery for that afternoon, as he needed to return to Camelford to fetch his assistant and the proper equipment for an amputation. He left the house with instructions for the servants to prepare household items for the upcoming surgery and a promise that he'd return by one o'clock.

Becky sat in her chair, unable to move, tears pricking at her eyes.

She would not cry. She would not think on the fact that she had done this to Jack.

Mrs. Jennings opened the door, her arms brimming with items the doctor had requested. She glanced at Becky.

"Ma'am, Mr. Jennings hadn't gone to fetch the post for several days, so he went today. There were several letters for you, but I thought you might be especially interested in this one." Fumbling with her armful of supplies, she withdrew a letter from her apron pocket. "It's addressed to Mr. Fulton."

Becky's heartbeat quickened. Standing, she took the letter from Mrs. Jennings and stared at it.

Who could it be from? What could it be? The writing was tall and elegant. It certainly didn't match that of anyone in her family, but who else knew Jack was here?

Becky glanced at Jack, who lay motionless on the bed, now deep in slumber. She laid a hand on his scorching hot, dry forehead. "Jack?"

No response. She laid a cool cloth on his forehead then turned away, still gripping the letter. Blindly, she left the room.

Across the hallway, she sat on her own bed—the bed she'd hardly seen in the last several days. She laid the letter down on the counterpane in front of her and stared at it.

It was addressed to Jack. She shouldn't open it.

But Jack was unconscious in the next room. Insensible with fever...and losing his arm.

She grabbed the letter and tore it open.

December 4, 1827

J,

In respect for our previous friendship, and my desire to see you well situated, I've taken some time to think about it, and I have decided to reduce the terms of our agreement.

Eighteen thousand.

Despite your refusal to pay a shilling when last we met, I feel this is a very fair compromise indeed. I am certain you will agree.

But the remaining terms still stand. We're running out of time, my friend.

T.W.

Becky read the letter again. And again.

Jack had refused to pay him a shilling? *When?* Had he given up in his attempt to steal her money before he'd come to Cornwall? The day he'd found her here was the day after Tom Wortingham had penned this letter. Which meant Jack had still wanted her even after he'd told Wortingham he wouldn't give him a shilling.

Could he...?

No, a firm voice within her said. She'd shot him. Whatever had happened between Tom Wortingham and Jack, it had no bearing on her relationship with him now.

In any case, it didn't seem to matter. The man still demanded eighteen thousand pounds. That was the amount that would save Jack from the noose.

If he survived the gunshot wound she'd inflicted on him. If he survived the amputation.

Clutching the letter to her chest, Becky closed her eyes.

She didn't know how long she sat there, rocking back and forth, her body racked with shivers as she tried not to picture the procedure that would soon be performed in the next room. Mrs. Jennings brought her a mutton pie for luncheon but she just stared at the food, not touching it.

Jack's arm. His beautiful, powerful arm. The muscles in his biceps and forearms that she'd loved to run her fingers over. Those long fingers that had brought her pleasure, again and again.

He'd lied to her. He'd seduced her and misled her. But none of that took away the fact that he had once been a healthy, whole human being, and she had taken that from him.

We're running out of time, my friend.

She scrambled to her writing desk and yanked out a piece of stationery. Dipping her pen into the inkpot, she scrawled two letters—one to her solicitor, and one to Kate and Garrett. In the letters, she instructed Garrett and the solicitor to draw up a promissory note for the sum of eighteen thousand pounds and deliver it to Mr. Thomas Wortingham of London, lately of the vicarage of Hambly in Kent.

She closed and sealed the letters and hurried downstairs to search for Sam. She found him in the small paddock at the corner of the woods, brushing down one of the horses.

"Sam, I must order you to return home, immediately." When his face darkened with an instant denial, she held up her hand. "Before I asked you to leave only because I felt you should return to my brother, but now it is truly a matter of life or death."

She thrust the letters at him. "This is the last thing I'll ever ask of you, Sam," she said quietly. "But you must deliver these letters for me. It is a matter of utmost importance. Please."

Jennifer Haymore

He shook his head slowly. "Mr. Fulton...?"

"I shall remain here in Cornwall with him until...until he recovers. Please tell my brother and Kate...Just tell them I wish I could be with them for Christmas, but it is unlikely."

Sam sighed. "I don't feel right leaving you with only the old man to care for you."

She raised a brow. "You doubt my ability to care for myself?"

"Uh..."

"I have the gun," she said quietly.

He deflated a bit. "Well," he muttered, "that's true."

"I can take care of myself. You must leave right away. And hurry, Sam. There isn't much time."

Slowly, Sam nodded. "As you wish, my lady."

She returned to the house and stumbled inside blindly, colliding with Dr. Bellingham at the top of the stairs. He took her by the shoulders and gently thrust her away, and she saw another man stood behind him.

"Dr. Bellingham! Oh, goodness..." Her heart leapt into her throat. "How...how long have you been here? Is it one o'clock already?"

"Forgive me, my lady." He cleared his throat, looking uncomfortable. "It's not quite one. We were somewhat early. This is my assistant and my brother, Mr. Rutger Bellingham."

She automatically dipped a curtsy at the man, and as he bowed toward her, she turned back to the doctor.

"I woke Mr. Fulton when we arrived. I wished to inform him about our decision regarding the amputation of his arm. I spoke to him about the surgery."

"Yes?" she breathed.

"Well, he was quite lucid, my lady. He refused the procedure. Given his clear state of mind, I feel I cannot, in good conscience, perform it."

Relief, mingled with renewed fear, rendered her unable to speak for a long moment. "Has his fever...?"

"It is higher than ever."

"You told him the risk?"

He nodded gravely. "There is some suppuration, and I have applied a hot poultice and spiritous embrocations to the wound to encourage it. If I don't cut it away, the infection will spread through the limb and into his body." He sighed. "If it spreads, it will likely do so very quickly, and..."

His voice dwindled, but Becky understood. She nodded. "He will die. Abruptly."

"Yes, my lady."

"Is he still awake?"

"Just barely."

"Can I see him?"

The doctor inclined his head. "Of course."

She entered Jack's room. He lay very still, but his eyes were open and he stared at the ceiling.

She swallowed. Walking toward him was like walking through syrup, and she had to push herself through every step. "Oh, Jack."

As if it took great effort, he turned to her, his eyes bright and feverish.

"No...amputation," he whispered through chapped lips.

"Are...are you certain that is what you wish? Dr. Bellingham said he told you the risks." She swallowed hard. "We believe mortification has begun. It will spread through your body. It might well kill you."

Looking away from her, he managed a one-shouldered shrug.

She grabbed his good hand. It was hot and dry.

"I...I don't want you to die."

"Why not?"

Dr. Bellingham stood in the doorway, and she glanced at him, dismissing him with her eyes. He nodded and left the room, closing the door gently behind him.

Because I love you.

But she couldn't say that. She couldn't. Not now.

"Because you don't deserve to die," she said instead.

"Don't I?"

"No," she murmured. "You are young and strong... and...and you deserve to live."

"No amputation," he rasped out.

She tried not to cry. She tried very hard. But it was no use. The tears began again. He watched them roll down her face dispassionately, then he closed his eyes.

"Please don't die. Please. I want you to live."

"Do you mean that?"

"I do. Please, Jack. Please don't die," she sobbed.

"Why?" he demanded, his voice stronger now.

"Because...I could not bear to be in this world without you. I could not bear to live a single day knowing that you were gone. Knowing that I was the one responsible. Knowing that if I wasn't so cruel, so unforgiving, that you would still be healthy and whole." She heaved in a breath. "Because I loved you once. Because somehow I know you are different from William. Because some part of me still insists that you loved me, too."

She pressed the hot back of his hand to her cheek, cooling the dry skin with her tears.

"I will try not to die, Becky," he whispered finally, closing his eyes. "I'll try my damndest."

Late that night, Jack's fever broke. Becky sat at his side, unable to sleep. She watched as the sweat beaded on his forehead and rolled down his face. She bathed him with clean towels. When she brushed her fingers over his skin, she found it damp and cool.

It was a difficult night. He tossed and turned, moaning in pain whenever anything touched his skin. She changed the dressing, noticing the wound was still an angry red, and it was swollen and hot. She alternated between squeezing drops of clean, fresh water and drops of watered-down brandy into Jack's mouth, a prescription she read had once saved a man's life after he'd been shot in the Peninsular Wars.

As a steely dawn began to drift through the motheaten curtain, Jack opened his eyes. The brown orbs were solemn now, no longer bright with fever.

"Hurts," he announced in a scraping voice.

She pushed a limp lock of hair away from her face. "Your fever broke last night."

He glanced at his arm. It was useless, for now, but it was still there. Sometime during the night, the swelling had diminished considerably.

"It's a miracle," she whispered.

He turned back to her. "You said you wanted me to live."

Emotion welled in her chest, so thick she could scarcely breathe. Looking away from him, she rose, her knees wobbling. "I...I'll go get you something to eat."

She hurried from the room. After instructing Mrs. Jennings to make Jack some broth, she went into the bedchamber adjacent to the master's chamber and spent the rest of the day scrubbing it until it sparkled.

Late in the afternoon, she finally summoned the courage to go to Jack. The doctor had him sitting up in bed, and some color had returned to his cheeks.

She tried to smile at him. "You look well."

He nodded. "I am better."

"That's...good." Awkwardly, she went to sit on the chair she'd hardly left for the last week.

"Where have you been all day?" he asked.

She looked at him, then quickly away. Heat crept over her cheeks. Why couldn't she bring herself to tell him the truth? That she'd arranged for his blood money to be sent to Mr. Wortingham? That he no longer needed to worry about his neck? That she was a coward and had avoided him all day?

"I've been working about the house."

She should tell him now. But...perhaps it wasn't necessary. She would tell him when he was a little better. When she could conjure the nerve to do so.

"Ah."

She licked her lips, and he looked away.

"I don't blame you, you know," she blurted. "For killing the marquis."

His tired gaze drifted back to meet hers. "You don't?"

"No. If what you said was true, then it was right of you to kill him. If he hurt his wife...if he murdered her...he didn't deserve to live."

"No," he agreed without intonation. "He didn't deserve to live."

She nodded. "I...I just wanted to make it clear. William...before Garrett killed him...I stabbed him. In the gut." She blinked hard. "He was...he was holding a gun, was going to kill...I had no choice." She hated talking about this. She hated reliving it.

"So I understand what it is like," she finished. "To make that decision, to choose between allowing evil to flourish and ending it."

"I know you understand," Jack said. "You made that choice again, because I was another man who deceived you, who lied to you. You were right to try to stop me. Stop the evil I represented."

"No!" she choked out. But then she clamped her lips shut and stared at him bleakly. Finally, she said, "It was different with you. I wanted...despite everything, I wanted you to live."

And Jack wasn't evil, not like William Fisk and the Marquis of Haredowne. Despite what he'd done to her. She didn't know how she knew that—she just did.

He closed his eyes. "I'm tired."

He was dismissing her, she realized. He didn't want her in the room with him. It made sense. She'd caused him untold agony and nearly been responsible for his death, after all. What was she expecting? His heartfelt thanks? That would be ridiculous.

She rose. "Of course. Can I bring you anything?"

"No. If I need something, I'll call for Mrs. Jennings."

She forced herself to nod. Mrs. Jennings had taken to sleeping in the bedroom across the corridor, for Jack and Becky had often needed her at night in the past week.

"Yes. Of course. Well. Good night, then."

"Good night, Becky."

Jack watched her go, her willowy figure gliding over the threshold before she closed the door gently behind her.

It always hurt him to watch her walk away, but this time there was a finality to it that tore at his chest.

He gave a long, shuddering sigh. His shoulder ached, but it wasn't terrible. It had hurt far worse this morning than in the previous days. He knew it would heal now.

All he'd needed was to hear her say she wanted him to live. Those few words were enough for him to cross the barrier, to fight with everything he had to conquer the infection that threatened his body.

Yet he had broken her. He saw it in her posture, in the shoulders that she'd held so straight when she'd trusted him. Now they sagged beneath the weight of her sadness. He saw it in her face, in those changeable eyes that no longer sparkled with passion but were somber and dark. In the flat line of her brow, and in her pale complexion. He didn't know how long it had been since she'd discovered his betrayals and his lies, but she must have lost half a stone in that time, and on a frame as slight as hers, half a stone was an enormous amount of weight.

Mrs. Jennings bustled in with a steaming bowl. "Well, then, young man. I've heard you're feeling a mite better. Are you feeling up for some supper?"

He eyed the dish in her hand warily.

"'Tis only a bit of mutton broth. Do you think you can manage it?"

He needed food. He needed his strength. He'd been

chained to this damned bed long enough, and he wanted out. He wasn't made to be an invalid.

"Yes. I can manage it."

"Very good, then." She settled in the chair that Becky always occupied. Guilt stabbed at him for asking her to leave. But watching her, the way she was now, broke his heart. He wanted to hold her close and tell her all would be well. That he loved her and cared for her, that he'd take care of her. That he'd make her happy.

But he had no right to touch her. And he damn well had no right to say any of those things to her.

Mrs. Jennings fed him several spoonfuls of the broth in silence. Then she said, "I was very much in love with Mr. Jennings."

He eyed her, wondering if, at her advanced age, she might be slightly addled.

"Just like my mistress loves you." A ghost of a smile flitted across her face. "Before we married, Mr. Jennings did something that made me very angry indeed, and I punished him. I didn't shoot him, though perhaps I should have." She paused, empty spoon held in midair, and looked down at him, her face a prunelike mask of disapproval. "You must have disappointed her greatly."

He closed his eyes.

After a short silence, in which Jack heard only the sound of the spoon scraping the bowl, metal pressed against his lips. He opened his eyes and lips and took the proffered soup.

"She is a sensitive girl," Mrs. Jennings said softly, as if she didn't want Becky to hear from wherever she was. "I've only known her less than a fortnight, haven't I? Yet she wears her emotions plain on her chest, clear as day for anyone with half a brain to see."

Jack swallowed the salty broth.

"Can you see them? Her emotions, I mean?"

"Yes, Mrs. Jennings," he murmured. "I see them."

Becky was right to have shot him. Not once, even when he was closest to death, even when the pain was at its worst, had he questioned her choice or her motivation.

He'd betrayed her in the worst way possible—he'd demanded her trust and then he'd crushed it beneath his boot heel. If someone did the same to him, he wouldn't spare that person a second glance. He'd shoot and then turn away and let him rot.

And yet, every time he'd opened his eyes, she'd been there. Caring for him. Helping him. Praying for him. She'd wanted him to live, even after what he'd done to her.

"She is a melancholy girl, but she is a good lady," Mrs. Jennings said. "We are old, you see, and we've not kept her home as fine as she'd have wanted. Yet she didn't complain, not once. She got on her hands and knees and worked alongside Mr. Jennings and myself. And when our weary bones was tired, she entreated us to rest."

"Did she." Jack wasn't surprised. Of course she was a fair mistress. He wouldn't have expected her to be any other way.

Mrs. Jennings eyed him. "Aye, sir. She did. And then I've watched her care for you..."

"She was the one who shot me," he reminded her with no animosity.

"Aye, and I daresay you deserved it," Mrs. Jennings

declared. "Lady Rebecca, she wouldn't harm a fly. Unless that fly did something of a very bad sort."

He sighed.

Mrs. Jennings raised the spoon. "She cared for you because she couldn't bear to see you suffer. And you will survive it now, and that brings her peace. But would you like to know what I'm thinking, sir?"

"What's that?" Jack asked dryly.

"I'm thinking it'd be more than trifling sad were she to be hurt again." Taking the spoon, Mrs. Jennings scooped up the last of the broth. "Very sad indeed. I don't think she'd survive it. Further, I think you're one of the few people, for whatever reason, who is capable of killing her."

Jack savored the warmth of the broth in his mouth. He swallowed and remained silent for several long moments.

He knew what he had to do.

"I don't want her hurt, either, Mrs. Jennings." He took a shuddering breath. "I'm not going to allow it to happen again."

Becky tossed and turned until, finally, at dawn, she gave up. With a sigh, she went to her window and pulled the curtain aside.

A fine layer of ice covered the ground. Beyond, the ocean was as silken and gray as a seal's coat, rippling against the cliffs below. Becky pulled a chair to the window, propped her chin in her hand, and stared out as the sun burned through the wisps of fog and the sky lightened to a brilliant, jewel blue.

Soon it would be Christmas. The first Christmas she'd ever spent away from her family. The first Christmas in four years she'd spent apart from Kate and Garrett.

It was a lonely feeling. But when it came to her family—not only Kate and Garrett, but all of them—she knew that the feeling was mutual. They loved her unconditionally, and they would be missing her as much as she missed them.

She traced circles in the fog inside the windowpane. She'd told Mr. and Mrs. Jennings to wake her if there was any change for the worse in Jack's condition. No one had come into her room last night, which meant either that he was stable or that he had continued to improve.

Jack would heal. When he was well enough, they would separate. She would return to London, and he... Well, it didn't matter what he did. He would take his own path. Whatever he chose to do was of no concern to her.

Or, at least, it shouldn't concern her. If it did, it was a sign of her weakness. It had been far easier to let William go, but Jack...he had wended his way through her, and try as she might, she couldn't pry him free.

Sighing, she turned and dressed herself in one of the two dresses she had brought with her to Cornwall. This one was a deep green color reminiscent of holly. It reminded her of the season and was far more festive than her brown habit, which was now stained with grease and dirt from all the cleaning she'd done in it.

After she brushed, braided, and pinned her hair, she stared into the looking glass for a long time. She looked haggard and thin. Her straight hair hung in wisps around her face, and her eyes looked dark and large, set deep in her sallow face.

Too much guilt and fear, sadness and disappointment resided there. She shouldn't feel that way, truly. She had

Kate and Garrett. Aunt Bertrice loved her in her gruff way, and Sophie and Tristan would never turn her away. Her nieces and nephews were all enamored of her. She was the favored aunt, and she loved them all.

She shouldn't feel this crushing weight of loneliness in her chest.

She turned to the door. Toward the man who had not so much been the source of her loneliness as deepened it, turned it into a physical ache.

So much…she'd wanted so much for him to love her. She closed her eyes, remembering those few days that she'd believed. How happy she'd been. How free she'd felt.

How could she capture that feeling ever again?

She exited her room, crossed the corridor, and slipped into Jack's room. To her surprise, he opened his eyes as soon as she pushed the door open.

"Good morning," he said.

"Good morning." She paused at the threshold, uncertain if he'd ask her to go away.

After a brief silence, he said, "Come in."

She walked over to her chair, pulled it back from the bed several inches, and sat.

He studied her for a few moments. "You look tired."

"I am fine." She gazed at his arm, narrowing her eyes at the fresh bandages. "Was Dr. Bellingham here?"

"Yes. He just left." Jack took a breath. "We knew you were asleep, so we were quiet."

She nodded. No point in correcting him.

He glanced down at his shoulder. "He splinted my arm, put it in a new sling, and he left more laudanum."

She knew, from her personal experience with her broken arm, that injuries like theirs weren't splinted until the swelling was down and they were on their way to healing. "That's excellent news."

"Yes."

"Does...does it hurt?"

"No. Well...I won't lie and say it doesn't hurt at all. But..." his eyes captured hers, held them in a snare, "...it hurts less than the knowledge of how much pain I have caused you."

A cement wall, established purely by an instinctual need for self-preservation, built up so quickly between them, she hardly had time to take a breath. She couldn't answer. She wouldn't—couldn't—believe him. She tore her gaze from his and stared at the foot of the smooth old gray silk counterpane. Once upon a time, her grandparents had used it on this bed. It was one of the few pieces of linen in the house that had been well preserved.

"Becky?"

She tried not to twist her hands. She shifted uncomfortably in the chair.

"What is the date?"

She jerked her gaze back to him. "It's the fourteenth of December."

"The fourteenth of December," he repeated in a whisper. Sorrow passed over his face; a look of exhaustion. Of defeat. Then he closed his eyes. "It's near Christmas, then. I've kept you from your family. If you leave soon, you can be in London by Christmas."

"No, Jack. I will remain here until you are well."

Chapter Twenty-two

Jack improved rapidly. The doctor removed the sutures, his arm wound closed and scabbed, and he seemed to be in less pain. His color was good, and he grew stronger by the hour.

Four mornings after his fever broke, Becky went to see Jack only to find the bed mussed but empty. Frowning, she left his room and called in the corridor. When there was no response, she hurried downstairs and into the kitchen, where Mrs. Jennings was baking bread.

"Have you seen Mr. Fulton this morning?"

"Why no, my lady, I haven't."

Panic beat in Becky's chest. Where was he? Where could he be?

She searched the remaining rooms of the house, then looked for him outside. She called his name across the grounds, and even went as far as Mr. and Mrs. Jennings's cottage. All was serene and quiet on this sunny, crisp winter's morning.

She stumbled back into the house, worried, horrified that he might have left Seawood. Where could he have gone? It was so cold, and he hadn't taken the horse, so he must have departed on foot. He'd told her that when he'd come from London in search of her, he'd come by post to Launceston, begged a ride from a farmer to Camelford, and then walked the rest of the way. There were limited options for transportation between here and Camelford, and the village was five miles away. She wasn't sure he could walk that far now, not with his injury, not in this cold.

Lifting her skirts, she hurried upstairs to see if he'd left any evidence of where he'd gone.

There it was. A sheet of stationery on his pillow. How could she have missed it earlier?

She reached trembling fingers toward it. It was written in a shaky hand—Jack had used his healthier left hand to pen the note.

December 17, 1827

    Dearest Becky,

    I've remained under your attentive care long enough. I will not place you in further danger by staying at your home. Tom Wortingham promised to release the evidence two days ago, and he will stay true to his word. The authorities are now hunting for the murderer of the Marquis of Haredowne.

I know what I have done to you is unforgivable, but I cannot help myself but to be so bold as to beg you, one final time, to forgive me. My intentions at the beginning, even though I felt an undeniable longing for you from the start, were dishonorable. Detestable.

Two months ago, I believed that nothing was more precious than my own neck. Now, I know how wrong I was. I've learned that nothing will ever be more important to me than the few stolen moments in which I was gifted with your trust—and with your love.

Good-bye, my love. Be safe. Be happy.

Jack

Staring down at the paper, Becky sank onto the edge of the bed.

She'd sent letters with Sam on the afternoon of the thirteenth of December. Jack's letter said he was a fugitive as of the fifteenth.

The date imposed by Tom Wortingham was the fifteenth of December. There was no way that Sam could have arrived in London in time. She was too late. If Wortingham truly had revealed his evidence, the authorities would be scouring the countryside for Jack. They could be on their way to Cornwall to take him into custody this very instant.

"Oh, I am such a fool."

When Mrs. Jennings had given Becky the letter from Tom Wortingham, she'd said they hadn't fetched the mail for several days. Wortingham's letter must have been sitting at Camelford, waiting for days while Jack was in the throes of his fever.

Becky read the letter again and again. She took it everywhere she went, thought about nothing but its contents. Mr. and Mrs. Jennings shot her concerned glances the day long, but they otherwise left her alone.

At sunset, Becky sat at her window, staring out over the sea. A storm was brewing and the wind blew hard, whipping a white froth across the surface of the water.

Where had Jack gone? She hated the thought of him alone out there, yet she tried to remember that he was a strong man who'd seen worse weather than this at sea. He was perfectly capable of taking care of himself. The fever and his wound had weakened him, but he wasn't an invalid. He was solid, innately strong, and he could manage a winter storm well enough.

Still, she tried not to think about how he'd get a coat on over his wound or a glove on his hand, or the fact that he might not have been able to walk as far as Camelford.

Pulling his letter from her pocket, she read it once again. Slowly, this time. She analyzed each word.

There was no pretense in Jack's words. He'd been honest with her from the moment he'd walked into Seawood. At some point before coming to Cornwall, he'd gone to Tom Wortingham and informed him that the scheme was over. His remorse for what he'd done was palpable. He didn't blame her for shooting him; he'd considered it a well-deserved punishment for what he'd done.

Even though he no longer had a reason to proclaim his affection for her—for it was too late for him to make use of her money—he'd said he loved her.

And that look of defeat on his face when she'd told him it was the fourteenth—he'd known then that he was doomed, that he would soon be a fugitive. Still, he hadn't said a word. He hadn't asked her for a penny, or even for her help. And when he'd gone, he hadn't taken a thing with him that wasn't his own.

Maybe once he'd been dishonorable and selfish. Maybe once he'd tried to manipulate and seduce her, but no longer.

He'd stayed in her house for a few days after his fever broke, but now that she thought back on it, she realized he'd been preparing himself for his imminent departure. In the last twenty-four hours, he'd eaten heartily and exercised his body by walking around the house, and while he wasn't dismissive toward her, he didn't engage her in meaningful discussions. He remained politely aloof.

She hoped he would escape from the authorities. She hoped he would run far away. She prayed that he would be happy and safe, in a place where the shadow of his past deeds didn't loom over him. It would always loom over him here in England, even if nobody ever discovered the truth of what had happened between him and the Marquis of Haredowne. There were too many terrible, heartbreaking memories here for him.

But she would miss him. Lord, she missed him already.

Her hand opened, and his letter fluttered to the floor.

Squeezing her eyes shut, she leaned forward, pressing her palms and cheek against the cold panes of her window.

For the past two weeks, she'd sheltered her heart with pride and anger. But both were melting away.

She loved Jack. She loved him, and she didn't want to be without him. She believed his letter. He truly had no reason to lie to her, not any longer.

He'd shown that he was an honorable man. He'd made a terrible mistake, but he'd owned up to it. Then he'd suffered. He'd struggled to survive because she'd begged him to. And then, believing the authorities must be searching for him, he'd left her to keep her safe, holding onto his promise of survival.

The next morning, she sat in the kitchen with Mr. and Mrs. Jennings, staring at her porridge. The cold lump in her stomach didn't mix well with her breakfast, and she pushed her bowl away.

"Come now, my lady," Mrs. Jennings soothed, her wrinkles deepening with concern. "You need your strength."

Sighing, she tugged the bowl back toward her and took another spoonful of the buttery mush. As she tried to force it down, a booming knock sounded at the door.

Jack!

She flattened her hands on the table and leaned forward, trying to calm her suddenly pounding heart.

No! No, it couldn't be him. He wouldn't return. It had to be someone else. Her gut clenching, Becky looked up at Mrs. Jennings in alarm. In turn, Mrs. Jennings glanced pointedly at her husband, who shuffled out to see who it was.

Becky sat frozen, listening to the low sound of voices in the entry hall. Then she bolted out of her chair. "Garrett!"

She flew into the entry hall and straight into her

brother's arms. Garrett squeezed her briefly, then gently pushed her away, and she realized he was soaking wet and now she was, too. The storm had rolled in late last night, and rain fell in heavy sheets outside.

His gaze fixed on the stairway, and he shook her gently. "Where is he, Rebecca?"

Tristan stood at Garrett's side. "Mr. Fulton—" He hesitated, then pressed on, removing his gloves and taking her hand in his own. "Becky, Fulton's been accused of murdering a peer."

"You...know?" she breathed.

Tristan gave her a crisp nod, but there was sympathy in his dark eyes. "The Lord Mayor of London came to see us. Evidence was presented to the authorities on the fifteenth of December—incontrovertible proof of Fulton's guilt, including written evidence and two living witnesses."

Becky sucked in a breath. Jack had been right—Tom Wortingham certainly hadn't wasted any time in following through with his threats. "What about Sam?"

Tristan gave her a blank look. "Sam is here with you, isn't he?"

He confirmed what she'd already known—there was no way Sam could have arrived in London in time. Sam had crossed paths with Tristan and Garrett and none of them had known it. Surely Sam was at home in London by now, along with her now-useless order to deliver Tom Wortingham a promissory note for eighteen thousand pounds.

"No. He's in London. I sent him home." She shook her head, biting down against the tremble in her lower lip. "Why are you here?"

"Kate received your letter and recalled me to London," Garrett said. "I was heading to Yorkshire to search for you. I arrived home a few days before the mayor came to us."

"We all knew Fulton had come to Cornwall to search for you and must have arrived by now, yet we hadn't heard a word from either you or him," Tristan added. "We misled the authorities, claiming that we thought you might be in Yorkshire, but I daresay they'll puzzle out the truth soon enough."

"And they'll come here."

"Yes," Tristan said. "They could be here in a matter of days."

"Rebecca, where is he?" Garrett's voice held an edge of danger.

"Gone," she said miserably. "Jack Fulton is gone."

Tristan and Garrett had brought a traveling carriage so that they could make better time to Cornwall by changing out their teams and using lanterns to light the way at night. By noon, the carriage and a fresh team were forging through the rain toward London, with Becky, Tristan, and Garrett bundled inside.

As she left Seawood and Mr. and Mrs. Jennings behind, Becky had a melancholy feeling she might never see it again. The house still belonged to her, and it would always be special to her as the first place she had asserted her independence. She had learned some valuable lessons there.

On the other hand, the place held many sad memories of her family, of her mother, and now for Becky herself. It would always be the place where she'd shot Jack—where she'd almost killed him.

As the carriage drew farther away, the tightness in Becky's chest eased, and she felt a little lighter. She could assert her independence anywhere now. She didn't need Seawood to do it. She could leave the house behind without any regrets. Perhaps she'd even sell it—but not to someone who'd neglect it as she had. Only to a family who'd appreciate the forlorn beauty of the place, who'd turn the house into a home.

Becky gazed at the sheets of rain falling outside the window as they passed through the village of Camelford and straggled down the lonely stretch of road leading toward Devonshire.

"Becky," Tristan said, after nearly an hour of silence had pervaded the close interior of the carriage, "we need to know if Jack Fulton hurt you."

She jerked her head up and stared at him, wide-eyed. "What? No!"

Garrett leaned forward on the mud-brown carriage seat. He sat on the backward-facing bench across from her and Tristan. "It is fairly definite that Fulton murdered the Marquis of Haredowne. Tristan and I—" his eyes slid toward their cousin, "—well, we have reason to believe he misled you. He was after your money to pay off the witnesses to the murder to keep them quiet."

"Did you know something about this?" Tristan asked. "Is that why you vanished the night before your wedding?"

"I know everything." Taking a deep breath, she continued. "I discovered he planned to take my money after dinner that night. I heard Stratford and him discussing it—"

"Stratford?" Garrett gnashed his teeth. "That bastard—"

"Please. Listen to me." Becky faced her brother, her spine straight. "You both must know how I felt hearing the truth, after everything that happened with William. I felt like such a fool."

Tristan shook his head. "No, you weren't a fool. Fisk tricked us all. Just as Fulton did."

"But Jack is different," Becky whispered.

Garrett's lips twisted. "I don't think so."

She glanced down at her lap, then up again, knowing she must tell them everything. Clasping her hands tightly together, she said, "I shot him, Garrett. I hated him for what he'd done, and when he came here ... I shot him."

Tristan's eyes widened. "Is he ... ?"

"No ... There was some putrefaction in his shoulder, but he fought it. He was recovering but still weak when he left."

"Do you know where he went?"

"No. He slipped out at night." Becky swallowed hard. "But, you see, after I shot him, I discovered that he'd already gone to the man—the witness to the murder who was trying to blackmail him. He'd threatened to reveal the truth about Jack and Haredowne if Jack didn't give him twenty-five thousand pounds, and Jack told him he wasn't giving him a shilling." She twisted her hands in her lap. "He told him he wouldn't take my money. And—" she blinked, "—he regretted manipulating me, Garrett. I know he did. That was why he left. Because he understood exactly what he'd done and how it affected me. Because he knew the authorities were coming to arrest him, and I told him I wanted him to live, and escape was the only way for him to do it."

Her cousin and her brother stared at her, their expressions wary. Becky dug in her reticule and pulled out the letter from Tom Wortingham. "Read this. It's proof that Jack..." Her voice dwindled, but the remainder of the sentence resonated clearly in her mind.

Proof that Jack loves me.

The fair weather that Becky and Sam had experienced on the trip to Cornwall did not hold for her return to London. The road was muddy and flooded in spots, and the going was so rough and their progress so slow Becky thought she might go mad.

Jack occupied her thoughts so thoroughly she couldn't focus on anything else. Every day, every moment, she wondered where he was. What he was doing. Whether he was safe, warm, sheltered. Whether his arm continued to heal.

During the long hours in the carriage, she told Tristan and Garrett everything. She explained what had happened between Jack and Anne Turling and the Marquis of Haredowne, all she knew about Tom Wortingham and his history with Jack, and all of Jack's actions toward her before they'd left London and after he'd arrived at Seawood.

Her cousin and her brother took all the information in, Tristan shrewdly analyzing while Garrett's jaw remained tight and his eyes cold and hard. Nevertheless, by the time they rattled, damp and muddy, into Mayfair on the twenty-second of December, Tristan and Garrett had both admitted that they believed Jack was remorseful and that he'd redeemed himself by refusing to give Tom Wortingham Becky's money.

Kate was at the steps to greet them when they arrived at Garrett's house. Without waiting for a footman to hand her from the carriage, Becky leapt out of it and ran to hug her friend. Together, they went inside, and while Kate clucked about, making sure she was fed warm milk and hot soup, they talked about all that had passed.

"I'm so sorry I didn't explain anything to you before I left London," Becky said. "I just… Well, for once I wanted to solve the problem by myself, without hiding behind you and my brother. I wanted you to have a lovely Christmas, to spend it with your son…"

Reaching forward, her dark eyes serious, Kate took her hand. "I was so worried about you."

"I know. It was wrong of me to disappear without a word." Becky tried to smile at her friend. "Even when you fled from Calton House that morning four years ago, you left me a letter to explain what you'd done. But I didn't even give you that courtesy."

Kate sighed. "I knew you wouldn't have left unless it was important. And it comforted me to know that you took Sam with you. I knew he'd keep you safe."

She released Becky's hand and Becky took another mouthful of the savory soup the footman had placed before her.

"Is Sam here?"

"Yes, he arrived about a week ago. He brought the letters you wrote to Garrett and your solicitor asking him to draw up a promissory note. I begged your solicitor to wait until Garrett returned from Cornwall, though. Given all that had happened, I thought it might be too late for such an action."

"You were right to do so," Becky said. "Thank you."

Kate smiled. "Sam is well, and he's gone back to his regular duties."

Becky returned her smile. She'd known Kate would never have used Sam's loyalty to Becky against him, that he'd always have a position in the duke's household. "How is little Henry?"

Kate's smile widened to a grin. "He is the most delicious, precious baby in the world."

At twilight, Kate and Becky drew on their coats, hats, and mittens, and wandered into the back garden for a short evening walk. The garden at Garrett's London home was nothing compared to the vast acreage of the gardens at Calton House. Tended for many years by Sophie, who loved roses, the small London garden consisted of several tight rows of rosebushes that would bloom bountifully in the spring but now were nothing more than lonely dead sticks straggling upward from the icy ground.

"Do you miss Jack, Becky?"

Becky stopped walking and stared up at the darkening sky.

Taking her hand, Kate squeezed it hard. "It is clear to me that he loves you."

Becky raised her brows. She'd told Kate almost everything, but she hadn't mentioned love—she'd diligently avoided that particular topic.

Kate continued. "I know now that his initial intentions weren't honorable . . . but there is a certain look . . . the way a man looks at a woman when he's in love with her. When he thinks no one is watching him. It can't be denied, and it can't be counterfeited. I'm sure of it."

"Did Jack look at me like that?"

"Oh, yes. All the time."

"I want to find him," Becky said quietly. "I want to be with him, more than anything in the world."

"But Jack Fulton is a fugitive. You are sister to a duke of England."

"Yes. You're right on both counts."

"Oh, Becky..." Kate's eyes filled with tears. "I feel so terrible that this has happened to you."

Becky looked into her sister-in-law's eyes. "I want to be with him, Kate."

"Are...are you saying you should leave the country with him? Live in exile? Never see your family again?" Kate's voice was so tight it sounded as if someone was squeezing her throat.

The mere thought of leaving Kate and Garrett and the children filled Becky with pain. "I don't want to leave you." She paused, then took a deep breath and said quietly, "You would follow Garrett anywhere, wouldn't you?"

Biting her lip, Kate looked away. "You know I would. I'd follow Garrett to the ends of the earth."

Becky squeezed her sister-in-law's hand hard, and they stood quietly for a long moment, looking up at the bright landscape of stars.

"I must find him," she finally whispered. "But how?"

Tristan stayed for dinner that night, and Sophie joined them, but as they prepared to return to their own house, Becky drew Tristan aside.

"I know it might be too much to ask after all you have done for me," she murmured, "but I was hoping you might ask around. See if you can learn anything about where Jack might be."

He stared at her for a long moment, then he smiled. Tristan was a handsome man, and when he smiled, a dimple appeared in one of his cheeks and gave him a jaunty, boyish appearance.

"Of course, Becky. I'll see what I can find."

Chapter Twenty-three

Jack had taken a great risk by coming here. The danger crackled around him. They were looking for him, and he knew what would happen if he was found. The evidence was incontrovertible. He'd killed a peer. He would hang.

He'd only come into London at dawn this morning—Christmas Eve morning. He'd lingered in shadows and kept away from anyone remotely resembling a constable. Now, he stood on the bank of the Thames in the gloom. The temperature was below freezing, and the clouds hung low and gray in the sky. Faint steam wisped up from the river, and through the mist and the clusters of anchored ships, he could see the weathered side of the *Gloriana*.

Home. The ship was home to him—or at least it should feel that way. Yet he couldn't help not wanting to go back. He'd come to London with the intention of starting a new life, and returning to the *Gloriana* felt like moving backward. It felt like he was going into exile all over again.

This time it was worse, though. He wasn't going into exile. He was going into hiding. And this time, it would be forever. The *Gloriana* would leave London at noon today headed for Kingston, Jamaica, and he'd never return to England.

The cold stabbing through his wound, he pulled his hat low and sauntered onto the dock, looking for all the world as if he belonged there. The barge drew close, its occupants, wearing dark coats, hunched over in the cold as they rowed closer.

One of the rowers—it was the boatswain McKinley—raised his head, and a big smile split his face. "Ho there, Jack!"

He raised his good hand in a silent salutation as the other sailors called their greetings.

Taking a deep breath, he walked to the water's edge and boarded the barge as it drew alongside the dock. The action was natural to him but it was made awkward by his injury—he wasn't able to use his arm for balance, and he would likely have toppled had the hands of the sailors not reached out to support him.

"What happened to yer arm, there, Jacky lad?" asked one of the older sailors. Johnson was his name. He followed up the question by spitting a wad of tobacco over the side.

"Shot," Jack said tersely. He ignored the raised eyebrows of the men. They'd just have to be kept in suspense, or think that one of the men pursuing him had shot at him. No way in hell was he talking about what had happened since he'd been in England. They all knew that the case of murder against him had resulted in another warrant for his arrest, and he knew, via a message from Captain Calow, that the crew of the *Gloriana* had been questioned about his whereabouts. No one had known where he was at the time, but these men were his friends—his brothers—and even if they had known his whereabouts, they wouldn't have given him away.

He settled onto one of the benches, and the men fell into silence as they rowed to the ship.

He stared back at the dingy buildings lining the waterfront, at the dark figures of pedestrians hurrying through the cold to get home to their loved ones in time for Christmas.

One of them glanced at him, and a chill raced from the base of Jack's neck all the way to his toes. Even from this distance, he could recognize the pale stare of Tom Wortingham. Tom was still following him, apparently, but Jack couldn't fathom why. It was over. As promised, Jack hadn't delivered a shilling to Tom. And, as promised, Tom had exposed the truth to the authorities.

Turning away from the dock, Tom drew his collar high around his neck and disappeared into the landscape like a specter.

Jack closed his eyes and turned away from the place that had, once again, rejected him.

Becky rose early on Christmas morning. Kate, Aunt Bertrice, and the children were running to and fro making last-minute preparations for the holiday, but Becky felt little inclination to join in the excitement this year. She sat in her favorite velvet chair in the salon, a recent issue of the *Edinburgh Journal of Medical Science* lying in her lap. She usually devoured the journal as soon as she received one of the quarterly issues, but this morning the words seemed to dance on the page.

A soft knock on the salon door interrupted her restlessness, and Becky breathed a sigh of relief at the diversion. "Come in."

It was a maid. "My lady, Lord Westcliff is here. He wishes to speak with you, if you're available."

Becky laid the journal aside and jumped up from the armchair. "Tristan?" She smoothed her skirts. "Of course I will see him. Where is he?"

"He awaits you in the drawing room, my lady."

Becky hurried to the drawing room, threw open the door, and rushed in. Her cousin rose from one of the palm-print chairs.

"Oh, Tristan, do you have news of Jack?"

He nodded somberly. "Merry Christmas, Becky. Please sit down."

She nearly dove into the sofa in her haste. "Please, tell me what you have learned."

Tristan took a breath. "Well, as you asked, I've been searching for information regarding Fulton's whereabouts. I recalled the name of the ship he'd sailed on before he returned to England. So I went to the docks to review the record of vessels that had gone into and out of the Port of London in the last few weeks."

"And?" Becky held her breath. "Did you find any mention of the *Gloriana*?"

"Yes. It so happens that the *Gloriana* has been anchored near the London Docks since the beginning of the month."

Becky's fist flew to her mouth. "Is he on the ship?"

Tristan frowned. "I'm not certain—"

"Would he risk coming to London?"

Tristan shrugged. "He might. Especially if his best

means of escape from England was anchored in the Thames."

Becky rose. "Will you take me there? Please, Tristan—"

Tristan raised his hand. "Wait, Becky. The *Gloriana* has already left London. They sailed with the tide yesterday at noon."

His words sucked the air from her body. Deflated, she sank back onto the sofa, staring at him hopelessly. "If he was aboard—"

"Then he is gone."

"Where...where were they headed?"

"The West Indies. Jamaica."

The West Indies. A world away. Becky rose on trembling legs. "I—I'm sorry, Tristan, but I must be by myself for a while."

He stood, too. Reaching out, he pulled her into a quick hug. "I understand. I'm sorry." He tipped her chin up so she faced him. "I'll see you tonight at dinner."

"Yes...all right," she murmured. She stumbled away from him, then headed upstairs. She found her heaviest coat and told Kate she was going for a walk. Josie would chaperone her, but her lady's maid knew her well enough to know when she wanted to be left alone, and she'd keep her distance.

It looked as if it might snow. Frigid air bit at Becky's cheeks as she strode through Mayfair, but she hardly noticed. She walked with a brisk stride toward the banks of the Thames. She knew she'd never find the *Gloriana*. Even if the ship was still in port, the docks were too far away, beyond neighborhoods too dangerous to walk through. But something drew Becky in that direction. If only to look at the river and daydream that Jack might be near.

She walked as far as the Tower of London before she considered turning back. It was growing late and she should return before her family began to worry. She couldn't miss too much of Christmas. She glanced over her shoulder and saw Josie a few paces behind her, scowling. Clearly the maid believed they'd already ventured too far.

Becky walked past the Tower gates. Garrett would have been held prisoner here if he'd ever been accused of William's murder. But Jack wasn't a peer. More likely, he'd be imprisoned at Newgate, where the lowest of the criminals were held.

She'd walk just a little longer. She couldn't face Christmas with her family—not quite yet. Another few minutes, and then she'd turn around and go home. Sinking deep into her thoughts, Becky strode on.

She couldn't wait for Jack and the *Gloriana* to return from the West Indies. That would be a fruitless endeavor—not only would the *Gloriana* be gone for months, but when the ship did return, he probably wouldn't be aboard. He couldn't return to England.

That meant Becky would have to follow him. Secure passage to Kingston. As soon as possible.

Something hard poked her side. Startled, Becky jerked back, but a long, strong arm slid around her waist, pinning her against a tall body. Metal flashed at her waist, hidden from other pedestrians by the wide, faded black cape he'd swept around them both.

"Shh." The man squeezed one side of her waist and dug his pistol into the other. "Keep walking, if you please, my lady."

Gasping, she looked up at the man's pallid face. She knew instantly who it was.

Instinct told her to scream, to yank herself away and run to safety. But she held those compulsions at bay. The barrel of a gun was digging into her side. He could very well shoot her dead right here on the street.

Surely this man would know Becky wouldn't venture out on the streets of London on her own. She hadn't paid any attention to Josie since she'd glanced at her back at the Tower, yet she didn't dare look behind her. Becky didn't want to give her captor any hint that a third party might be watching.

So she simply said, in a quiet voice, "You're Tom, aren't you? Tom Wortingham?"

The man had a long, slender neck, and his Adam's apple undulated when he swallowed. Giving the appearance of looking straight ahead, gray eyes slid in her direction.

"Let's move along, shall we?"

He had a gentleman's accent. But she shouldn't be surprised at that, should she? Jack had said he was a vicar's son.

"Very well." She kept her breaths strictly regulated, kept her focus between the pavement in front of her and the man tugging her against him. He smelled of parchment when it turned yellow and began to flake at its edges. It wasn't a disgusting smell to Becky—it reminded her of old books. But it wasn't particularly appealing, either.

And the man himself wasn't appealing at all. He was too thin, and his skin had a yellowish, unhealthy hue. Was he a drunk? Nausea twisted through her as she contemplated the

additional danger he might pose to her if he was. Yet he
didn't smell of spirits.

His lips curved into a skeletal grimace. "You've made
it easy for me, my lady. We're almost home."

"Home? Where...?" Her voice dwindled away. She'd
walked nearly as far as the London Docks, she realized.
She'd passed the construction at St. Katharine's Docks,
quiet today due to the holiday, without paying any heed
to how far she'd gone.

Wortingham snickered softly. "You'll see soon
enough."

She found his politeness quite odd. She wondered if he
had the will to do it. Actually pull the trigger, shoot her,
if she called for help or tried to run. She could feel a
tremble in the touch of his fingers. Forcing her legs to
continue moving, she studied him covertly. He did look
afraid, but Jack had said he was desperate.

They walked along a street lined with dock warehouses—
close to where Tristan had said Jack's ship had been
anchored. But the *Gloriana* was already gone. Keeping
her voice steady, she asked, "You will hold me for
ransom?"

Wortingham hesitated, then said, "How much did our
friend Jack tell you, my lady?"

"I discovered the crux of it on my own. I daresay I'd
eventually learn the contents of any letter sent to my
home, and you were kind enough to send two—one to
London and one to Cornwall."

He gave a slow nod and spoke in a low voice, mindful
of the other pedestrians, though as they drew into the
neighborhood beyond the docks, the number of people
on the street thinned. "I shall send a note to His Grace

requesting a certain amount to guarantee your safety. I won't ask for much, and your brother is one of the richest men in England, isn't he? I just require a few thousand pounds—it will be nothing to him. Once he sends it along, I'll set you free. You'll go on your way, and I'll go on mine."

"Well, that sounds simple enough." Becky's voice sounded strong, but she felt lightheaded, and her knees had gone watery. Biting the inside of her cheek, she concentrated on giving the appearance of strength. How much farther would she have to walk with a gun pressed to her side? It bit hard into her skin. She'd have a round bruise above her hip when this was all over.

He's in trouble, Jack had said. Tom Wortingham had been a gentleman once. He must have been threatened with dire consequences if he did not pay off some large debt, otherwise he wouldn't go to such lengths, take such risks out in the open on Christmas Day.

"Here we are." Wortingham stopped at the door of a drab building that ran the length of the block. They must be in Shadwell or Wapping. Becky had never been in this area of London before. It was grayer and darker than the angry sky, and the stench of sewage and rot steamed up from the street and filtered through the air.

Where was Josie? Still Becky didn't dare look behind her. Had Wortingham done something with her? Had she run away as soon as she saw the stranger accosting her mistress? But Josie wouldn't do that... would she? Becky had thought her more spirited than to shrink away at the first sign of trouble. Yet Becky had never really seen her maid in a precarious situation before. There was no telling what she had done or where she was. Becky was tempted to ask Wortingham if he'd done something to her, but that would only put Josie in more danger, so she kept her lips sealed.

She glanced up at Wortingham's long face again. For whatever reason, he didn't frighten her as much as William had at the end. He didn't mean to rape her, she thought. He didn't even mean to hurt her, although he might threaten to, to be certain Garrett sent him the money.

But those were foolish thoughts. It certainly was possible he *did* mean to rape her and to kill her afterward. She didn't know him from Adam. He could be more evil than even William had been.

Yet he'd been Jack's friend for many years. They'd grown up together in Kent, had counted on each other. Until, apparently, a woman had come between them.

"Come along, my lady." Wortingham unlocked the brown-gray door and pushed her inside. She stumbled into a dark entry hall, ripe with the stench of urine, and he slammed the door and locked it behind them.

"You are not going to hurt me."

Even in the dim light, she could see that he wouldn't meet her eyes. "I'll do whatever I must do. If your brother proves troublesome—"

"He won't," she assured him quickly. "You'll get your money. Whatever you want."

He pushed her toward a narrow flight of stairs. "You first, my lady. I'll be right behind you."

Keeping the pistol firmly trained on her lower back, he nudged her up the stairs and down a long, narrow, poorly lit corridor. At the end of the corridor was a door that was in even worse repair than the rest of this dismal place. It hung crookedly on its hinges and was splintered near the handle.

She hesitated, turning her head to look at him over her shoulder. "I could scream," she said quietly. "Someone would hear me. Help me."

He shook his head. "Sure you can scream, but no one will come. No one pays attention to such things in places like these."

Against her will, her teeth began to chatter. She clenched them together, hard.

"But I'd advise you not to scream at all," he continued. "The sound tends to grate on a man's nerves. If you find it necessary to scream, I shall have to devise a way to silence you."

He fumbled with the broken door. Finally, he forced it to open with a loud, complaining squeal of bent hinges.

She saw the gun for the first time as he waved her inside. She knew enough about weapons to know that it was an expensive, well-made pistol, with an ivory grip and an engraved brass barrel.

"Sit down," he said.

The room was tiny, with a desk at one end and a dingy bed at the other and little space to move between the two. She stepped toward the desk, but he gave a harsh laugh. "No, not there. I require the chair. I've a letter to write."

Keeping her back straight, she lowered herself on the edge of the narrow bed, folding her hands in her lap.

"How did you know where I was going?" she asked.

"Oh, I didn't." Holding the gun in one hand, he pulled out the desk chair with the other. The chair was a spindly thing, with a frayed cloth seat and mismatched legs. "I've been waiting at your brother's house since yesterday morning. As soon as Jack sailed away, I knew you were my only remaining hope."

She tried not to flinch at his mention of Jack's name. She sensed that he watched her carefully even as he readied a sheet of stationery and dipped his pen into the inkwell.

"There must be another option. Something that doesn't entail a hanging offense. Something legal, perhaps."

He laughed heartily at that. "No, ma'am. I am far past that kind of hope, I'm afraid."

"Do you owe money?" she asked.

"Oh, yes," was his ready answer.

"To whom?"

"People it's best you know nothing of, my lady."

"You're a gentleman. How could you become involved with such a breed of people?"

His lips curled downward, but then he shrugged. "Why not? What is a gentleman with nothing? No money, no woman, nothing to call his own. One hides behind his demons, because to come out is to expose oneself, to face the disaster of one's life, isn't it?"

"But when you hide behind demons," she murmured, "you risk becoming one."

"Perhaps that is better than facing a failed life."

"And now they threaten you, these demons. They want money from you, but you cannot pay."

His features pinched. "That was Jack's responsibility."

She just stared at him, unable to argue.

"You cannot understand how deeply he is indebted to me," Wortingham continued. "He took everything from me, and then I protected him, for years. He was foolish to expect to owe nothing in return." He gave a humorless chuckle. "And now he is gone again. Vanished, like a coward. Again."

Becky pressed her lips together until they felt tight and bloodless. "Are you being threatened?"

He paused in the middle of scrawling, cocking his head at her and once again pointing the barrel of the gun in her direction. "I require the funds by the first of the year, or…" He shook his head. "Ah, but you ask too many questions, my lady. I daresay none of this is any of your concern."

She stared at the pistol. "I suppose not. I suppose you should write that letter quickly, for it seems we're both in a hurry. I'd like to be home with my family in time for dinner." She paused. "It is Christmas, you know."

Her own bravado shocked her. She was completely at this man's mercy, but even though her trembling had betrayed her, she'd shown very little fear. She'd changed in the past four years. Perhaps she had truly become brave, after all.

"Is it Christmas? I'd quite forgotten."

He was a rather poor liar, for a criminal.

He'd finished the letter. He folded it carefully. "Here's the challenging bit, my lady. There's a boy who lives with his mother down at the other end of the corridor. He's willing to run odd jobs for me for a penny or two when the occasion calls. We shall walk down the passageway, knock on his door, and give him an urgent missive to be delivered to the Duke of Calton. Will you be able to stand there, quiet as a mouse, while I relay the instructions to him?"

"I…think so."

"I'll count on your honesty, my lady." He hesitated.

"In truth, I'd expected you to have fainted by now, or at least succumbed to screaming for help. I suppose I can see what it is that Jack saw in you, after all."

She didn't have time to question that statement. They both turned to the sound of pounding footsteps outside, Wortingham swinging the gun toward the door just as it crashed inward.

A man leapt into the room, and Becky's breath caught in her throat. She'd expected the running feet to belong to her brother. Garrett wasn't the man who'd burst through the door, though.

Jack.

Tom Wortingham didn't even have a chance to get a good aim at Jack before Jack kicked the gun out of his hands. The gun went flying past Becky's legs and slid under the bed. Wortingham lunged out of the chair as if to retrieve it, but Jack was on him.

It was no contest. In less than five seconds, Jack had him down and was throwing punches at his face. Holding his injured right arm tight against his body, he pounded the other man with his left fist.

Blood flew out in a spray from Wortingham's mouth, and he moaned loudly, now completely defenseless against Jack's onslaught.

Oh, God. Jack was going to kill him.

"No!" Becky leapt toward the two men and grabbed Jack around his waist. He tried to throw her off, but she wouldn't let go. She clung to him, refusing to release him, pulling with all her might until they half rolled off Wortingham. "No, Jack! Please, stop!"

Suddenly, he clutched her shoulder and stared into her face, his light brown eyes wild with rage, with fear. For her, she realized with a jolt. He'd been afraid for her.

"Did he hurt you?" He shook her. "Did he hurt you, Becky?"

"No," she gasped out. "No. He didn't hurt me."

Some of the pressure released from her shoulder, and Jack wrapped his good arm around her and yanked her against him. "Oh, God," he said brokenly. "He had a gun... he might have..."

"No," she soothed, burying her face in the curve of his neck. "No, he didn't touch me."

Tom Wortingham, his face bleeding, was trying to crawl around them, his long arm reaching beneath the bed. Slipping his arm from around Becky, Jack thrust him away. Tom crashed against the chair, and a chair leg snapped as man and furniture went down in a flailing heap.

Jack retrieved the gun. His face took on a grayish hue when he pulled it from underneath the bed.

He turned his gaze to Wortingham. "So this is what you've been threatening me with? My father's pistol?"

Tom struggled to a seated position on the floor. "You know I retrieved it from the alley that night. I meant to hand it in as evidence against you, Jack, but I had enough evidence for a prosecution without it. And it's all I've got now, really." He waved his hand around the tiny, gray room. "You see I haven't got much."

"And you believe that's my fault."

Pressing his fist to his bloodied mouth, Tom stared at Jack, his shoulders shaking. "You're not supposed to be here. You sailed away on the tide. I saw you go."

"I didn't go anywhere." Jack looked at Becky. "The moment I boarded the *Gloriana*, I knew I couldn't leave

England without being sure...I knew he might come after you. I couldn't...leave you."

Before she could respond, he turned back to Tom, rage inflating his shoulders. Tom cowered on the floor, staring at Jack with true fear in his gray eyes.

Becky laid a hand on Jack's arm. "Jack?"

"What is it?"

"I don't want to hurt him."

He sighed, long and low. "Nor do I." His eyes were sad, and weary. Still holding the gun, he pressed his injured arm closer against his chest, wincing as he did so. "I know what we must do."

Chapter Twenty-four

All three of them looked up at the sound of shouts and footsteps in the corridor. Jack's good hand tightened around the gun. He hoped it wasn't one of Tom's agents. He hoped he wouldn't have to shoot anyone. He didn't even know if he could shoot a gun left-handed.

They all looked through the doorway, past the sagging door, which was now beyond repair.

"It's Garrett," Becky whispered two seconds before her brother burst into the room. Jack lowered his weapon as the duke reeled to a halt, looked from Becky to Tom to Jack.

"What...?"

Becky rushed to him and grabbed his shoulder. "Garrett...is Josie all right? Where is she?"

"She's at home."

Becky released an audible breath of relief. "What happened?"

Still keeping a wary eye on Jack and Tom, the duke

explained. "She ran into the house, wheezing for lack of breath, and said you'd been abducted from the street. She followed you and the man—" he narrowed his eyes at Tom, "—him?—as far as this building. She was able to describe exactly where he had brought you. I rode out here immediately. Once I was able to get inside, it wasn't difficult to find you."

Jack shook his head. Tom Wortingham was completely lacking in common sense. He hadn't even considered the fact that a lady would always bring a companion with her when she went for a walk.

"We have this situation under control," he told the duke.

"Fulton." Calton's voice was dry, and his gaze rested on the sling holding up Jack's injured arm, telling Jack he knew exactly how that injury had come to be there. "Thought you were en route to the West Indies."

"No."

The duke's cool gaze slid to Tom. "And you are...?"

A bead of sweat rolled down Tom's cheek. He looked frantically from Jack to Becky, unable to meet the duke's cold eyes, much less answer him.

Jack glanced at Becky, and she gave him a subtle nod. The small gesture of trust flooded him with hope. "This is Tom Wortingham, an old friend of mine. He has unfortunately found himself in desperate circumstances and has been on the verge of taking desperate measures."

Understanding dawned on the Duke of Calton's face. Tom made a strangled noise. Jack's old friend had no idea what he was about to do. He probably thought Jack would throw him to the wolves.

Well, that was exactly what he was going to do. But certainly not in the way Tom expected.

"Fortunately, we have a solution. He needs to get out of London immediately, you see," Jack continued, "and Becky and I have a plan to help him."

"Is this true, Rebecca?" the duke asked.

Becky gave her brother a grave nod.

"However, we are in need of your assistance, Your Grace," Jack said.

The duke's brow creased. "Oh?"

"Yes. The use of a carriage, perhaps? And one or two burly men to ensure Mr. Wortingham arrives safely at Gravesend."

In anticipation of poor weather tonight, Captain Calow planned to anchor the *Gloriana* at the bottom of the Thames. As soon as the weather promised to hold fair, the captain would haul anchor and be on his way. Calow was a strict disciplinarian, and always in need of more men. He especially enjoyed reforming weaklings into strong, resilient sailors, as he'd done once upon a time with a downtrodden eighteen-year-old Jack Fulton.

Tom would join the crew of the *Gloriana*. The experience would either kill him or save him from himself. Either way, Tom would be given the choice. If he proved strong enough, he could begin anew.

The duke studied them all. Jack, who met his icy blue gaze head-on. Tom, who shifted from foot to foot and mopped blood and sweat from his face with a dirty linen handkerchief. Last of all, Becky, who didn't speak, but moved to stand at Jack's side in a clear gesture of solidarity.

Tom Wortingham spoke little beyond the necessities. He went without complaint, packing a sheaf of paper and his pen and ink into a sack, along with a shirt, pair of trousers, and nightshirt. They left Wortingham's lodgings together and took a hackney coach back to Mayfair.

They went directly to the stables at Garrett's house and arranged for the carriage and men to escort Wortingham to Gravesend. Garrett retired into the house as one of the men nudged Wortingham inside the carriage. He sat, staring grimly at the rear-facing seat, as the man climbed in beside him and slammed the door shut.

Becky stood at Jack's side at the Curzon Street gate and watched the carriage carrying Tom Wortingham disappear around a bend in the road.

Becky turned to Jack. The streetlamp cast a pale glow over his long, dark coat and the black hat he wore low over his forehead. Yet she knew his eyes were latched on to her. She could feel them.

They gazed at each other, not touching, not saying a word.

It was really Jack, in the flesh. He was here, in London. He hadn't sailed away. His handsome face stared down at her, his eyes dark. For the first time since he'd burst back into her life today, she soaked him in.

He'd come back for her.

Finally, she blurted, "When you were sick...I tried to pay Mr. Wortingham. I sent my servant to London with a letter authorizing the delivery of the funds."

He gazed at her, his lips parted.

"But I didn't know you had only until the fifteenth of December. I was too late. I'm so sorry."

"I am the one who is sorry." His voice, low and

smooth, soothed the lump of emotion welling in her throat.

The world narrowed to a tiny capsule of space surrounding them. There were no pedestrians annoyed by them taking up space on the pavement. There were no rattling wheels or clomps of horses' hooves. The city tang of London disappeared to be replaced by Jack's salty, masculine scent.

There was only Jack and her. And Becky never wanted it to be any other way.

"I thought you had gone," she whispered, staring into his deep brown eyes. "Sailed away."

"I couldn't go. Not...not without seeing you one more time. To be sure—" He stopped abruptly.

Becky clenched her fists at her sides. "To be sure of what?"

"To be sure that there was no chance of your forgiving me. No chance for us. To be together."

"I was so angry with you," she said. "I thought I could never forgive you. But...oh, God, I *have* forgiven you, Jack."

"I'm not the man I was when I first met you."

"I know."

"I love you. So much."

She suddenly felt shy. It was hard to say, to admit to it after so many days of anger and hurt, and guilt. "I love you, too."

Once the words escaped her mouth, she felt light. Lighter than she had in years.

Slowly, a smile curved his wicked, handsome lips. She glanced at his arm, which he held protectively against his torso. "Is your arm—?"

"It is better."

"Did you hurt it when you fought Mr. Wortingham?"

"No."

"I'm so sorry I shot you."

"I was never angry at you for it, Becky."

"I know." She tried to smile, but her lips wobbled, and the expression disintegrated before it could take shape.

Ever so slightly, his face darkened. "I must leave England. I must leave this place—my homeland—forever."

Fear for him flared in her chest. "Every moment you spend here increases your danger." Truly cognizant of their surroundings for the first time, she glanced up and down the street, then to the gate, where one of Garrett's men watched them.

She turned up to the twilight sky, and a snowflake fell on her eyelash, clinging for a second before it melted away. "Look, it's snowing."

He tilted his face upward. "So it is."

She took hold of his good arm. "Come inside with us. It's safe and warm in the house."

This would be Becky's last Christmas in London. And she wanted nothing more than to say a proper good-bye to her family, with Jack at her side.

Becky's family welcomed him into the house warily, but within moments it was as if Jack wasn't a fugitive from the law who'd deceived their beloved sister, who'd tried to swindle them of their money, who'd hurt and betrayed them all. Amazingly, miraculously, they treated him as a member of the family. As a brother.

Becky sent for Lady Devore to join them for Christmas dinner, for the lady possessed no family in London, and

Becky wanted to say good-bye. The ever-thoughtful duchess pulled Jack aside to ask after Stratford, and hearing he would be spending the holiday alone, she hastened to send him an invitation as well.

After dinner, the Duke of Calton's family and their guests assembled in the drawing room. The duke and duchess reigned over the proceedings. Lord Westcliff and his wife, Sophie, were there, and Gary, Westcliff's son by his first marriage. Lady Bertrice was present as well, dressed in a green gown reminiscent of the enormous tree that brushed the ceiling. Lady Devore had arrived just before dinner, and Stratford had arrived as they were eating the turkey with sage and onion stuffing and mince pie.

Jack remained at Becky's side as if he were glued there. When she went to the wassail bowl, he followed her and fetched himself a glass as well. When she leaned toward the fire to warm her hands, he did the same. When she looked out the window to gaze out at the street-lamps casting a golden glow over the snow-covered street, he stood beside her. During dinner, at which the whole family was present, even the children, Jack asked Lord Westcliff to change seats with him so he could be near Becky. The viscount had agreed with a smile.

His sitting beside Becky had been against protocol, of course, but Jack had learned by now that this family cared very little for protocol. He rather thought they approved of his desire to sit beside the woman he loved.

After they'd retired to the drawing room, his gaze kept wandering toward the fir tree standing in the center of the room. It was brilliantly lit with tiny tapers and small wrapped gifts tied to all its branches. Becky, noticing his stare, chuckled. "Do you like it?"

"Well, yes, I do." He turned to her. "But... why?"

"When Tristan and Garrett were boys, they spent a Christmas at court. They did not have very happy childhoods, either of them, but that Christmas, Queen Charlotte had a tree erected at Windsor Castle. It was tied all round with strings of almonds and raisins, lit with candles, and each of the children who visited was given one of the toys from its branches. Ever since, Garrett has erected a tree of his own at Christmas, to make the day special for everyone, but most of all, I think, to delight the children as he was once delighted." She grinned. "And I think you are delighted as well."

"I think I am," he said, turning to her. He *was* delighted. By the tree, by the smell of plum pudding, by the smiles on the faces of the children. But mostly by the fact that Becky was at his side. And she showed no intention—or desire—to leave it.

She wouldn't leave him. Not now. Finally, there were no secrets between them.

"He'll give the children their gifts tomorrow. But for today, we just enjoy the beauty of the tree and its decorations."

"I am enjoying the beauty of the tree, and the beauty of this night," he said quietly. He took her hand in his and turned it over, tracing the delicate back with his thumb. "But I'm enjoying the beauty of my companion far more."

Her smile was dazzling. "You shouldn't flatter me."

"Nothing I say to you is flattery, Becky. I swear on my life, everything I ever say to you from this point forward is truth. I will never insult you with anything less."

She blinked those eyes—shaded indigo in the candlelight—at him. "Thank you."

Stratford sauntered up to them, holding a glass of wassail. He took up Becky's hand and kissed it, then slanted a glance at Jack. "So the truth is finally out."

"All of it," Jack agreed.

Stratford released a breath. "Glad to hear it." He grinned at Becky. "The chap was madly besotted, and terrified of botching it."

"Well," she said quietly. "He did botch it, and rather badly. But—" she returned his smile, "—I think he's atoned for his sins."

"Good." Lowering her hand, Stratford sobered. "So...you'll be leaving England then?"

"Yes," Jack said. "There's no other way—not now. We need to go quickly. We'll be leaving for Portsmouth tomorrow."

"Where are you headed?"

"America," Becky breathed. Jack squeezed her arm.

Stratford raised a brow. "So far away?"

"Yes. Becky's always wanted to visit America. We don't know if we'll stay—maybe we'll end somewhere else. But we thought we'd try it. Explore a little."

Stratford didn't respond. A melancholy expression crossed his face. "I'll miss you, old chap."

Becky excused herself to play a carol for the children on the pianoforte, and as she walked away, Jack asked him, "What about you?"

"Me?"

"Yes. What will you do?"

Stratford blew out a breath. "Ah, what I've always done, I suppose. Sleep my days away and drown my nights in debauchery and vice."

"Do you know what I think?"

"What's that?"

"I think you need to find a woman."

Stratford laughed bitterly. "I have women aplenty." He rubbed his thumb along the lip of his cup of wassail. "I don't know how to change my life, but I've tried just about every woman I could, and none has changed a damn thing."

"But you want it to change, don't you?"

Stratford shrugged. "Not really. What for?"

Jack's gut clenched. He reached out with his good hand to grasp Stratford's shoulder. God, but he didn't want the earl to end like Tom Wortingham. "Good luck, man."

Stratford nodded. "And you, too. I daresay you'll be needing it more than me."

"That might be true."

He took his leave of Stratford and headed to the pianoforte as Becky readied herself to play. Just as he approached her, the Duke of Calton asked for a private word.

Becky looked up at her brother in alarm, but Jack gave her a reassuring smile. He'd seen this coming, and he was ready for it. Her brother—her entire family—cared deeply for her, and it was his responsibility to convey the fact that he cared as deeply as they did.

Exiting the room to the opening strains of "God Rest You, Merry Gentlemen," he followed the duke into the dark, wood-paneled study where he'd first proposed to Becky. The duke slid behind the desk and lowered himself onto his chair. He grabbed the decanter sitting on the desk's edge and held it toward Jack. "Brandy?"

"No, thank you."

The duke set it down. He didn't pour himself a glass, either. "Sit, Fulton."

Jack lowered himself into the closest chair, and keeping his injured arm pressed tightly against his chest, he placed his good hand on the arm.

"Wortingham was blackmailing you. Why?"

"I never asked him details about why he needed the money, but he said it was a gambling debt. I just thought..." Jack closed his eyes.

"What did you think?" the duke asked.

Jack shook his head. "As angry as I was with Tom for making those demands, a part of me understood him. I hoped that somehow... if I could get the money, I could heal him, mend his mind, bring him back to the person he once was." He laughed without humor. "And in doing so, I could finally leave the past behind. *Stupid*. There was only one thing that could bring me out of my past."

"What was that?"

Jack met the duke's gaze. "Becky."

Calton made a noncommittal noise in his throat. "The authorities are hunting for you."

"Yes, they are."

"You put us all at risk this night by coming to my house."

"I am sorry for that."

The duke leaned forward. He hadn't blinked, hadn't taken his eyes from Jack.

"Rebecca has told me everything. Everything that passed between the two of you." He spoke very slowly. "She wishes to marry you."

Jack nodded slowly. "I certainly hope so, sir. I wish to

marry her, as well. That hasn't changed, not since the first time we spoke in this room."

"I'm going to make you an offer."

Jack raised his brows. "Are you?"

"Leave this house. Leave my sister in peace, and I'll ensure you get out of England safely. With your pockets brimming."

Jack went stiff all over. "No."

The duke cocked his head. "Don't you wish to know the amount?"

"No."

"It's more than Rebecca will bring you."

Jack ground his teeth. "Do you think—after all that has passed—that I want her damn money?" Rising, he thrust a frustrated hand through his hair. "God damn it."

Steepling his hands in front of him, the duke leaned back in his chair. "It is a good offer."

Jack stared at him, too furious to speak, not trusting himself to move.

"Think on it."

Jack slapped his good hand on the desk and leaned forward until his nose was inches from the duke's. "I'm not going to think on it. I don't want your damned money or your damned freedom. I want Becky."

The duke appeared unaffected by Jack's show of temper. "You intend to take her away from her family. From those who love her and want nothing more than to keep her safe. With you, her happiness, her life, and her livelihood will be at risk. What man wants that for his sister?"

"Her happiness is my only priority. *I* will keep her safe."

"And when have you proven that you can be trusted to do that? You have hurt her."

"No more," Jack ground out. "You have my word."

"And what is your word worth?"

"It is all I have. Your sister, despite everything, trusts me. And if that's all I ever have, that will be enough. It's all I care about."

"Good." The duke straightened, and so did Jack. "Frankly, if what you told my sister is true, and you killed the Marquis of Haredowne in defense of a woman, then I cannot fault you. It is an honorable man who will go to any lengths to protect an innocent."

"I will do anything for Becky, but I will never call myself honorable. It is not an honorable man who marries a woman in order to use her money to pay off his blackmailer."

"Sit down, Fulton."

Jack returned to the chair he'd occupied before, and the duke's light blue eyes pinned him to it. "You *didn't* marry Rebecca for her money."

"I didn't succeed. But I would have."

"Mm. But I will never think that was the primary reason you wanted her." Calton folded his hands on his desk. "If you lacked scruples so entirely, you would have given up on her the moment she demanded more time, right here in this room. You would have pursued and seduced someone else, or found another way to obtain fifteen thousand pounds for your old friend. But you didn't. You wanted my sister for more than her money."

Jack met the other man's stare. If he'd met Becky without Tom Wortingham's threats hanging over his head, he still would have wanted her. It had been more than her money from the very beginning. Deep inside, he'd known it all along.

Again the duke peered at Jack with those disconcerting eyes. "But do you love her? As much as you loved the girl you killed the marquis for?"

He winced. This was the hard part. He wouldn't speak ill of Anne, and yet he wouldn't hold her on a pedestal. He couldn't allow anyone to think he cared for Becky any less than he had once cared for Anne, because it simply wasn't true. "Anne was my first... she will always hold a place in my memories. But Becky is here now. She is real. She is my life."

Calton drew back sharply, looking shaken. "I understand perfectly."

All of a sudden, Jack understood, too. The duke had loved Sophie, Lady Westcliff, from the time he was young. But now he'd found his partner for life in his duchess.

"Look, I haven't gone about this in the proper way," Jack said. "God knows you cannot wish for a scoundrel, a criminal, and a liar to become part of your family. But I love your sister. Again, I would ask you to allow me the honor of becoming her husband. The deceit I engaged in—it was to my own detriment, and not only physically." He gestured at his bandaged arm. "I will never forgive myself for lying to Becky. For hurting her." He took another breath, this one shaky. "But by God, I'm going to spend the rest of my life making it up to her."

Calton paused, and then he said slowly, "But not in England."

"No. A life in England...I wanted it. I tried. But it is not meant to be."

"You must leave before the authorities learn that you have been here."

"Yes."

"Where will you go?"

Jack glanced away, then back at the duke, meeting his eyes squarely. "I took the liberty of arranging passage to America under an assumed name. A ship departs next week from Portsmouth."

Calton shook his head. "You expected she would submit to this plan?"

"I hoped...I prayed that she'd find it in her heart to forgive me my sins. I couldn't go away without being sure." Something in him softened as he remembered the look of anticipation and excitement in Becky's eyes when he'd drawn her aside earlier and told her his plan.

"What name will you assume?"

Jack tightened his fingers over the armrests, steadying himself. "James. Jack and Rebecca James. I hope you will not think it presumptuous of me, but I have watched your family for the past month, and it is so unlike mine. I can only hope the family Becky and I will build in America will be as strong, stable, and loving as the one you have built here in England."

Even if it was only the two of them—if Becky was infertile as she suspected—he maintained that hope. They would build a happy life together. Each would be all the family the other truly needed. And far away, Becky would always have her loved ones in England.

The duke nodded. "No, it isn't too presumptuous. In

truth it will comfort me to know that my sister will be known by her true name. I've suffered her as a Fisk for four years too long. But—" the duke's eyes narrowed, "—you *will* marry her properly?"

"Yes. I promise you that will happen as soon as we arrive on American soil."

"Are you suggesting that you and my sister live in sin for the entire duration of the voyage to America?"

"Well..." Jack shifted uncomfortably.

The duke's eyes narrowed until only the thinnest line of blue showed. "No."

"No?"

One edge of the duke's lips tilted upward. "The special license you obtained last month is still valid, is it not?"

When Garrett and Jack returned from their conference, Garrett called for quiet, then announced, "The curate has been summoned. Jack Fulton will marry Rebecca tonight."

Becky's jaw dropped. She stared wide-eyed at her brother before Kate, Sophie, and Cecelia whisked her out of the room. As they hurried out, though, Becky caught Jack's eye. He was smiling at her, his eyes full of love. It surged into her, through her, and she smiled, too. She still had a silly smile pasted on her face when the ladies tumbled into her room.

Becky stood in the center of her bedchamber in a blissful daze as the women bustled about.

Sophie sent for the dress she'd worn when she remarried Tristan four years ago, and that had been altered for Becky when she'd planned to marry Jack at the beginning of the month.

Josie, who'd been hurrying to pack Becky's belongings to take with her on the voyage to America, took charge of the proceedings, ordering the other women about as if they were the servants and she the mistress. None of them cared; instead they jumped to search through Becky's stockings drawer, her clothes press, her rack of shoes, her box of jewelry.

The sapphire blue silk Becky had worn for Christmas dinner pooled around her feet, and Becky leaned down to tuck the arrowhead Jack had given her into her garter. When she straightened, four women were staring at her, frowning, and she laughed. "It's for luck!"

Shaking her head and muttering about the eccentricity of the James family, Kate went to her own room to find a certain hairpin that matched perfectly with the dress. The other ladies scattered around, returning to their various tasks.

As Becky tied the leather strip that held the little carved man from Fiji around her neck, Josie leaned close and whispered into her ear. "My lady, you haven't need of anything for your flux, do you?"

Becky's heart tumbled over in her chest. Dropping her hands, she turned slowly to her maid. "What day is it, Josie?"

"Why, it's Christmas, of course. The twenty-fifth of December."

Becky's flux came like clockwork every twenty-eight days, and Josie always kept track of what day she was on in the cycle. "How many days am I late?"

"Fourteen, my lady," the maid said primly.

"A fortnight!" She pressed her hand to her stomach and stared at her pink-cheeked maid.

Josie grinned. "I daresay it's a good thing you're marrying tonight."

Becky's breath caught. "I daresay it is."

Kate burst in, victoriously holding up the pin she'd found. When her eyes met Becky's, she dropped her hand. Her dark brows snapped together. "What? What is it?"

Forgetting the other women in the room, Becky rushed to her sister-in-law and hugged her tight. "Oh, Kate, I think I am with child."

Kate burst into tears.

Becky drew back. "Don't tell me you are unhappy! You know I thought... I thought after William that I was barren."

Kate drew out her handkerchief and blew her nose. "No, my dearest," she said between sniffs, "I am so happy for you. You will make a lovely mother. I'm just—well, I just had a baby myself, and I'm terribly emotional. Forgive me for weeping; what a heartless response."

"No, of course not." Becky hugged her tighter. "Not heartless at all."

"Oh, Becky, darling." Sophie's amber eyes glowed with pleasure. "What lovely news this is."

Becky met Cecelia's dark, serious eyes. Her friend smiled warmly and took her hands. "This is what you want most of all... Jack, and now this. I am so very happy for you."

Fifteen minutes later, the women made their way downstairs, smiling but with tears in their eyes. Sophie's wedding dress was a beautiful gown of brilliant white Italian silk, its skirts full and flounced, and above the flounces, an embroidered wreath of silver and white flowers trailed around the skirts up to the bodice.

Kate opened the door for Becky. Dropping her skirts, Becky stepped into the drawing room. All conversation ceased as everyone turned to her.

The curate stood beside the Christmas tree. Garrett and Tristan stood to his left, and the children were seated on the sofas and chairs. Jack stood beside the curate, tall and handsome in a simple black waistcoat and tailcoat and white shirt and cravat. His smile carved deep grooves in his cheeks as he looked at her, his gaze lingering on the artifact from Fiji at her neck.

Becky paused just inside the door, the happiness surging so powerfully inside her, she thought she might burst with it.

Jack reached out his good hand. "Are you ready?" His voice was calm and quiet, but it resonated through the room, and Becky could feel everyone's questioning eyes on her.

"Yes." She stepped forward and took his hand. He squeezed her fingers, and the curate began.

Jack said he'd take her as his wife. He promised to love her, comfort her, honor and keep her as long as they both lived. After Becky made similar promises, the curate asked who would give her away, and Garrett stepped beside her and laid a hand on her shoulder. "I will."

The curate turned back to Jack and recited the vows. Jack repeated them solemnly. She watched his face, watched the passion—and the honesty—in his brown eyes as he spoke.

"Please take Mr. Fulton's right hand, my lady."

She took his hand gently, conscious of his injury and careful not to hurt him. He held her hand limply—he couldn't quite close his fingers yet—but warmth and comfort spread from his fingers through hers. She gazed into his eyes as she recited her own vows.

When it was done, Jack pushed a ring onto her finger. It was a beautiful gold band that glittered in the candle-light. "My mother's," he whispered.

"Please repeat the following words," the curate said, and then he began the vows.

"With this ring," Jack recited, "I thee wed and with my body I thee worship—"

Becky smiled.

"And with all my worldly goods I thee endow."

Rebecca fought the urge to giggle, but her lips twitched. She was still the one with the worldly goods, and she would be the one endowing them on him—and willingly, too.

Jack saw the expression on her face and grinned through the remainder of the speech. "In the name of the Father and of the Son and of the Holy Ghost. Amen."

The curate then spoke for a long while, his voice droning in her ear, but all she could do was smile gid-dily up at Jack. Finally, they were pronounced man and wife.

Becky gazed up into her husband's face. He smiled down at her, and then, drawing her close with his left arm, he bent and kissed her.

It had been so long since they'd kissed. It was a life-time ago. His lips were soft and warm, and they tasted like plum pudding and wassail, but there was a deeper taste, too. The rich, salty, masculine taste of Jack. She loved that taste, and forgetting everything else, she explored it, cupping her hands behind his head and sinking her fingers into his soft, sun-kissed hair.

Jack. *Her husband*. It was finally true. And she'd never been happier.

Gently, he pulled away. Becky blinked, and he came into focus. Dark shadows loomed behind him. Garrett, she realized, was scowling at them. Tristan, too, though his expression was somewhat more benevolent. Kate, Sophie, Cecelia, Lord Stratford, and the children crowded around to congratulate them. Her cheeks heated, but Jack smiled at her, and she couldn't help grinning back.

Epilogue

On New Year's Eve, the weather was cool but not frigid. Last week's wind had given way to calmness, and most of the Christmas snow had already melted. After they made certain their luggage had been packed in their cabin, and their servants—Josie and Sam had volunteered to go with them to America—were properly situated, Jack and Becky huddled together on deck beneath a blanket. The sailors went about their duties behind them, silent for the most part except for an occasional harsh order from a superior.

"Good-bye, England," Becky whispered as the *Washington* slipped through the waves and the busy Portsmouth waterfront vanished into the fog.

Jack tightened his arm around her. Since they'd married, he'd felt a swirling combination of jubilation and guilt for taking Becky away from everything and everyone she'd ever known. The guilt had intensified when he'd witnessed their tearful good-byes.

"I'm sorry, sweetheart. I know how much it hurts you to leave your family."

She smiled wistfully. "They are all that I've ever had, until now. But I know that they will always be here for me. We will write to one another. I hope that someday, when we are settled, some of them will visit us."

"I hope they will."

She leaned against his left side, her warmth permeating the thick wool of the blanket he'd wrapped around their shoulders.

"Jack?"

"Yes?"

"Do you think Tom Wortingham will survive?"

Jack sighed. "I honestly don't know. In his warped way, Tom cannot forget Anne. He always loved her, but she never returned his affection. Not in the way he wanted. And he was never able to move beyond that."

"Even if she had returned his affection," Becky mused, "he was only a vicar's son, and she was untouchable."

Jack's chest went tight in mourning for the loss of his one-time friend. "Yes, exactly. His actions were his means of vengeance, rooted in jealousy and competitiveness. And what did he gain from them? He had no money, no vocation, for he never followed his father's footsteps and took orders. He dwelled only in the past. How long can a man live in such a state?"

"But now there is hope for him."

"There might be."

"What about you?" she asked quietly. "Do you dwell in the past?"

In a way he had. When he returned to England the

memories had surged back, and Tom's blackmail had
pushed those memories to the forefront. But now they
were sailing away from Tom, away from the past, away
from England. He was gliding toward a new life, with a
woman he loved beyond his wildest imaginings.

Jack sighed, and with the release of breath, he released
the last vestiges of those feelings he'd kept bottled up
inside for so long. Anger, grief, guilt, bitterness, despair.
All of it blew away, leaving him clean and whole, and
ready to live again.

"No," he murmured. "I don't dwell in the past. Not
anymore."

She sighed contentedly, and he continued. "Tom has
existed in a perpetual state of anger and resentment. He
believes happiness is unattainable."

"That is sad." She slid him a glance, her eyes reflecting
the blue-gray of the ocean. "Yet despite his unhappiness,
I cannot bring myself to like him. He caused you to be
accused of a crime for which I cannot fault you. No one
could, if they knew the story behind it."

"The law could."

Becky shivered, and he moved to stand behind her,
wrapping the blanket around them both, careful of his
shoulder, which still hurt like hell whenever anything
touched it. She clutched its ends together in front of her
while he slipped his good arm around her waist and
rested his chin atop her blue velvet bonnet.

"Are you warm enough, sweetheart?"

"Yes." She paused, and her stomach drew inward as
she sucked in a breath. "Jack?"

"Hm?"

"I...should tell you something."

His skin prickled at the hesitation in her voice. "Oh? What is it?"

"I..." Dropping the blanket, she turned within the circle of his arm and looked into his face. Her changeable eyes had deepened and darkened. "I think... well, I might be with child."

Everything went still and hollow. Nothing seemed to move. Even the ship seemed to pause in its glide through the waves.

Finally, he found his voice. "Is... is that what you want?"

"I..."

"I mean, are you happy?"

Pressing her lips together, she nodded.

He touched a fingertip to her stomach. "Our child?"

"Yes. I am not certain it has truly happened... but I've read about the symptoms—" a pink flush suffused her cheeks, "—and they are all there. I'd been distracted and hadn't noticed..."

He pressed his hand flat over the thick, dark layers of her stays, bodice, and coat. Shouldn't she have told him sooner? Was she frightened he wouldn't want to marry her if he discovered she was with child? He shook his head, confused.

"How long have you known?"

"Since Christmas. Moments before I came downstairs to... marry you." She shifted uncomfortably and looked up at him, a frown creasing her brow. "Everything has been too hectic since then, what with arranging for everything and saying our good-byes to everyone. I was waiting for the right time to tell you." She hesitated. "Are you unhappy?"

"God, no. No, Becky. I…" He swallowed hard. "I've never been happier."

She buried her face in his coat. "I'm happy, too," she murmured, her voice muffled. "So happy."

"I love you," he said fiercely.

The ship seemed to resume its smooth motion, and he saw glimpses of the shoreline through the fog as they moved away from England and toward their new life. One he would spend every moment savoring.

She shuddered.

"Are you still cold?"

"A little."

"Let me take you below. Your maid said there would be some tea ready. That should warm you."

She looked into his eyes, and her lips curved into a beautiful smile. A seductive indigo sparkle lit her eyes. "Nothing can warm me as you do, Jack."

Her words heated him from the inside out. His heartbeat thrummed through his veins, flushing his skin. "Well, then," he said with a grin, "I'd best lock the door."

He led her down to their sumptuously appointed cabin, and as promised, he drew the bolt behind them. Turning back to face the interior of the room, he smiled at Becky as she untied the ribbons of her bonnet. Steam wafted lazily from a silver tea service set on the table, but he ignored it.

Jack tugged the bonnet from his wife's head, tossed it aside, then pulled her into his arms and proceeded to warm her.

Thoroughly.

After five years in the West Indies,
Serena is back in London.
But so is the one person she never
expected to see again . . .
Jonathan Dane—her very own
original sin.

⁓

Please turn this page
for a preview of

Confessions of
an Improper Bride

the first book in Jennifer Haymore's
sensual new series!

Available in 2011.

Off the coast of Antigua
July, 1822

Serena had not slept well since the ship had left Portsmouth. Eventually, the roll of the *Victory* always lulled her into a fretful sleep, but before then she'd lie awake for hours next to her sleeping sister, her mind tumbling over the ways she could have managed everything differently. How she might have saved herself from becoming a pariah.

Tonight was different. She'd started off the same, lying beside a sound-asleep Meg and thinking about Jonathan, about what she might have done to counter the force of the magnetic pull between them. Sleep had never come, though, because a lookout had sighted land yesterday afternoon, and Serena and Meg would be home tomorrow. Home to their mother and younger sisters, and bearing a letter from their aunt that detailed her disgrace.

Meg shifted, then rolled over to face Serena, her brow furrowed, her gray eyes unfocused from sleep.

"Did I wake you?" Serena asked in a low voice.

Meg rubbed her eyes and twisted her body to stretch her back. "No, you didn't wake me," she said on a yawn. "Haven't you slept at all?"

When Serena didn't answer, her twin sighed. "Silly question. Of course you haven't."

Serena tried to smile. "It's near five. Will you walk the deck with me before the sun rises? One last time?"

The sisters often rose early and strode along the deck before the ship awakened and the bulk of the crew made its appearance for morning mess. Arm in arm, talking in low voices and enjoying the peaceful beauty of the sun rising over the bow of the ship, the two young ladies would stroll along the wood planks of the deck, down the port side and up the starboard, pausing to watch the sun rise over the stern of the *Victory*.

What an inappropriate name, Serena thought, for the ship bearing her home as a failure and a disgrace. She'd brought shame and humiliation to her entire family. "Rejection," "Defeat," or perhaps "Utter Failure," would serve far better for a ship returning Serena to everlasting spinsterhood and dishonor.

Serena lit the lantern and they dressed in silence. It wasn't necessary to speak—Serena could always trust her sister to know what she was thinking and vice-versa. They'd slept in the same bedroom their whole lives, and they'd helped each other dress since they began to walk.

After Serena slid the final button through the hole at the back of Meg's dress, she reached for their cloaks hanging on a peg and handed Meg hers. It was mid-summer, but the mornings were still cool.

When they emerged on the *Victory*'s deck, Serena tilted her face up to the sky. Usually at this time, the stars cast a steady silver gleam over the deck, but not this morning. "It's overcast," she murmured.

Meg nodded. "Look at the sea. I thought I felt the ship being tossed rather more vigorously than usual."

The sea was near black without the stars to light it, but gray foam crested over every wave, and up here on deck, the heightened pitch of the ship was more clearly defined.

"Do you think a storm is coming?"

"Perhaps." Meg shuddered. "I do hope we arrive home before it strikes."

"I'm certain we will." Serena wasn't concerned. They'd been through several squalls and a rather treacherous storm in the last few weeks. She had faith that Captain Moscum could pilot this ship through a hurricane, if need be.

They approached a sailor coiling rope on the deck, his task bathed under the yellow glow of a lantern. Looking up, he tipped his cap at them, and Serena saw that it was young Mr. Rutger from Kent, who was on his fourth voyage with Captain Moscum. "Good morning, misses. Right fine morning, ain't it?"

"Oh, good morning Mr. Rutger," Meg said with a pleasant smile at the seaman. Meg was always the friendly one. Everyone loved Meg. "But tell us true, do you think the weather will hold?"

"Oh, aye," the sailor said, a grin splitting his wind-chapped cheeks. "I think so. Just a bit o' the overcast." He looked to the sky. "P'raps a splash o' rain, but nothin' more to it than that, I daresay."

Meg breathed a sigh of relief. "Oh, good."

Serena pulled her sister along. She probably would have tarried there all day talking to Mr. Rutger from Kent. It wasn't by chance that Serena knew that he had six sisters and a brother, and his father was a cobbler—it was because Meg had hunkered down on the deck and drawn his life story out of him one morning.

Perhaps it was selfish of her, but Serena wanted to be alone with her sister. Soon they would be at Cedar Place, and everyone would be angry with her, and Mother and their younger sisters would divide Meg's attention.

Meg went along with her willingly enough. Meg understood—she always did. When they were out of earshot from Mr. Rutger, she squeezed Serena's arm. "You'll be all right, Serena," she said in a low voice. "I'll stand beside you. I'll do whatever I can to help you through this."

Why? Serena wanted to ask. Serena had always been the wicked daughter. She was the oldest of five girls, older than Meg by seven minutes, and from birth, she'd been the troublemaker, the bane of her mother's existence. Mother had thought a Season in London might cure her of her hoydenish ways; instead it had proven her far worse than a hoyden.

"I know you will always be beside me, Meg," she said. And thank God for that. Without Meg, she'd truly founder.

She and Meg were identical in looks but not in temperament. Meg was the angel. The helpful child, ladylike, demure, and always unfailingly sweet. Yet every time Serena was caught playing with the slave children or running on the beach with Bertie Parsons, the baker's son, or hitching her skirts up and splashing into the ocean, Meg stood unflinchingly beside her. When all the other people in the world had given up on her, Meg remained steadfast, inexplicably convinced of her goodness despite all the wicked things she did.

Even now, when she'd committed the worst indiscretion of them all. Even now, when their long-awaited trip to England for their first Season had been cut sharply short by her stupidity.

"As long as you stand beside me," Serena said quietly, "I know I will survive it."

"Do you miss him?" Meg asked after a moment's pause.

"I despise him." Serena's voice hissed through the gloom. She blinked away the stinging moisture in her eyes.

Meg slid her a sidelong glance. "You've said that over and over these past weeks, but I've yet to believe you."

Pressing her lips together, Serena just shook her head. She would not get into this argument with her sister again. She hated Jonathan Dane. She hated him because her only other option was to fall victim to her broken heart and pine over him, and she wouldn't do that. She wouldn't sacrifice her pride for a man who had been a party to her ruin and then turned his back on her. That would show weakness, and Serena was anything but weak.

Serena turned her gaze to the bow of the ship. The lantern lashed to the forestay cast a gloomy light, revealing a muddy fog swirling over the lip of the deck.

Smiling, she turned the tables on her sister. "You miss Mr. Langley far more than I miss Jonathan, I assure you."

Meg didn't flinch. "I miss him very much," she murmured.

Of course, unlike her own affair, Serena's sister's had followed propriety to the letter. Serena doubted Commander Langley had touched her sister for anything more than a slight brush of lips over a gloved hand. They danced exactly twice at every assembly; he'd come to formally call on Meg at their aunt's house three times a week for a month. In the fall, Langley was headed to sea for a two-year assignment with the Navy, and he and Meg had agreed, with her family's blessing, to an extended courtship. He'd done everything to claim Meg as his own short of promising her marriage, and Langley wasn't the sort of gentleman who'd renege on his word.

Unlike Jonathan.

Stop! Serena commanded herself.

She patted her sister's arm. "I wager you'll have a letter from him before summer's end."

Meg's gray eyes lit up in the dimness. "Oh, Serena, do you think so?"

"I do."

Meg sighed. "I feel terrible, you know."

"Why?"

"Because it seems unfair that I should be so happy and you..." Meg's voice trailed off.

"And I am disgraced and ruined, and the man who promised he'd love me for all time has proved himself a liar," Serena finished in a dry voice. Nevertheless, it hurt to say those words. The pain was a deep, sharp slice that seemed to cleave her heart in two. Even so, Serena hid the pain and kept her face expressionless.

Meg's arm slid from her own, and tears glistened in her eyes. Meg knew exactly how Serena was feeling, so it didn't matter that she struggled so valiantly to mask her feelings. Meg always knew. She always understood. It was part of being a twin, Serena suspected.

Meg stopped walking and turned to face her. "I'll do whatever I can...you know I will. There is someone out there for you, Serena. I know there is. I *know* it."

"Someone in Antigua?" Serena asked dubiously. Their aunt had made it quite clear that she would never again be welcome in London. And Meg knew as well as she did that there was nobody for either of them in the island they'd called home since they were twelve years old. Even if there were, she was a debauched woman. No one would want her now.

"Perhaps. Gentlemen visit the island all the time. It could certainly happen."

The mere idea made Serena's gut chum. First, to love someone other than Jonathan Dane. It was too soon to even allow such a thought to cross her mind, and every cell in her body rebelled against it. Second, to love anyone ever again, now that she was armed with the knowledge of how destructive love could be. Who would ever be so stupid?

"Oh, Meg. I've no need for love. I've tried it, and I've failed, through and through. A happy marriage and family is for you and Mr. Langley. Me...? I'll stay with Mother, and I will care for Cedar Place."

A future at Cedar Place wasn't something she'd been raised to imagine—from the moment they had stepped foot on Antigua, Serena and her sisters had told one another that this was a temporary stop, a place for the family to rebuild its fortune before they returned to England.

But now Cedar Place was all they had left, and it was falling into ruin. Before her father had purchased the plantation and brought the family to live in Antigua six years ago, Cedar Place had been a beautiful, thriving plantation. Six months after arriving on the island, Father had died from malaria, leaving them deeply in debt with only their mother to manage everything. And Mother was a well-bred English lady ill-equipped to take on the work of a plantation owner. Serena had doubts Cedar Place could ever be restored to its former glory, but it was the one and only place she could call home now, and she could not let it rot.

Meg sighed and shook her head. "I just think—Oh!"

She stumbled, slid, and went down in a flurry of skirts, leaving a glimmering slick of grease in her wake.

And then the ship dipped down the trough of a wave, and Meg slid beneath the deck rail and disappeared over the edge. As if from far away, Serena heard a muffled splash.

With a cry of dismay, Serena lunged after Meg until her slippered toes hung over the edge of the deck and she clung to the forestay.

Far below, Meg flailed in the water, hardly visible in the shadowy dark and wisping fog, her form growing smaller and finally slipping away as the ship blithely plowed onward.

After living for six years on a small island, Serena's sister knew how to swim, but the heavy garments she was wearing—oh, God, they would weigh her down. Serena tore off her cloak and ripped off her dress. She kicked off her shoes, scrambled over the deck rail, and threw herself into the sea.

A firm arm caught her in midair, hooking her about the waist and yanking her back onto the deck. "No, miss. Ye mustn't jump," a sailor rasped in her ear.

It was then that she became conscious of the shouts of the seamen and the creaking of the rigging as the ship was ordered to come round.

Serena tried to twist her body from the man's grasp. "Let me go! My sister is out there. She's... Let me go!"

But the man didn't let her go. In fact, another man grabbed her arm, making escape impossible. She strained to look back, but the ship was turning, and she couldn't see anything but the dark curl of waves and whitecaps, and the swirl of fog.

"Hush, miss. Leave this one to us, if ye please. We'll have 'er back on the ship in no time at all."

"Where is she?" Serena cried, sprinting toward the stern, pushing past the men in her way, ignoring the pounding of the sailors' feet behind her. When she reached the back of the ship, she tried to jump again, only to be caught once more, this time by Mr. Rutger.

She craned her neck, searching in vain over the choppy, dark water and leaning out as far over the rail as the sailor would allow, but she saw no hint of Meg.

"Never worry, miss," Mr. Rutger murmured. "We'll find your sister."

The crew of the *Victory* searched until the sun was high in the sky and burned through the fog, and the high seas receded into gentle swells, the ship circling the spot where Meg had fallen overboard again and again.

But they never found a trace of Serena's twin.

THE DISH

Where authors give you the inside scoop!

♥ ♥ ♥ ♥ ♥ ♥ ♥ ♥ ♥ ♥ ♥ ♥ ♥ ♥ ♥

From the desk of Jill Shalvis

Dear Reader,

When I started this series, about three estranged sisters who get stuck together running a beach resort, I decided I was out of my mind. I have a brother, and we like each other just fine, but I don't have sisters. Then at the dinner table that very night, my three teenage daughters started bickering and fighting, and I just stared at them.

I had my inspiration! "Keep fighting," I told them, much to their utter shock. I've spent the past fifteen years begging them to get along.

After that night, it was a piece of cake to write the sisters—Maddie, Tara, and Chloe—with their claws barely sheathed, resentment and affection competing for equal measure.

All I had left to do then was find the three sexy guys who could handle them.

It just so happened that, at the time, my neighbor was having an addition put on her house. For six glorious weeks, there were a bunch of guys hanging off the roof and the walls, in a perfect line of sight from my office.

Which is really my deck.

So I sat in the sun and wrote while in the background cute, young, sweaty guys hammered and sawed and, in general, made my day.

And on some days, they even took off their shirts. Those were my favorite days of all. But I digress . . .

I was working very hard, planning out conflicts and plot pacing and trying to nail down my hero. And given what I was looking at for inspiration, it shouldn't be any surprise at all that the hero for this first book in the Lucky Harbor series, SIMPLY IRRESISTIBLE (on sale now), turned out to be a master carpenter.

And a very sexy one at that.

I'm actually writing book two right now. I keep going out on the deck, sitting and patiently waiting, but my neighbor hasn't hired any more sexy carpenters. Darn it.

Enjoy!

Jill Shalvis

www.jillshalvis.com

♥ ♥ ♥ ♥ ♥ ♥ ♥ ♥ ♥ ♥ ♥ ♥ ♥ ♥ ♥

From the desk of Jennifer Haymore

Dear Reader,

When Jack Fulton, the hero of A SEASON OF SEDUC-TION first entered my office to ask me to write his story, I was a little confused about his motives.

"Okay." I stared at him dubiously. "From what you've said, it sounds like you met a woman and fell in love. What's the issue here?" Honestly, I couldn't figure out why he'd come to me in the first place. I'm here to write about characters with real, serious problems, and his seemed straightforward enough. Actually it didn't seem like a problem at all.

"For one thing, she's the sister of a duke, and I'm a sailor."

Hmmm . . . a Cinderella story in reverse. There might be something here. Yet . . .

Frowning, I skimmed through the application he'd laid on my desk. While I had to admit that when he'd walked in I'd gotten a brief vision of the rolling sea, the guy didn't comport himself like a salty seaman at all. I tapped the papers. "Says here you're from a distinguished family. Your father and brother both sit in Parliament. You're a gentleman."

Fulton sighed. "By blood, maybe."

"Hmm." I know how thick bloodlines ran in nineteenth-century England. The fact that he was a gentleman from a reputable, wealthy family with noble roots would go far in aiding his bid for a duke's sister. If he were a chimney sweep or something, it might be different. But I didn't feel this was quite enough.

He leaned forward in his chair. "Lady Rebecca doesn't trust anyone. She doesn't trust me. And because of that, she pushes me away."

"Why doesn't she trust anyone?" I asked.

"Because of her previous husband."

"What about him?"

A muscle twitched in Fulton's jaw, and his hands gripped the chair arms so tightly I could see his knuckles whitening. "William Fisk was a bastard," he gritted out. "He didn't love her. He married her for her status and her money. He planned to steal it all away from her."

I had to agree, this Fisk dude *was* a jerk. Poor Lady Rebecca. Still, I couldn't see the relevance of any of this. I shook my head. "Look, I don't think this is the story for me. The lady might have some issues with trust, but don't we all? If she loves you and you love her, you can work it out. I guarantee it."

Clearly agitated, Fulton thrust a hand through his brown, sun-streaked hair. He rose and began pacing my tiny office, from one end to the other and back again. I watched him patiently, but secretly hoped he would leave soon. I had a lot of work to do.

Finally, he spun around, pinning me with dark eyes. "You don't understand."

I shrugged. The issue seemed clear enough to me.

"There's a problem. An *insurmountable* problem." He stalked toward me, placed his hands flat on my mahogany desk, and leaned forward until his nose was an inch from my own.

"You see," he began, his voice quiet but with an edge of something hard and brittle, like a thin sheet of glass about to shatter. "She shouldn't trust me. She shouldn't believe a word I say."

"Why's that?" I murmured, staring up into his narrowed, dark eyes.

"Because," he said, very, very quietly, "my motives when it comes to Lady Rebecca Fisk are exactly the same as her first husband's."

Once I heard that, I was hooked. I knew I had to take this story on. I invited Fulton back into his chair, and after some arduous work and heavy arguing, we finally hammered out the fair solution to his problem, and A SEASON OF SEDUCTION was born.

Please come visit me at my website, www.jennifer
haymore.com, where you can share your thoughts about
my books, sign up for my newsletter and some fun freebies,
and read more about the characters from A SEASON OF
SEDUCTION.

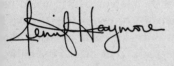

♥ ♥ ♥ ♥ ♥ ♥ ♥ ♥ ♥ ♥ ♥ ♥ ♥ ♥

From the desk of Annie Solomon

Dear Reader,

One of the most interesting things I did for TWO
LETHAL LIES (on sale now) was the research. Nor-
mally, I don't enjoy that part of the writing process, but
I had some interesting experiences with this book.

In one scene, for example, I wanted my heroine,
Neesy, to disable a car. But she had to do it quickly—
before the bad guys could get her—without tools, and in
a way that could just as easily be reversed so the car
would start once the evil ones were gone. Sound easy?
Well, the car was a 1959 Oldsmobile, and I couldn't find
any reliable source, online or off, who could help. So I
went to the only experts I knew: Click and Clack, the
Tappet brothers from the radio show *Car Talk*. We had a
great time on the air, and they came up with a good solution. But after all that? The scene was cut!

Although the Net didn't help with that problem, it
was a godsend for others. When I decided to do a section

of the book at Disney World, I was a little nervous. I'd been to the park once, but it was years ago; I had only vague memories. But when I went online to see what information I could find, I was amazed. I discovered not only maps and the pictures from the Disney site, but lots of videos taken by visitors themselves, which would be much closer to the experience of my characters. And then I hit the jackpot—a mini-documentary about the secret tunnels beneath the park. That shaped the entire section. And it was so cool to write about something most people don't know.

I found lots of other things that helped me set the story of Mitch, his daughter Julia, and his love, Neesy, in reality. The Drake Hotel is a well-known hotel in Chicago—and Princess Diana really did stay there! Hanover House in New York City is based on the Sloan Mansion, a turn-of-the-century home with fourteen-foot ceilings and seventeen bathrooms. I put Roger Carrick in the Omaha-Nebraska section of the FBI so I could write about Muscatine, the small town on the Mississippi that I visited last year. I met lots of great folks and had a wonderful time. And it's true, as Roger says—corn *is* everywhere.

If you'd like to see pictures of the places I've been, watch the videos, hear me on the radio—even take a gander at the scene that bit the dust—it's all on my website, www.anniesolomon.com. Stop by, check it out, and say hello. I'd love to hear from you!

Happy Reading!

Annie Solomon

Want to know more about romances at Grand Central Publishing and Forever? Get the scoop online!

GRAND CENTRAL PUBLISHING'S ROMANCE HOMEPAGE

Visit us at www.hachettebookgroup.com/romance for all the latest news, reviews, and chapter excerpts!

NEW AND UPCOMING TITLES

Each month we feature our new titles and reader favorites.

CONTESTS AND GIVEAWAYS

We give away galleys, autographed copies, and all kinds of fun stuff.

AUTHOR INFO

You'll find bios, articles, and links to personal websites for all your favorite authors—and so much more!

THE BUZZ

Sign up for our monthly romance newsletter, and be the first to read all about it!

If you or someone you know
wants to improve their reading skills,
call the Literacy Help Line.

WORDS ARE YOUR WHEELS
1-800-228-8813